THE
DARE

BOOKS BY CAROL WYER

The DI Natalie Ward series
The Birthday
Last Lullaby

The DI Robyn Carter series
Little Girl Lost
Secrets of the Dead
The Missing Girls
The Silent Children
The Chosen Ones

Other titles
Life Swap
Take a Chance on Me

Mini Skirts and Laughter Lines
Surfing in Stilettos
Just Add Spice
Grumpy Old Menopause
How Not to Murder Your Grumpy
Grumpies On Board

Love Hurts

THE DARE

CAROL WYER

bookouture

Published by Bookouture in 2019

An imprint of StoryFire Ltd.

Carmelite House
50 Victoria Embankment
London EC4Y 0DZ

www.bookouture.com

ISBN: 978-1-78681-851-5
eBook ISBN: 978-1-78681-850-8

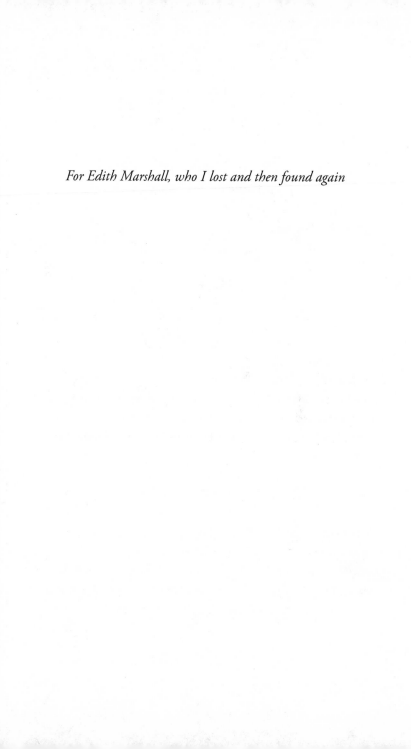

For Edith Marshall, who I lost and then found again

PROLOGUE

The large hand on the wall clock inched closer to the number six. As it did so, he struggled to control the jackhammering in his chest. *Soon*. He poured the oil into his hands, smoothed it over his chest and shoulders, and stared into the large mirror that allowed him to see the creature in all its glory. The tattooed snake glistened in the light from the window, seemingly alive, with scales refreshed and shining. Its head hung below his right collarbone, its jaws wide open. The scaly, black body disappeared over his shoulder to coil down the length of his back and reappeared on the left-hand side of his ribcage, where it curled around his waist, its tail disappearing under the waistband of his jeans. It had been a while since the snake had been pacified and fed.

Soon.

He dragged on his shirt to conceal the dark beast and paced the carpeted floor, halting by the music box, lovingly handcrafted and mounted on a wooden stand. It was astonishing what was sold at car boot sales. One person's junk could be another person's treasure. This was his.

He traced the holes and protrusions along the barrel of the music box and ran his fingers along the pieces of metal – the eighteen-note Yunsheng movement, resembling a book of thin, metal matches – that would create the tune. He lifted the music box with care, fingertips lightly grasping the delicate hand crank, and turned it unhurriedly until the drum rotated, the silver strips struck the drum, and the tinny tune – a recognisable nursery rhyme – filled the otherwise silent room. He smiled at the irony. How appropriate that he had chosen this one.

The clock hands moved again. It was now after 3.30 p.m. School was over for the day and it was finally time. He cranked the handle and hummed along as it played, his hooded eyes scanning the street for his next victim. She'd be passing by soon. Very soon.

Boys and girls come out to play,
The moon does shine as bright as day;
Come with a hoop, and come with a call,
Come with a good will or not at all.

CHAPTER ONE

MONDAY, 16 APRIL

'Get a fucking move on!' Jane Hopkins shouted, even though the giant John Deere tractor ahead currently holding up the lengthy queue of traffic wasn't the real reason she was thirty minutes late getting home. She rested her elbow against the window and let out an exasperated sigh.

At this rate, she wouldn't get home until after five. She turned up the volume on the radio to take her mind off her frustration at travelling at such a snail's pace. In reality, there were only three miles left. Getting worked up about a few extra minutes was pointless, except she was always at home when Savannah got in, even though the kid knew where the spare key was hidden and was quite capable of letting herself in. It was a matter of principle. Jane's own mother had always been at work when Jane came home from school, and as a former latchkey child, she hadn't wanted Savannah to experience the same thing. That was why Jane worked nine to three thirty and only four miles away from home – four long miles. She tried to relax her jaw. She was grinding her teeth subconsciously again as she usually did when she was wound up. The tractor refused to pull off into the only lay-by between here and the T-junction.

'Bastard,' she muttered. There was no way anyone would be able to overtake the vehicle heading through the centre of Hapfield. She was stuck crawling along with everyone else, all doing ten miles per hour. She'd already left a message on her daughter's mobile to say she was going to be late but she rang again, and Savannah's breezy, recorded voice filled the car.

'Hiya! It's Savannah here. I can't talk now, so leave a message.'

'Hun, I'm still running late. Won't be long. There are crisps in the cupboard if you're peckish but don't eat too many. I thought I'd cook your favourite, lasagne, for tea.'

It was her own fault she wasn't at home as usual with a smile and the offer of something to eat, and now there was added guilt to that she was already experiencing. *If his wife ever finds out…* She blocked out the thought. The tractor was finally turning off, its indicator flashing for an eternity while it waited for a gap in the oncoming traffic so it could manoeuvre. The exasperation of the drivers ahead of her was evident in the way they floored their accelerators as soon as the wretched machine had disappeared. She joined them and within five minutes was pulling up on her drive.

She jumped out of the car and slammed the door with a bang. The bloody workmen had clocked off early. They were supposed to be there until five. It was quarter past four. *Lazy shits.* Muddy caterpillar tracks ran to and from the bricked driveway. The garden was still a mess – a quagmire that Jane couldn't imagine would ever look anything other than a mudbath. A mountain of rolled turf sat in the far corner, each piece like an inside-out, hairy green carpet. She scowled at it and wished she'd never employed the duo – they'd offered the cheapest quote but were turning out to be the most unreliable workmen she'd come across.

There was no sign of Savannah. Jane had half-expected her thirteen-year-old to be leaning against the front door with a sour look on her face, but she must have collected the key from under the special rock and let herself in. She opened the door and shouted, 'Savannah! You home, sweetie? Sorry I'm late. Traffic was dreadful.' She winced at the half-truth. Of course, she'd never be able to tell her daughter the real reason she was late. 'Savannah!'

There was no reply. The girl was probably already glued to her phone. That was the routine: come in, chuck her bag at the bottom of the stairs and head to her room, where she'd peel off her hated school uniform and become so involved in some game or other, she wouldn't hear her mother shouting that tea was ready.

Jane stopped in her tracks. There was no school bag.

'Savannah!' She climbed the stairs and opened the door to her daughter's bedroom. The unicorn on the dressing table grinned its happy smile at her. The bed hadn't been made. It was always difficult to wake Savannah up. She really wasn't a morning person, and since they'd moved to this house, it had been even more difficult to get her up each day. The neighbour owned a terrier that spent most nights outside, barking at shadows. The night before it had yapped solidly until 3 a.m. Both Jane and Savannah had risen at 8 a.m., fatigued and in bad moods, and Savannah hadn't wanted to go to school at all.

'Please, Mum. Let me take a day off. I feel ill,' she'd pleaded.

She'd looked pasty but Jane hadn't given in. *Why not?* asked the voice that sometimes acted as her conscience. *You know fucking well why not. I didn't want to take a day off work and miss out on screwing my boss in his office*, she snarled back at it.

Jane scooted back downstairs and checked her mobile in case her daughter had tried to contact her. The only message on her phone brought a hot flush to her cheeks as she read then deleted it. She rang Savannah's number again. It went immediately to answerphone.

'Savannah, it's Mum. Ring me when you get this message.'

She ended the call, and a mix of vexation and anxiety caused the hairs on the back of her neck to rise. Savannah was never late from school. She was always home by 4 p.m. The school was only a twenty-minute walk – thirty tops if you were a schoolgirl talking to your best mates and dragging your heels – and it was the golden rule that Savannah was only allowed to walk home unaccompanied by her mother if she came straight home. Jane wasn't a strict parent but that was one rule she held fast – she wasn't going to have Savannah grow up with the same deep-seated resentment and feelings of rejection that Jane had experienced. At least Savannah would know her mother cared enough about her to be there at the end of every day to listen to grumbles and offer a pot of tea and a smile. Not that she seemed to give much in return these days. Savannah barely managed a hello before disappearing upstairs.

It was four thirty. She ought to be home by now. Jane pocketed the mobile and strode to the window overlooking the street. Beyond it was wasteland, nothing but open space waiting for development. Several cars snaked past. She turned her head to the left, the direction Savannah would come from. No sign of anyone walking towards the house.

She marched to the front door and stood outside, then walked the length of the driveway and stood at the edge of the pavement to get a better view up the road. Her next-door neighbour was approaching, her dog on a lead. Jane couldn't face talking to her about her barking mutt, so she turned away and looked in the opposite direction towards the railway crossing and the park that skirted behind her home. Nobody. She scooted inside the house before the woman reached her.

She tried Savannah's phone again and got the same answerphone message. It was no good; she had to find out where her girl was. She kicked off the high heels she'd been wearing, swapping them for a pair of trainers beside the back door, and headed in the direction of the school. Where could her daughter be? Had she buzzed off into town with her friends? She made a snap decision to ring one of the mothers, Isobel Gilmore, a snooty cow but one who'd invited Savannah around to hang out with her daughter, Sally, when no one else had been so welcoming.

'Hi, Isobel. It's Jane Hopkins here – Savannah's mother.'

'Oh, hi.' The response was lukewarm. Jane wasn't surprised. She and Isobel were polar opposites although their children rubbed along well enough.

'Is there an after-school activity today?' She hated asking the question and could imagine Isobel rolling her eyes. Jane really would be the worst type of mother if she didn't know what was going on at the school. All the other mothers knew what was happening.

'No. Nothing on Mondays.'

'Okay. Thanks.'

Isobel obviously picked up on her tone. 'Is something wrong, Jane?'

Jane didn't want to give away too much information. The news would be halfway across town before she'd hung up and made it to the school gates, only twenty metres away. Once the jungle drums started sounding, their noise would reverberate around the entire network of local mums and Savannah would be the butt of jokes the following day.

'No, nothing.' She glanced across at the locked gates as she spoke, then changed her mind. What the heck if Savannah was teased in the morning. She ought to have come straight home. 'Well, yes. Savannah hasn't come home yet. I wondered if she was with Sally.'

'No. I'll ask Sally when she last saw her.' There was a mumbled exchange and Jane struggled to hear what was being said. An oil tanker drove past her, and the driver honked his horn and made a suggestive sign. She turned away, mobile clamped to her ear. Isobel was back. 'No, she hasn't seen her since school.'

'Okay.' Jane didn't know what to say or do next. She had a weird sensation of floating away from reality. Savannah didn't have many friends. Sally Gilmore and Holly Bradshaw were the only two girls she hung about with. It had been a struggle for her moving to this school.

Isobel defrosted a little, her voice warmer. 'Don't worry. She'll turn up. She's probably got waylaid with friends and forgotten the time. Sally did that once. Gave me a proper scare. Let me know when she gets home.'

'Can you ask Sally to try her on social media? Ask her to call me. Please.' Jane knew she was overreacting. Savannah was only half an hour late.

Isobel must have thought the same. 'Sure. If she hears anything at all, I'll ring you.'

Jane half-ran and half-walked back to the house, hoping to see the girl by the door, school bag on the path beside her, on her phone. There was nobody. She opened the door and called out Savannah's name but was met with silence again. She rang Holly Bradshaw's mother, Karen, who worked at the local pharmacy and sounded irritated at the call.

'I'm not off shift yet. Holly's with my mother,' she said.

She gave Jane her mother's address, several streets away. Torn between waiting for her daughter and seeking out Holly, Jane frantically searched for some paper. Using the back of an electric bill, she scribbled a note that she left on the bottom stair so Savannah would see it as soon as she came in.

Ring me now.

She raced out to her car, threw herself back into the driver's seat and drew out into the traffic. Her conscience whispered two words: *Your fault.*

'Fuck off,' she replied out loud.

After a ten-minute drive, she pulled onto a driveway outside a smart, modern bungalow that was three times the size of her own house and parked behind the black convertible Mini stationed there. A woman with jet-black hair answered the door, a restraining hand on the collar of an exuberant spaniel, and gave her visitor a steely look. Jane wasn't going to be put off.

'I'm Jane Hopkins. Savannah Hopkins' mother. I'm sorry to bother you but I need to speak to Holly. Savannah hasn't come home and I wondered if Holly had any idea of where she might be. Please? I'm worried about her.'

The woman hesitated for a moment before saying, 'You'd better come in.'

She led the way into a warm, bright, welcoming kitchen and ordered the dog to lie on its bed.

'Holly, this is Savannah's mother. She's looking for Savannah.'

Holly Bradshaw was dark-haired, rosy-cheeked and sulky-mouthed – the opposite of Savannah. She looked up at Jane through long black eyelashes, her lips pulled down, and then she spoke. 'Not seen Savannah since school ended. She was in a strop and went off without us.'

'What do you mean?'

Holly shifted uncomfortably on the kitchen stool, her plate of chips in front of her.

Her grandmother stroked her hair and encouraged her to talk. 'Tell Mrs Hopkins.'

Holly shrugged. 'She was in a bad mood. She and Sally had a falling-out and she went off. That's all.'

'What did they fall out about?'

'I dunno,' said Holly, and then she appeared to lose interest in the conversation, turning her attention back to the chips in front of her.

'Where did you last see her?'

'Aldi. The car park at Aldi.'

It was the route Savannah and her friends took each day, leaving Watfield Secondary School, crossing the supermarket car park and then taking the pedestrianised street that joined onto the road leading to her house.

'Did she go off alone?'

'Yeah.' Holly shrugged like it was no big deal.

Jane wanted to wring more out of her, but there didn't seem to be any more. Holly speared a chip and ate it. Her grandmother gave the girl a beatific smile, oblivious to Jane's discomfort. With nothing further to be said, she showed Jane out, allowing disapproving eyes to graze Jane's tight top and overly short skirt. Jane knew what she was thinking. She'd come across this sort of woman with her petty prejudices before. She gave a polite smile in return and wasn't surprised when the door shut smartly behind her. She closed her eyes for a second and heard the echo of her daughter's voice, indignant and upset at the same time. It was her first week at the school – the first and only week she'd allowed her mother to meet her at the gates...

'What does pikey mean?'

'Why are you asking?'

'Some girls told Holly not to hang about with me cos I'm a pikey.'

'What did Holly tell them?'

'To get lost.'

'Good on her.'

'You haven't answered my question. What does pikey mean?'

They walk down the road, Jane smoking a cigarette and holding her head as high as she can. 'Someone who lives in a caravan – a traveller.'

'Oh. But we don't. Why would they think that?'

She throws her daughter a look. 'Don't listen to them. They'll get over it.'

Savannah bites her bottom lip and nods.

Jane was used to such taunts. She'd grown up in a tough environment on a council estate in Dudley, and after meeting her husband Lance – Savannah's stepdad – they had moved about the country with his traveller family for a while before settling in Watfield, only the year before. Their thick Black Country accents had stood out from the Staffordshire dialect of the region. It seemed stigmas stuck and tittle-tattle travelled, no matter what you did to try and better yourself. Holly's grandmother was one of those who listened to the rumour mill. You could see it in her steely silver eyes.

Jane drove back home via the Aldi car park, where she got out. She pulled up the screensaver photograph of Savannah on her mobile and stopped customers leaving the store. Had any of them seen a young girl with a blonde ponytail, wearing the red jumper and black trouser uniform of the local school? She was met with head shakes and shrugs. She should have come here sooner.

She rang Savannah's number yet again. No reply. It was now coming up half five. *Over one and a half hours late.* She scurried past the supermarket towards the Caffè Nero nestled between the fruit shop and a Poundland store and peered through the window. A group of youngsters in the same uniform as Savannah was gathered at the far end of the café. She hurtled through the door and towards them. Savannah wasn't among them.

'Have you seen Savannah Hopkins?' she asked.

The two girls and a boy in front of her were older than her daughter. They looked up from their mobile phones, unglued their lips from striped straws poking out of plastic smoothie cups and shook their heads.

'Don't know her.'

'Here.' Jane shoved the photograph in front of them.

The girls looked blankly at it. 'She at Watfield Secondary?'

The boy's mouth tugged downwards. 'Fink I seen her yesterday by the science block.'

'Not today?' Jane needed to get outside, look for her daughter, not waste time talking to these kids. Her brain was buzzing, the noise drowning out all other sound. She saw the boy's lips move but didn't hear him.

She raced outside and along the pedestrianised street, her head swivelling left and then right and left again. Her heart was a leaden weight in her chest that threw itself against her ribcage as she ran. Savannah wasn't anywhere in sight. She rang the girl once more and still got no reply. She didn't care that people were staring at the wild-eyed woman in a top that was too tight for her, a short, black-leather skirt and trainers. She had to find her daughter. This was her fault. If she'd been at home at the usual time, she'd have realised Savannah was missing sooner and come looking before now.

She raced down the road, veered left past a block of flats and halted outside the building she hated most in the town. The police station was an old-fashioned brick building, complete with traditional blue lantern and marked with the word 'Police' – the sort that might have appeared on a television period drama. She'd been inside twice since she'd moved to Watfield: both occasions were to collect a repentant Lance, who'd been taken into custody for being drunk and disorderly. That was before she kicked him out seven months ago.

She took a deep breath and pushed open the door. Inside was an unmanned wooden counter, pitted with age, that separated the public from the station itself. A transparent screen was drawn across. She hammered on it loudly, all sense of reality now deserting her.

'Hurry the fuck up. My daughter's missing.'

CHAPTER TWO

TUESDAY, 17 APRIL – MORNING

'Leigh! Get a move on. I haven't got time for this.' Natalie searched about for her car keys.

Her son, Josh, dressed in school uniform with his shirt hanging fashionably outside his trousers and striped green-and-black tie in a loose knot, had his back against the front door and was thumbing his smartphone, backpack hanging from one shoulder. He spoke without looking up. 'She's probably looking for her games kit.'

'Shit!' Natalie raced up the stairs to assist her daughter, who was tugging willy-nilly at clothes that had been stacked neatly in the airing cupboard and were now in a jumbled pile.

'I can't find it. Where is it?' Leigh asked.

Natalie shook her head. 'Sorry. I forgot to put on the washing machine last night.'

'Mu-um!'

'I know. I got in late and I know I should have but… I'll get it out again. You can wear it again today, can't you?'

'It'll stink.' Leigh's bottom lip stuck out.

'It won't. You only wore it for a while for netball, not for a marathon. You'll be wearing clean socks and pants. I bet no one will notice.'

Leigh stomped into her bedroom, kicking at shoes left on the carpet and making a meal of collecting her socks and trainers and stuffing them into a blue drawstring bag, observed by her mother.

Natalie had no time for histrionics. 'Look, it would have helped if you'd actually put your dirty washing in the wash basket after the last time you wore it rather than the night before you needed it. You'll have to take it as it is. I'll spray it with some deodorant. Now, come on or we'll be late.'

'*You'll* be late, you mean.'

Natalie was tempted to haul her daughter to task over her sulky comeback but the fact was, it was true. Natalie had a meeting with her team at nine and needed to drop her children off at the school they both attended before she could get to it. Normally, her husband David orchestrated such chores. It was easier for him because he worked from home and had become a chauffeur for the children, along with cook and several other roles when Natalie was involved in an investigation or working late. Today, however, he was on his way to a seminar in Birmingham, hoping to network with fellow translators and get much-needed work sent in his direction.

She pounded back downstairs into the laundry room behind the kitchen and opened the washing machine door. She yanked out the rumpled games kit and sniffed it. Her nose wrinkled. It would have to do. After rushing back upstairs to the bathroom to spray it with some lemon-scented spray David had bought her for her last birthday, she thundered downstairs and shouted again for Leigh, who was still in her bedroom.

'Leigh, for goodness' sake!'

'I'm coming! Keep your hair on.' The girl sauntered downstairs, took her clothes from her mother and stuffed them into the blue bag.

Josh slid his mobile into his jacket pocket. 'You ready at last, then?' he asked.

'Shut your face.'

'Leigh! That's no way to talk to your brother. Josh, tuck your shirt in.' Natalie checked around for anything she might have forgotten, made sure she had her briefcase and followed her children out to her Audi. Locking the door behind her, she inhaled deeply. She couldn't imagine doing this every day without losing her sanity.

Both children were silent on the journey from the village of Caster-gate, where they lived, to the secondary school on the outskirts of town. Leigh stared fixedly out of the window and ignored both Natalie and Josh, who gave up trying to jolt her out of her mood and went back to staring at his mobile. Natalie also tried to make conversation but, in the end, decided it wasn't worth the effort. Even Josh was only in grunt mode. *Teenagers!* For a while she felt grateful to have David to take up the strain then reminded herself why there *was* strain. If he hadn't been gambling and lost their savings, she wouldn't have had to take on the extra responsibilities of working to pay the mortgage. It had been tough recently – tougher than usual: she'd believed David had started gambling again. In early March, she'd not only found out he'd been on a gambling website but that he'd taken out a loan for £5,000. The revelation had been the final straw for Natalie.

'Natalie, for God's sake, calm down.' David's face is passive. He's not at all repentant.

She can't calm down. She wants to hammer her fists against his chest and scream at him. How bloody dare he do this to her again? What was he thinking of, taking out a loan for such a large amount when there's only her salary holding everything together, and why?

'Five... thousand... pounds, David. Explain why the fuck you've taken out a loan for that amount of money if it isn't to fund your gambling habit. Go on, you lying heap of shit. I bought your crap about only checking out the gambling site I found pulled up on your computer, and I believed you because, as you pointed out, you hadn't touched our savings. You were so bloody high and mighty about it all and now... this!'

'I know what it looks like, but you've got it wrong. I took out the money to pay for a holiday to Florida for us all. You've been working so hard and I didn't know what to get you for your birthday, so I thought a family holiday would be the perfect present. Time for each other and the kids. I wanted to surprise you with it. I couldn't surprise you if I took the money from our bank account.'

She freezes. Is he lying? His face says not. He has tears in his eyes and his slim shoulders have slumped. He is a man beaten – destroyed by her cruel words. He reaches for her hands but her arms hang limply by her sides like a rag doll. Is he telling the truth? As if some silent telepathy has passed between them, he turns and heads for his office to return less than a minute later with a holiday brochure. He hands it over and she sees that the corners of some pages have been turned down. She opens it dumbly and studies the resort near Disney World. He's circled the hotel name, Sunshine Palace, in red, along with the prices for high season: the cost of the holiday for four is almost £5,000. She closes it and returns it to him.

'You understand…' she begins.

He interjects with a weary shake of his head. 'I understand that you don't trust me in spite of everything I've said and done. I understand that whatever I do, I'll always be guilty in your eyes for having let you down.' He turns away and drops the brochure in the wastepaper bin, where it lands heavily.

Natalie has no response. It's true. Ever since he gambled away their savings, she's been expecting him to fail. She's been treating him like a suspect, waiting for him to make a mistake, but on this occasion, she's been wrong. She's still angry he's taken out a loan, even for a holiday. After all, it will be her that foots the bill at the end of the day, but she's still at fault for thinking the worst. 'Listen, I'm sorry. Really. You can see how it looked.'

'What made you snoop and find out about the loan, Natalie?' he replies. His forehead creases deeply, and along with the grey in his hair, David resembles a man in his mid-fifties rather than late forties.

She opens her mouth but says nothing. They both know the answer: she doesn't trust him. That's why she hunted for evidence that would prove he was gambling.

He shakes his head sadly. 'Will you ever have faith in me again or have we gone past that?'

Her heart begins to thud solidly in her chest. The power is in her hands. Whatever she says next will determine if they can continue as a couple and will affect the whole family. 'I'll try, David. I'm naturally suspicious. You know that. It's who I am. The thought of it all happening again terrifies me so much sometimes, I forget to be rational. I'll try to be more trusting. I'm truly sorry to have jumped to conclusions.'

The answer seems to satisfy him but instead of discussing it further, he merely nods and moves off to his office.

Natalie joined the line of other taxi mums and dads trying to find a space near the drop-off point. Her mobile lit up and she glanced at it. It was a text message from one of her sergeants, Murray Anderson. She lifted the phone up so she could see the screen and read quickly, all the while trying to concentrate on the bumper of the Volvo in front of her in case the car came to a sudden halt. She was to ring the station urgently.

Leigh was becoming restless, her bag already half on her shoulder. 'Can't you just let us out here like Dad does?' she moaned.

'It's not the designated area,' Natalie replied, mindful of the road markings that indicated she shouldn't stop until another fifty metres on. The new system had only recently been implemented. It was to ensure the safety of the numerous children dismounting from vehicles but it had certainly slowed down the entire process of dropping off. Leigh, sat next to her, exhaled noisily and rolled her eyes. Natalie ignored the gesture. It was an agonising five minutes before she found a space and Josh and Leigh piled out.

'Have a good day,' she called but was ignored as Josh immediately joined a group of lads approaching the entrance on foot and Leigh raced off through the gate, kit bag bouncing against her back.

Natalie checked her mirrors to pull back out into the traffic, caught a glimpse of Josh tugging his shirt back out of his trousers and sighed. It was an ongoing battle with her children. They were becoming fiercely independent and listened to her demands less and less. She'd never stepped out of line at that age, she mused. Frances, on the other hand… She wiped away all thoughts of her estranged sister.

Back in the stream of traffic, she used the hands-free to call Murray.

'Hi. Got your message. What's up?'

'Word's in that a young girl who went missing yesterday afternoon has been found dead. You need to check in with Superintendent Melody.'

'I'll be there in ten minutes.' She switched on the flashing blue lights that ran along the front of her grille, warning other vehicles of her presence, and accelerated in the direction of Samford.

Samford Police headquarters, a state-of-the-art building built in 2016, was one of only four investigative hubs across the county and contained a criminal investigation department, public protection and forensic staff from the north of Staffordshire, as well as local officers and Natalie's team. She swiped her identity pass to gain access, greeting the desk officers with a quick wave, and raced up the wide staircase to Superintendent Aileen Melody's office on the top floor.

Natalie's footsteps were muffled in the thick carpet. Although the superintendent's office was directly above her own, and shared the same dimensions, it was obvious only the senior officials were housed on this floor, with its water cooler in the corridor, modern art that adorned the pale-blue walls and leather chairs dotted on the wide landing. Natalie halted outside the door and listened before knocking. Inside, Aileen's soft, southern-Irish voice had taken on a steely tone and she was shouting at somebody either with her or on the end of the phone. Natalie waited until the ranting ceased and then knocked.

'Come in.'

Aileen, a slim woman with auburn hair cut short to frame her delicate face and intense green eyes, looked up from the folder on her desk, her brow knotted. There were no preliminaries.

'Thirteen-year-old girl by the name of Savannah Hopkins went missing on her way home from Watfield Secondary School yesterday afternoon. Missing Persons were searching for her. Her body turned up less than an hour ago. I know you're heavily involved with another case but I'm reassigning your team and I want you to head this.'

Natalie stood with her hands behind her back. Any murder investigation was a challenge, but when it involved children it presented an even greater test: trying to separate emotion from the investigation. Natalie had been involved in several such cases and each one had tested her mettle. She waited for instructions, which came quickly.

'Get everyone up to speed as quickly as possible and head over to Watfield. This is all we have at the moment.' She pushed the folder in Natalie's direction. A photograph of a pale-faced girl with blonde, shoulder-length hair and chestnut-brown eyes that seemed to radiate sorrow was pinned to the front of it. Natalie nodded her assent and took the file, reading through it quickly. There was no need for any further conversation.

As she turned to leave the office, she glanced at the photograph Aileen kept on her desk of her two nieces, both about the same age as this unfortunate girl, and understood why her boss was impatient to find the perpetrator quickly.

CHAPTER THREE

TUESDAY, 17 APRIL – MORNING

Natalie's unit consisted of three dedicated and gifted individuals: DS Lucy Carmichael, DS Murray Anderson and PC Ian Jarvis. Ian, the most junior and youngest of them, had suffered a serious stab wound to the chest during an investigation in March and had only recently returned to work. She was determined to keep him only on light duties and away from harm.

She found them gathered in their office, awaiting instructions. Work had ceased on the case they'd been investigating and Lucy was packing up the information they'd amassed on a car-theft gang operating in the area. She pushed the lid down firmly on the cardboard box and handed it over to the officer waiting to collect it. The man nodded in Natalie's direction and mumbled, 'Morning, ma'am,' before leaving.

Lucy wiped her hands on her trouser legs and sat down. Natalie didn't waste any time. She passed around the photograph of the schoolgirl and spoke quickly.

'At half five yesterday afternoon, Mrs Jane Hopkins of 21 Western Park Road, Watfield, reported her thirteen-year-old daughter, Savannah, missing. Jane is known to local police following several incidents that took place last year when local officers were called out to scenes of domestic violence at their residence. Her husband, Mr Lance Hopkins, was charged in September last year for drunk and disorderly behaviour. By the way, he's Savannah's stepdad, not her biological father. Shortly afterwards, he left the family home, and to date, we have no known address or details on the man. Yesterday evening, the Missing Persons squad conducted a thorough search of Western Park Road, the immediate area and nearby parkland. Savannah's body was discovered less than an hour ago when officers searched the park area behind her house for the second time. Superintendent Melody wants us to head to the scene immediately. As you know, we are no longer handling the car-theft investigation. This is our priority. Let's go.'

Watfield's only park, some fifteen acres and almost square in shape, stretched from the western side of Watfield to the railway line and was bordered at one side by a river, with the main road leading into the town centre on the other. It had maintained much of its original layout from the 1920s, when the park was first opened, and consisted largely of open grassland, playing fields, a football pitch and a skatepark, as well as small areas of woodland planting and a play area. As Natalie and Lucy drew into the car park opposite the sole entrance on Western Park Road, they couldn't miss the television vans and crews that had already begun to assemble.

Small crowds had gathered either side of the wrought-iron gates, nestled closely together as if seeking human contact. Natalie had seen this before at crime scenes: a herding instinct that, in the face of tragedy, brought people together. Grim-faced police officers stood guard along the length of the park in front of the railings, with legs planted and hands behind backs. Natalie parked next to the squad car, driven by Murray. Ignoring the cameras, the team suited up in protective clothing and strode as one towards the officers stationed beside the park gates, where they held their IDs outstretched so names could be noted in the logbook. A chorus began behind her.

'Detective, have you found Savannah Hopkins?' The calls and shouts from the journalists were ignored. Natalie lifted a hand to show she wasn't prepared to talk to anyone and slipped into the park, accompanied by her officers. She needed no directions for which way to head. There were only two footpaths: the one to her left led towards the river, but judging by the white paper uniforms in the distance to the right, that was where she'd find Savannah Hopkins.

Yellow-and-black crime-scene tape cordoned off an area close to the path, encompassing a bench, bushes and a large willow tree. Several officers, along with the familiar solid figure of Mike Sullivan, head of Forensics, were gathered outside the makeshift tent that housed the girl's body. Mike was not merely a colleague: he was David's best friend, and he and Natalie·had embarked on a brief affair a year and a half ago, when Natalie had first discovered her husband had a gambling addiction. While she had put the liaison behind her and tried to work things out with David, Mike's marriage to his wife Nicole had failed – not because of what had occurred, but due to the pressure of work.

Natalie's team arrived at the tent, where she greeted Mike and his men. 'What have you got so far?'

He gave a small sigh. 'We believe she's been strangled. There's bruising commensurate with strangulation, and undoubtedly the pathologist will be able to confirm our initial speculations.'

'Any idea who the pathologist will be?'

Mike shook his head; his thick, dark hair was unkempt, as if he'd forgotten to run a comb through it in his haste to get to the crime scene. 'Could be either Ben Hargreaves or Pinkney Watson. Not had word yet.'

Natalie favoured Pinkney, with whom she'd worked on many cases, but Ben had proved his worth during an investigation the year before – another involving children. She sighed heavily. She couldn't put it off any longer. It was time to look at Savannah. She stepped into the tent and took in the sight of the young girl stretched out beside a blue litter bin, the type often seen in schoolyards and parks with a moulded compass top, four apertures and Victoriana gold banding and lettering. Savannah was slight, only five feet tall, with slender arms and legs. Her face was as white as alabaster, with a sprinkle of light freckles across her cheeks and a small mole above her pale-rose lips. The bruises Mike had mentioned were evident – purplish-blue in colour – and her hands, clenched in two balls, bore scrapes on the knuckles. She was dressed in skinny black jeans that accentuated her lean frame and a dark-grey hoodie bearing the Superdry logo. Her Converse trainers, laced neatly, looked new, the soles hardly worn. Natalie allowed her gaze to rest on the girl's face, the sharp cheekbones, the naturally thick eyebrows that arched over closed, violet eyelids. A glimmer caught her attention. Savannah was wearing a small silver star in her right ear but nothing in her left.

'You found the other earring?' she asked Mike.

'Not yet.'

Natalie dragged her eyes away from the child on the ground. 'She's not wearing a school uniform, yet she disappeared immediately after school ended. Looks like she changed out of it.'

'We've not come across her uniform, school bag or mobile phone, but obviously we're conducting a full search. There's nothing in the bin of note although we're going through the contents to make sure.'

Natalie crouched and studied the girl. The clothes looked new. Had she changed from her uniform in order to meet somebody? She tore her gaze from the marks on the girl's neck, stood and addressed the team. 'Her clothing appears to be undisturbed but, obviously, we'll need to establish if she's been raped.' Her voice was clear and calm but it was at odds with the hammering in her chest. She took a step backwards and spoke to Mike again. 'Okay if we walk the area with you?'

'Sure.'

They followed him from the tent into the park. Natalie cast a look back towards the park gates. There were no surveillance cameras by them or in this park. A killer could have come in without being spotted, although the entrance needn't have been the entry point. A person might have access by crossing the railway lines or the river, or via one of several gardens that bordered the park. The questions were already mounting up: Had the perpetrator been lying in wait for Savannah, or stumbled across her? Had they kept her hidden from the search parties, then murdered her? Or had they strangled the girl elsewhere and returned to dump her body a short distance from her home?

A young man in a badly fitting brown suit with a camera slung around his neck, and a woman in jeans and a short red jacket were in conversation with one of the officers safeguarding the spot. *Newshounds.*

The river was approximately 100 metres away. Directly to the left of the tent was a wooden bench bearing a plaque that stated Fred had enjoyed sitting here in his favourite spot, with the dates of his birth and death. Somebody had scrawled *H 4 R* and a love heart on the rear.

'Think the bin is significant?' Murray's voice was quiet as befitting the scene.

'She might have tried to run away from her assailant and he struck when she reached the bin. We can't read too much into it at this stage.'

His words, however, had touched on something – a recollection, not of a case she'd been involved in but one that had taken place while she was stationed in Manchester. A teenage girl had been strangled and discarded among rubbish bags at the rear of a restaurant, only doors away from where she'd lived.

'Murray, video this so we have something to go on. Lucy, you and Ian canvass the occupants of the houses that back directly onto this park. I'll speak to her mother.' They moved away, leaving Natalie alone with Mike.

Mike shoved his hand into his pocket and pulled out a packet of chewing gum. He unwrapped and popped a piece into his mouth. Natalie glanced at his fingers, yellowing with nicotine. His marriage break-up had taken its toll on him. She suspected it was more the absence of his daughter, Thea, than his spouse that had hit him deepest. His four-year-old was his world.

'Ben,' he said, spotting the arrival of the pathologist who hastened towards them, head lowered.

'Been stuck in traffic.' Ben's Brummie accent was thick and his words delivered quickly. 'Some breakdown just outside Sandown that had to be cleared away. I'd have been here sooner otherwise.'

Mike shook his head. 'No worries. You're here now.'

Ben shrugged a response and placed his large leather case on the ground, produced a small cloth from his jacket pocket and wiped his glasses with it. His long black hair was in a stubby ponytail this morning and his chin smoothly shaven – a contrast to Mike, who seemed to have perpetual stubble no matter what time of the day. Ben raised his mask so only his dark eyes were visible and entered the tent.

'What are your initial thoughts?' Natalie asked Mike.

His jaw moved up and down as he chewed. 'There's no evidence of a struggle here – no broken branches or grass scuffed. There's no sign of grass stains on the soles of her shoes. In fact, they look hardly worn, and she got those bruises on her hand from hitting something hard – a wall, a door. There's nothing here that I can see that would have made those marks. I think she was kept somewhere, killed and dumped here. Killer carried her and placed her at the spot. There are no drag marks.'

Natalie nodded soberly. The killer could have left her anywhere out of sight, but instead of concealing her body, they'd left it in full sight, right next to a litter bin. *Is the bin significant?*

'Horrible, just horrible. What a bastard,' Mike said.

Natalie understood his outburst. No matter how hard they both tried to leave emotion out of it, they were mindful of their own

children and their safety. It was written on Mike's face, the way
he hung his head and his eyebrows sat heavily above his eyes, and
Natalie couldn't help but think briefly of Leigh's sulky but pretty
face as she'd raced off to school only a short while ago. Savannah
had left home yesterday morning and that had been the last time
her mother had laid eyes on her.

'I'd better go and talk to her mother.'

'I'll keep you in the loop,' he replied, his gaze drawn to two of
his team searching by the bench.

Natalie walked back towards the entrance, where the red-
jacketed woman was waiting eagerly with a microphone. 'Detective,
can you confirm you have found Savannah Hopkins?'

Natalie ignored both the woman and the photographer snap-
ping pictures of her and kept her steady gaze on the road ahead.
Lucy and Ian, along with extra officers, had moved the crowds
off, and apart from a few lingerers who shuffled slowly along the
pavement opposite, the street was clear. Natalie paused and turned
back towards the reporter. 'There'll be an official statement later.
In the meantime, please show some respect and move away so we
can do our job.'

She hadn't meant it to come out quite so harshly but it had
the desired effect. The woman backed off. Undoubtedly, she'd
understood what Natalie was implying: a young girl had been
found murdered and her family were in pain.

CHAPTER FOUR

TUESDAY, 17 APRIL – MORNING

Natalie recognised the aged white VW Polo outside 21 Western Park Road. It belonged to Tanya Granger, one of the family liaison officers who worked in the area. Tanya, with her bright-red hair, was five foot four, stout and plain-faced but had a big heart and possessed a comforting persona – a warmth that emanated from her, which helped the victims' families.

Natalie inhaled deeply. This was always the hardest part: looking at the distraught faces who'd been sideswiped with terrible news of their loved ones, who hadn't yet fully processed what was happening, yet having to press them for information that might lead to an arrest.

The house was set back from the road, the last in a row of identical terraced Victorian houses, each with long frontages, traditional storm porches, timber doors and bay windows. Number 21 had a large garden plot that ran beside the length of the pavement towards the park – separated by railings identical to those surrounding the park – and to the rear of the property. A small digger was parked in the middle of the garden, and shrink-wrapped pallets of paving slabs had been left near the driveway. The garden was some way off completion, with caterpillar tracks running across the earth and plants in large wooden crates awaiting planting. Closer to the side of the house there was further evidence of work with scaffolding against the wall.

Natalie approached the building and spotted movement the other side of the bay window. Within seconds Tanya appeared at the door and Natalie gave a quick nod. Tanya shook her head, a sign that the mother was in a bad way. It was to be expected. Natalie couldn't begin to imagine what she was going through.

'She's in shock. Blames herself and the local police, and she won't sit down. She's been pacing about for the last half hour like a caged animal,' said Tanya. She led the way into the sitting room and introduced Natalie to the slight woman with huge eyes sunken in her ashen face, who stood in front of the bay window and shook her head as soon as Natalie opened her mouth. Her voice was quiet but steely.

'Don't. Please don't say you're sorry about Savannah. Don't say anything. I don't want your platitudes.'

Natalie gave a brief nod. 'I'm sorry to have to speak to you at such a bad time but we need to act quickly.'

'Your lot didn't act quickly enough, did they? I told the officers she'd gone missing yesterday afternoon. They had time to find her before this…'

'I can only extend my sincere apologies that she wasn't found in time. I wasn't involved in the search but I am heading the investigation into her death, and I assure you I shall do everything I can to bring those responsible for her death to justice.'

'Those responsible. Who exactly do you mean, Detective? We're all responsible – me, her friends, the police and everyone else in this sodding town who went about their business and noticed nothing, with no thought other than for themselves. I'm responsible because I'm her mother and should have kept her safe, and your lot should have listened to me when I begged them to look for her and not dawdle about. We're all bloody responsible, so who are you going to charge? Savannah should be here, at home, not there.' She waved her hand in the direction of the park.

'I am genuinely sorry you feel let down.'

'*Let down?* I'm so much *more* than let down,' she hissed. 'I am…
empty… sucked dry of emotion. Can you possibly imagine what
it feels like to know your daughter is dead at the other side of the
park? She's there and I'm here and I can't accept what's happened.'

'I understand how difficult this is for you, but I have to do my
job and I need to ask you a few questions about Savannah.'

Jane seemed not to hear. Deep creases had formed on her
forehead, the product of internal pain.

'Do you have children, Detective?'

'A boy and a girl. My daughter's recently turned fourteen.'
Natalie sensed revealing such personal information would help the
woman connect better with her.

Jane regarded her with more interest and wrapped her arms
around her skinny frame. 'Are you close to her?'

'Not as much as we used to be. She's become more independent
of late.'

The answer seemed to resonate with Jane. 'They grow up too
quickly, don't they? One minute you're best friends, holding hands
when you go out shopping together, and the next, you're blocked
from their lives. Savannah used to tell me everything – shared every
secret – and loved, well, she loved me unconditionally. Her stepdad,
that was a different matter. Lance was never really parent material.
I suppose that's why she and I got along so well – conspirators
against him and allies when he was in a bad mood. I thought we
still shared a bond… a mother–daughter bond. In spite of my
marriage break-up and teenage growing pains, I believed she'd tell
me if she was in trouble or if she was scared of anything. I truly
believed it, Detective.'

Natalie wasn't sure where Jane was going with this monologue
but she let her have her say. It was obviously something she felt
strongly about.

'Savannah didn't say anything that gave me cause for concern or
an explanation as to why she wouldn't be coming home yesterday

as usual. She'd have told me if she was going to be late. She didn't have many friends and she'd have said something if she was going to meet one of them. She always came straight here. She had her little secrets but she knew I'd worry if she didn't come home. What I'm saying is, somebody grabbed her and took her away and I don't have any idea who would do that. I told the police. I *knew* something bad had happened but they tried to calm me down me and insisted on checking with all her classmates before manning a search. They wasted time. If only they'd listened to me, we might have found her alive. A mother knows, doesn't she? A mother senses when something bad has happened.'

Natalie was about to reply when, without warning, Jane folded onto her knees and crumpled in a heap on the patterned carpet. The sobs came next – huge, gulping, painful sobs that filled the room — and were followed by cries of anguish. Tanya raced to the woman's side and comforted her. Natalie had to wait before Jane could speak again to give her permission to look at Savannah's bedroom. Leaving the distraught woman in Tanya's capable hands, she withdrew to the entrance hall and made her way upstairs to the girl's bedroom.

The single bedroom was distinctly bohemian with white walls and dark wooden furniture, ethnic-print blinds, colourful bed linen and a matching makeshift canopy draped over two ceiling-hung poles. Soft toys sat on white shelving, crammed in next to schoolbooks and a collection of Suzanne Collins' *Hunger Games* and Ally Carter's Gallagher Girls series. A toy unicorn smiled merrily at her and gaily coloured necklaces hung over a mirror on a white dressing table cluttered with fabric boxes, inside which were items of jewellery: small earrings, necklaces and friendship bracelets.

Leigh's room was a chaotic mess of clothes and shoes, thrown onto any free space. Savannah's was less so, although the bed was unmade and the wardrobe housed numerous cardboard boxes, piled one on top of the other, and was cluttered with garments, several heaped on the same clothes hanger. Natalie pulled one hanger out. There was a brand-new sparkly top from a trendy boutique in town along with a pair of jeans from another shop, both bearing price tags. Savannah had placed a baggy woollen jumper over them, which struck Natalie as strange when there were other empty hangers on the rail. She dragged out a soft bag that had been shoved to the rear of the wardrobe and peered inside. It contained all manner of plastic goods, stationery items, animal-shaped erasers, key rings, bracelets, face jewels, mobile phone cases. There were more boxes all jam-packed under the bed, each filled with make-up – some unused – and nail varnishes, pens and items that were important to a teenage girl, haphazardly thrown into each. *Out of sight*, thought Natalie.

Searching through Savannah's drawers, she unearthed an unworn sequinned T-shirt, screwed up in a plastic bag and hidden under underwear, and in yet another drawer, a disposable lighter and half-smoked packet of cigarettes. A picture of the girl was forming in her mind. No matter what Jane believed, Savannah had been keeping secrets from her mother.

Downstairs, a slightly calmer Jane had accepted a glass of water and was now sitting down at the kitchen table. Natalie dropped down in the chair opposite her.

'What can you tell me about your daughter?'

Jane sighed wearily. 'She was a good kid. She didn't have the easiest time coming here to Watfield. It took a while for her to settle, and then after Lance pissed off, she had to put up with some more crap from the other kids in her class. We've both had a hard time.'

Jane's face had the drained, lean look of somebody who'd found life difficult. She pulled at the skimpy top she was wearing that revealed a tattoo of a rose on her left breast. She was in control again although her cheeks were now smudged black from the heavy mascara she'd been wearing. 'People didn't take kindly to travellers moving into the area,' Jane continued. 'Not that we're really proper travellers. Lance's family are and they move all over the country, but I wanted a proper home for us all, and when this house came up for auction, we put a bid in. It needed a lot of work but it was our first bricks-and-mortar home.'

Natalie waited for Jane to continue – whatever she said might help Natalie to build a picture of the girl. Jane shifted in her chair. 'Lance didn't like it here and couldn't adjust. In the end, he left. Savannah and I stayed. I used all my inheritance to buy this place because I thought it was the right thing for us both. I thought Savannah would benefit from living in a community, in a town. Christ, how I wish we'd never moved here. If we'd stayed put, this wouldn't have happened. This is all my fault.' She dropped her head into her hand.

'Did Savannah ever see her biological father?'

Jane released a sigh. 'She never knew him. He was killed in a motorbike accident soon after I discovered I was pregnant. Savannah and I lived with my mum in Dudley where I was brought up, until her death in 2015, when Savannah was coming up ten. Soon after she passed away, I met Lance. His family had moved onto a disused site near my flat and we bumped into each other. He was helpful, carried my shopping upstairs because the lift had broken and I lived on the top floor. We hit it off. The travellers stayed on the site for a few months before they were forced to move on, and when they did, Savannah and I went with them.'

'Have you any idea where Lance is?'

Jane shook her head. 'He went in search of his family. Could be anywhere.'

'Do you have a phone number for him?'

'No. His old pay-as-you-go number isn't working. I think he must have changed his phone and decided not to give me the new number. It's been tough since we came here. I hoped living away from the travellers would bring us closer, but it turned out to have the opposite effect. Lance hated it and, in the end, we knew we couldn't make it together. We're too different. I wanted stability for Savannah and for myself and he just wanted his old life back. I had no reason to stay in touch with him.'

'Not even for Savannah's sake?'

'Lance isn't great with kids, especially teenagers. He never touched her, if that's what you're thinking. He wouldn't have done that.'

'I understand he was cautioned for violence.'

'He never hurt her. I swear. He hit me a few times, bust my lip once after a major row, but I didn't press charges at the time. He started drinking heavily and made a nuisance of himself in town and got pulled for fighting in a pub. I had to bail him out. It was getting embarrassing. I was trying to make a new life for us all and he kept messing it up, and by then I'd had enough of him.' The words came out automatically as if she'd told the story many times and was tired of it.

'After he left, Savannah didn't try to contact him, did she?'

'No. She was sick of the arguments too. She wasn't bothered about him going. They'd never been close. It's a different life, being with a travelling community. You don't live as individuals and family units. You all rub along together except I couldn't and Savannah struggled too. The other kids wouldn't accept her. They were all born into that life and were related – we were outsiders even though we lived with Lance. There were quite a few pressures: his ex-girlfriend and child lived on-site with another member of the group, and Lance's mother didn't take to me. Things got strained between me and Lance, and that's why I insisted we move to Watfield. This house was a bargain and we could afford it. His family didn't seem upset when we left. I guess they knew he'd return to them. They understood him far better than I did.'

'What about Savannah? Didn't she miss them all?'

'She didn't appear to. We talked about it a few times and I think she was relieved to have some stability in her life. She was fed up of never settling in one place and she didn't like Lance's mother either, or the other children on-site.'

'You don't think she was in touch with any of them, do you?'

'Not that I know of. It's unlikely.'

'Did she settle here?'

'It took a long while for her to become accepted at Watfield Secondary – you know how ignorant people can be. There were ups and downs, for us both. She was such a quiet girl but she seemed to come out of her shell the last few months and she'd made proper friends.' She choked back a sob.

'Can you give me their names?'

'She hung about mostly with Sally Gilmore and Holly Bradshaw – they were both in her class. I asked them if she was with them yesterday, but they hadn't seen her. Holly said Savannah and Sally had had an argument and Savannah had walked off.'

Natalie wrote down the names of the girls. They might be able to tell her more about Savannah and explain why she had new clothes in her wardrobe, hidden from view. 'Did you give Savannah pocket money?'

'She got five pounds a week. She complained it wasn't enough but I'm not made of money. I have bills to pay.'

Natalie nodded. There was no way Savannah could afford all those clothes and cigarettes on that amount of money.

'Savannah was wearing a Superdry top, black jeans and Converse trainers when we found her, not her school uniform. Could she have come home and got changed then gone out again?'

Jane's brows furrowed. 'I don't think so. I'd have seen her uniform hanging on the back of the door, where she normally leaves it. I bought her that outfit for her last birthday. Cost me a fortune but she was so pleased with it.' She swallowed hard. 'Her school bag wasn't at home either. She might have let herself in and gone out again but she'd have told me – left me a note or rung me. She wouldn't have just gone off.'

'You hadn't fallen out over anything?'

'No. Not at all. We got along fine. We had our moments, but what mother doesn't have run-ins with her daughter? She wouldn't go off without letting me know where she was. She wouldn't do that. And she wouldn't have turned off her mobile.' She shook her head in bewilderment.

'What about other relatives? Is there anyone else who has had contact with her?'

'My father did a bunk when I was a kid and hasn't been in touch since. There's no one else. There was only Lance.'

'Did you stay in touch with any of your old friends from Dudley?'

'I burnt those bridges when I moved away with Lance's family. Nobody wanted to know me after that.' She squeezed her eyes shut. Sadness, like an invisible shield, radiated from her. Natalie wondered how Savannah felt about her mother's hermit-like existence. It must have put some strain on their relationship.

'Does Savannah own a pair of silver star earrings?'

Jane wiped her eyes, staining her forefinger with silver-blue eyeshadow. 'Yes.'

'Was she wearing them yesterday morning?'

'She's not allowed to wear jewellery to school. Why? Was she wearing them?'

'She was.'

'She loved those earrings. They were her favourite. I don't understand any of this. Why did she change out of her uniform?'

'That's one of the things we're trying to work out. Did she mention a boyfriend?'

Jane stared at the shiny eyeshadow on her finger as if she couldn't work out where it had come from. 'Boyfriend? No. She wasn't interested in boys as far as I know.'

'What was she interested in?'

'The usual things: make-up, clothes, shopping, online games, films, books and singing. She practised singing all the time. She made up her own dance routines too. She wanted to be a pop star.'

'She went online? I imagine she had social media accounts. Do you own a computer?'

'I can't afford expensive stuff like that. I'm stretched as it is. She had a mobile. Don't they all at that age? She used it for online activity, mostly Snapchat or Instagram and to play games, and she used the school's computer if she needed it for schoolwork.'

Natalie probed further, trying hard not to upset or annoy the woman. 'I expect you monitored her online activity.'

'Of course I did. Any games or apps had to be bought through my account, and it was a pay-as-you-go so she had limited data. It had parental controls too. I watch the news and I know what can happen to vulnerable teenagers online. I wanted her to stay safe.' She swallowed hard again and tears sprang once more to her eyes.

'I noticed you are having some work done to the house.'

Jane nodded. 'A bit of landscaping and some repainting. Lance made a start on it but left the garden half-done. It looked such a mess. I got a local firm to sort it.'

'Were they working yesterday?'

'Yes, but they weren't here when I got home. They're supposed to work until five but they'd clocked off early.'

'Which company are you using?'

'Tenby House and Garden Services.'

Natalie made a note. 'And the names of the men working here?'

'Stu and Will. I don't know their surnames.'

'What time did you get home yesterday?'

A muscle twitched in Jane's jaw. 'Quarter past four. I'm usually at home before Savannah, who was always home by four – I didn't like her to come home to an empty house – but I was stuck in traffic.' Jane's voice weakened. Her face had taken on a look Natalie had seen before – that of a person whose life has just been shattered.

'Where do you work?' Natalie tried to keep the woman engaged. It wouldn't be long before she broke down again.

'Wilton's Building Supplies, on the main Ashbourne road.'

Natalie jotted down the address.

'I got held up. I ought to have been home by quarter to four.'

It wasn't her fault she'd been stuck in traffic yet something in Jane's tone made Natalie study Savannah's mother, who twisted a tissue in her hands with downcast eyes and whose face was racked with guilt.

'I'm going to leave you with PC Granger for now but I'll be back again soon. Have you got anybody who could come and stay with you?'

Jane shook her head.

'No friends?'

Jane swallowed hard. 'There's a friend – a work colleague.'

'I really think you need support.'

Jane nodded but fell silent.

'PC Granger will answer any other questions you have. I really am most dreadfully sorry.'

CHAPTER FIVE

TUESDAY, 17 APRIL – MORNING

Natalie drew a deep breath before looking up and down the street. The interview with Jane Hopkins had been most uncomfortable, and part of her had wanted to reach out and comfort the woman, but all she could offer was a promise she'd try her hardest to track down Savannah's killer. It hardly seemed enough and would never bring back Jane's daughter, yet it was Natalie's duty to find answers. Her officers would be nearby. They had to amass as much information as possible. This was the golden hour, the point when memories were freshest and they stood the greatest chance of getting leads. She needed to set to work quickly.

Spotting Murray ahead of her, she strode in his direction and caught up with him on the pavement outside another ramshackle house. She handed him the details of the workmen. 'I'm heading back to the station to speak to the officer in charge of the search last night. I need you to track down these two at Tenby House and Garden Services. They ought to have been on-site when Jane got in yesterday afternoon but they weren't. Get their surnames and bring them in for questioning.'

Ian and Lucy appeared from nowhere and joined them. Lucy shrugged her shoulders. 'Not got anything. Most people were out at work yesterday afternoon. Those that weren't saw nothing, and no one seems to have been about early this morning either.'

'Same here. Nobody saw a thing,' said Ian.

'Okay, Ian come back with me. I'd like you to check up on a few people, namely Lance Hopkins, his family and Savannah's mother, Jane. There was something I picked up on – a hesitancy when I asked her about getting home late. I'm sure her journey home should only have taken fifteen minutes but she didn't get back until quarter past four. She claimed she got held up in traffic but that's odd for that time of day. It's not exactly rush-hour traffic in these parts. Lucy, try Savannah's teachers and her friends – these two in particular: Sally Gilmore and Holly Bradshaw. I've had a quick look in her bedroom and there are a few new items, some with tags still attached, and I don't think she got the money for them from her mother. Someone might have given them to her as a present, or she might have stolen them. She changed out of her uniform at some point and even put in her favourite earrings. It's unlikely she went home to change because she didn't leave her uniform or school bag behind. Her mum says she's wearing an outfit that she got for her birthday and I suspect she might have put it on to meet somebody. We need to find out if there was anyone she was seeing behind her mother's back – a boyfriend perhaps. At the moment, we've no idea where her uniform, bag or mobile are. Oh, and Ian, put a trace on her phone – see if we can locate it or where it last transmitted a signal. We'll reconvene at twelve o'clock.'

Back at the station, Natalie lost no time in catching up with DI Graham Kilburn, who'd been heading the initial hunt for Savannah. A gaunt-faced man in his early sixties with grey straggly eyebrows and a bald head, Graham looked like a man who'd had enough of life and his job. He pulled out a packet of cigarettes from his pocket, offered one to Natalie – who declined – and tapped one out, placing it between his lips with the expertise of a serious smoker.

'Mind if we go upstairs? It's been a hell of a night.'

'No problem.' Natalie hadn't smoked for a year and a half. She'd given it up the same day she'd slept with Mike but still enjoyed the smell of a freshly lit cigarette. It was difficult some days not to take it back up, especially as many of her colleagues were smokers, but she was determined not to give in. They had enough expenditure in the house without her adding to it. Her mind flicked to the cigarettes hidden in Savannah's drawer and her mother, who had no idea of what her daughter did in her free time. *Do any of us?* She didn't really know what Leigh got up to when she was out of sight.

From the roof she watched the morning traffic heading towards the city centre, bustling, busy, unaware of what was going on inside the walls of the police HQ.

Graham lit up and inhaled. 'All the paperwork you need is on your desk. Local uniforms were alerted to the girl's disappearance at five thirty when Jane Hopkins went to the station to report her daughter missing. We weren't notified until two hours later after they'd conducted enquiries. They had her down as medium-risk because there was some cause for concern given the volatile relationship between Mrs Hopkins and her husband, Lance, who was known to them. Although her husband left in September last year, a neighbour, Amy Stephenson, believed she'd seen him hanging around the house only two weeks ago. We couldn't corroborate that claim as there'd been no other sightings of him.'

'Did you discover where he's moved to?'

'Unfortunately not. We interviewed Jane Hopkins but drew blanks and she was fairly sure Lance wouldn't have taken Savannah. Their split wasn't acrimonious so he wouldn't have taken her out of spite or to get back at his wife, and according to her, he'd never been especially close to Savannah. We searched the house and Savannah's bedroom for clues as to her whereabouts but found nothing helpful. Her mother wasn't able to tell us if anything was missing from her room and insisted the girl hadn't run away. By all accounts, she wasn't a popular girl and only had two friends – Sally Gilmore and

Holly Bradshaw. She'd been arguing with Sally before going off "in a mood". We reviewed footage from CCTV cameras in the town centre and spotted the girls at the back of Aldi supermarket but lost sight of Savannah after she moved away from Sally and Holly at around three forty. We checked with all shopkeepers and had information from an assistant in the phone shop, Nick Duffield, known as Duffy, who recalled seeing Savannah pass the shop still wearing her uniform and carrying a black backpack at around three forty-five. He assumed she was headed home.'

'How come he recognised her?'

'She and her friends visit the shop most weeks. It undertakes computer repairs and sells mobile phones. It also sells accessories, phone cases and such-like, and two of the girls have pay-as-you-go phones and go in regularly for top-ups to their data allowance.'

Natalie thought back to the plastic phone cases she'd found in the box in the wardrobe. Savannah had at least five different cases. 'What did the girls argue about?'

'It was over a bracelet that Savannah had given Sally. She'd wanted it back but Sally had lost it and they rowed about it. Sally said Savannah was in a lousy mood because she'd been involved in a brawl with another girl, Claire Dunbar, at school that day. She often got ribbed for her accent and for being part of a travelling community before settling here. Sally told us Savannah was fed up with the name-calling. It was at this point we wondered if she'd run away rather than been snatched. We went through the usual procedures: tried ringing her phone, conducted door-to-door enquiries along Western Park Road and then roads in the vicinity. Some neighbours wanted to assist and formed search parties to help officers cover the park and wasteland. We called off the search at midnight, and at eight o'clock this morning we received an anonymous call saying Savannah had been spotted in the park. I sent a unit out and they discovered her body almost immediately.'

'You'd already covered the area where she was found?'

'Yes.'

'And you have no idea who made the call?'

'It was from an unidentifiable phone. I sent the information to the technical support team but they haven't been able to trace it. It's no longer transmitting. This was the worst possible outcome. I'd really hoped Savannah was cooling her heels and would come home once she got over whatever was bothering her. Most teenagers come back within twenty-four hours. The evidence – the argument, the fight, unhappy at school and home – it all seemed to be pointing to her running away rather than an abduction.'

'Unhappy at home?'

'Holly said Savannah had been crying a lot recently, and when they'd asked her what was wrong, she wouldn't tell them but said she hated her mum.'

Natalie made a mental note to talk to Holly about this. 'You tried to track her phone?'

'We did but we had no joy.'

'Thanks, Graham. You've been really helpful.'

He puffed out the last of the smoke between pursed lips and pinched the tip of his cigarette between thumb and finger before pocketing it. 'You never forget them. The ones you didn't find. They haunt you.'

Natalie understood what he meant. She felt the same way about past victims. She had to bring to justice those responsible. Those she'd let down were forever in her thoughts.

                    *

Sergeant Lucy Carmichael waited in the doorway while the secretary buzzed through to Watfield Secondary School's head teacher. Holly Bradshaw and Sally Gilmore were both at school in spite of the terrible news of Savannah's death. Lucy shifted from one foot to the other and cast about the cramped office. There was something about schools that brought out the rebel in her. She'd never been a high achiever, and had it not been for her best friend, Yolande, now married to her other best friend, Murray, she'd have dropped out altogether. The corridor was painted in similar dingy hues of off-brown and creamy yellow that brought back recollections of her and Murray standing outside the head's office awaiting punishment for smoking. She pushed aside her childhood memories of miserable schooldays and foster parents who had given up on her wayward nature. She wasn't the same person. Nowadays, she had Bethany and a baby on the way, and she was a sergeant in the police force with opportunities to advance her career. Lucy Carmichael had come a long way since those dreadful days.

Lucy's mobile rang. It was Natalie who wanted to pass on the news about Savannah's fight with Claire Dunbar.

'Find out what you can about it and talk to Savannah's other friends about her relationship with her mum. Ask if they argued a lot or maybe ask how she really felt about her mother,' she said.

'Would you rather I brought both girls to the station?' Lucy asked.

'No. Best if they're kept in familiar surroundings. They might feel intimidated if we interview them here. We can always talk to them again.'

Lucy ended the call and pocketed the phone. The secretary looked up and gave her a small smile.

'Mr Derry is free now.'

The head teacher was in his thirties, not much older than Lucy, with pewter-grey eyes and a heavy monobrow that undoubtedly caused sniggers among the schoolchildren. He shook his head sadly although his face remained impassive. 'Terrible news about Savannah.'

'I wondered if you had any information which might help us form a picture of her.'

His shoulders lifted and dropped in his oversized grey cardigan and he opened wide hands. 'Tricky in that I didn't know her very well. This is a very large school and to know each child is impossible although I've seen her out and about the grounds, usually alone. She was very timid. Soon after she arrived, I recall I spoke to her in the corridor to see how she was settling in, and she adopted the startled look of a rabbit caught in headlights, wouldn't meet my eye and scurried away as soon as she could. Kirsty Davies was her form teacher and she'll undoubtedly tell you the same as all the other teachers here: Savannah was a quiet girl, one of those who barely registers on your radar. I don't mean to sound unkind. I'm merely trying to explain how anonymous she was. She kept in the background and never drew attention to herself.'

'I understand she was friendly with Sally Gilmore and Holly Bradshaw. I'd like to talk to them and possibly other classmates.'

He looked at his watch pointedly. 'I'm afraid they're with a grief counsellor at the moment. I don't really think we should disturb them. They were shaken by the news.'

'Savannah Hopkins was murdered. I think that takes precedence, Mr Derry. I don't need to remind you time is of the essence and we must gather whatever information we can.' It felt odd standing up to this figure of authority but Lucy maintained a steely gaze and the head teacher offered a tight smile of contrition.

'Of course. Do you need to speak to them together or separately?'

'Separately. I'd like to start with Sally Gilmore then Holly Bradshaw and finally Claire Dunbar.'

'Claire Dunbar? She's in the year above. Why do you want to talk to her?'

'She and Savannah were involved in a fight yesterday. I'd like to ask her what it was about. Is there somewhere I could interview them? And would you be prepared to sit in with us, please? They are minors and have the right to an adult presence.'

'Certainly. How about conducting your questions here in my office?'

'That would be most helpful.'

Mr Derry spoke to his secretary outside and returned with an extra chair for Lucy to use. 'Where would you like this?'

'Would you mind if I sat at your desk and you moved to the rear of the room?'

'If you'd prefer,' he replied and placed the chair in front of a bookcase cluttered with box files. 'Sally and Holly are on their way.'

'Thank you. I'd also like to chat to Kirsty Davies.'

'I'll arrange that once you've finished with the girls.'

A light rapping on the door announced Sally's arrival. Her voice quavered. 'Sir. I was told to come here.'

'Come in, Sally. This is Sergeant Carmichael. She wants to ask you a few questions about Savannah.' Mr Derry's bright voice made Lucy cringe.

Sally seemed to shrink back, her red-rimmed eyes widening.

Lucy spoke up before the girl became too scared. 'Hi, Sally. This won't take long. I need your help. I don't know much about Savannah and I hoped you'd be able to tell me about her.'

Her gentle tone seemed to work. Sally edged forwards and dropped onto the seat in front of the head teacher's desk. She clenched a tissue in her fist and kept her gaze lowered. Lucy spoke quietly.

'Yesterday, you and Savannah had an argument. Can you tell me what it was about?'

Sally sniffed a few times and nodded. 'She gave me a bracelet because we were friends. It came undone and I lost it. She noticed I wasn't wearing it and thought it was because I didn't want to be her friend any more, and she asked for it back. I told her I lost it but she didn't believe me and said I was deliberately keeping it. She got really snotty about it and then said I wasn't a proper friend cos proper friends wouldn't lose things and stormed off.'

'Did she often lose her temper?'

'No but she was in a bad mood because of Claire Dunbar. Claire called her a thieving gypsy and said Savannah's stepdad used to steal from people's garden sheds.'

'I imagine that upset her.'

Sally shrugged.

'I'd be pretty upset if someone accused me of stealing when I didn't.'

Again, Sally shrugged. Lucy didn't push the subject.

'Did Savannah give you any idea of where she was going?'

The girl's head moved only slightly. 'No.'

'You must have been good friends for her to give you a bracelet. I expect she shared some of her secrets with you.'

She gave another slight lift of her shoulders and her eyes anchored on a fountain pen on the desk. Her knuckles whitened as she clenched the tissue more tightly.

'I don't want you to tell me everything she shared with you but maybe you know something that will help me find out who did this to her. Can you help me, Sally?'

Another sniff, a flutter of eyelashes and a soft, 'Maybe.'

'Did she have a boyfriend or was she seeing somebody regularly?'

'I don't think so. She never said.'

'But you must have talked about boys and relationships. I talk about people I fancy with my friends. Was there anyone she really liked?'

'Justin Bieber and a boy in our class called Toby, but he's got a girlfriend and besides he doesn't like Savannah.'

'Why doesn't he like her?'

'Dunno really. I suppose it's cos she was shy, especially around boys.'

'She didn't mention anyone else, outside of school, or possibly online?'

'No.'

'Did she talk about her stepfather, Lance?'

'Only to say she was glad he'd gone. He used to get really drunk and hit her mum.'

'Did he hit her too?'

'I don't think so. She'd have said.'

'I heard she was mad at her mum. Do you know anything about that?'

Another shrug from the girl. 'I get mad at my mum some days.'

'Help me, Sally. Why was Savannah angry with her mum?'

The girl blinked several times before speaking again. 'She got a new boyfriend and Savannah said he was really creepy.'

'In what way was he creepy?'

'I dunno. Creepy. Staring at her when her mum wasn't around, saying stuff to her, being slimy and trying to touch her then pretending it was only because he was being friendly, staring at her tits, that sort of thing.'

'Did he touch her?'

'She didn't say he did, only that she wished her mum had never met him.'

'Did she tell you his name?'

'Um, it was Phil, I think… He stayed over at their house a couple of times. Savannah didn't like him at all.'

Lucy considered what she'd just learnt. Savannah might simply have been jealous of this new man in her mother's life and made up some of these allegations. However, he'd require investigating. 'Did she seem different yesterday at all? Did she seem excited or worried or nervous – before the fight with Claire?'

'I didn't notice. She was always really quiet. She didn't like people noticing her. Sometimes I forgot she was even in class.'

'Did she bring any clothes into school with her? She might have shown you them – a hoodie and jeans?'

Another shrug. 'I didn't see any clothes. She was acting a bit weird yesterday. She didn't go to lunch with us as usual. She disappeared after our art lesson and when I asked her where she went instead, she said, "Nowhere," and that she'd stayed in the form room.'

'Did she often disappear like that?'

'No, she usually hung around with us. She was okay when you got to know her. She liked the same things as us… It's a bit awkward, y'know. My mum doesn't like Savannah's mum. I liked Savannah but I wasn't really her best friend. I hung about with her cos she was good at being invisible.' She suddenly stopped talking.

'What do you mean, Sally?'

'Nothing. I'll miss her.' Her eyes filled with tears and she lowered her head.

Lucy was certain there was more but Sally wasn't going to say anything further.

'Sally, thank you very much. You've been a big help and a good friend to Savannah.'

'Can I go now?'

'Of course, unless there's anything more you want to tell me?'

Sally pushed back her chair and stood to leave. Her eyes were dewy but she looked at Lucy. 'She was okay and I really did lose the bracelet.'

Holly was waiting outside the head's office and came in as soon as Sally left. She had bright eyes and a pretty, round face and to Lucy's surprise, didn't appear to be unduly distressed by the news of her friend's death. She answered Lucy's questions without hesitation and confirmed much of what Sally had already told Lucy, including the news Savannah disliked her mother's new boyfriend.

'Why didn't she like Phil?'

'She was angry at her mum for letting him stay over without asking her. The first time he stayed, Savannah didn't even know he was in the house, not until he walked into the bathroom while she was taking a shower. She said he deliberately hung about, gawping at her, and didn't leave, even though he said he was really sorry. She thought he was really creepy – hated him coming around.'

There it was, that same word – creepy. Lucy wanted to find this Phil and quickly.

Holly stared openly at Lucy. She appeared to be more coopera-tive than Sally.

'Did he ever touch her?'

'I don't think so.'

'I heard she was crying a lot, recently. Do you know why?'

'She was unhappy.'

'What about?'

'Other kids being horrible to her, and she was upset because she thought after her stepdad left, it'd be her and her mum again like it was before he arrived, but instead her mum found a boyfriend.'

'She was close to her mum, then?'

Holly pulled a face. 'Not *close* but she liked it being just her and her mum. She used to talk about how it was before they moved away with the travellers, when they lived with her gran in Dudley. I think she was happier then.'

'Did she ever mention running away?'

'No.'

'Not at all?'

Again, Holly shook her head.

'Holly, Savannah had a lot of new stuff in her bedroom – clothes and things with price tags on them. Do you know how she got them?'

The girl lowered her eyes.

'Holly,' Lucy urged quietly. She tried again. 'Were they presents from somebody?'

Holly shook her head. 'She nicked them.'

'Stole them?'

'Yeah. She took stuff from supermarkets, shops, anywhere really. She always got away with it. I never took anything. Honest,' she suddenly added, swivelling to face the head teacher. 'I told her she shouldn't but she didn't care.'

'She smoked too, didn't she?' Lucy asked.

Holly's cheeks flushed pink. 'Maybe.'

'Did you see her smoke?'

'Once or twice.'

'How could she afford cigarettes?'

Holly lowered her voice to a whisper. 'Sometimes she sold the things she stole to get the money.' She kept her head down and would no longer meet Lucy's gaze, leaving her to assume Holly was also party to the smoking, if not the shoplifting. At least she'd established how Savannah had come by some of the goods Natalie had found in her room.

'Did she sell the things at school?'

Holly glanced in the direction of the head teacher and then nodded once.

Mr Derry cleared his throat as if he wanted to speak but Lucy glared at him.

'Can you tell me who she sold stuff to?'

'I don't know who.'

'Don't you have any idea? Maybe they could help me find out more about Savannah.'

'I really don't know. I didn't ask her.'

Lucy found that hard to believe but she was mindful of the head teacher's presence, which might be hampering Holly's willingness to say more. In spite of further questions, Lucy could get no extra information from the girl who either didn't know the answers or wasn't prepared to share them. She also claimed she didn't know where Savannah had been going or who she might have met up with. Holly's expression became more determined with each question. Lucy wondered if Holly's and Sally's mothers knew what their daughters got up to when they weren't at home. She allowed Holly to leave and waited for Claire Dunbar, the girl who'd started the fight with Savannah, to arrive. She already had some idea of how Savannah behaved and why; she could take that information back to the team for further discussion, and a name – Phil.

*

Claire Dunbar looked older than fourteen, with short, wavy, black hair that accentuated her sharp features and dark, groomed eyebrows. She wasn't especially tall but she exuded a confidence as she slipped onto the chair that had been vacated by Holly and spoke before Lucy could begin questioning her.

'I know why you want to talk to me but I want to say Savannah started it.'

'I take it you are referring to the fight you had with Savannah Hopkins, yesterday afternoon.'

'It wasn't much of a fight – she spat at me because I called her some names, then she suddenly threw herself at me, slapped me and grabbed at my hair. I fought back and then some of the older kids got involved and hauled her off me.' Her dark eyes flashed angrily.

'So why did she attack you?'

'She was in Pretty Things boutique in town on Saturday. I saw her stealing a top. She slipped it into her bag and then left the shop without paying. I told her she was a thief and she went mental at me.'

'Why didn't you say something to an assistant while you were in the shop?'

'I was with my mum and gran.'

'That isn't really an explanation, Claire.'

Claire looked down suddenly. 'I don't know. I should have but I didn't. It happened very quickly.'

It didn't make sense. Why hadn't Claire spoken up about it at the time? They weren't friends. She had no reason to protect her.

'But you're sure you saw her steal it?'

'Definitely. I challenged her about it yesterday.'

'In front of others?'

Claire squirmed in her seat. 'Yes.'

'In the schoolyard?'

'Yes.'

'At lunchtime?'

She received a nod.

'How many people were there approximately, Claire?'

'A crowd. Twenty, maybe.' She lowered her eyes.

Lucy suddenly understood why Claire had kept the information to herself. She'd wanted to embarrass Savannah in front of everyone she could.

'You said you called her names. What did you say to her exactly?'

'I don't remember.'

'Come on, Claire, I'm sure you *can* remember. We all say things in the heat of the moment. We sometimes say things we don't mean.' Lucy waited, hoping the girl would say more, and she did.

Claire squared her shoulders and said defiantly, 'I told her she was a thieving gypsy… but it's true. I didn't say anything that wasn't true.'

'Except she wasn't a gypsy.'

'She and her mum lived with the gypsies, and Savannah's step-father was one. Everyone at school knew they were gypsies and she did steal. I saw her. And my mum told me Savannah's stepdad used to steal too from sheds but the police never did anything about it. I didn't say anything wrong.'

'What else did you know about her?'

Claire shook her head. 'Not a lot. I didn't have anything to do with her. Saturday was the first time I really noticed her.'

'You said she spat at you.'

'Yeah. It was disgusting. It went down my face. She said I'd be sorry for calling her names.'

'Did she say anything else?'

'No, she suddenly went ballistic and tried to yank my hair out.'

'Did either of you get injured?'

'It was mostly pushing, pulling and shouting. She scratched my neck though.' Claire moved her collar to reveal a red mark.

'And the fight was broken up?'

'Somebody pulled her off me. I don't know who. She shouted she'd make me sorry and walked off with Sally Gilmore and Holly Bradshaw.'

'Did you see her again yesterday after that?'

'No. I'm in a different year to her. I didn't see her.'

'What did you do after school?'

'My mum picked me up and we went to visit my gran.'

'You didn't go out at all after that?'

Claire shook her head. 'No. We had tea with Gran and then we went home.'

'Had you ever been involved in a fight with her before?'

'It was the first time. I didn't pay her much attention until yesterday.'

'Did she get into fights with others?'

'Not that I heard of.'

'I understand she was called names quite often.'

'If she was, I didn't hear about it.'

Lucy pressed on but there was little more to glean. She would take what she knew back to the station and see if it helped them.

*

Everyone was gathered again in the office bang on twelve and ready to pool information. Natalie had read through Graham's report, which he'd summarised on the roof, and together with Ian had begun compiling a picture of Savannah's life. She rolled up the sleeves on her white shirt and leant across her desk to address everyone.

'There are a few grey areas concerning Savannah's life. It appears contrary to what her mother told me: she was unhappy – with school and home. Lucy, what have you found out?'

'That seems to be the case. I spoke to Sally and Holly and both confirmed Savannah didn't get along with many people. Several pupils constantly tormented her with jibes and called her derogatory names. Claire Dunbar called her a thieving gypsy yesterday, a statement she felt was justified having spotted Savannah lifting a T-shirt from the boutique in town on Saturday. A fight started and was broken up by older pupils before any teachers got involved. Claire claimed Savannah spat at her and told her she'd be sorry for what she said, then stalked away. Claire didn't know what she meant by that.

'Their form teacher, Kirsty Davies, confirmed Savannah was a pupil who kept her head down. She'd also noticed that the last few weeks Savannah had become slightly more argumentative than usual but put it down to her age. It might be a coincidence but it appears Savannah's change in attitude coincided with the arrival of Jane's new boyfriend, who has started staying over at their house. Name of Phil.'

Natalie cocked an angled brow. 'Phil, eh?'

'He walked in on Savannah when she was showering and she told her friends he was creepy. She also mentioned he stared at her a lot and she was uncomfortable with him about the place. Could be plain jealousy or there's more to it.'

'Track him down and interview him.' Natalie nodded in Ian's direction. 'Ian?'

Ian cleared his throat. 'The phone company is unable to track Savannah's mobile. It's been switched off. Last call was made on Friday lunchtime to her mum. They've sent a list of text messages and calls but quite honestly there's nothing of note on it. She only appears to have used it to stay in contact with her mum. She used Snapchat to talk to her friends but the technical department is looking into that. Nothing on it yet.

'Jane Hopkins checks out in terms of what she's told us about her past life. Her mother is dead and Jane dropped off the radar late 2015 when she went off with Lance and his family. There's a copy of the marriage certificate – July 2016. According to Lance Hopkins' P60, he works as a labourer. His tax returns are up to date, with the last one filed in Watfield last year. I haven't got a location on his current whereabouts. He's had four charges brought against him for being drunk and disorderly – one in Manchester, one in Newcastle upon Tyne and the two most recent in Watfield, last year. Their property was purchased the back end of 2016 at auction for £56,000. It was described as "in need of complete renovation". Jane was left a legacy of £60,000 when her mother passed away in 2015. This was used to buy the house, which is in her name only, not Lance's. Finally, there is an anomaly in her statement. She claimed to have left work soon after her usual time of three thirty and got held up in traffic. Even if she'd been held up behind a bicycle it couldn't have taken forty-five minutes to get from Wilton's Building Supplies on the main Ashbourne road to her house in Western Park Road. It's only four miles away. It doesn't add up. Either she's wrong about the time she left or she's withholding information.'

'We need to discuss that further with her,' said Natalie. She glanced at Murray, who'd been standing by the door, arms across his broad chest. 'Okay, onto the two labourers working on Jane's garden – Murray, what do you have on them?'

'Their names are Stu Oldfields and Will Layton. They're downstairs, waiting. Both insist they didn't see Savannah yesterday afternoon but Ian went through the statements you received from DI Graham Kilburn and found a witness, Mrs Margaret Mullens, who mentioned seeing them with Savannah and another schoolgirl, smoking outside Savannah's house last Wednesday about five p.m. I rang her about it and asked if she'd thought to report the incident to Savannah's mother, but she claimed it wasn't her business to even though she was confident all parties were smoking. I'm under the impression she was afraid of confrontation and avoided the family altogether. She didn't know much about them other than the police had been called out to the house on a couple of occasions and she saw Savannah walking to and from home now and again.'

'Okay. We'll talk to her again if we need to. Ah, here's Mike.'

Mike was striding purposefully towards the office, file in his hand. Murray opened the door for him.

'Hi again. I thought you'd like an update. I'll start with the negatives: we haven't found Savannah's school uniform, bag, mobile or indeed the star-shaped earring, missing from her lobe. That might mean the killer has them or they got lost near where she was murdered. Now onto what we do know. We're certain she was murdered at a different location then brought to the park and positioned by the waste bin. The pathologist, Ben Hargreaves, has confirmed Savannah was strangled and that the bruising on her knuckles was most likely caused by repeatedly striking something hard. He reckons death occurred sometime between eleven o'clock last night and four or five o'clock this morning.

'We've collected specks of what appears to be paint from broken skin on her hands and are currently examining them. It seems, at first glance, these are paint flecks attached to wood, presumably from a wooden door, box or crate, but I'll confirm that once we're certain. She wasn't molested in any way, and apart from the bruising to her hands and neck, shows no other signs of struggle or harm. Ben's examining her now and will send a report directly to you. Sorry to be brief but I must get back to the lab.' He passed the file to Natalie, gave her a lopsided smile and left.

Natalie faced the team once more. 'Ian, you need to keep digging. Find Lance Hopkins. Lucy, talk to Jane Hopkins and get hold of whoever this Phil character is. Murray, you'll help me to interview that pair you brought in. I'll take Stu, you take Will.'

She slapped the file onto the table. If Savannah had been killed at eleven last night, she'd been dead thirteen hours. The press would have released the story by now, headlines splashed across every newspaper, and Jane Hopkins would be caught in the media circus surrounding her daughter's death. If she'd thought it had been difficult to settle in a new town after living with travellers, she was going to find it even tougher being the subject of people's critical opinions, not to mention living with the guilt that she wasn't at home when she ought to have been.

CHAPTER SIX

TUESDAY, 17 APRIL – MORNING

The snake glided side to side as he performed lateral raises with the dumbbells. He'd positioned himself in front of a full-length mirror with another behind so he could observe as it moved silently, rippling along the muscles in his back as he lifted then lowered methodically and repeated the movement.

The reptile was fed, but after such a long fast, its hunger had grown out of proportion and it was already demanding more to assuage its voracious appetite. The hunt, the kill and the final act of leaving its prey drained of life had only served to invigorate the beast; the desire to murder again, and to do so quickly, was all-consuming, yet he must be cunning. He was playing a dangerous game. Savannah Hopkins had only just been discovered and already he was planning on snatching another to feed this obsession. His eyes glittered at the prospect. He'd waited too long for this wonderful opportunity.

He lowered the weights to the floor and flexed his pectorals. The serpent's jaw gaped wider, its hooded eyes searching, watching and waiting. *Soon.* He reached for the oil and performed the familiar ritual of tipping it into one hand and rubbing gently in controlled circular movements, coating both palms with the almond essence before spreading it across the black boa constrictor, admiring the dark-grey triangle between its nose and eyes and the subtle saddle markings close to its tail. He rubbed the oil across his chest and the snake's jaw opened wider, revealing tiny hooked teeth that could grab its prey. The boa doesn't have fangs. It's non-venomous and kills its prey by constriction, squeezing the circulatory system hard until blood can no longer reach the victim's brain and it dies within seconds due to ischaemia. His pink tongue flickered across his lips. *Like Savannah.*

Before long, there'd be another victim to satiate the hunger. The snake was going to strike again.

CHAPTER SEVEN

Natalie dropped onto a seat in front of the young man with shaggy, dirty-blond hair and matching shovel-shaped beard. He was tall, legs stretched right out under the desk so his boots were stuck out close to Natalie's chair. His muscular hands with thick fingers and cracked nails were currently curled around a blue disposable lighter. This was Stu Oldfields, the twenty-four-year-old builder and labourer who was part of the Tenby House and Garden Services team assigned to work on Jane Hopkins' house.

He spoke immediately. 'I told the detective last night that I didn't see her yesterday, not before or after school.'

'So I understand, but I also heard you left work early yesterday afternoon. Why was that?'

His hand clenched and unclenched the lighter. 'We had to pick up some supplies. The shop closed at four thirty. Early closing on Mondays.'

'Where was this shop?'

'In the retail park the other side of Watfield – KSC Building Supplies.'

'What exactly did you have to collect?' She asked the question casually and was interested to see him hesitate before answering.

'Cement... four bags, guttering, ten lengths of three metres and... some Thistle multi-finish plaster.' It was quite a specific answer to her question. She hadn't asked for quantities.

'What did you do after you purchased the supplies?'

'We headed back to the yard.'

'Which yard do you mean?'

'The yard at work.'

'At Tenby House and Garden Services?'

'Yeah. We took the supplies back, well… I didn't. Will did. It was almost clocking off time so he dropped me off at my place first. I live nearby in Mulberry Close.'

'I expect you have a receipt to confirm what you bought and time of purchase?'

'Got it on account. The boss, Noel Reeves, will have the details of what we bought. Won't be a time on it though. It'll have been sometime before four thirty.'

'How long did it take you to get the supplies and load them onto the van then drive to the yard?'

He scratched at his chin and glanced away for a moment. 'Not long.'

'Was there anybody else at the shop while you were there?'

Another scratch and a ponderous wait before he said, 'I didn't see anyone. I wasn't paying much attention, to be honest.'

Natalie kept her gaze steady. 'So, what time did you get home?'

He pulled a face. 'Can't say for sure. Will dropped me off at my house and I went straight up for a shower. Then I played on my Xbox until my mum got home. I didn't check the time.'

He seemed ill at ease and Natalie was certain he wasn't telling the truth.

'Your mother can vouch for you being at home when she got in?'

'I don't know. I was in my room. She must have known I was there. I went downstairs at about six thirty or so for something to eat.'

'But she didn't see you?'

He picked up the lighter again. 'I know what you're suggesting but I *was* at home. Ask Will.'

'I shall. Did you talk to Savannah much?'

'Now and again. I was busy a lot of the time.'

'What did you talk about?'

'Not much. Music, films, stuff.'

'You shared the same interests?'

'Not really. It was just chat – banter – nothing serious. One time, I was whistling along to the radio and she said she liked the song. I was just making an effort to be nice to her. I'd ask her anything like what she was having for tea or if she'd seen *Isle of Dogs*. That's what I'm like. I'm nice to the people where I work. I was nice to Jane too.'

'I have a witness who saw you smoking with Savannah and another girl at Savannah's house last Wednesday at about five p.m.'

'She's wrong.'

Natalie's mouth stretched into a smile. 'I didn't tell you it was a female witness.'

'I assumed it would be a woman,' he replied. The giveaway was his hand, now covering his mouth as he spoke.

'No, you didn't. You knew who I was referring to.'

He dropped his hand, drummed his fingers against the desk in a light, disjointed beat. His chin jutted forwards. 'Once. It was once. Jane had nipped out to get something and Savannah was hanging about the house with one of her mates. She came outside and asked if we fancied a smoke. She'd got a packet of cigarettes and we both took one. It was only a crafty fag at the back of her house, but some woman in her fifties walked past and stopped for a second when she saw us. Savannah hid her cigarette but we thought she'd noticed us. Savannah was worried the woman would tell her mother but I told her not to worry. I didn't think she would. Not judging by the way she scurried off. That's all. It was one time.'

'And you think it's okay to accept cigarettes from underage girls and encourage them to smoke?'

'It was no big deal. I started smoking when I was a kid. Savannah told us she'd been smoking for two years. She wasn't a young thirteen-year-old; she was quite grown-up in some ways – quiet but not like some who are a bit juvenile and silly.'

'She might have appeared that way but actually she was still a minor. I'm going to cut to the chase here. Did you have any form of relationship with her?'

'No!'

'Did you make any advances towards her?'

'What, try it on with her? No way. I'm not stupid. Imagine if something like that got back to my boss? I'd get the boot. I didn't, and she didn't flirt or anything with me, either. Ask Will. He knows nothing happened. Besides, she's not my type at all.'

'What about her friend?'

'I didn't try it on with her either.'

Natalie noted his indignation and also that he couldn't leave his lighter alone, his fingers rubbing the plastic as he spoke. She changed tack. 'Yesterday afternoon, you and Will left the job early to collect building supplies.'

His head bounced up and down as she spoke. 'Boss sent Will a text message asking us to get the materials so we had to knock off early.'

'You were dropped off at home and you didn't see or speak to Savannah Hopkins at all? Is that correct?'

'That's right. A police officer came around last night, told me she'd gone missing and quizzed me about her, things she might have told me, whether I'd noticed anyone else around the house, if she'd seemed unhappy – that sort of stuff.'

'Did she?'

'A few days ago, she seemed more downbeat·than usual. I asked her if she was okay and she said she was sick of the kids in her class and the whole town. Said she'd like to leave Watfield.'

'Did she mention where she might go?'

'London. She really wanted to become a singer. She thought that was the place to go. We all have daft ideas like that. I wanted to be a footballer at her age. When the officer told me she was missing, I figured she'd run away.'

'When was the last time you saw Savannah?'

'Friday afternoon. Jane sent her out with two mugs of tea. Jane always makes sure we get enough tea and biscuits.'

'How was she?'

'Same as usual – quiet, a bit shy.'

'She was a quiet, timid girl but she came outside and offered around cigarettes and poured her heart out about wanting to be a singer to you, a complete stranger.'

'Maybe she just liked me and felt she could tell me things. Girls generally like me.'

This fresh element of smugness served only to irritate Natalie, who needed to corroborate his version of events. Murray was in the adjacent room interviewing his work colleague, Will. She'd see if their accounts tallied.

'I'm going to leave you for a moment. Could you wait here, please?'

'Can't I go yet? I haven't done anything.'

His insensitivity was irksome. 'You're helping us with our enquiries into the murder of a thirteen-year-old girl who you knew, so for the moment, sit tight.'

She tapped on the door to interview room B and Murray emerged. They kept their voices lowered.

'Stu says they went to collect supplies yesterday afternoon and he was dropped off at home. Didn't see Savannah,' she said.

'Same story as Will – they went to pick up some cement and guttering and he took it back to the yard. Said it didn't need both of them to offload the supplies and since they were driving past Stu's house, he deposited Stu there and then carried on without him. Will was in the yard until almost five fifteen. The owner,

Noel Reeves, was present at the time, chatted to him for a while about their current job and likelihood of finishing by the end of the month so they could move on to another job in Watfield.'

'Have you checked with Mr Reeves?'

'I rang him a few minutes ago. Will appeared at about quarter to five and stayed until well after five. He also confirmed he asked them to collect the materials from the suppliers before they shut shop at four thirty.'

'Okay. What about smoking with the girls? Did Will admit to that?'

'Said the girls were giggly and asked if they wanted a cigarette. He knew they were underage, but since he didn't offer them the cigarettes, he didn't think it was wrong. Didn't speak much to Savannah but said she seemed to gravitate to Stu and had spoken to him on a couple of occasions.'

'Mind if I have a quick word? I can't shake off the feeling Stu's not being straight with me. His body language is all wrong.'

'He could be nervous.'

Natalie pulled a face. 'No, it's more than that.'

Murray's interviewee, Will Layton, was older than Stu, a bull-necked man in his late twenties with lips pressed into a thin line. He rested his elbows on the desk, his eyes narrowing at her arrival.

'Good afternoon, Will. I'm DI Ward. I've been talking to your colleague, Stu, about Savannah Hopkins. I'd like to hear your version of events. You both left work early yesterday and I'd like you to run through where you went.'

'I already went through everything with DS Anderson.'

'And I'd like you to go through it again for me.'

'We had to collect some cement and guttering from the suppliers at the other side of town. I got a text from Noel asking us to pick up the stuff before four thirty, when they shut, and take it to the yard. We left Jane's house at about four, drove to KSC Building Supplies, picked up the gear and headed back to the yard. That's where we leave the van each night – outside the offices. I dropped Stu off at his house, which is a couple of streets away, and delivered the goods. I knew nothing about Savannah being missing until later when I heard down the pub that the coppers were looking for her.'

'You don't use Wilton's Building Supplies for your building materials?'

'We don't have an account with them, and besides, they sell mostly to the public. We're trade. We use KSC.'

'How many bags of cement did you buy?'

'What?'

'How many bags of cement did you purchase?'

'Four bags of general-purpose cement.'

'Weight?'

'Err, twenty-five kilos each.'

'And what sort of guttering? Plastic? Steel? Length?'

'Galeco galvanised steel, ten lengths of three metres. Why do you want to know all this?'

Natalie didn't respond to his question. 'Anything else?'

'No. That was it.'

'What about plaster?'

His eyes darted from Natalie to Murray. 'They didn't have exactly what we needed so we didn't get it. The boss said he'd go to Stoke-on-Trent to get it this morning.'

'And what make of plaster was it?'

'Thistle multi-finish. They'd run out.'

'I could check those details with the suppliers.' She cocked her head and gave him a small smile. Stu's version had been slightly different.

Will kept his silence.

'And Stu was with you all the time?'

Will looked away. She'd got him cornered.

'You know there will be CCTV footage from the building suppliers proving you went inside alone. Do I need to request it?' His chin lowered, a submissiveness. She'd guessed correctly. Stu had claimed they'd picked up plaster but there had been none, a fact he'd have known if he'd accompanied Will. 'You're not only lying to us, you're perverting the course of justice by being uncooperative. We're investigating a murder, a cold-blooded murder of a young girl, and we don't have time for timewasters like you. I don't care what your motives are for lying on his behalf; what I want is the truth. Stu wasn't with you, was he?'

He glowered at her, eyes glittering before finally replying, 'No. I went to the suppliers alone.'

*

Lucy was inside 21 Western Park Road, trying hard to get Jane Hopkins to talk. The woman was a sobbing mess, hair lank and flat to her head, and eyes hollow in a grey face. Tanya Granger was with her, an arm around her shoulders. The house phone rang and Tanya patted Jane's arm gently then stood up. Lucy was aware of Jane's eyes following the liaison officer, who answered the call and quietly told the reporter at the other end not to ring again.

'Another one?' Jane said, sniffs interrupting her words. Tanya nodded.

'Jane, I really need to ask you some questions. Are you up to it?'

Jane's staccato inhalations quickened.

'Jane. I have to ask you about Phil.'

The breaths became soft sobs once more.

'We know you've been seeing somebody called Phil. Help me out, Jane. I have to eliminate him from our enquiries.'

'It wasn't him… He didn't kill her.' Jane fought for control, hands twisting at a fleece blanket on her knees.

'Jane, if you won't tell me anything, I'll have to find him and take him to the station for questioning.'

Her eyes widened. 'Don't. Please… don't.'

'Then tell me what I need to know. Who he is?'

'Phil Howitt. He owns Wilton's Building Supplies, where I work.'

Lucy had checked Jane's background and believed the owner to be called Wyn not Phil Howitt.

Jane explained. 'He hates being called Wyn. He's always been Phil to everyone. He got the nickname because he looks like Phillip Schofield, the television presenter.'

'How long have you been involved with him?'

'Since the office party last Christmas,' she replied softly, fingers plucking at the edge of the blanket. 'He's married and has two little kids. You mustn't question him. His wife can't find out about us. He had nothing to do with Savannah's disappearance or murder.'

'I'm afraid that's for us to investigate and decide.'

'He wasn't involved.'

'What makes you so sure?'

Tears tumbled down her cheeks. She raised her haunted eyes. 'I was with Phil when Savannah went missing. He's the reason I was late home. We were having sex in the back office and I didn't leave at my usual time. I left almost half an hour later.'

'You told DI Ward you were held up in traffic.'

'It was a half-truth. I got stuck in a long line of traffic behind a tractor, and none of us could overtake, but if I'd left on time, that probably wouldn't have happened. It's my fault. This is all my fault.'

*

Natalie and Murray sat in front of Stu Oldfields. Murray kept his eyes anchored on the man, arms folded, filling his seat with his huge frame.

'What's happened? Why are you looking at me like that? What's Will told you?' The confidence had disappeared.

'I think you've a fair idea of what he told us,' said Murray.

'The fucker. He promised he'd back me up.'

Natalie took over. 'I'm afraid the new information we've received changes quite a few things, Stu. You no longer have an alibi for yesterday afternoon. You didn't go to buy supplies with Will, in fact you left Jane's house fifteen minutes before him at quarter to four. He told us you headed towards town. That's the same route Savannah would have taken to return home. You must have seen her coming in the opposite direction.'

Stu's head swayed wildly from side to side. 'It isn't what you think.'

'And what might I be thinking?' said Natalie sharply.

'I didn't kill Savannah.'

'Let me tell you what I actually think, Stu. I think you've wasted a lot of my valuable time by keeping back the truth. Savannah was murdered. You told the officer in charge of investigating her disappearance that she'd hinted about running away and you possibly muddied waters for his investigation.' She held up a hand to silence him when he began to retort. 'Shut up. I'm speaking now. You've lied, withheld information, been vague with your responses and now you're telling me you didn't see Savannah, even though you left her house and walked into town at about the time she was returning home. From where I'm sitting, you'd better have a cast-iron alibi or you're suddenly our number-one suspect. Where did you go?'

'I didn't kill her.'

'That's not what I asked you,' Natalie snapped.

He lifted the lighter and twisted it around between his fingers. 'I met up with somebody.'

'Who?'

'I can't say.'

Natalie slammed her palm against the desk. 'For crying out loud! Do you want to be charged for murder?'

'I didn't kill her.'

'Who did you meet up with?'

He stared at the lighter. Natalie waited, lips pursed, eyes drilling into him. When he didn't meet her gaze, she sat back in her seat.

'Right, Stu. I haven't got time to piss about. I'm not going to play your stupid games. I could do this the hard way. I could waste my team's valuable efforts tracking down your movements by tracing your mobile, using CCTV footage, any number of ways... all of which will take time. Eventually, we'll determine exactly what route you took, where you went and who you were with. If you're not guilty of either abducting or killing Savannah, you can save me a lot of hassle and allow me to do my job properly, which is tracking down her killer. If you don't cooperate, I can charge you on a number of offences, and ultimately, if you're lying, and you did bump into Savannah or go off with her, I can charge you for your part in her murder. How do you want to play this? Let me give you a helpful suggestion – one way will make me so furious I'll have you banged up in a cell within minutes; the other might just see you going back home later today. Which is it to be?'

He refused to look up.

'DS Anderson, charge Stu with perverting the course of justice and stick him downstairs in a cell. Stu, you'll need to contact a lawyer.' She scraped back her chair and marched to the door. She was pinning everything on him responding to this heavy-handedness but he kept silent. She stood outside in the corridor and lifted her head to the ceiling. *Bloody Stu Oldfields.*

CHAPTER EIGHT

TUESDAY, 17 APRIL – AFTERNOON

Natalie threw open the door to the office and flung her file onto the nearest table. 'Little bastard won't talk. He's wasting our fucking time!'

Ian watched her as she paced the room before he spoke. 'We might have something else to go on. I've been reading through all the files DI Graham Kilburn gave you, along with the statements we took from witnesses this morning, and one of the last people to see Savannah near the Aldi supermarket was a bloke called Anthony Lane. I ran his name through the police database, and guess what? He's on the register. He's a known sex offender and was charged in 2008 for exposing himself to young girls.'

'Okay, we'll talk to him.'

The internal phone rang. It was Murray. 'Stu's just told me where he was yesterday afternoon.'

'Where?'

'In the park behind Savannah's house. He was with a girl right up until six thirty and then he went home, had dinner with his mum and watched telly.'

'Who was he with?'

'He's reluctant to give us her name. Apparently, she's a schoolgirl.'

'From the same school Savannah attended?'

'No. She's from Lincoln Fields Secondary School which is at the far side of town.'

'He needs to tell us who she is. I'm guessing she's underage or he'd be more cooperative. Press him, Murray.'

She put down the receiver and faced Ian. 'Seems Murray's got him talking at last. If Stu's alibi checks out, he'll be out of the frame for this and we're down a suspect. Have you got an address for Anthony?'

Ian scribbled it on a sticky note. As he did so, her mobile phone rang.

Lucy's voice crackled, like she had a poor signal. 'Jane's confessed she's in a relationship with Phil Howitt, owner of Wilton's Building Supplies. They were having sex in his office yesterday afternoon, which was why she was late leaving the premises. She says he can't have had anything to do with Savannah's disappearance.'

'We still need to talk to him. We don't know if she was actually snatched coming home from school or much later. She might not have been taken at all. She was dressed to meet somebody. Just because he was with her mother at four doesn't mean he didn't meet up with Savannah afterwards.'

'My thoughts exactly, which is why I'm sitting outside the office of Wilton's Building Supplies, about to go in and question him.'

'Good. Savannah told Sally that Phil was creepy. There might be a solid reason for that. Find out how well they got along, if at all.'

'Roger. On it.'

The line went dead and Natalie turned her attention to the address Ian had passed her. Anthony lived a few minutes away from the supermarket. 'Nothing on Lance yet?'

'Not a thing.'

'Let me know as soon as you locate him. I'm going to talk to Anthony. What was the name of the other guy who saw her on her way home?

'Nick Duffield but he's known as Duffy. Works in the phone shop in Watfield.'

'I'll question him too while I'm in town. Ask Murray to check out Stu's alibi once he coughs up who it is.'

'Reckon he'll tell Murray who he was meeting, then?'

'For certain. That's why I left Murray alone with him. I got the impression Stu was slightly afraid of him. If anyone can extract that information, it's Murray.'

*

Phil Howitt was only in his mid-forties but with a full head of platinum hair that was at odds with his heavy, dark brows. He studied Lucy carefully and shook his head sadly. Jane had been correct when she said he resembled the television presenter Phillip Schofield. 'What a truly dreadful thing to have happened. I spoke to Jane last night. The poor thing was in bits. I can't imagine how she must be feeling. And Savannah – a lovely girl. I can't believe this has happened to her. Have you any idea who might have killed her?' His eyebrows wrinkled with unease and sorrow.

Lucy had come across people like him before – overly concerned. He pulled back a chair for her to sit down in a gentlemanly fashion and continued making tut-tutting noises. 'We were all distraught to hear the news. Jane's a valued employee.'

Lucy glanced at the digital picture frame on his desk that flashed up photographs one after another – a baby dressed in a white christening gown; two toddlers beaming for the camera; the same two children holding hands, both dressed in matching hats with pom-poms; one child on a bike – all of them proving Phil Howitt was a family man. He followed her gaze and confirmed her thoughts. 'That's Izaak and India. Izaak's four and India almost three now. Time flies so quickly. You have any children?'

Lucy and Bethany were expecting their first baby in a few months but she wasn't going to share that information with a man she'd never met before. 'No.'

He moved behind the desk and sat down. 'How may I help you?'

Lucy decided not to beat about the bush. 'I understand you and Jane Hopkins are in a relationship.'

He steepled his forefingers and pressed them against plump, pink lips.

'It's not serious.'

'But you are involved with her?'

'I really don't see what bearing my relationship with Jane has on your investigation, and I trust you will be discreet about whatever knowledge you've amassed. I may have my indiscretions but I also love my wife and family. I wouldn't want them to be upset in any way.'

Lucy cringed inwardly. However, she wasn't here to break up his marriage. 'It's important I eliminate you from our enquiries. You are connected to the victim and her mother, therefore we have to question you.'

'I suppose so.'

'You've stayed overnight at Jane's house on a number of occasions.'

'Is that a question or a statement?'

Lucy ignored the flippancy. 'Have you?'

'Yes. I spent a few nights at Jane's.'

'That must have been tricky to arrange without your wife becoming suspicious.'

'Not really. There are numerous trade events and conferences that she believes I'm attending. But that's not really any of your business. Why do you want to know if I've stayed at Jane's house?'

'When did you last see or speak to Savannah?'

'Last week. Thursday morning. At breakfast. Before you ask, I got along well with her. She was somewhat of an introvert but there was no animosity there. We chatted a few times when I was there, but as you can imagine, I didn't see much of her. I spent my time with Jane. I wasn't under any impression Savannah was unhappy about the situation. Jane didn't say anything about it and the girl was always pleasant to my face.'

'Was Savannah aware you are married?'

'I certainly didn't tell her.'

'There was one occasion when you walked in on her while she was showering.'

He removed his fingers and laughed lightly. 'Oh, lord, yes! That was highly embarrassing – for us both. I was caught completely unawares. I apologised, of course, and backed out immediately.'

'That's not what Savannah told her friends. She claimed you hung about the bathroom staring at her.'

His mouth flapped open. 'That's preposterous! Of course I didn't. What a ridiculous statement to have made.'

Lucy noted the large gestures that accompanied his words and eyes that scanned the room quickly. He was nervous. 'She also gave her friends reason to believe things weren't as comfortable between you as you have suggested.'

'Why would she do such a thing? Was she attention-seeking? I certainly did nothing to warrant such reaction.'

'She told her friends you often stared at her and made her feel uncomfortable.'

'That's *utter* nonsense.'

'Did you ever proposition her in any way?'

'For crying out loud! What do you take me for? I have a wife and two young children. I'm not some debased character who gets his rocks off staring at teenage girls.' He ran a slim finger around the collar of his white shirt.

Lucy kept up the questioning. 'Yesterday afternoon, you and Jane were in your office—'

'We don't need to discuss the intimate details but yes, we were in this office.' He glanced at the black leather sofa behind Lucy, which she'd noted on her arrival.

'What time did Jane leave?'

'Almost four o'clock.'

'And you?'

'Not until gone five thirty. I had paperwork to complete.'

'Did anyone see you between Jane leaving and you departing?'

'No. My personal assistant, Maisie, was off yesterday, and as you can see, I'm on the top floor. Nobody comes up here unless they need to speak to me.'

'Not even when you left?'

'Again, no. I always use the back staircase that leads directly to the staff car park at the side of the warehouse, and you'll notice there are no windows overlooking it. Most of the employees were either in the warehouse or the shop, which is accessed by the public car park to the front of this building. Nobody would have seen me.'

'They might have seen you leave in your car.'

'Only if they happened to be in the car park at the time and that's highly unlikely. They'd have been inside. The place doesn't shut until eight.'

'What time did you get home?'

'I didn't go straight home. I changed into my running gear in the office and then drove to Jubilee Park where I jogged for almost an hour. After that, I went home.'

Jubilee Park was five miles outside Watfield – a huge expanse with numerous jogging routes, popular with serious athletes training for marathons and die-hard running enthusiasts.

'Did you see many people on your route?'

'One or two. I didn't pay them much attention. I had my music turned up and my mind was elsewhere.'

'Can your wife vouch for you returning home at about six thirty, then?'

His face wrinkled apologetically and he gave a small shrug. 'Unfortunately, she can't. She and the children stayed over at my mother-in-law's last night. She lives in York. I'm expecting them back later today.'

'Did anyone spot you arriving at your house – a neighbour perhaps?'

'Not that I noticed. You can't think I'm involved in any way, can you? I absolutely had nothing to do with Savannah's death. Jane said she disappeared on her way home from Watfield Secondary and I was here then, right until five thirty.'

'We believe Savannah was meeting somebody and she was murdered later – around eleven. As you have no alibi for that time, we need to confirm your whereabouts.'

He stood up abruptly and pressed his fingertips to his head. 'No. No. This isn't right. I had nothing to do with it. There are some cameras along the road. Maybe you could search for my car on them. That would vindicate me, wouldn't it?'

'You better give me the route you took and approximate times you made the journey, and I'll also need to take a DNA sample from you.'

'You can't possibly believe I killed her.'

'As I explained, we have to eliminate anyone who knew the victim.'

'I suppose so. Look, about earlier. I don't want to seem heartless. Jane and I… it's complicated.'

'I'm sure it is, sir.'

'No. It really is. Jane works for me and, well, she can be quite persuasive.'

'That isn't any of my business. I'm only interested in your movements from yesterday afternoon onwards. Were you in contact with Savannah at all?'

'How do you mean?'

'Do you have her mobile number?'

'Erm, no.'

'You seem uncertain.'

'I definitely don't have it. Why would I have her number? I've told you everything I know. I'm not responsible for her death.'

'But with nobody to confirm your whereabouts, we have to prove where you were and establish you did not meet with Savannah or that you weren't in the vicinity of her house yesterday.'

He lifted his fingers again, rubbed at his neck. 'I might have driven past the house.'

Lucy remained poker-faced. 'What time would this have been?'

'Late. Elevenish. Jane rang me as soon as the police started hunting for Savannah. She was obviously distressed and asked if I'd visit her – give her moral support. I told her it wasn't a good idea to draw attention to our relationship. In truth, I though Savannah had just gone off with friends or was in a mood and would return. Jane kept calling me, so in the end, I went around to comfort her, but when I saw the police activity near the park, I drove away.'

'What made you think Savannah had taken off with friends? From what I gather, she didn't have many friends.'

'She could be a little moody at times. I don't claim to understand teenage girls. I assumed – wrongly as it happened – that she was with friends and would come home. Sadly, she hasn't.'

'Earlier you said she was an introverted girl who was pleasant to your face. Now you are suggesting she was moody.'

'Teenagers are capable of being both pleasant and moody at times,' he snapped.

'And you witnessed her being moody on occasions?'

'You're taking my words out of context. I'm only telling you what I imagined to be the truth. I thought Jane was overreacting to her daughter's disappearance and I was wrong. Okay?'

'Could I take a look at your phone, sir, to confirm the times Jane rang you?'

He sighed dramatically and passed her a silver iPhone. She glanced through the call log. There were several calls from what she assumed to be Jane's number from six o'clock until the early hours of the morning, and none from any other number. It appeared he was telling the truth. However, he could have made contact with Savannah using social media. 'I'd like to take your phone back with me. I'll have it returned as soon as possible.'

Phil frowned and got to his feet. 'Now, hang on a minute. You have no right to confiscate it. I need it for work and there's nothing on it that will help you with your investigation. I've already told you where I was. I've assisted you with your enquiries and I demand you return my property immediately or I shall report you to your superiors.'

His demeanour had transformed; the pleasant look had departed, replaced by a scowling mask. Why had he suddenly become so anxious about his mobile? There was only one reason Lucy could think of: there was something that might incriminate him on it. She pressed on. 'If you feel I've acted inappropriately, then you'll have to report me, but given you have no concrete alibi as to your whereabouts, you were in the vicinity at the time of Savannah's murder and I have reasonable doubt regarding your actual relationship with Savannah, I am within my rights to examine this device. It will be returned shortly. I'd like to take your laptop too.'

'Whoa! That's enough now. You're not taking it.'

'You can't prevent me, sir.'

'Like hell I can't. It's my laptop.'

'Sir, I insist you sit down and not prevent me from doing my job. I wouldn't want to have to charge you.'

The eyes blazed fiercely but he stepped backwards, pressed his knuckle to his mouth momentarily and composed his features once more. 'I had absolutely nothing to do with Savannah's death. I want that noted. Nothing whatsoever.'

'Understood.' Lucy picked up the laptop and tucked it under her arm.

'I'm still inclined to report you. I'm not happy with the way you've conducted your interview or with you seizing my possessions as if I were some criminal.'

'I'm sorry you feel that way, sir. However, I'm satisfied I've carried out my investigations in a professional manner. I'll see they're returned to you as soon as possible.'

Lucy turned on her heel, heart thumping. Her intuition sensed she was onto something and she was keen to find out why he'd been so unhappy with her taking his electronic devices. She needed to get them back to the lab pronto.

CHAPTER NINE

At the same time Lucy was interviewing Phil Howitt, Natalie stood outside an unassuming, two-storey brick building and rang the doorbell to number 4, a ground-floor flat. Anthony Lane, a known sex offender, in jogging bottoms and a loose, long-sleeved T-shirt, opened the door, a half-eaten piece of toast in his hand.

'Yeah?'

Natalie held out her ID card for him to study. 'DI Natalie Ward. I'm here about Savannah Hopkins. I'd like to ask you a few questions about yesterday and what you actually saw.'

He stuck his head out and glanced up and down the street before saying, 'Come in.'

With the door shut behind her, Natalie couldn't escape the aroma of toast and bacon that filled her nostrils. Anthony waved her into the kitchen and to a small square table shoved into the corner of the room. He cleared away a plate stained with tomato ketchup, chewing the remainder of his toast as he did so. Natalie waited for him to invite her to sit before pulling out a well-worn wooden chair and dropping onto its shiny surface.

Anthony joined her. He wiped crumbs from his mouth and spoke. 'I saw her in the Aldi car park behind the main entrance, with two other girls. I don't know what they were discussing but she suddenly threw up her arms and marched away. The other girls nudged each other and laughed.'

'What did you do afterwards?'

'I went into the supermarket to do my shopping and walked home. I watched some television and then decided to go to the pub – the Spread Eagle, near the monument. On my way there, I spotted police in the pedestrian area of town and asked a copper what was going on. He told me they were looking for Savannah and I told him I'd seen her. That's it. I described her to him and what I'd seen outside the supermarket, and they took notes.' He bit at a ragged thumbnail, ignoring the lengthy, greasy fringe that had tumbled forwards into his eyes.

'Did you know Savannah or her friends?'

'I've seen them about town. A lot of the schoolkids from Watfield Secondary come into town once classes end. I see them milling about sometimes if I'm out and about.'

'Are you often "out and about"?'

'A man has to eat. I need to shop somewhere and I live near the town centre, don't I? I work at the brewery and get in about three thirty. I tend to shop when I get in – choose something I fancy for my dinner.' He lifted his thumb back to his lips and nibbled at some skin around the nail.

'You understand why I'm interviewing you, don't you?'

'Let me take a wild guess. My past. I'm the go-to person when anything happens to children, aren't I? I'm the supposed kiddy-fiddler that people shun and I happen to be a registered sex offender. That's it, isn't it? You lot never give a bloke a second chance. I never touched any of the girls, you know. I was charged for exposing myself. I never laid a finger on any of them and it all happened ten years ago.'

'That's a mighty big chip you've got on your shoulder, Anthony. I actually wanted to talk to you because you're one of only a handful of people who recalls seeing Savannah yesterday afternoon before she went missing.' She let her words sink in. He grunted a response.

'Was she dressed in school uniform?'

'Yes. They all were.'

'Did you overhear any of their conversation?'

'No. I was concentrating on getting a trolley from the trolley park so I didn't hear what they said.' He kept his eyes anchored on his thumb.

'Were the girls still there when you came out?'

'No, and I didn't see them or Savannah on my way home. I walked back past the church.'

'Anthony, I think you know more than you're telling me.'

'Why would I keep anything back?'

'You tell me.'

His eyes widened to reveal flecks of orange in his dark irises. 'You're one of those officers who believes people like me should never be accepted back in society, aren't you?'

'There's that chip again. No. I'm one of those officers who thinks somebody who is only buying food for one person doesn't need a large trolley for a supermarket shop.' She sat back in the chair and folded her arms.

'So single people only buy small amounts, do they?' he sneered.

'That's not what I'm suggesting, but you carried whatever you bought from the supermarket back home and I expect it couldn't have weighed too heavily. You wouldn't have used a trolley for a small amount of shopping.'

She had him on the ropes. He blinked furiously several times at being caught out. He stood up and paced to the kitchen sink. 'I didn't see Savannah, all right?'

'What else did you hear or see? What were the girls talking about?'

'I didn't hear anything.'

'Anthony, I can interview you at the station or you can tell me everything now and make life easier for yourself. Do you really fancy getting into my car in front of your neighbours? Tongues will wag if they see you being led away. People will assume all sorts of things about you. You don't want that, do you?'

'For fuck's sake. That isn't fair. I've kept my head down for years. I don't try to annoy anybody and I'm trying to lead a normal life. I just happened to be at the supermarket—'

'Anthony, cut the bullshit. What did you overhear the girls saying?'

Her sharp words worked. His nose wrinkled and then he spoke again. 'All three were smoking. They're usually around the back of the supermarket at that time. I see them hanging about most days. Savannah was angry about something; she was waving her cigarette about and shouted, "Bastard!" and then suddenly she noticed me. Anyway, she called me a pervert and I didn't hang around long after that. I rushed into the supermarket and grabbed some cheese. While I was at the checkout, I saw her march away, like I told you. On my way out, I overheard one of the other girls say she was a stupid cow. I guessed she meant Savannah. That's everything. Honest.'

'You saw Savannah on a few occasions?'

'Usually at the supermarket or in the side street. She was always with the same two friends.'

'How come you seem to know her better than the other girls? You haven't mentioned them by name.'

'No special reason.'

A muscle twitched in Natalie's jaw. 'You need to level with me, Anthony. I meant what I said about taking you to the station and I shall if I'm not satisfied with your responses. I'm sure your neighbours will be keen to tell everyone they saw you being marched to a police car. So, let's try again. Why was Savannah of more interest to you than her friends?'

His narrow shoulders slumped. 'A few months ago, I noticed her stealing some stuff from the clothes section in Aldi. She rammed a top into her backpack and strolled out and nobody stopped her. I was kind of interested to see if she'd do it again and to know if she'd get caught, so I started hanging about the supermarket car park until she went inside, then I'd follow her and see what she took. She got away with all sorts of goods. It was just a casual interest.'

'You watched a teenage girl stealing? That sounds highly suspicious to me. Did you ever challenge her about it or act like a responsible adult and report her like you ought to have done?'

'I know I should have but part of me wanted her to get away with it. Supermarkets are rich, right? They can afford to lose a few items. I admired her boldness.'

Natalie kept her cool. 'I'd say that was being party to theft.'

'No. I wasn't. I was merely an observer. She was good at it too – lightning quick. She'd lift things under people's noses. It was like she was invisible to everyone around her. I wish I could creep about unnoticed. It would make life more bearable.'

'Oh, please, you're breaking my heart with your hard-luck attitude. I'm investigating Savannah's murder, and the fact you got pleasure from watching her shoplift is, quite frankly, sick. Do you have anything else to help me work out where she went?'

His lank hair fell further across his face, covering some of the acne marks he sported from his youth as he shook his head.

'I'll be back if I need any further information from you. I'd strongly suggest you stay where we can find you. Don't leave town.'

'See, you're like most of the folk around here. You wouldn't use that tone with me if I wasn't on the sex offenders' register.'

'Whatever,' said Natalie, wearily, and stood up in one swift movement.

*

Back at Samford Police headquarters, Lucy had returned to the office and was instructing one of the technical team who was now in possession of Phil Howitt's iPhone and laptop.

'How quickly can you examine it?' asked Lucy.

The woman shrugged lightly. 'Mike told us to prioritise anything from your team, so as soon as we find anything, I'll get back to you.'

'Great, thanks.'

Once the technician had gone, Murray looked up from his screen. 'You're keen, Lucy. Hoping to get fast-tracked for promotion?'

She gave him a silent two-fingered sign that made him chuckle.

'You okay, Ian? You look a little pale. You're not overdoing it, are you?' she asked.

Ian muttered something unintelligible.

'He's being brave and wearing his big-boy pants today,' Murray said.

Lucy smiled. 'More like bloody Superman pants. He did save your life, you know? Or at least saved you from getting carved up.'

'Shut up, the pair of you,' Ian snapped.

'Oh, okay.' Murray's eyebrows arched high on his forehead. 'Pants must be too tight,' he added with a wicked grin.

Lucy mouthed, 'What's up with him?'

Murray lifted both hands and pulled a face.

Ian spoke up. 'I'm trying to concentrate, that's all, so stop distracting me.'

Murray swung back towards his desk, teasing over. Before the incident in March, in which Ian had stepped in for Murray during a takedown and been knifed, the men hadn't seen eye to eye. Ian had only been back a few days and already the cracks were reappearing in their relationship. In Lucy's opinion, it was more than a football rivalry that caused them to bicker – both men wanted to be the alpha male. Ian had gone up in her esteem. He hadn't made a fuss over the injuries that had kept him in hospital for a couple of weeks and on painkillers since. He'd insisted on returning to work as soon as he possibly could, and to Lucy, that showed guts.

The team resumed their roles, banter over. Not long after, Natalie rang in and spoke to Murray to give him an update.

'Anthony Lane saw Savannah smoking in the car park behind Aldi with two girls who I assume are Holly Bradshaw and Sally Gilmore. Also spotted her shoplifting a few times. Can you try and locate him on any CCTV cameras in town? He claims he left the supermarket and went home via the church. See if you can verify that for me. I'm about to talk to Duffy from the phone shop. What else have we got?'

'Lucy's brought back Phil's laptop and phone. Said he was acting cagey so she asked the tech team to examine them.'

'Interesting. I'll be back as soon as I've spoken to Duffy. Shouldn't be too long.'

*

Natalie ended the call and opened the door to the brightly lit phone shop. It was similar to the one she'd visited with Josh and Leigh, who'd both insisted on trying out the latest smartphones but had ended up with affordable models, much to their chagrin. A glass-fronted cabinet filled with accessories and some second-hand laptops stretched the length of the shop to the right. Along the wall opposite were shelves containing various phones, each attached by coiled leads preventing them from being stolen. Behind the counter stood an athletically built man in his late twenties with wavy blond hair, striking cheekbones, a clean-shaven jaw and a genuine smile. He reminded Natalie of an actor Leigh had once had a crush on after watching the Harry Potter films. He was examining a laptop, gently prodding it with a screwdriver. He looked up.

'Can I help you?' he asked. Natalie approached and showed her ID card. The smile vanished. 'You've come about Savannah, haven't you?'

'I have. You were one of the last people to see her. I understand she and her friends often visited the shop.'

He gave a sad smile. 'We're the only mobile phone shop in Watfield and we do computer repairs as well so a lot of the kids in the area come here for one reason or another – to get something fixed or for top-ups.'

'Top-ups? I thought that was mostly done online nowadays.'

He shook his head. 'Not around here. We have many customers who buy five- or ten-pound cards a month for their pay-as-you-go phones. I don't just mean schoolchildren.'

Natalie nodded. 'What more can you tell me about Savannah? I know she was in here a few times, so did she talk to you very much?'

'Savannah was one of the quieter ones. I've been working here over three years, since January 2015, and some days you can't move in the shop for schoolkids. They all chat to me. Savannah arrived in Watfield just over a year ago. There was a lot of gossip about where she'd come from – something about being a traveller – and her stepfather Lance was a right piece of work. I had a run-in with him a couple of times.'

'What about?'

'Accused me of selling him a dodgy second-hand phone. It wasn't. We do sell second-hand phones but they're all in perfectly good working order. We overhaul them before they go back out.'

'Have you seen him recently?'

'Not since he left town.'

'And how often would you say Savannah came into the shop?'

'At least once a week. That's not unusual. Mobiles and gizmos are to teenagers what bright, shiny objects are to magpies. They want to know what the latest phone can do and find out about apps and stuff on them, even if they don't own one. They'd sometimes come in to ask questions about their own mobiles, especially if there were problems with them, or get new covers – we have some wicked plastic covers. I have a friend who makes them,' he said, pointing at a pile in a plastic basket on the counter.

'What did Savannah come in for?' Natalie asked, trying to get the man back on track.

'She had an old Samsung mobile. It wasn't as up to date as some of the others' phones. She'd mess about with the new models to see what they could do and get a top-up card now and again.'

'Did she talk to you about anything in particular?'

'Not really. She'd occasionally ask about the phones or games I play. I'm a gamer and some of the kids come in to find out how to level-up on the more popular games.'

'Any special game?'

'She'd just ask what I was playing and ask if it was any good.'

'Did you overhear anything that might give us an idea of where she was headed yesterday afternoon?'

'I didn't hear anything to help you. Sorry. I saw her walk past the shop at about three forty-five and she stopped by the window and waved at me. I was busy sorting out the display cabinet at the time so I didn't open the door and say hello.'

'She didn't look unhappy?'

'No. No more than usual.'

'She was alone?'

'Yes.'

'You didn't notice anyone following her?'

'Nobody.'

'You're sure of the time?'

His forehead wrinkled slightly. 'Definitely. I'd just checked the time before she went past the shop. I've no idea what happened to her afterwards. I joined up with a few other locals to help look for her but – well, you know what happened. We didn't find her. I heard the dreadful news this morning. I feel really bad about being one of the last people to see her. Maybe if I'd been by the counter, she'd have come inside to say hello and this wouldn't have happened. I'm afraid I have nothing else I can tell you.'

'Okay. Thank you. One last thing: were you alone in the shop yesterday?'

'Yes. Although, my boss, Mitchell, was working upstairs in his flat. He came down almost immediately after I saw her, to take over from me. I had to leave early for a dentist appointment.'

'Is he here at the moment?'

'No, he's had to get some parts for a broken laptop. He should be back any minute but I know for a fact he didn't see Savannah. His office is at the rear of the building so he couldn't have seen her walking past.'

'Does he live alone?'

'Yes. His long-term girlfriend passed away a few years ago, just before he moved here and took on this shop.'

Natalie made a note and thanked the young man again.

He cleared his throat as she was leaving and spoke. 'Savannah was a nice girl. I think she was a bit misunderstood. The others – her friends – took the mickey out of her when she wasn't with them.'

Natalie spun around again. 'Why?'

'She wasn't a local like most of them, and her mum's got a bit of a reputation, and, of course, her stepfather was known around town. They were labelled as a rough family. Savannah got tarred with the same brush.'

'What do you mean by having a reputation?'

Duffy cast his look downwards for a second. 'A bit easy, tartish. Word gets about in a town like this one. They were very much outsiders and didn't do a lot to help themselves become accepted. I don't know more than that.'

Natalie thanked him again and moved aside to allow a man who looked to be in his forties, carrying a large cardboard box, to enter.

'This is my boss,' Duffy called out.

She faced the man. 'I'm DI Ward, sir. I was asking about Savannah Hopkins.'

He put the box on the shop floor carefully and held out a slim hand. It was warm to the touch. 'Mitchell Cox. I own the shop. This was such a horrible thing to happen. Duffy and I joined the search party for her.' He shook his head sadly.

'You didn't see her at all, did you?'

'No. I was fixing a laptop in my office until I came downstairs to run the shop. Duffy had an appointment for four o'clock. I didn't see a thing.'

'You knew Savannah?'

'Not very well. Duffy usually deals with the customers unless we're very busy. I tend to work more on the technical side. I'd seen her in the shop but I'd only served her once, I think.'

'You didn't ever serve her parents?'

'No, I can't say I did. Sorry I can't be more helpful. It really is a terrible thing to happen – it's such a nice town too. The people are really good sorts. We've never had anything like this happen before.'

'Do you have any CCTV? Maybe you have her on camera.'

'We have surveillance equipment but the recording only lasts twenty-four hours. It's on a loop. It's largely to deter shoplifting. Some of the phones are quite valuable. The camera's there.' He pointed it out to her.

'You have no others?'

'There's nothing else. We don't generally have any trouble, and every valuable item is tagged electronically. We have retractable security grilles on the window, the place is fully alarmed and I live above the shop. One camera is enough.'

'You never spoke to Savannah?'

'Only to serve her. I'm regarded as a bit of a dinosaur by the younger generation. I'm afraid I don't keep up with what they like. Duffy here knows all about the latest mobile trends more than I do and what appeals to the younger generation. I stick to the older clients who need an upgrade or some technical advice.' He gave a half-hearted smile.

'And you were in the shop all afternoon?'

'I locked up at six, ate my meal upstairs and was roused by police knocking as I watched television. There was quite a commotion and many of the locals came out to help hunt for her. I joined them. Up until then, I was here.'

Natalie moved aside to allow a couple of young girls to enter the shop. Duffy threw them an engaging smile as they approached the counter. She thanked Mitchell for his time and hastened to her car. It was coming up to five o'clock, over one full day since Savannah had disappeared. She needed to take stock of what information they'd gathered.

CHAPTER TEN

TUESDAY, 17 APRIL – EARLY EVENING

Natalie arrived back at the station to find her team in deep discussion. Lucy looked up as soon as the door opened. 'Natalie, we've uncovered something of concern on Phil Howitt's laptop. They were in encrypted files.'

Natalie tossed her large bag onto the nearest chair and crossed the room to join the team gathered around a laptop. She released a heavy sigh at the photographs of naked young girls on the screen. Some were as young as eight or maybe ten. 'Bring him in for an interview. Did he have an alibi, Lucy?'

'Not a concrete one. Ian's been trying to track his car passing through any CCTV camera points but we haven't spotted it yet. Phil drove past Jane Hopkins' house late last night but he didn't stop off. He says he was put off by the police presence.'

Natalie snorted. 'I bet he was. Anyone located Lance Hopkins?'

Ian shook his head. 'Dropped off the radar. I spoke to Amy Stephenson again. She's the neighbour who claimed to have seen him hanging around but she now thinks she might have been wrong.'

Natalie let out a hiss of exasperation. 'It would make our lives easier if people could be sure of what they did and didn't see. Okay, keep looking for him. He needs to be told about Savannah and we also need to confirm his whereabouts for yesterday. Murray?'

'Stu Oldfields, the labourer, said he met up with fourteen-year-old Harriet Long. She's not at the same school as Savannah. She attends Lincoln Fields Secondary at the far side of Watfield, on the main A50 road. They've been seeing each other for the last couple of weeks, but he's adamant he never had sex with her. I'm not so convinced by his denial. He was definitely nervous about confessing he was with her yesterday. If it had been platonic, he'd have no reason to hold out about it. I haven't been able to contact her yet. He gave me her mobile number but she isn't answering. I tried her mother's contact number and got no response either. I drove over to their house but no one was in, and a neighbour, Kate Baldwin, told me Harriet's mother works shifts at a logistics company out at East Midlands Airport and doesn't get in until after midnight. Kate also said the girl was feral and could be anywhere. She goes out with friends and hangs about the street a lot, being a troublemaker.'

'Feral?'

'That's what she said. Wouldn't say any more than that.'

'You left a message on Harriet's phone?'

Murray nodded an affirmative. 'And on her mother's.'

'Oh, sod it, we'll have to try again later and, in the meantime, hope one of them contacts us. The trouble is, if Stu's already spoken to Harriet, she could well cover for him. Ian, have you got anything positive for me?'

He shook his head. 'I went through CCTV footage and found Anthony Lane outside Aldi in the car park as you suggested but he's not on any footage near the church later as he claims. The camera there is playing up and we only have sporadic shots of people up until seven p.m. and then it goes blank completely.'

'Are there no other cameras in the area?'

'None.'

Natalie's cheeks puffed up and she slowly released the air before speaking again. 'That means Anthony, Phil and Stu all have flimsy alibis at the moment. Right, we'll work with what we have for now. By the way, the Hopkins family had a reputation for being a bit *rough*. I'm not sure how many people they annoyed but there's a chance Lance or Jane pissed someone off. Might be worth prodding that possibility. Ah, Mike!'

Mike Sullivan waved a manila folder in her direction. 'This is straight from the lab – the bruising and scrapes on Savannah's knuckles were caused by repetitive blows to a hard surface, namely wood. The splinter we uncovered was oak wood painted dark grey. I think she'd been imprisoned and had been trying to get out.'

'Like bashing against a locked door?' Ian offered.

Lucy's heavy eyebrows lifted to meet her blue-black fringe. 'Or a coffin-like box.'

'Could be either but we didn't find any other fragments on her clothing, and if she'd been lying down in a box, I'm pretty sure we'd have found something elsewhere. Her clothes were clean apart from some very light grass staining where she'd been positioned. Ben's emailing his report over any minute. He's certain she was strangled and then moved to the park and placed where we found her.'

'By the waste bin. Like she was rubbish,' said Lucy, softly.

Natalie rested her fingers on her chin and digested the news. 'The park is significant. It has to be. The wastepaper bin… the fact her home was only the other side of the park. There was a similar case in Manchester a few years ago. A fourteen-year-old girl was strangled and her body left by rubbish bags to the rear of her parent's restaurant. Nobody was charged with her murder. Ian, can you get information on that investigation? I'd like a list of suspects and full details on it.'

Mike spoke again. 'Sorry to report we have collected a vast amount of evidence which we're sifting through, and so far, none of it appears to be connected to Savannah's death. It's a huge park and a popular one, so we're having trouble working out what might be relevant and what isn't. We've got no trace on her mobile. We suspect the SIM card has been removed. The mobile provider has given us a list of calls and text messages. Details are in the file but she rarely made actual phone calls, and when she did they were reserved for her mother. The majority of her conversations were via Snapchat and mostly to her two close friends – Sally and Holly. Nothing sinister in them and no suggestion she intended running away. She was a regular user, even during the day but especially evenings. However, the last time she used that application was Sunday evening at nine, when she and Sally talked about what they'd done all day. Again, nothing in their conversation for us to go on. She didn't use her phone at all on Monday, the day she disappeared.'

'I was under the impression teenagers were never off their phones,' said Murray.

Ian tapped at his screen and spoke. 'I've been hunting for other online presence but she doesn't even have a Facebook page. She has an Instagram account and that contains a lot of photos of make-up and clothes. Nothing else. She seemed to have been quite the loner.' He spun the screen towards Natalie so she could see the pictures.

Mike also glanced at them then said, 'I'll leave the report with you to fathom out why she didn't use her phone yesterday and who she was meeting. I'll be in the lab if you need me.'

'Cheers, Mike,' said Natalie, taking the folder from him and browsing through it. Savannah was certainly a strange girl. What thirteen-year-old had only two friends and hardly ever used her mobile for communication? Leigh was almost always talking to her friends and sharing photos. Natalie had had the conversation with her several times about being careful with whom she shared information.

Mike left and there was a ping, signalling the arrival of an email. Murray spoke up. 'The pathology report is in.'

'What does it say?' Natalie asked.

Murray's eyes flicked over the document. 'In summary, there was bruising and ligature marks in connection with manual strangulation – soft tissue thinning due to fluids being driven out by mechanical compression, fractures of the thyroid and hyoid, vocal cord and lymph node haemorrhage, salivary gland congestion and also congestion haemorrhage in the conjunctivae. There are no defence marks and the only other bruising is on her hands.'

Lucy heaved a sigh. 'Sounds like Savannah was overpowered and strangled with force.'

Natalie stared into space for a moment. 'She was going to meet somebody. I'm sure of it. Why else would she change from school clothes into a new outfit?'

Lucy nodded. 'That sounds logical. Forensics haven't found her school clothes or bag.'

Ian piped up. 'The killer might still have them. Some sort of trophy.'

Natalie agreed it was possible. She glanced at the office clock. It was just past six o'clock and she hadn't yet rung her husband to let him know she'd got held up. 'Lucy, I think it's time to talk to Phil Howitt again.'

'I'll bring him in.'

Natalie read through Ben's report on Savannah's death then stood up sharply. She ought not to leave it any later. David was used to her dreadful hours but she couldn't leave him in the dark as to what she was doing. She went upstairs and watched the evening traffic below, its continuous rumble a soundtrack that drifted to the roof terrace, where she stood with her mobile to her ear. She'd done a lot of thinking on this roof. It was where the smokers came to get their fix and where others came for a break from stressed offices. It was also where she and Mike would occasionally meet for a more intimate chat, during which they'd discuss their families.

Recently, they hadn't managed to bump into each other here. She knew the reason why: she'd deliberately avoided the roof. She was aware of the times he was likely to be there, dragging on a cigarette, yet she hadn't climbed the stairs to chinwag in case she revealed the true extent of her concern over David. It was difficult enough at times being mere colleagues, having shared a bed together, and although both had put the affair behind them, at times, the attraction was still there. Mike was a good-looking man and, at the moment, she was vulnerable. His charms might easily sway her so it was better to avoid him. She was so lost in thought, she almost didn't hear David speaking:

'Hi gorgeous. Everything okay?' His voice was cheerful. The television was on in the background.

'Hey. Look, I'm sorry, I'm going to be held up. I'm tied up with a murder investigation.'

'Shit! That's rough. Don't worry about us though. I bought a takeaway for the kids and I've got a bottle of wine on the go.'

'Wine? You celebrating?'

'Could say that. The news will wait until you get home. I'll save the wine – sounds like you might need a glass or two.'

'Did the conference go well?'

'Superbly. I'll fill you in about it when I see you. I'll wait up until eleven and then I might turn in.'

'Are the children there?'

'In their rooms. They wolfed down the takeaway and disappeared before they had to clear up.' He laughed.

'I'll try and get back before eleven. I've a suspect to interview and then I'm sending everyone home.'

'Okay. Good luck. Love you, Nat.'

'Love you too.'

Her response had come out easily. It was nice – a relief – to hear David so upbeat. The last few weeks had been so full of tension between them it had taken a toll on her mentally. It was good to get back to being the old David and Natalie. She hoped his news was about work and he'd secured some new contracts. They could do with the income but David also needed a boost to his self-esteem.

She headed for the door, and as she did so, Mike walked outside, unlit cigarette between his lips. He patted his jacket pocket for his lighter, removed the cigarette and spoke. 'Fancy seeing you here.'

'I had to ring David.'

He smiled. 'I've not seen him for over a month. Work's been a nightmare and every spare minute I spend with Thea. It's about time he and I went out for a drink.' She drew to a halt and opened her mouth to say something and his eyebrows lifted in response. 'He is okay, isn't he?'

'Yes. Busy. I think he's got some new clients. I have to go. Suspect to interview.'

He studied her. 'You look tired. You sure everything's okay?'

'It's fine. Work-life and home-life tend to pull you in all directions. I had to get the kids up this morning and drop them off at school and it was pretty damn stressful. I'm glad David usually does it. I wanted to scream at the parking officials. They made us queue up and wait for ages to drop off inside the bloody designated drop-off zone.'

Mike laughed and picked a tiny piece of tobacco from his lips. 'I have all that fun to come. Any advice?'

'Buy a massive four-by-four so you can mow the other parents out of the way or you'll never get to work on time.' She gave him a smile and he held her gaze for a second, then she gave a brief nod, spun on her heels and took the stairs again. It was better for both of them if she didn't engage in too much chit-chat with Mike Sullivan.

Phil Howitt was a broken man. Tears stained his cheeks, and as his head moved pendulously from side to side, they trickled and plopped onto the table.

'Please, please,' he urged.

His lawyer sat in silence beside him, keeping his counsel.

Natalie sat back in her chair and gazed coolly at Phil, unaffected by his sudden outburst.

'I don't need to spell this out for you. You have illegal images on your laptop that are not only disturbing but raise certain questions. You have two children of your own, Mr Howitt, and you were spending time at your girlfriend's house – a woman with a teenage daughter who voiced anxieties about you to her friends.'

He turned towards his lawyer. 'I went through that with DS Carmichael. I didn't touch Savannah. I was always nice to her. Ask Jane. There was one occasion when I accidentally walked into the bathroom while she was showering and I retreated immediately.'

Lucy, who was next to Natalie, spoke up. 'But Savannah said otherwise. You know that. I told you that when we last spoke.'

'She was lying!' His voice rose to crescendo and his lawyer lowered his gaze.

Natalie interrupted his outburst. 'Calm down, sir. We have no way of knowing what happened in the bathroom given Savannah is dead. You freely admitted you were within the vicinity of her home last night at about the time we believe she was murdered.'

'I had nothing… nothing to do with her murder. I was going to see Jane. She'd been messaging me and finally I decided to go and comfort her. That's what happened. Please. Believe me. I swear on my children's lives I didn't kill her.'

Natalie winced at his statement. 'I'd like access to your vehicle to have it checked out.'

His mouth flapped open. 'No. This is all wrong. You'll look for proof she was in my car and you'll find it and charge me. Savannah was in my car but only because I gave her a lift to school, last Thursday, after I'd stayed the night with Jane. It was pouring down with rain so I offered her a lift even though the school wasn't too far away. She accepted but asked me to drop her off just before the school, so I let her out at School Lane.'

'Why did she want to get out there?'

'I don't know. Maybe she didn't want anyone to see her with me. I really don't know. I didn't ask. Look, I was just being kind. Don't read anything more into it. What's going to happen to me?'

'We need to establish you aren't responsible for Savannah's death.'

'I'm not. What about the photos?'

'We'll be passing all information to the child pornography team that handles such matters and who will undoubtedly charge you.' Natalie looked at the lawyer as she spoke to include him. He gave a quick nod.

'But it was only a few pictures. I didn't download them myself. They came in an attachment from a friend. I wasn't interested in them.'

'Then why did you keep them on your computer in encrypted files?' Lucy said, quickly.

'I forgot they were there.' His words were feeble and his bottom lip trembled.

Natalie was convinced he was lying. This wasn't what she was investigating. She needed to establish if he was responsible for Savannah's death.

He suddenly wailed, 'Oh God. What am I going to tell my wife? The children?' The tears fell again.

Natalie was becoming irritated and sidestepped the question. 'I can't answer that for you. My sole mission here is to determine if you had any involvement in Savannah's disappearance and subsequent death.'

'No, no, no! I had nothing to do with it. Please.' The sobs became louder and Natalie terminated the interview.

Natalie marched back to the office alone. A sense of end-of-the-day had fallen over HQ with much of the earlier hustle and bustle now over. A small cough came from downstairs and echoed around the empty foyer. There was little more they could accomplish today and they all needed a break. Natalie was feeling jaded and she still had to swap hats and become the wife and mother she was, once more. The multicoloured settee that stood outside their glass-fronted office was empty as usual, and beyond it she made out the hunched forms of Murray and Ian, both working at desks. She slid her pass through the card reader that opened the door and strode inside.

'Phil Howitt claims he knows nothing at all about Savannah's disappearance, and if I had to lay a bet on it, I'd probably say he isn't responsible. He's a spineless bastard but I don't think he's a killer. Anything here?'

'I've tried to contact Harriet Long and her mother again but I'm only getting answering services. Want me to run past their house?' Murray asked.

'Leave it until morning. She'll probably cover for Stu even if he's fibbing about his whereabouts. You reckon he was with her?'

Murray nodded. 'Yeah. I'd say he was dead scared I was going to charge him for having sex with a minor, rather than anything else.'

'Best to make sure. We'll try her house first thing when her mum's home too. Ian, how are you getting on?'

'I sent a request to Manchester regarding the strangled teenager as you asked. I'm waiting to hear back. Still trawling through footage and not got anything on Lance Hopkins, although I've put out an alert on his family and asked for police forces to let me know if the travellers are on their patch. He could well be with them.'

'Good. Cheers, both. Let's wrap it up for tonight, then. We'll get back onto it first thing.' She picked up her bag and wished them both a good night.

As she marched across the car park, a light rain began to fall and she thought about Savannah accepting a lift from Phil Howitt even though she'd told her friends he was creepy. Could he be responsible? She threw her bag into her car and breathed deeply. She was tired – too tired to make a good call. She'd believed Phil to be in a state because of the discovery of child pornography on his laptop, but what if he was deliberately making more of that to disguise what had really happened? Natalie put the car into gear and drove away. She needed some sleep – a glass of wine and some sleep.

CHAPTER ELEVEN

THEN

They call it the wasteland, a vast, undulating area where children race each other on bicycles, speeding down steep gradients of the hillocks like daredevils, or wander about in small gangs, idly exploring or merely lurking until it's time to return home. The bigger kids monopolise the far side of the wasteland, huddled in groups, smoking cigarettes, taking drugs or drinking illegal concoctions either stolen from shops or nicked from their parents' hidden stashes. That particular area is taboo to the younger children. Anyone under the age of thirteen is restricted to the greener area completely overlooked by the eleven huge apartment blocks.

He loves the wasteland – it's a secret garden of delights. One time, he skipped off school and stole a BMX bike from the corridor in one of the blocks of flats. He rode flat out, flying over the humps, pretending the bike was a horse, champing at its bit, eager to race, before dumping it in a marshy part of the wasteland and meandering back home, exhilarated by the rush of speed.

Another time, in the lengthier grass, he discovered a large, brown toad. He marvelled at how composed the creature seemed, even when he tired of its repetitive croaks and prodded it to make it leap, and then, bored of the game, flattened it with a large, grey stone. The toad had made no effort to escape, accepting its fate in the knowledge it had met its match. A warm sensation similar to the one he experienced that day on seeing the crushed animal, and knowing he was the one to extinguish its life, floods his veins, making him smile and his toes curl in delight. He hunted for more toads after that but none had appeared, so he turned his attention to the other creatures on the wasteland: the unfortunate ginger and white kitten that readily approached him, encouraged by his outstretched hand and soft, coaxing noises. It came up to him, trustingly, allowing him to stroke it, winding its silken tail around his bare calves. It hadn't expected the rock to smash against its skull. Even now he's still astounded at how tiny the cat's head had been and how easily it had crushed. It had been like tapping the top of his boiled egg.

After school, the wasteland becomes home to the teenagers and children from the flats, huge grey monstrosities built in the 1960s to deal with overcrowding. He lives on the third floor, in the block closest to the wasteland, along with his mother and baby brother. From his bedroom window he can see almost all of it, from the long, grassed area, where some kids make out with each other, to the other side, the part protected by high fencing – a dumping ground – that really fascinates him. From his vantage point nothing escapes him, and recently he's noticed figures slide under the wire netting and head into the distance to explore the goods that have been deposited there. His mother has forbidden him from going to that part of the wasteland, claiming it's too dangerous, but her words only serve to fuel his desire to join the older kids who return with treasures from their sorties – broken metal toasters, huge bits of wood, rubber tyres and other delights that he wants to check out.

He is a loner, a tiny boy for his age, who – with his ghostly white face and skinny arms – presents no threat to any of the other children, who either ignore him as if he's invisible or snigger at his high-pitched voice and sticklike limbs.

He's off school yet again today. This time it's tonsillitis that's made his throat raw and has knocked him out for over a week, but today he feels well enough to eat something and sit in the room they use for both meals and watching television. His mother's turned on the set and he's watching He-Man attacking his arch-enemy Skeletor, whose yellow skull is hidden under a hood, making him even scarier than he already is. He prefers the blue-skinned Skeletor, who is cunning, performs magic and is an expert in martial arts, to the hero of the cartoon.

'I have to go out for an hour. Will you be okay on your own?' his mother asks.

'Yeah.'

'You make sure to stay indoors. You're not well enough to go out. I don't want you off for another week.'

He nods again, vaguely aware of his mother putting his baby brother into the carry cot, and the door to the flat shutting with a loud click.

The cartoon ends and he wanders across to the window overlooking the wasteland. A group of girls from his tower block are running and shrieking. They're often together in their clique, led by Faye Boynton, a thirteen-year-old tomboy who lives with her two older brothers and their dad, on the same landing as him. She's tough. He's seen her fighting on several occasions, and witnessed the damage she can cause. She gave one boy a broken nose and a split lip that needed several stitches.

The girls are headed to the dump. He screws up his eyes and watches as Faye keeps lookout and one of the other girls yanks at the bottom of the fence then slips under. Faye goes last and the trio dash away, out of sight. He can't understand why his mother doesn't want him to go to the dump. It's obviously a great place to mess about. One day soon, he is going to explore it, regardless of what his mother says.

CHAPTER TWELVE

TUESDAY, 17 APRIL – NIGHT

He listened to the screams and smiled to himself. Harriet hadn't been a match for him. She'd been overpowered so easily – too easily. A delicious feeling of warmth filled his veins and he was aware of the snake moving across his skin. Soon it would get its reward.

She begged to be let out, her fists bashing against the door. It was pitch-black inside her prison and she was terrified. *Good!*

He refused to answer her. She could suffer in the full knowledge nobody was coming to her rescue, and she could tremble with fear, knowing that when she was finally released, she would meet her end. The snake would wrap itself around her throat and squeeze the very life from her. He had one more thing to do – a little treat for the detectives who were searching for the girl and him. If they were clever enough, they'd find it, although by the time they did, it would be too late to help Harriet.

A twisted grin lifted the corners of his mouth as he felt for her mobile phone and lifted it from his pocket. He searched for the camera app, chose the video function and then began recording the cries.

*

The front door opened as soon as Natalie approached it and she found herself swept into her husband's arms. An aroma of garlic and red wine rushed up to greet her and she found her face being grazed by slight stubble. His lips were on hers in a brief embrace, and before she knew it, she was being ushered inside to the warmth and the rich, spicy aromas from an Indian curry.

The hall lamp glowed welcomingly, diffusing gentle beams of light across the table, where she dropped her car keys. The door to the lounge was open and a burst of laughter exploded from the television. With soft, furry slippers now replacing her work boots, she padded to the room where David was waiting for her, smile on his face. He turned the sound down on the television.

'That was quite some homecoming,' she said invitingly.

'And I haven't finished saying hello properly,' he replied. A bottle of wine stood open on the coffee table in front of the worn settee along with two glasses. 'Sit down.'

She did as bid and watched him as he poured out the wine, lifting it to the light to check for sediment. This was the David she'd married – a man with a sense of fun, eyes burning intensely, a slim body that was still in good shape for a man in his late forties. He handed her the glass with a wink. She sniffed the wine – a full-bodied, oaky aroma.

'Go on, taste it,' he said, picking up the bottle and hiding the label with his hand.

Natalie raised it to her lips and sipped, allowing the rich, fruity flavours to wash over her taste buds. It was good – very good and expensive. She made an approving sound that made him grin further.

'What is it?'

'Guess.'

'I can't. I'm not a wine buff. It's good, fruity and hits the spot. Must be something that cost a fortune.'

'Correct. It's a 2008 Masi Costasera, Amarone della Valpolicella Classico.' He revealed the label, like a magician producing a rabbit from a hat.

She recognised the name. It was an Italian wine that they'd enjoyed for their fifteenth wedding anniversary – a gift from Eric, David's father.

'David! That must have set you back at least twenty pounds!'

'Thirty,' he replied smugly and lifted his own glass. 'To my fabulous wife!'

'What are we celebrating exactly?' she asked cautiously.

'An advance on a contract – a thousand pounds upfront.'

Natalie took in his flushed cheeks and her heart filled with happiness for him. Gone was the sulky man who'd been moping about the house for months, hiding away in his office and hating the world for not giving him a chance. She was extraordinarily pleased for him. He deserved this break. She raised her own glass happily. 'To my talented husband.'

'Cheers!'

She sipped again, holding the wine long enough to enjoy the sweetness before allowing it to slide smoothly down the back of her throat. Tiredness and frustration gave way to a mellowness. It had been so tough with David fighting to get translation work. This was good news.

'How much will you earn in total?'

'Another grand so that'll be two in total,' he said with a shrug, 'and further opportunities if this client is satisfied and spreads the word.'

'I'm truly happy for you,' she said, meaning every word.

'Yeah. Me too. It's so good to finally bring home some money and feel like a breadwinner again.' He slugged his glass back and licked his lips, lifting the bottle immediately for a top-up.

Natalie savoured hers more slowly and consciously untightened the muscles in her neck and shoulders. 'Kids okay?'

'The usual. Josh managed several grunts and almost a complete sentence at teatime. I thought when his braces came off he'd be keen to flash his teeth, but if anything, he's quieter.'

'Hormones.'

'Most likely and I suspect there's a girl on the scene. He couldn't tear his eyes from his mobile tonight, and Leigh wasn't very hungry. She said she had some difficult maths homework to do but when I offered to help her out she said she could manage.'

'They're growing up, David. They weren't very happy that I drove them to school today. Apparently, I shouldn't have waited in that confounded drop-off queue. I have to say it's a stupid new system. There wasn't anything wrong with the way we did it before.'

'True. You can be stuck for flipping ages now. Some of the parents get really het up about it. I witnessed a full-blown row between two mothers vying for the same space the first week it was enforced. They spent so long shouting at each other and the officials, we were all late for school! I usually tip Josh and Leigh out beforehand. They walk the last few hundred metres.'

'That's what Leigh told me after she'd rolled her eyes a hundred times and sighed in that irritating bored manner she's recently adopted.'

'But you didn't do it?'

Natalie shook her head. 'Nah. I'm a copper, aren't I? Have to play by the rules. I waited until we got to the actual drop zone. Besides, I'm not going to be dictated to by a stroppy fourteen-year-old.'

David chuckled. 'And you were never stroppy, of course.'

'Not at that age. I wouldn't have said boo to a goose, let alone played up.'

He studied her for a moment, a smile playing across his lips. 'My, how you've changed.'

She couldn't help but return his smile. His good mood was infectious.

He put his glass down and spoke again. 'There's some takeaway left over if you fancy it.'

'That'd be good. Not eaten since a sandwich at lunchtime. What did you save me?'

'Your favourite – butter chicken and a naan.'

She smiled at his thoughtfulness. This could be the turning point they'd been waiting for. If David got more work, things could only get better.

He stood up. 'I'll reheat it for you.'

'You don't have to do that. You've had a long day too. You left at the crack of dawn.'

'I'm not tired. Guess I'm still on a high.'

She listened to his soft whistling as he went about microwaving the curry and reflected on this turning point in their relationship. There had been sour moments and uncertainties ever since she'd discovered David had taken out a loan, but finally the niggling doubts were subsiding. With his focus on work again, David wouldn't be tempted to gamble, and she had to admit, he was a good father. She sometimes took for granted everything he did. She polished off the last of her wine and poured another glass. Her job was stressful but coming back to a happy, safe family made it bearable.

David returned sometime later with a bowl of steaming food and the flat, white bread on a side plate. 'Voila!' He passed it to her and she breathed in the delicious aromas. She stabbed at an extra-succulent piece of chicken and popped it into her mouth, all the while making appreciative noises. David sat down again and turned his attention to the television. After a couple of mouthfuls, she said, 'Mike says he hasn't seen you for ages and you need to arrange a night out.'

'True. I'll give him a call and sort out—' The gentle ring of the doorbell stopped him in his tracks. 'Who's that at this time of night?'

Natalie's stomach sank. She had a fair idea who it might be and her suspicions were confirmed when she heard Murray's voice. He shuffled into the lounge behind David.

'Sorry, Natalie. I wouldn't have come if it wasn't urgent,' Murray said.

'What is it?'

'Harriet Long's mother, Melissa, rang me during her break. She'd picked up my phone message and tried to get hold of her daughter but she wasn't at home. Melissa's boyfriend, Kyle, told her he thought Harriet was staying overnight with a friend – Emily Rowley – except that isn't the case. Emily didn't invite her to stay. Harriet's phone goes straight to answerphone and Melissa doesn't know where she is. She's tried all the girl's friends. Looks like Harriet's disappeared.'

Natalie pushed her food to one side.

'We'll need to talk to Stu Oldfields again. If they are an item, she might be with him.' She looked over at David. 'Sorry about this.'

'It's okay. I'll see you when you get in.'

Natalie raced out to the hall while Murray walked on ahead to the car. She yanked on her boots once more and turned to face David who'd followed her out. 'It's good news about your contract.'

'Yeah.' This time the smile didn't reach his eyes but he held onto the door and watched as she and Murray pulled away from the kerb.

'Sorry to drag you—' Murray began.

'No need to apologise. You were right to jump on this. What about Harriet's mother? Is she at home?'

'She was on her way there when she rang me. She's called the Missing Persons team too.'

Natalie shook her head. 'We'll speak to her as soon as we've tried Stu.'

'Odd, isn't it? We want to talk to Harriet about Stu's alibi and *whoosh*, she disappears.'

'I know. It doesn't bode well.'

The road, like a huge, black tongue, was swallowed up by Murray's Jeep Renegade as it sped towards Watfield. They passed shadowy shapes, blurred images of bushes and trees, and onto unlit roads. Natalie sank deeper into thought. She had to act quickly.

A missing girl was a concern. A missing girl who was tenuously linked to the murder investigation of another girl was an even bigger worry. Natalie didn't believe in coincidences. There was some factor linking Harriet Long and Savannah Hopkins, and at the moment the one connection they were aware of was Stu Oldfields.

The entrance to Watfield was marked with a painted sign and a notice claiming it was twinned with a city in Germany that Natalie hadn't heard of. Crossing a large roundabout in the direction of the city centre, they came upon a residential area with large detached houses set back from wide pavements planted with leafy trees. Gradually these gave way to denser settlements of smaller houses and finally opened out to a retail park. Natalie spotted a large sign for Tenby House and Garden Services, where Stu worked. The satnav indicated they had almost reached his house, and within minutes they were drawing up outside a bland, terraced house on Mulberry Close.

Murray accompanied Natalie to the door, and an external security light came on automatically as they approached the house. A flicker of blue light coming from curtains that weren't quite pulled together alerted them to the fact somebody was upstairs watching television. Natalie rang the doorbell and waited. A scuffling sound preceded the sliding of a chain bolt and the door opened quietly. Stu looked out, a deep frown between his eyes.

'Yes?' he asked.

'Hello, Stu. We're here about Harriet Long.'

He glanced behind him and spoke in a whisper. 'My mum's in bed. I don't want her to wake up.'

'Can we come inside then?'

'Not really. I don't want her to suddenly come downstairs and find you.'

'You don't quite understand. I'm *insisting* we come in.' Natalie pushed forwards and, surprised by her actions, Stu took a step backwards.

'Okay, but please don't wake my mother.'

Murray followed them both into the kitchen, where he pulled the door to after himself.

'What do you want to know?' Stu said.

'Is Harriet here?'

'No, why would she be here?'

'She's not at home and no one knows where she is. You're seeing each other so I thought it logical she might be with you. Is she?'

He shook his head slowly. 'No. I haven't spoken to her since yesterday. She hasn't been answering my messages. I assumed she was ghosting me.'

'You thought she'd broken things off between you without telling you?' Natalie asked.

'Yeah… ghosting,' he repeated.

'Can you prove that?'

'I can show you the messages I sent her but she didn't text back. Normally she replies straight away.'

'Would you fetch your phone so we can double-check that? In fact, I'd like DS Anderson to accompany you upstairs.'

'He doesn't need to come upstairs. Harriet isn't here,' Stu said.

'If you have nothing to hide, then it shouldn't be a problem.'

'Nah. It's late and my mum's asleep. Don't you need a warrant to search people's homes?' he asked, suddenly adopting a more aggressive response, with legs suddenly planted wide.

'We're not searching. DS Anderson would merely like to accompany you while you help us with our enquiries, so, do you mind?' She kept her eyes trained on him and he caved under her steely gaze.

'I guess not,' he mumbled and led the way, Murray trailing behind.

A few minutes later they both returned and Stu held out his phone. Natalie glanced at the call log, flicked through the applications quickly and noted there was nothing from Harriet. The fact there weren't any messages didn't mean they hadn't been deleted. She needed the technical team to examine the device. A floorboard creaked and Stu let out a sigh as the kitchen door opened quietly.

'Stu, what's going on?'

'Nothing, Mum. The police wanted to ask me some more questions about Savannah.'

A woman in a deep-blue dressing gown that swamped her tiny frame glared at Natalie. 'It's gone midnight.'

'I'm very sorry to interrupt you so late. Your son has been helping us with our investigation.'

'You spoke to him earlier. Why are you back again at this time of the night? Can't it wait until a more civilised time?'

'Another teenage girl's gone missing and we need to act quickly to find her.'

'Oh, that's terrible. Another girl. I'm sorry but I don't see what it has to do with Stu.'

'I knew her too, Mum.' Stu rubbed a hand over his head, his eyes downcast.

'Oh! How come? Was she a client's daughter as well?'

Stu shook his head and threw Natalie a pleading look that she ignored. His mother had no idea of his involvement with Harriet, but he could explain that one himself. Natalie pocketed the phone.

'I'll have this returned as soon as possible,' she said.

Stu's shoulders slumped but he didn't argue.

His mother stepped forwards. 'Why have you taken his phone? Stu, what's really going on?' she asked, sharply.

Murray spoke up. 'Your son is friends with the missing girl, Harriet Long. We've confiscated his mobile to check exchanges between them in case there's anything that might give us a clue to her whereabouts. Have you ever met her, Mrs Oldfields?'

A deep frown line appeared on her forehead. 'This is the first I've heard of her.'

'She's never been to this house?' Natalie asked.

'Not to my knowledge. Who is this girl you've been in contact with, Stu?'

Stu's face had turned ghostly white. 'A friend, that's all, Mum.' He faced Natalie again. 'I swear I haven't a clue where she is. Honest.'

'If she turns up here, let us know immediately.' Natalie threw a stern look at the young man before leaving.

Back at the car, Murray slid back behind the wheel. 'I don't think he knows where Harriet is. She couldn't have been hiding upstairs. His bedroom was barely large enough for a single bed and he had an open wardrobe – no doors, just a curtain across it. There was no place to hide. The bathroom door was ajar and the only other room was his mother's bedroom,' he said.

'Damn! I was hoping she'd be there. Let's try her family.'

Harriet's house was on the outskirts of Watfield in a suburb known as Bramshall that backed onto woodlands. It was the third house, and the only one with lights on, in a line of terraced cottages. Melissa Long came to the door, her gaunt face streaked with tears.

'Have you found her?' she asked, eyes wide.

Natalie shook her head and introduced herself and Murray, and they were shown into a sitting room filled with children's paraphernalia: a small trampoline, a baby chair, a child's sit-on tractor, an activity mat and a box stuffed with books, cars and vibrant plastic objects. A baby with a runny nose and damp eyes sat on a man's knee and hid his face against the man's chest when Natalie and Murray walked in.

'I'm DI Ward and this is DS Anderson. You must be Kyle Yates.'

The man with black hair and a fringe that hung in front of his coal-black eyes stroked the child's head. The child sniffled loudly and stuck a thumb in its mouth, head turned away from the visitors. 'That's right.'

'We'd like to ask a few questions if that's okay.'

'Are you from Missing Persons too? They've already asked us loads of questions,' he said.

'We're handling another investigation, and Harriet's name came up in it as a possible witness to an alibi, so we're also trying to locate her.'

'I rang Harriet's mother yesterday afternoon and left a message on her phone, sir,' said Murray.

The man nodded, eyes slightly unfocused.

Melissa spoke up. 'Has Harriet done anything wrong? Is that why she's gone?'

Natalie replied, 'No. We just needed confirmation that she'd been with somebody Monday afternoon so we could eliminate that person from our enquiries. She wasn't involved in anything to our knowledge.'

'But you *are* helping to look for her?'

'We are.'

Melissa chewed at a thumbnail and paced to the window, where she looked out onto the dark street.

Natalie turned once more towards Kyle. 'I understand this is a difficult situation and you've probably answered these questions before, but we'd appreciate your help. When did you last see Harriet?'

'This morning before I went to work.'

'When did she tell you that she was going to be staying overnight with a friend?'

'Only as we were leaving. She said she wouldn't be home because Melissa had okayed it for her to stay over with her best mate, Emily, so they could work on a science project. She also said Melissa had asked her to tell me because she'd forgotten to. I didn't think anything of it. I believed her.'

'But you didn't confirm the arrangement with Melissa?'

He stroked the child's hair again and looked at Melissa, who'd turned to face them. 'I'm so sorry, love.'

Melissa shook her head and blinked back tears. 'It's not your fault.'

He directed his explanation to Natalie and Murray. 'It was mental here this morning. We have three kids: Harriet, the baby here and a three-year-old, Jack, who wouldn't change out of his Spiderman pyjamas to go to nursery. Melissa was sorting them out, and Harriet and I were both running late. We left at the same time and she mentioned she wouldn't be home just as she hurried off to catch the bus.'

'And you didn't speak to Melissa or message her at all today to confirm the arrangement?' Natalie asked.

'No.'

'Surely you would have wanted to make sure of the fact?' Natalie kept her tone light but her eyes fixed on the man who wouldn't look up.

He shifted uncomfortably. 'This little one is teething and had kept us up all night so we were all tired. I didn't ring Melissa because I knew she'd be trying to sort out the children or maybe even grab a little shut-eye before her shift. It never even crossed my mind to double-check Harriet had asked if she could stay at Emily's. She's stayed over with her a few times, so it wasn't odd. I just never thought...' He glanced in Melissa's direction again, then hung his head.

Melissa sniffed, her eyes glassy with tears.

Murray, who'd been making notes, spoke again. 'You didn't see, speak or text Melissa even after you'd finished work?'

'Not until she rang me earlier.'

Melissa interjected. 'I work midday to midnight three days a week, over at East Midlands Airport, so I have to leave home at quarter past eleven at the latest. The babies stay with Kyle's mum. We're not allowed to use mobiles at work unless it's during our break. Kyle doesn't usually ring me.'

Kyle carried on speaking. 'I collected the boys from my mum's at about five and came straight home. I didn't know Harriet wasn't staying at Emily's until Melissa rang to say the police wanted to talk to Harriet.'

'You didn't text or phone Harriet to check on her at all? Make sure she'd got to Emily's? Ask how her project was going?' Natalie asked.

Kyle kept his head lowered. 'Harriet's not the sort of girl you check up on. She probably wouldn't have answered even if I had rung her,' he said.

Natalie was quick to respond to the statement. 'What do you mean by that?'

'She's independent, isn't she, Melissa? Besides, I'm not her dad.'

'He means Harriet can be a bit of a handful, that's all. She knows her own mind and doesn't always do what Kyle asks. I can't understand why she'd lie about staying at Emily's house. She's never done anything like that before,' said Melissa. She pulled out a cigarette from a packet with trembling fingers.

'Has she taken any of her clothes or anything personal?' Natalie asked.

Melissa shook her head. 'The other officers asked the same question. I looked in her bedroom as soon as I got in. You think it hadn't crossed my mind she'd run away? I don't think anything is missing. She has a stuffed elephant – had it for years – but it's still there, and a necklace that she got for her birthday. She can't have run away. If she'd gone, she'd have taken both of those with her. None of this makes any sense. I think something's happened to her.'

'Has Harriet mentioned a boyfriend to you?' Murray asked.

'No. She hasn't got a boyfriend, has she, Kyle?'

Kyle shrugged. 'Not talked about one to me.'

Natalie gave Melissa a small smile of encouragement. 'Did she mention the name Stu?'

Melissa blinked a couple of times and shook her head. 'Definitely not. Kyle?'

'No. Never heard of him,' he replied.

'Can you think of anybody at all – a relative, friend – who she might be staying with?'

Melissa stared at her unlit cigarette. 'I can't think of anyone. My parents live in Glasgow and we haven't seen them for a couple of years; her dad's in prison. She doesn't have anything to do with him or his family. There's Kyle's mum who lives nearby but she didn't see Harriet today. I tried a couple of her friends. Not many people are still up at this time of night but those who answered hadn't seen her. Emily's mum told me she'd not been invited to stay.'

Natalie watched as Kyle stroked the baby's angry red cheek with one finger. He kept his eyes on the child all the time, assiduously avoiding her gaze. 'I'd like a list of her closest friends to contact.'

'We gave all the names we could think of to the other officers.'

'That's fine. I'll get the names from them. Does Harriet have access to a laptop or iPad?'

'Kyle has a games console and we have mobiles but we don't own any computers.' Melissa slipped the cigarette between her lips and pulled out a lighter from her trouser pocket.

'Did Harriet mention Savannah Hopkins at any time?' Murray asked.

Melissa flicked the lighter a couple of times but it wouldn't spark. She extracted the cigarette from between her lips. 'That's the girl who was killed on Monday, isn't it? No. She didn't say anything about her.'

'She didn't know Savannah?' Natalie asked.

'No, but we know her stepdad, Lance Hopkins, don't we, Kyle?'

Kyle's eyes were fixed on the top of his baby's head. 'Yeah. He came around looking for work – gardening, DIY, that sort of thing.'

Natalie could sense Murray stiffening at the news. They'd found a connection.

'Did he do any work for you?' he asked.

'Fixed some guttering that was leaking. He was only here for one morning,' said Kyle.

'When was this?'

'Last year. Early July.'

'And you knew he was Savannah's stepdad?' Natalie found it odd they would know that if Lance had only worked for them for one morning. Kyle spoke up.

'There was a lot of talk at my local pub about the family when they first arrived in Uptown.'

'Why?'

'Because they were travellers,' Kyle replied with a shrug. 'The locals love to gossip about outsiders.'

'And you didn't see Lance again after he worked on your house?' Natalie asked.

Melissa shook her head. 'He overcharged us and we told him to piss off. He wasn't very happy about it but he did a crap job and we weren't going to pay him what he demanded. Kyle gave him what we thought it was worth and told him to sling his hook and so he did. Not seen him since.'

The baby wriggled in Kyle's arms and began to fret. He shushed it. 'I feel pretty shit about all of this. I feel like it's my fault.'

Melissa spoke sharply. 'It isn't your fault, all right?'

'I wish I'd said something earlier to you and then we'd have known she was missing sooner.'

'We don't know when she went missing, Kyle. She might not even have gone to school. She might have bunked off. You know how she can be.'

It was true. Until they knew Harriet's precise movements, none of them would know when she had gone missing.

Natalie directed her next question at Melissa. 'Has she bunked off school before?'

'Only a couple of times. The first time she had some test she hadn't revised for and the second she went into town with a friend. I found out about it and read her the riot act. She can be headstrong at times but she isn't a bad kid, not at all. She might have skived off yesterday. I can't watch over her twenty-four-seven, can I? Not with two little ones to handle and a job,' said Melissa. She managed to light the cigarette at last and inhaled before waving it in Natalie's direction. 'I bet I can guess what you think of me but let me tell you, I love my daughter and I'd do anything for her. I watch out for her and I've brought her up properly. It's not been easy with her dad in jail but we're all fine and Kyle is good to her. She's happy at home. She hasn't run away.' Her voice had become tremulous. She lifted her head up to the ceiling and groaned then rubbed her neck. 'This is a fucking nightmare! Please find her.'

The baby began squirming and started sobbing.

Kyle spoke again. 'I have to take this little chap back to bed. Do you have any more questions?'

'Not for the moment. We're going to do everything we can to track her down,' said Natalie. They needed to locate the girl and quickly.

With Kyle out of the room, Melissa blinked back tears and addressed Natalie. 'I'm sorry I snapped at you. I can't imagine what's made her go off like this and I'm really worried about her.'

'I completely understand. Please try not to worry too much.'

Upstairs the baby's cries increased and Melissa ran a hand over her face. 'Oh God! I hope she's okay.'

A knock at the door brought her back to her senses and Natalie took advantage to leave. 'I'll answer it for you. You stay here,' said Natalie. She beckoned Murray and they left the woman staring once more out of the window.

Graham and another officer were on the doorstep, his face as solemn as the first time they'd met.

Natalie spoke before he went into the house. 'Do you happen to know if Harriet made it into school today?'

'Yes. I spoke to her head teacher. She attended all the lessons. It seems she vanished soon after school ended. We suspect she didn't catch the school bus home. The driver didn't recall seeing her get on the bus. He's fairly new to the job and doesn't know any of the kids by name, but when we showed him her photograph, he couldn't remember seeing her at all. He's certain he'd have recognised her if she had taken the bus.'

'It's the same pattern as yesterday, then?'

'Looks that way, although I hope we're wrong and she's simply run away.'

'Me too,' she replied as Graham slipped into the hallway.

Natalie and Murray returned to the car. 'What now?' he asked.

'We believe Savannah changed out of her school uniform to meet somebody, and now we know Harriet made up a story about her friend Emily and planned to be out overnight. She can't have intended roaming the streets all night so I'm guessing she also intended meeting up with someone. Maybe it's even the same person. We've got two people associated with both girls: Stu Oldfields and Lance Hopkins. We've no idea where Lance is, which is a worry, and the fact his name has cropped up yet again bothers me. We really must locate him. At the moment, Stu's our most likely suspect. He knew both girls and Harriet was his alibi.'

'In which case he'd want her to be alive to confirm that, wouldn't he?'

Natalie nodded. 'But only if she could back him up. What if she couldn't because she wasn't with him?'

'A girl who's disappeared can't testify either way,' said Murray.

'Exactly.'

As they drove back towards the Samford Police headquarters, Natalie mulled over their conversations with Kyle Yates and Melissa Long. The fact Kyle had consistently avoided looking in their direction niggled at her. He'd deliberately kept his focus on the baby, even during questioning, and Natalie couldn't help but feel he was hiding something.

CHAPTER THIRTEEN

WEDNESDAY, 18 APRIL – EARLY MORNING

Lucy had been quick to respond to Natalie's phone call, made as she and Murray drove back to Samford, and had arrived at HQ just before 3 a.m. Ian hadn't yet responded but Natalie half-expected he was drowsy on medication and might well have not heard his phone.

The lack of sleep didn't seem to have affected Lucy, who looked fresh and alert as she pushed her long blue-black fringe from her forehead and studied the screen closely. Over the last hour, they'd lifted CCTV footage from cameras along the route that Harriet might have taken home and spotted her climbing onto a local bus headed for the town centre. Now they were searching more footage from the same shopping area Savannah had walked on Monday.

Forensics had examined Stu's phone and established he'd been telling the truth about Harriet ignoring his calls and texts. She'd not replied to any of his messages sent on Tuesday and although he'd rung her three times on Monday, there was nothing to prove they had arranged to meet after she'd finished school that day. Natalie had left instructions for the tech team to look into Harriet's online presence for clues. She drained her coffee cup and sat back in her chair. In spite of the caffeine, her brain was fogging up with tiredness once more and she still had no information on Lance's whereabouts. She'd put out a general alert on Lance's family in the hope that if they could locate the travellers, they might be able to get hold of him.

Murray suddenly stabbed at the screen. 'There. That's her.'

They bent forwards and examined the girl with black hair fashioned into two buns, one each side of her head, more closely. At about five foot eight, Harriet was a striking girl who looked far older than her years and made the Lincoln Fields Secondary uniform of black jacket, white shirt and grey skirt with flat black boots look fashionable. Lucy pointed out the red rucksack dangling loosely by her side as she walked from the bus across the car park at Aldi and into the passageway leading to the pedestrian precinct and almost missed the figure that moved behind the girl until Murray shouted, 'Stop!'

Natalie raced across to see what they'd found.

Murray pointed at the screen. 'We've found another connection – that's Anthony Lane. He was one of the last people to see Savannah.'

'The guy who's on the sex offenders' register?' Lucy asked.

'That's the one.'

Natalie spun around and reached for her jacket. 'Murray, you come with me. Lucy stay on this. Keep looking out for any other sightings of her... and if anything else crops up, let me know straight away.'

Anthony Lane rubbed at his chin, stubbled with growth. 'I've not the foggiest idea who this girl is, DI Ward, and I resent you dragging me out of my bed at four thirty in the morning. This is victimisation, pure and simple.'

Murray stepped closer to Anthony, forcing him to retreat a step in the kitchen where they were all standing. He held up the photograph of Harriet Long right in front of Anthony's face.

'This isn't victimisation. You were spotted on camera following *this* girl at four thirty yesterday afternoon. She is missing. Now, if you can give us a reasonable explanation as to why you were trailing her, we'll go away. If not, we'll be continuing this conversation at the station,' he hissed.

Natalie let him have his moment. Murray, with his solid frame and ability to look angry at any given moment, was useful in such matters and had the desired effect.

Anthony responded quickly. 'I'd no idea who was walking in front of me. I'd been to Aldi to buy food and then I popped down the road to post a birthday card. I couldn't tell you who was walking in front of me. My mind was elsewhere.'

'Who was the card for?' Natalie asked.

'Why do you want to know that?'

'So that I can speak to that person and ensure the card is post-marked for yesterday evening when it would have left Watfield.'

'Oh, sure. My nan. She lives on the Isle of Wight.'

'You grandmother?' Murray sneered.

'Yes, my nan. She's ninety-five tomorrow.' Anthony tugged at his dressing-gown cord, looking defensive.

There was no evidence of anyone else in the tiny flat but Natalie asked Murray to look around all the same. Anthony began to protest then changed his mind.

Natalie kept up her line of questioning. She held the photograph of Harriet up in front of his eyes. 'You recognise her at all, Anthony?'

He screwed up his eyes and peered at the picture. 'Can't say I do.'

'You might have seen her hanging around with some of the Watfield Secondary kids.'

'No.' He shook his head and released a bored sigh that annoyed Natalie.

'Anthony, you don't have a concrete alibi for Monday when Savannah disappeared and now you're implicated in this girl's disappearance by virtue of the fact you were walking right behind her in Watfield.'

'I told you where I was on Monday. And I don't know this girl,' he said, stabbing at the picture with his fingertip.

'Does her name, Harriet Long, mean anything to you?'

'Never heard of her.' He folded his arms and stared at his bare feet.

Murray reappeared. Harriet wasn't in the flat. Natalie could take the man to the station but she had no reason to charge him. It was a dead end for now. A sudden wave of tiredness washed over her, reminding her she hadn't slept for twenty-one hours. She fought the urge to yawn and told Anthony she'd be back if they had any further questions.

'If you keep hassling me, I'm seriously going to complain to your superiors. And I'll have something to say about your officer too. He's a bully,' he said.

Murray snorted in disdain.

'Complain if you feel you've been treated unjustly,' Natalie replied. She had no energy left to argue. She stomped back to the Jeep and dropped into the passenger seat. The wine she'd drunk with David was leaving her mouth dry and her head aching. She released a heavy sigh. 'Sodding heck. It's too early in the morning to come up against dead ends and argumentative witnesses. I almost dragged him to the station because he was pissing me off. Stop off at the drive-through at Costa, will you, on the way to the station? I desperately need some caffeine and I suggest you nip home and get some rest for a couple of hours after you drop me off at the station.' She rummaged in her bag for some mints or gum to freshen her mouth, and as she did so, her phone buzzed. She lifted it to her ear.

Lucy was on the line. 'DI Graham Kilburn's been in touch to say they've got a full search party out in Bramshall, extending into the woodland, and he's alerted the media. He's appealed for anyone who saw Harriet to come forward. It'll be going out on the local news channels next bulletin. One other thing. I think I've spotted her on a camera close to the phone shop where Nick "Duffy" Duffield works. I'm just trying to get a clearer image to make sure it's her. I told DI Kilburn of my findings.'

'Cheers, Lucy. I'm on my way back now.'

*

It was 5.10 a.m. when Natalie, armed with takeaway coffees and two muffins, arrived back at the office. She shoved a cup and bag in Lucy's direction. 'White, no sugar and I think the muffin is cherry,' she said, sitting down next to her colleague and delicately picking the paper from the sticky sponge. She pulled off a large piece and stuffed it into her mouth. It was deliciously sweet, undoubtedly laden with sugar that she ought not to eat given her slightly spreading waistline, but at this time of the day she needed all the calories and sugar rush she could muster. Lucy muttered thanks and took a quick slurp of her drink. She'd blown up the image she'd captured from one of the cameras and was trying to get a clearer image. She turned the screen in Natalie's direction.

'This is the original CCTV footage taken outside WHSmith. Look, there's a woman pushing a buggy, but if you examine it more closely you can see she's shielding another person walking in the same direction, right beside her, almost like her shadow. If you look carefully, you can see a person's leg and they're wearing a black boot. If you study the enhanced image you can also make out a shape which I'm certain is a red backpack. I think that's Harriet.'

Natalie checked the time clock in the corner of the image: 4.50 p.m. 'What time did she get off the bus?'

'Half past four.'

Natalie waved her half-eaten muffin as she spoke. 'It took her twenty minutes to reach that point. That seems a long time. It's only a five-minute stroll from the bus stop to WHSmith. She must have stopped somewhere along the street – most likely at a shop.'

'Those were my thoughts so I made a list of the shops along that route, and that's when I came across the phone shop. Another coincidence?'

'You know my thoughts on that subject. We'll talk to Duffy again.' She finished the muffin and wiped crumbs from her hands on her thighs. 'Nothing from Ian?'

Lucy glanced up. 'He might be with Scarlett. He let slip something yesterday but you know how cagey he is over his personal life.' Scarlett was Ian's ex-girlfriend and mother to his baby although she'd left him shortly after the baby had been born.

Natalie knew that private lives needed to be protected and Ian's was no exception. After being almost fatally stabbed during an investigation only a few weeks earlier, it seemed that Scarlett had reappeared on the scene, but none of them knew if it was permanent. It was really difficult to juggle two worlds, especially with the horrendous hours they sometimes kept.

'We'll check with all the shop-owners but we'll start with Duffy at the phone shop.' She yawned and stretched. A shower would help her regain focus. She could take one at the station or nip home and get changed. She opted for the latter. She'd feel better if she had on fresh clothes. 'I'll talk to DI Kilburn and then I'm going home to grab a shower.'

'I wouldn't mind getting a couple hours' sleep. I'll be back for eight,' said Lucy.

'No problem. Murray will be back on duty soon and MisPer are searching for Harriet.'

*

Emily Rowley peered at her mobile screen. She'd been chatting to friends all night about Harriet in WhatsApp groups. There was a real buzz as they gossiped about her and tried to guess her whereabouts. Emily knew Harriet better than most. Harriet was an out-and-out attention-seeker. She'd try out all sorts of nutty stuff to prove she was the daughter of a hardened criminal – somebody who could take on anything – and she certainly had everyone's attention now.

If she was honest, Emily was a little in awe of her friend who didn't care for rules and regulations and would deliberately flout them whenever possible. Then there were the challenges she'd recently become interested in. It had started with the Ice Bucket Challenge, when she'd got Emily to tip ice-cold water over her as she stood in a bikini, then posted the video on Facebook. That had been fun but then she'd tried out other dares, some of which Emily thought were a bit too stupid like the car-surfing dare and the horrible choke dare. She'd asked Emily to do that one with her, but Emily had refused so Harriet had done it alone with a makeshift noose to cut off oxygen and filmed herself. She knew no fear.

Emily had a good idea of what her friend was up to. They'd talked about it and she knew by the light in her eyes that Harriet was keen to give it a go. If Emily was correct, Harriet was in hiding somewhere and would stay out of sight for the next two or three days. Harriet was doing the Disappear dare.

Emily hadn't slept all night, torn between telling the police what she suspected and keeping her bestie's confidence. Harriet would hate her for ruining the dare and might not forgive her for telling everyone. Then there was the possibility that Harriet might actually be in danger. If she told the police she was hiding because of a dare, they might not hunt for her. Emily sighed heavily and logged onto the Disappear website yet again. She'd tried it throughout the night and seen nothing. If Harriet was going through with the challenge, she'd be sure to leave a video on the site. If she did, at least Emily would know she was in hiding and not in danger.

She clicked onto the participants' page and found a new video had been uploaded. She pressed play. It wasn't the grinning face of a boy or girl, whispering about how they were at a secret location, and it wasn't her friend. There were no images, only darkness, but it took her breath away. Somebody was bashing against a door. They were screaming to be released and it was a voice she recognised immediately: Harriet's. She watched it through again. Harriet was crying and yelling and sounded petrified. What should she do? It was only six o'clock in the morning and her mum would be asleep. She'd be mad that Emily had been online at this time of the morning but she ought to tell somebody. She thought about her other friends who might be online. She could tell them and ask their advice. No, this was serious. She had to tell the police who were searching for Harriet. Harriet was in trouble and Emily had to help her friend. Without further thought, she swung her legs out of her bed. She scurried out of her bedroom and knocked on her mother's door.

*

Natalie tiptoed around the bedroom silently. She was accustomed to searching for things in the dark on the many occasions she'd been called out on a case at some ungodly hour. The nightlight plugged into a socket in the hallway cast sufficient light for her to retrieve a blouse and underwear and make her way to the en-suite bathroom that David used more often than her. This morning, a shower rather than a soak in the bath was in order, and if she only put it on half power, she was unlikely to disturb her husband. Not much penetrated David's slumber. Natalie envied him his ability to drop off at whim and not rouse until the alarm woke him. She'd been suffering bad bouts of insomnia that she'd initially put down to the stressful nature of her job but now seemed to be part of some physical change in her body.

In the bathroom, she peeled off the clothes she'd worn since the morning before. The trip to school and sitting in traffic with other parents seemed a lifetime ago. It was such normality that she missed. Since being made DI and transferring to Samford, there'd been much less time for her family. She'd asked Kyle if he'd texted Harriet to see how she was getting on with her science project, yet she rarely managed to message her own daughter and son. She ought to make more time. She consoled herself with the knowledge that David was always around for them. They never came home to an empty house. David would make sure they ate at the right time and did their homework and didn't get into difficulties when she wasn't about.

Warm water trickled over her shoulders, and as she soaped herself she sighed. She'd begun to pile on the weight. Irregular hours and a crap diet, usually from the snack machine at work, were taking their toll. It was something else she needed to address. Over the last year she'd put on almost a stone. She certainly wasn't the same woman who'd had a fling with Mike Sullivan. That woman had suddenly become middle-aged and out of shape.

She was towelling herself dry when her phone buzzed, and she was taken aback to hear Graham's voice. She held her breath. Were they too late?

'Something important has come to light and you need to see it immediately. Can I email it to you? It's a clip from a website called Disappear. Harriet's friend Emily spotted it and told her mother, who alerted us. I'll stay on the line.'

'Spotted it?'

'She had an idea Harriet was doing the Disappear challenge – where you vanish for a few days, for no apparent reason other than to scare your family – and monitored the website for any videos posted. She found it at about six this morning.'

Natalie gave him her email address and waited for the email to arrive. She opened it and clicked through to the website and the video that had been posted. It was pitch-black and nothing could be clearly made out, but it soon became apparent it was a video of a girl trapped and banging on a door, screaming to be released. It lasted twenty seconds but those twenty seconds chilled Natalie to her marrow.

Graham's voice was quiet and brought her back to the here and now. 'You watched it?'

'Is it…?'

'Emily says it's definitely Harriet's voice.'

'Did she know Harriet intended disappearing?'

'It appears so.'

'And she said nothing to you!' Natalie was perplexed.

'She wasn't sure. They'd only talked about it. She claims she didn't know Harriet had actually gone through with it.'

Natalie bit her tongue. The girl had been loyal to her friend, and for all sorts of reasons, known only to her, she had kept quiet. It was no good getting angry about her lack of cooperation. At least she'd alerted them now and they knew Harriet was trapped somewhere. At least, that's what Natalie hoped because the alternative didn't bear thinking about.

'How did they come across the website?'

'Social media. Harriet was into social media challenges and heard about it. She showed Emily the website. What do you reckon about the video? Think she really is in trouble or messing about?' Graham asked.

'She might have had an accomplice film her and be playacting, but there appears to be genuine fear in her cries. We can't afford to treat it as a prank video, not given the similarities between her disappearance and Savannah's.'

'The video doesn't give us much to go on but I've upped the level to high priority and we're conducting air and land searches in the vicinity.'

'We'll look into this website, Disappear, and find out what time the video was uploaded and who uploaded it. See if we can pinpoint their location. I'd like to talk to Emily as soon as we've done that and I've updated my team.'

'I'll request she stays at home until you've spoken to her.'

'Thanks. I'll keep in touch.'

Natalie grabbed her clothes and dressed quickly. She couldn't calm the hammering in her chest. Was the video a fake? She hoped it was. She hoped Harriet was carrying out some ridiculous challenge and was safe. Because if she wasn't, then Natalie could only assume the killer had filmed the girl.

CHAPTER FOURTEEN

Natalie clattered into the office, phone pressed to her ear as she spoke. 'Is that all you can tell me? This is a matter of some urgency,' she hissed angrily at the negative response and slammed the phone onto her desk. All she'd learnt was that the Disappear website was located in Germany and there was lengthy protocol to follow to be able to confirm who ran it and who had uploaded the video of Harriet. A couple of weeks ago, she'd have been able to involve their technical department at HQ and persuade them to prioritise it, but there'd been a huge shake-up and now all such matters were handled elsewhere in Staffordshire, at a brand-new special IT centre of excellence, set up in partnership with a high-tech aerospace engineering company. It employed a vast number of staff – technicians and digital forensic officers – all highly trained and extremely busy. Natalie wanted results rapidly. Mike had worked closely with the technical team before they'd been rehoused; he'd know who the best person would be to ask. Mike was well-respected and might even pull strings to help get the information quickly. She dialled his number.

'Hey! You're up with the larks.' His voice was thick with sleep.

'Not been to bed. Another teenage girl from the Watfield area has gone missing, and a video of her trapped somewhere has appeared on a website called Disappear. It seems to be located in

Germany and I can't find out who is behind it or who uploaded the video. I'm going to ask the IT centre for assistance but you know the guys there better than me. Who would you recommend for such matters?'

'You need Bart Kingsley. He's a website genius. Try him.'

'I don't suppose you could ask him for me?'

'Sure. I'll get onto it immediately. Email me the website details and I'll see what I can sort out for you.'

'Thanks, Mike. Appreciate it.'

'No problem. I need to get up and get to the lab. We're still trawling through all the evidence we amassed at the park. Another missing teenager, eh? That doesn't sound good at all. I hope this isn't related to the Savannah Hopkins investigation. Who is she?'

'Harriet Long. I don't think she knew Savannah. We were trying to track her down because she was apparently with one of our suspects on Monday afternoon. We wanted to get confirmation of that but she vanished before we could speak to her.'

She heard Mike suck in his breath. 'So it is related. I hope you find her, Nat.'

Only two people ever called her Nat – one was David, and Mike the other.

'MisPer are on it but I have a truly horrible feeling about this, Mike.'

There was a pause. Mike knew about some of her past cases involving teenagers and children, and how badly a couple had ended. After one particularly awful investigation, involving teenage girls who were found strangled, their bodies strewn with petals, Natalie had undergone a course of therapy and still had nightmares over it. Although David had been by her side at home, Mike, being in the same profession, truly understood the panic she experienced every time she was assigned a similar investigation and comprehended how desperate she became to resolve it before it reached a grisly end.

'One step at a time, Nat. You'll find her.' His words had the desired effect.

She forced herself to inhale slowly. The office door opened and Ian appeared.

'Thanks, Mike. Catch you later.' She terminated the call.

For somebody who'd had a night's sleep, Ian looked worse than she felt. He began with an apology. 'I didn't get your message until my alarm went off. I took some painkillers as soon as I got in and they wiped me out. Sorry, Natalie.'

She wasn't annoyed. He probably shouldn't have come back to work so soon after the stabbing incident anyway. He had been seriously injured. Still, he was no use to her if he was out of sorts. 'You feeling okay to work today?'

'Definitely. I'm fine.'

'Okay, good.' She was about to bring him up to speed when Murray arrived. He threw open the door and spoke.

'Melissa Long has just made an urgent appeal on the local radio to her daughter, begging her to come home.'

'So the news is out then,' said Natalie.

Ian looked perplexed. 'What have I missed?'

'Quite a lot,' said Murray.

'You can bring him up to speed in a second. There's been a development. First off, Harriet's phone pinged at five forty-five a.m. The signal was triangulated and covered an area close to her home in Bramshall so MisPer have moved back there to hunt for her. Secondly, a video's been posted on a website called Disappear. Are either of you familiar with it?'

No one had heard of it. Ian sat down and began typing immediately. He was the best of all of them on all matters to do with the Internet. Murray and Natalie edged closer to him and watched as a black screen manifested itself.

'That it?' Murray said.

'No, wait,' Ian replied as, one by one, words in large red font manifested across the screen:

Do… you… dare… to… disappear?

The words vanished and a fresh screen appeared, this time with a lengthier message.

Have you got the wits and courage to outsmart everyone?
Can you remain hidden and fox even your best friends?
12… 24… 48… or even 72 hours.
How long can you stay under the radar?
Clever enough to vanish?
Then we dare you to…
Disappear.

Ian pressed the word 'dare' that was now flashing and was taken to an information page with hints from those who had taken up the challenge.

Ian read out some of the tips. 'This guy – Erik from Stuttgart – says you should make sure you take nothing of sentimental value with you or your parents will believe you have run away. You want everyone to think you have completely vanished off the face of the earth. This person, KJ, says it's important to keep your mobile switched off when you are not filming yourself because it can be traced. Best to buy a burner phone and leave your usual one at home.'

Natalie rubbed at her forehead. 'What the fuck is this nonsense?'

Murray spoke out. 'It's a dare. The website is daring people to disappear. Wasn't there a craze a while back for kids to go missing for twenty-four hours? It's along those lines.'

'Shit, yes. I heard about that.'

Ian clicked onto a section called 'Hall of Fame', featuring a leader table of names of those who had managed to hide for the longest periods of time, then another section, 'How did you do it?' This was a page containing videos of teenagers who'd filmed themselves during hiding, and the most recent was the video Natalie had received from Graham.

'We believe that's Harriet,' she said.

'Then it seems she's deliberately hiding.'

Natalie shook her head. 'No. I don't think so. It isn't like the other videos here. Surely, she'd have posted one of herself hiding not screaming behind a door. This is different. Somebody wants us to believe she's hiding. I think she's in danger.'

*

Harriet sensed it was daylight. Not that she could see anything, shut up as she was in the pitch-black of the cramped space. It was the sound of birds that had woken her – the first one like a note from a flute followed by another that sounded a little like a jangling of keys. At first, she'd thought the sounds were human, but as they intensified she understood them to be coming from birds who would only be singing if it was daytime. Her toes tingled with pins and needles and she tried to relieve the pain by wiggling them. Her body was clammy and cold, damp with sweat.

She'd dozed off. How long had she been asleep? Hours? Minutes? She strained to hear any movements or sounds that would indicate she wasn't alone. The noise of water rushing downstream or a faraway waterfall in her ears confused her momentarily, but she soon realised it was coming from her own body that was pumping her blood so quickly it made her feel faint. Was she alone or was her tormentor still close by?

She swallowed painfully, her throat dry from screaming so loudly. She'd yelled for hours but nobody had heard her. No one had come to rescue her. She fought back fresh tears that sprang to her eyes. She wanted to go home. She wanted to see her mum and cuddle the baby, who smiled at her when she tickled him, and hug her younger brother, who called her Hattie and told her he loved her even though she pretended to ignore him.

She wanted this horror to end. She hated being trapped in the dark. Harriet didn't like the dark. She'd never admit to her friends she was afraid of it – they all thought she was daring, the daughter of a criminal, and she lived up to that image. Harriet was always the first to rise to a dare – the girl who others looked up to with her devil-may-care attitude, who didn't give a shit when teachers told her off, who hung with the older kids and had smoked dope and taken E and had a proper boyfriend. The truth was she was always putting on a front. She hated being the show-off but it was the only way she knew how to behave.

If her classmates could see her now, they'd laugh at her. She was nothing without her bold make-up, false nails and attitude. She was Harriet Long, half-sister to two demanding brats and the person who was most ignored at home. She was the pain in the neck who argued about stuff even though she didn't mean to. She suddenly wanted to tell her mum she was sorry for being such a nuisance. She didn't know why she played up. She couldn't help it. Maybe it was because she craved attention that she did stupid things and annoyed her mum. Any attention was better than none.

Her mum wouldn't even know she was trapped here. She'd believe the story that she was with Emily. Harriet released a sob. She'd done some dumb shit in her life but this was the dumbest. Why had she told Kyle she was staying at Emily's? Now her mum wouldn't even be looking for her. She snivelled noisily, trying to focus on how she might escape even though, deep down, she knew it was hopeless. She was never going to see her mum again.

A creak!

Panic like invisible mist filled her chest, clogging her airways and causing her breath to come in little gasps. There was another, louder creak. Harriet began to tremble and her mind went blank, all thoughts consumed by some primeval sense that told her something even more terrible was about to occur.

*

Ian rang Natalie, who, together with Murray, was on her way to visit Harriet's friend, Emily Rowley.

'I've received a call from West Midlands Police to say a group of travellers have arrived on their patch. Officers are on their way to establish who they are and if Lance Hopkins is with them.'

She thanked him and punched out the remainder of the text message she'd composed for her daughter, Leigh, telling her she hoped she'd managed to get her maths homework done okay. She read it through and decided it sounded horribly formal. She heaved a sigh, added a 'love you' and sent it anyway. At least Leigh would know her mum was thinking about her. She typed another to Josh – a brief message saying she'd see him later and was sending love – and pressed the send button. When had it suddenly become so difficult to communicate with her two teenagers? She found it difficult to remember what it was like to be that age. If she was honest, she tried not to think about those years at all. They were filled with too many memories of her sister Frances. She slid the phone back into her pocket.

'What were you like as a teenager, Murray?'

'A right tearaway. Got into a shitload of trouble.'

'Would you have taken up a dare like this one?'

'Probably. You have no fear at that age. Everything's a laugh, isn't it? You want to show off to your friends, and if they're into something, you probably are as well. I did all sorts of crazy nonsense – tried to jump from the roof of a building to another one time. Well, that was the plan until we got spotted and a security guard marched us off the premises. In retrospect, I don't know what we were thinking of. It seems to be a phase that teenagers go through.'

Murray kept his attention on the road. Natalie figured he had a point. Teenagers had little fear or sense when it came to such challenges. There'd been a glut of them in recent years thanks to social media, including a fire challenge that involved soaking parts of the body with a flammable liquid and setting fire to it before jumping into a pool or shower to douse the flames, all the while filming it for Instagram, and a cinnamon challenge where participants ate a spoonful of the spice without any water, which had resulted in some of them choking and being rushed to hospital. Natalie worried her own children could be influenced by such challenges. If Harriet had taken up this particular vanishing dare, she might have tried others.

Emily Rowley was dressed for school and sat on a kitchen stool with her hands in her lap.

'Thank you for talking to us, Emily,' Natalie said.

The girl shrugged nonchalantly.

'You must be concerned about Harriet.'

'Sort of. Yeah. I watched the video online and I was scared something had happened to her.'

Emily's mother intervened. 'She told me straight away it was Harriet and I rang the police. She's worried, all right, aren't you, babe?'

The girl winced before reprimanding her mother. 'Mum!'

'Did Harriet say anything about taking up the Disappear challenge to you?'

'She talked about it a couple of weeks ago. I hadn't heard of it but she told me about the website, Disappear, and we looked at the ways you could go missing for a day or longer, and at some of the videos. She thought they were cool. I never thought she'd try it herself. I mean, she does all sorts of stuff but I never thought she'd try and vanish. After Harriet's mum rang and we found out she was missing, I wondered if she was doing the dare, and that's why I went on the website – in case she'd uploaded a video. She had but it wasn't like the other videos there. I expected her to have done a selfie video – you know, talking to the camera.'

'How did she find the website, Emily?'

'Chatting online. She's really into social media challenges and was discussing them with others and somebody mentioned the Disappear website.'

'Do you know anyone else who's done the dare?'

Emily shook her head. 'No. Harriet and I only talked about doing it. We discuss all sorts of dares but we don't do them. We just watch videos of people who have.'

'You say she's done other stuff – what exactly has she done?'

The girl's cheeks flushed. 'Just silly stuff. Loads of kids do it. Challenges. Dares.'

Natalie was under the impression Emily had joined in with some of it and didn't want to divulge too much in front of her mother.

'When did you last talk to Harriet?'

'Lunchtime yesterday.'

'She didn't say anything at all about going missing?'

'No.'

'Has she ever said anything about home life? Maybe talked about being unhappy?'

Emily shook her head. 'Not really. She misses her dad. She doesn't ever get to see him and she gets annoyed with her little brothers, especially Jack, at times.'

'Did she say anything about Kyle?'

She blushed. 'Only rude stuff about him being a bit of an idiot.'

'She doesn't get along with him?'

'She gets on with him but she doesn't think much of him. He's not a bit like her dad, and she thinks the world of him.'

'Was she behaving differently in any way to normal?'

'She was in a really good mood because she's got a new boy-friend. She wouldn't tell any of us who he was except he's really good-looking and he owns a car. I thought she might be going to see him because she did her nails at lunchtime. She'd brought some falsies to school – you aren't supposed to wear them there – and she stuck them on. She laughed and said the teachers wouldn't notice. She wanted her hands to look nice for later but refused to tell us why. She just winked. That's why I thought it was for her boyfriend. She has a thing about nails.'

'Did she say anything to you at lunchtime about taking up this Disappear dare?'

'No. After we looked at the site, I asked if she'd ever do it. She laughed and said there were better ways to spend your time than hiding from everyone.'

'Did you discuss where you would hide out if you took up the dare?'

'Yeah. I said I'd go to her house and hide in her bedroom, and she said that was dumb because it was way too obvious, and she'd go somewhere nobody would think of. She said she knew a secret place in Watfield she'd been to with her boyfriend, and she'd go there.'

An urgent phone call to Tenby House and Garden Services had resulted in them establishing Stu was currently on the M6 motorway with his work colleague, Will Layton. Natalie rang Stu on the mobile number his boss had given her.

'Stu, we need to speak to you.'

'I'm on the motorway.'

'It's a matter of some urgency regarding Harriet Long.'

There was a garbled conversation and then he said, 'We're not near any service stations so we can't pull off, and we're a good ten miles from the next junction. Can I talk to you on the phone?' His voice sounded anxious. Natalie would rather talk to him face-to-face but time was of the essence.

'Harriet told her friend Emily you had shown her a secret place. Where might that have been?'

'A secret place? I don't know what you mean.'

Natalie suddenly lost patience. 'I can have your vehicle stopped at any moment and you brought in for questioning so don't make this harder for yourself than it needs to be.'

'I'm not!' The indignant voice went up an octave.

Natalie tightened her grip on the phone. 'Stu, where did you and Harriet go when you met up with her?'

'A few places – outside her school, the chip shop near me or the retail park. She once caught a bus into town and walked down to meet me when I finished work at the Hopkins' house. We went to the park behind the house. The park behind the house... Wait a sec... That must be what she meant. It isn't actually a secret. It's a building in the park. It's boarded up now but we sat on the porch for a while. It's out of sight behind some bushes.'

Natalie looked at Murray, who nodded.

'What sort of building is it?'

'Dunno... looks like a house with boarded windows and a long terrace and a clock on the roof.'

Murray mouthed 'cricket pavilion' at her.

'Could it be a cricket pavilion?'

'What's one of those? I don't know what a pavilion is. Will?'

There was mumbling and he came back on the line. 'That could be it. It looks like that. Have you not found her?' The voice sounded unnerved.

'Not yet.'

'Do you think she might be there?'

'I hope so.'

She thanked him and ended the call then rang Graham, who was still heading the search for Harriet, with the new information. He knew about the pavilion.

'My team searched it when we were hunting for Savannah. It's most unlikely Harriet would be there. It's extremely run-down.'

'Well, it's all we've got to go on, so we'll take a look just in case she is actually hiding there.'

He sounded jaded. 'Okay. We're concentrating on the Bramshall area. We've covered the entire housing estate and nearby streets and are fanning out. Good luck.'

Floral tributes had been laid beside the park railings along with stuffed toys, photos and messages for Savannah, who would never see or read them. The park gates were closed and a sign saying the park was closed for the meantime had been placed on them. Natalie cast about for signs of life inside the park and, spotting no one, said, 'There's only one thing for it. Climb over.'

The railings weren't very high but it took careful manoeuvring to avoid the sharp, golden spikes at the top of each ornately painted upright. Murray landed with a heavy thump beside her. A lorry rumbled past them along the main road, the occupant oblivious to them both.

On their way to the park, Natalie had searched on her phone for information about the pavilion and established there'd been a bowls club pavilion in the park at one time. She spun 180 degrees. 'Where's this pavilion?'

Murray peered at the map on his mobile and pointed left. 'If I'm looking at the right place, it's in that direction.'

'There must be other ways of getting into this park,' she commented as they jogged along the pathway.

'You'd have to cross the railway lines and nip through a break in the hedge. There's only one entrance. Turn here.'

He swerved right and raced up an incline, Natalie close behind him. At the top of the slope she slowed and glanced down onto the houses below and the back gardens adjoining the park. One such house belonged to Jane Hopkins. Each had hawthorn hedging forming a barrier between the gardens and the park. It was unlikely anyone could have entered the park from any of these houses. If Harriet had come here, she must have climbed the railings like them and taken a chance she'd have been spotted by passing traffic. It didn't seem likely. If Harriet had wanted to hide, she wouldn't have chosen a route where she might have drawn attention to herself.

Murray had increased his lead so she picked up her pace again, passing a children's play area and a set of three swings. Murray drew to a halt and examined the screen again. Natalie caught him up, pleased to not be out of breath. He turned his head left then right. 'There.' He darted towards thick bushes and forced his way between them. Natalie brought up the rear, squeezing between the thick leaves overgrown over time to provide a screen for what lay beyond – a structure similar in style to a small wooden chalet complete with two steps leading to a wooden terrace running along its length. This was the old bowls pavilion.

Murray skirted around the back of the building, leaving Natalie at the front. She moved silently up the steps and along the wooden slatted floor, slippery with moss and damp. The floor in front of the boarded door showed signs of recent activity, undoubtedly footprints from officers who'd been looking for Savannah. Grey cobwebs covered in dark specks wafted against the solitary window, thick with dust and dirt. She made out smudges where others before her had peered inside into the gloom and one name scrawled in the dust: *Savannah*. She wondered who might have written it. Inside was nothing but darkness.

Murray reappeared and beckoned her. 'There's a rear entrance.'

She followed Murray to the rotten door that hung crookedly off a broken door frame.

They shuffled into the dusty room, assaulted by a sudden smell of decay, and stood stock-still. Something with claws scuttled away into the darkness. Murray pulled out his police-issue torch and shone the beam around the large room, ravaged by time. Shredded paper hung from an old noticeboard and mildewed floorboards had lifted up, revealing a large hole close to the door. She wrinkled her nose. The pungent, acidic scent was from mice. They were the ones who'd now made it their home. No human had set foot in here for many years.

'There's no one here,' said Murray, having run the beam around the room again.

Natalie had to agree. They hadn't found Harriet, and the adrenalin that had infused her with energy suddenly departed, leaving her weak-kneed. Savannah was dead and Harriet was still missing and time was running out. She pulled herself together quickly and dialled Stu once more.

'Have you found her?'

'She's not here.'

'Oh shit. I hoped she would be.'

'Stu, how did you know about this place? It's almost impossible to find unless you know about it.'

'Savannah told me about it.'

That would explain the name written in the dust. Savannah probably wrote it. 'Savannah did?'

'Yeah. She said she used to go there and hang about on her own when she was pissed off with her mum until she cooled off. She liked the fact nobody could bother her there.'

'How many times did you visit it?'

'Only the once.'

'Did Harriet ever talk to you about a website called Disappear?'

'No.'

'Did she mention doing any social media challenges?'

'No. What sort of challenges?'

'Never mind. How about a dare where she would vanish for a while?'

'Definitely not. We didn't talk about any of that stuff.'

'You're absolutely certain?'

'One hundred per cent certain.'

She hung up and asked Murray to drive into town. If Harriet had come in this direction – and according to the CCTV cameras, she might have – she'd have passed the phone shop. It was only a hunch but it was possible she'd stopped off there, maybe to purchase a burner phone as the Disappear website suggested.

They drove to the end of the pedestrian-only street and parked on the road, close to the phone shop. It was ten to nine and the 'closed' sign was still turned outwards but Natalie banged on the door and roused the owner who lived upstairs. Mitchell Cox was in a dressing gown and pyjamas and wore an expression of concern.

'I just heard a mother making an appeal on the radio for her missing daughter, Harriet Long.'

'That's correct. We were hoping you might have seen her yesterday afternoon at about half past four.' She handed him a photograph of Harriet.

'I know this girl,' he said, slowly, his head bobbing up and down. 'She's been here.'

'Did you serve her?'

'No. Duffy did.'

'Was she in yesterday afternoon?'

'Sorry, I've no idea who came into the shop. I was working upstairs. You need to ask Duffy. He'll be here any minute, if you'd like to wait for him.'

'If you don't mind.'

'Not at all. I'd better get dressed.'

He left Natalie and Murray standing in the shop, where Murray picked up a couple of the plastic phone covers, turning them over absent-mindedly and looking at the artwork. 'These are unusual.'

Natalie glanced across at the bright covers. They were exactly the sort her children would like for their phones. They changed their phone cases regularly, tiring of the old very quickly. She thought back to Savannah's phone cases she had stored away. 'Harriet and Savannah both came to this shop.'

'It is the only phone shop in Watfield,' said Murray, returning a black case with a strange white motif to the bowl. 'You know what teenagers are like with mobile phones and technology. Yolande's nephew is only three and he already knows his way around a smartphone.'

The door opened and Duffy came in, wiping his shining brown brogues on the doormat before coming in. It had started drizzling outside and his grey trousers were spattered with glistening droplets. He greeted them both, his brow slightly wrinkled.

'Hi. Do you know what's going on at the other end of Watfield? I got diverted around town. There are loads of police there.'

Murray responded, 'You haven't heard the news this morning? A teenager called Harriet Long went missing yesterday afternoon.'

A muscle twitched in Duffy's jaw. 'That's why I was sent the long way around town. You're looking for her?'

'That's right.'

'Shit! I hope she's okay?' He pulled off his leather jacket and threw it onto the counter. Under it he wore a beige jumper over a white open-necked shirt. On him the trendy ensemble worked well. Natalie was certain many of the girls would come into the shop purely to flirt with Duffy, whose easy manner was as attractive as his looks. She took over the questioning, leaving Murray to make notes.

'Do you know her?'

'I know a girl called Harriet. She comes into the shop now and again. Is it the same person?'

Natalie showed him the photograph and he nodded. 'That's her. She was here yesterday afternoon.'

'What time would that have been?'

'It was after the initial afternoon rush, which tends to be when Watfield Secondary School kick out. It was quiet when she came in, so it was probably around half past four.'

'What did she want?'

'Her mobile screen had frozen. She asked me if I could fix it. I turned it off and on again, and it rectified itself. She said she'd tried that but it hadn't worked for her. Said I had the magic touch.'

'That was all she wanted? She didn't buy anything or talk to you?'

He gave an apologetic smile. 'That's it. She chatted for a while.'

'What about?'

'Mostly about Spotify and music she was into and phone apps. She was saying how she liked Snapchat and how naff Facebook is.'

'Did she mention a website called Disappear?'

He shook his head. 'No.'

'Have you heard of it? Maybe one of the other schoolchildren mentioned it.'

He screwed up his face in concentration. 'Can't say I've ever come across it. Disappear? No. What is it? Some sort of game?'

Natalie turned the conversation back to Harriet. 'Did Harriet ever come into the shop with Savannah Hopkins?'

'Savannah? No. I never saw her once with Savannah. Why? Do you think her disappearance is connected to Savannah's?'

Natalie noticed the flash of concern in his eyes and pushed further. 'Did she tell you where she was going or say she was meeting anybody?'

'She didn't say a word.' He shook his head from side to side to affirm the statement.

'Did she seem upset or anxious?'

The muscle twitched once more in his jaw and he took a moment to respond. 'Not in the least. She laughed at a couple of my crap jokes. She seemed fine.'

'Can you tell us what time she left the shop?'

Duffy lowered his gaze and the muscle trembled several times. 'Could have been five or ten minutes later. I didn't check.'

'Did anyone come into the shop while you were talking?'

'Not a soul. It was dead quiet. A bloke came in soon after she left and it got busy around five.'

'And you were alone the entire time?'

'I wasn't completely alone. My boss was upstairs.'

There was something about Duffy's overly relaxed manner that troubled Natalie. 'You've never met Harriet outside of the shop?'

'Absolutely not. She was only a customer. I know next to nothing about her other than what music she likes to listen to. Do you think something serious has happened to her?'

'She's gone missing and we're concerned for her safety. If you see her again or hear from her, we need to know.'

'Sure.'

'If you know anything else, now would be a good time to tell us, Duffy. She's only fourteen. She's been missing all night.'

Duffy shook his head.

'You are fully aware that Savannah went missing under similar circumstances and was murdered.'

He swallowed hard and nodded. 'I know.'

'Can you tell us where you went after the dentist?'

'Home.'

'Is there anybody who can confirm that?'

'My mum.'

'You live with your parents?'

'For the time being. I'm saving up for a place of my own.'

'And were you at home all evening?'

'Until I went to help search for Savannah, yes.'

'Again, can anyone confirm that?'

He sighed dramatically. 'Yes. My aunt and nephew came around. I was playing computer games with him until we heard about Savannah.'

'Thank you. And what about yesterday afternoon?'

'I was here until the shop closed and then I went to a mate's house.'

Natalie kept her steady gaze fixed on him. The muscle in his jaw twitched once more.

'Has this mate got a name?'

'Jaffrey McCarthy. We play in a band. I play guitar. He plays the drums. We all practised in his garage until late. He can confirm that.'

'We'll need the band members' contact details. Have you anything else you want to tell us?'

Duffy's eyebrows lowered again and his chin jutted forwards. He looked directly at Natalie. 'I don't have anything to add but if I see Harriet, I'll be sure to let you know immediately.'

'Can't put my finger on it but there's something odd about that bloke,' said Murray as they walked back to the car. 'He's a little too perfect. I reckon he knows more than he's saying.'

'I got the same impression. He's either completely innocent or he's keeping quiet because he's somehow involved in their disappearances. He's the last person we know of who saw both girls before they vanished. That makes me suspicious, in spite of his claims.'

'But he went to the dentist immediately after Savannah left the shop. He couldn't have followed her or kidnapped her and then gone home.'

She thought for a minute. Duffy was a connection to both girls and they didn't know a great deal about him. They had to test his alibis. 'We're in town so we may as well check he's been telling the truth. The dentist is nearby, isn't it?'

'I'll get it up on Google Maps.'

'We'll make sure he really did have an appointment and then we'll take it from there and check out the rest of his story.'

The dentist was only a couple of streets away and they were waiting in reception to speak to somebody when Natalie got the call.

'Natalie, it's Graham. We were too late. We've found her. We've found Harriet.'

CHAPTER FIFTEEN

WEDNESDAY, 18 APRIL – MORNING

Rain was falling steadily and ominous grey clouds scudded across the skies. Tiredness mingled with the damp made Natalie shiver and she shoved her hands deep into her jacket pockets to warm them. Water dripped from her hair and trickled down the back of her neck but she ignored the discomfort. They stood on a short track off the main road, wide enough for three vehicles, beside an open gate that led into Bramshall woods. It would have gone unnoticed had it not been for the presence of several police vehicles that lined the road and drew attention to what was little more than a pull-in point to a gate. If she'd continued along the road and passed the lengthy woodland, she'd have come across the row of terraced houses that she'd visited in the early hours. Harriet's home had been within striking distance of her body. Now Melissa Long would be inside, coming to terms with the fact her daughter would never be coming home. The weight in Natalie's chest was genuine – her heart heavy with sorrow for a mother's loss.

There was an abundance of activity, with white-suited officers moving about the area, and the plethora of police vehicles had been joined by Forensics' white vans. She lighted on the woman in the red jacket, who stood a short distance away from the other news reporters, eyes trained on Natalie and Graham. Poor Harriet was undoubtedly going to make front-page headlines.

'She's through here. Careful how you go. It's slippery in parts,' said Graham.

Moving silently along a slightly trampled grassy path, they stepped over sodden ferns and broken branches shining with water droplets. The rain tapped out a rhythm on the leaves above them, an urgent drumbeat to accompany their steps. Natalie and Murray trailed in his wake and picked their way into the coppice, where after some fifty metres it appeared less dense and where Natalie made out forensic officers picking their way around piles of waste.

Graham faced her. 'I've given Mrs Long the news and requested an FLO to sit with her. I don't know what else to add. Two teenagers in two days. Normally teenagers who run away are found quickly and alive.'

Natalie felt his anguish and sympathised. They'd all hoped to find Harriet alive.

He pulled on the end of his nose then heaved a sigh. 'I have to leave you here. I've got to wind up the search operation and report back. I'll speak to you later.'

Natalie and Murray walked towards the forensic team, checked in with the officer in charge of the security log and slipped on the paper suits offered to them. Dense woodland shielded them from sight. Anybody coming here under the cover of darkness could be assured of not being spotted. It was cool and drips from the foliage plopped onto ferns in a staccato rhythm as she suited up. She paused to take in the carpets of wood anemones and yellow celandines that covered the ground under the trees, stretching as far as the clearing where rubbish had been dumped, suffocating nature's beauty.

Natalie pulled up the hood to cover her soaking hair. 'Okay?' she asked Murray, who responded with a slight lift of his head. They crossed the mossy ground towards the piles of rubbish, skirting around broken tiles, plastic guttering, a filthy mattress and broken tiles. A cream ceramic sink lay upside down next to a cracked and grubby toilet. A mound of white cement powder had transformed some of the ground into a pure white circle. Among the builder's rubble and household items were bags of household waste, bags ripped apart by scavengers and contents scattered – a broken toy doll, a plastic fire engine, a single glove, lying under banana skins and empty tins of soup. Even with the rain washing down on them the smell was evident – a sweet aroma of rot and filth. Natalie's heart sank at the sight of the girl in trousers and grubby white blouse, whose hair was still expertly twisted into two tight buns on her head and who was lying flat on her stomach, arms spread wide. A makeshift shelter had been erected to keep the worst of the weather off her.

Ben Hargreaves, the pathologist, was still examining Harriet's body. He checked the thermometer he'd been using to measure her internal temperature, then looked up at Natalie.

'Hello, Ben.'

'Morning, DI Ward… DS Anderson.'

'I suppose the obvious question is, was she strangled like Savannah?' she asked.

'There's bruising around her neck suggesting that to be the cause of death but, obviously, I need to confirm that.'

'Of course. Any idea of time of death?'

He lifted the thermometer as he spoke. 'As you know, the body's temperature cools by approximately one to two degrees each hour after death. If we take both that and the stage of rigor into account, we could assume she was killed a few hours ago, but I wouldn't be able to put a more exact time on it without further examination.'

'Have you any other thoughts? I need all the help I can get to catch the son of a bitch responsible,' said Natalie. She received a sympathetic smile.

'Well, she was found in this position on her front, but the presence of livor mortis on her back suggests she was killed elsewhere and moved sometime after death, probably an hour or two afterwards.'

Natalie knew a little about lividity. It was caused by the pooling and settling of blood in the blood vessels due to gravity occurring when the heart could no longer pump blood around the body. It appeared as a discolouration of the skin that started approximately thirty minutes after death. It developed more fully after three or four hours and entered what they called a fixed stage after eight hours, giving a good indication of when the victim had died and if the body had been moved after death.

Ben lifted Harriet's blouse to reveal milk-white skin and the purplish bloom that spread across her back and shoulders.

Natalie asked, 'Is it fixed lividity?'

'No, not yet, which supports my theory that she was killed sometime in the early hours and moved to this spot afterwards, certainly after livor mortis had begun.'

'The killer murdered her, kept her hidden for at least half an hour, then brought her here?'

'At least half an hour, probably longer. There's something else too. She was wearing false nails. Four of them have broken off recently and two have cracked, and there's slight bruising to the side of both hands and the outside of her little fingers.'

Murray balled his hands to imagine the scenario that would cause such bruising and said, 'From bashing against a door?'

Ben nodded. 'That would certainly cause it.'

'Is there anything more you can add?'

'Sadly, no, but I'll examine her fully as soon as she comes into the morgue.'

Natalie thanked him and walked away from the shelter. The rain was still tumbling onto gleaming leaves and small yellow flower heads that bowed and swayed under the weight of the water droplets as if nodding at Natalie. Stopping some distance from the body, she turned towards Murray. 'It's the same MO: a girl disappears, the girl is then found strangled near rubbish. First Savannah was found by a waste bin near her home and now Harriet's been strangled and left on a fly-tip close to her house. There's definitely a pattern emerging.'

'And she's not wearing a jacket or carrying the red backpack we saw her with on CCTV.'

'That's true. I wonder if we were right and the killer is hanging onto clothing as trophies. To my knowledge, Forensics still haven't recovered Savannah's bag or uniform yet. Have you seen Mike anywhere?'

'Is that him, over there?' He pointed him out.

'Oh, yes. I need to talk to him. We haven't tied up that loose end regarding Duffy so can you return to the dentist and confirm his appointment on Monday? I'll sort out transport back to the station and meet you there.'

'Roger that.' He set off, and she looked about the clearing. It wasn't huge but it was filled with garbage that couldn't have come from one person alone. She approached Mike.

'Hey!'

Mike looked up, eyes scanning her face for signs of dismay. 'I'm sorry, Nat. Really sorry.'

'I had that shitty feeling it was too late and I couldn't shake it off. Sometimes… sometimes you know you're not going to make it in time.' She looked away briefly then pulled herself together. 'She's missing a black jacket and a red backpack. She had both when she passed a CCTV camera yesterday afternoon.'

'Okay, we'll hunt for them. It's bloody difficult though. Talk about a needle in a haystack. Fucking killer knows how to make our lives difficult.' He glanced about the mess scattered in front of him.

'Is there any other way to reach this spot?'

'Quite a few if you're willing to trudge through several hundred metres of woods and uneven terrain, but no other easy access like the one we used. It's unlikely the killer carried her body through the woods to this point if that's what you're asking, but we're examining the entire area all the same.'

'It's mostly builder's rubbish rather than household waste.'

Mike agreed with her. 'Yeah, the sort of stuff people chuck out of houses when they're renovating them. Reputable builders usually take it to recycling depots or have skips or even take it back to their yards, not dump it. Could be cowboys or DIY-ers who use this spot as a fly-tip.'

Natalie could think of one firm that wasn't very far from this spot: Tenby House and Garden Services. Here was yet another potential link to Stu Oldfields.

An officer called across. 'Sir, we've found a mobile phone.'

Mike stopped his search and leapt to his feet, crossing the site at speed to the man who offered him the phone. Mike took it in his gloved hand. 'Get me the kit,' he ordered. Natalie waited while he dusted it for prints but he gave an exasperated hiss and said, 'It's been wiped clean.'

'Can we turn it on?'

'Sure.' He switched it on. A photograph of Harriet and her friend Emily.

Natalie glanced at Mike. 'It's definitely Harriet's but this doesn't add up. Her body's over there but her phone was in a different spot and it's been wiped clean. Why not leave it on her person or close to her? Where exactly did you find it?' she asked the officer.

'By the marker.' He pointed towards the middle of a pile of bricks.

Mike shook his head. 'You're right. It can't have fallen out of her pocket or even out of the killer's pocket. They won't have clambered over those bricks for any reason.'

Natalie walked towards the stick marking the spot, taking care not to slip on the upended and broken bricks, and knelt down. The marker was slap bang next to a black bag marked with one word: 'rubbish'. She was even more convinced it had been placed for them to find. 'The bastard's playing with us. Whoever it is has put the phone there for us for some reason.'

Mike's voice was wary. 'That might well be the case, Nat. The screensaver's disappeared and I've clicked onto a video entitled "Choke Dare". You need to see this.'

Mike joined her and held the mobile closer so she could see the screen, and her mouth opened at the sight of Harriet, a noose around her neck, hanging from a beam, her eyes growing large and pupils dilating. Natalie held her breath as she watched the girl begin to fade, her eyes rolling back into her head. Without warning, Harriet stepped back onto a chair, bent over and gulped in lungfuls of air, dry-coughed several times. Then she stood up, a wide smile on her face, and swaggered up to the camera. She laughed and said, 'I dared do it… Do you?'

'What the fuck?' Natalie said.

'I don't get it. Hang on. There's another video on the home screen named "Dare",' Mike replied and clicked onto it. Natalie recognised it as the same one that had been uploaded to the website, Disappear. She listened to Harriet's screams for the few seconds the video lasted.

'There's another one. "Ice Bucket Dare". I've heard of that one.' They watched as Harriet introduced herself and announced she was about to take the Ice Bucket Challenge. She removed her dressing gown to reveal a bikini and squealed noisily as icy water was tipped over her by an unknown person.

Natalie spoke once more. 'Her friend Emily said she was keen on social media challenges. There are all sorts of crazy ones and some are more dangerous than others.'

'At first glance there are only three videos. Do you want to look at the phone first and see if there's anything else on it that might be of use to you, or should I send it directly to the lab for analysis?'

'Best if you handle it. Can you make the second one any clearer? I'd like to know where it was filmed. It's too dark at the moment to make out where she is.'

'We can try to. Actually, I'm going back to the lab myself in a couple of minutes. I was working on some fibres we picked up at

Western Park. You want a lift to the station or is Murray returning for you?'

'I sent him to check out an alibi. A lift would be welcome.' She pressed hard on the point directly above her left eyebrow. It was tender and she had the beginnings of a blinding headache, and it was still only nine fifty in the morning. It had all the makings of a very lengthy and arduous day.

'You holding up?' Mike asked as they whizzed along the main road towards Samford. He'd been strangely silent up until that point, which had suited Natalie. Her thoughts had been on the investigation.

'I'm fine.'

'You look a bit—'

'Old and fat,' she finished his sentence for him.

He laughed. 'Not at all. Jaded. That's all. Don't be so hard on yourself, Nat.'

She sighed. She wasn't good at handling compliments.

'I know we signed up for all of this shit but it's bloody hard some days, isn't it?' he continued. He felt for a packet of Marlboro in the plastic tray between them. 'You mind if I smoke?'

'Go ahead. Wind down the window a bit though. I don't want to get too tempted to steal one from you.'

He smiled winningly, extracted a cigarette from the pack adroitly with one hand and placed it between his lips, keeping his other hand on the steering wheel. He felt about for his lighter and cursed. It had slipped out of reach. Natalie bent forwards, retrieved it and flicked it into action, holding it while he leant into the flame and illuminated the end of his cigarette. She breathed in his aftershave – a light citrus scent that brought back a brief memory of his arms wrapped around her.

He inhaled and lowered the driver's window a few centimetres. An icy breeze rushed in instantly, chilling the side of Natalie's face and bringing light rain that didn't appear to trouble Mike.

'The last time I saw David, he hinted you and he were going through a rough patch. Glad you're sorted,' he said.

Heat rose up Natalie's neck. She ought to have guessed David would have told his best friend about their troubles. 'Did he tell you why?'

'Only that you'd jumped to conclusions that he was gambling again and he was majorly pissed off with you.'

'Then you understand why we fell out.'

'Was he? Gambling?'

'No. I got it wrong.' She stared out of the window and watched the other drivers in their vehicles headed alongside. They passed a man in a mauve shirt and dark-blue tie, face red and lips moving as he spoke to an invisible person on the end of the phone. He lifted a finger and wagged it angrily. People didn't need to wait until they got to the office to become stressed these days. They could manage it on their way there, she mused. She felt horribly flat. It wasn't because of David sharing details of their marriage with Mike. It was because she hadn't reached Harriet in time. Could she have done more to save her? She'd been up all night but still she hadn't located the girl in time, and she was no closer to finding Savannah's or Harriet's murderer. The chances were it was one and the same.

Her mobile buzzed. 'Natalie, I've just left the dentist surgery and I thought you'd want to know that the receptionist checked the diary. Duffy definitely had an appointment for four p.m. and it was crossed off as attended. I also rang his friend, Jaffrey McCarthy, who confirmed he was with Duffy from about six until almost midnight. Tuesday night is when the band practises.'

She hadn't really expected any other outcome yet Duffy's mannerisms had convinced her he was withholding some nugget of information. 'Okay. Head back then. I need to brief everyone.' She ended the call, rested her head against the headrest and shut her eyes. 'I don't know which way to turn, Mike. I don't know if I'm close or miles away from working out who's behind these murders.'

'What have you got so far? Let's see if it makes any sense,' he replied.

She opened her eyes and spoke. 'Both girls visited the phone shop in Watfield immediately before they disappeared, but the guy they spoke to, Duffy, denies knowing them well and says he had no idea that they were planning on disappearing.'

'And do you believe him?'

'I don't know. He seems upfront but there's something about him that doesn't ring true.'

'Copper's instinct,' Mike said with a smile. She returned it.

'Now we've got the video we believe to be of Harriet, and a website – Disappear. Maybe she did upload that video as a prank or maybe the killer did. I can't be sure. The girl was willing to post a video of herself hanging, for fuck's sake, so she might have posted this one too for a laugh. I won't know until we can work out who uploaded it. Then there's the fact that both bodies were left near their homes and in places connected with dumping rubbish. The killer must have known something about both girls to know where they lived. It could be somebody they're acquainted with.'

'Seems logical and might take you back to Duffy.'

'But there's also Harriet's boyfriend Stu. Harriet was key to his alibi for when Savannah went missing. He works for Tenby House and Garden Services, which is close to where we found Harriet, and he might even use that fly-tipping area to dump waste.' She didn't pause to let Mike speak but continued with, 'And then, we have Anthony Lane, charged a few years ago for exposing himself to young girls, and who's been captured on camera following both Savannah and Harriet. Am I getting closer or just more tangled up?'

'For what it's worth, I think you're working it like you usually do. You're checking every option and that's the way you'll find whoever's responsible. It takes time.'

'I don't have time, Mike.'

'You can't make it happen any faster no matter how much you want to. You'll get there. Sometimes it takes longer than we'd like.'

She heaved a sigh. 'I hope you're right.'

'Sure I am. Come on. It isn't like you to doubt yourself.'

She rubbed at her face. 'Tiredness. I can't think clearly.'

'Grab a power nap. Even if it's only for ten minutes. It'll help. Go on. Try now. I'll wake you when we get there.'

She nodded and fell silent, closing her eyes again. She might have been wrong about David gambling again but she could ill afford to make similar bad judgements during this investigation and jump to incorrect conclusions. Lives were at stake and that led to her greatest anxiety, the one gnawing at her stomach at the moment, that there would be another victim.

*

He rubbed his hands, relishing the sudden heat produced by such vigorous friction. The police were bamboozled. They were scurrying about like headless chickens. Had they picked up on the clues left for them? He snorted. It was unlikely. He'd planned this meticulously and left nothing to chance. The police liked logic and order and getting a sense of what sort of person could be behind these ghastly crimes. He hadn't given them anything to go on. As far as they knew, the attacks were random, and they could have no idea of when he would strike again. They must be frantic with worry. What sort of person could succeed in two kidnappings and two murders within two days? He smiled broadly. He wasn't the timid little fraidy-cat now, was he? In fact, he would really show them all how brazen he could be. He'd pounce again. Today.

CHAPTER SIXTEEN

WEDNESDAY, 18 APRIL – LATE MORNING

Natalie finished reading through the information from Manchester regarding the murder of Alisha Kumar, who'd been strangled and dumped by rubbish bags. She highlighted a couple of facts before addressing the others, who were waiting for her to speak. She rubbed her forehead. The throbbing in her head was intensifying. She'd grab a couple of pills after the briefing. She stood up, a signal she was going to speak.

'We've got a load of information to sift through and this is going to be quite a task. Let's start with the two victims. They were both female, teenagers and from the Watfield area. Savannah went to Watfield Secondary to the south of the town, and Harriet, Lincoln Fields Secondary School to the north. At first, we believed they'd both run away. We knew Savannah was unhappy at home and school and annoyed with her mum because of her new boyfriend, Phil Howitt. As for Harriet, she missed her father, Shane, who is in prison, and was irritated at times by her little brothers. However, I think we ought to be moving away from the assumption they ran away, or at least consider the possibility they might have run off initially and their plans went horribly wrong. Unless we come across another reason for the girls to decide to take off, I think we should look at the possibility they did this for a dare. So, we need to know if Savannah went on the Disappear website. Maybe that is our connection.' She rubbed her head and carried on.

'As far as we can make out, they weren't friends or even acquaintances, and they didn't have anything in common, except both of them knew Stu Oldfields, a labourer for Tenby House and Garden Services, and Nick Duffield, otherwise known as Duffy, from the local phone shop.'

She paused to ensure everyone was keeping up. 'These two men have alibis for around the time Savannah disappeared although Stu's alibi is now in doubt. With Harriet dead, we can't prove he met up with her on Monday afternoon. I'd like to know his movements yesterday too. Not only has he got a flimsy alibi for Monday, he works only down the road from where Harriet's body was found. That fly-tipping spot in Bramshall woods appears to be used by builders rather than householders, so Murray, can you talk to Stu again and to Noel Reeves, the owner of Tenby House and Garden Services, and ask if they've ever dumped rubbish there? He'll probably deny it but push him on the matter. If they didn't, we'll have to widen the search to other builders. I can't imagine somebody from out of town would know about that clearing in the woodland. It has to be somebody with local knowledge.'

She stood up and moved to the window. There was almost too much information to process. They were going to be stretched to the limit. She might have to ask Superintendent Aileen Melody for assistance, although she could already imagine the response to her request. The force was ridiculously understaffed and overworked at the moment. She picked up her train of thought, wishing the banging in her head would subside.

'I'm not sure why Savannah changed out of her school clothes or why Harriet applied false nails but it seems significant. They might have intended meeting up with somebody, or simply got dressed up ready to post a video on this bloody website, Disappear. However, both of them must have had an idea of where they were headed and might have made arrangements to stay with someone. The question is who?

'One other person of interest is Anthony Lane, who we spotted on CCTV cameras in the pedestrian precinct, trailing both girls. Thanks to the camera on Church Road being out of action, we can't confirm his whereabouts either.' She had to stop for a moment. The headache was making her nauseous and she suddenly felt quite sick. 'Lucy, do you want to step in at this point? You have some info on Lance Hopkins, Savannah's stepfather.'

'That's right. West Midlands Police confirmed that there's a travellers' site in Erdington and spoke to Lance Hopkins' mother, Christine. She wasn't very helpful and said she had no idea of his whereabouts, but one of the others let slip Lance has been working at a building site in Sutton Coldfield the last few months. No one else knew anything about it or had any contact details for him.'

'How very convenient,' said Natalie, scowling at the news.

Lucy continued, 'Sutton is only twenty-fives miles away from Watfield, and he might have returned. The neighbour who thought she saw him near Jane Hopkins' house could have been right after all.'

Natalie spoke up again. 'If he was around, somebody else must have seen him. He had a grudge against the Longs – about non-payment for work he'd done to their property – but as for murdering their daughter over it, or even killing his stepdaughter, well, it doesn't make any sense at all. Still, we have to interview him.' Natalie rubbed her head again then rested her palms against the desk. The nausea was worsening.

Murray injected, 'Doesn't Lance Hopkins do building work – odd jobs and DIY stuff? He might know about the fly-tipping spot where Harriet was found.'

'Good point. Lucy, get onto West Midlands again and obtain a list of building sites where he might be working.'

Ian cleared his throat. 'I did some checking up on Lance. As you know he was charged with being drunk and disorderly and brawling in a pub last year. Turns out the person he was arguing and fighting with was Kyle Yates, who lives with Melissa Long, Harriet's mum. Might be important.'

Natalie's eyebrows lifted. 'Kyle definitely kept quiet about that when we spoke to him. That's interesting and it might account for why he couldn't look me in the eye. I'll tackle him on that subject. Okay. Maybe Lance does have more motive than we first imagined.' She wet her lips before continuing. She had one more line of enquiry she wanted to follow up.

'I don't want to make unnecessary work for us but there's something else we should look into. The case file I requested from Manchester is regarding Alisha Kumar, a fourteen-year-old girl who went missing back in 2014. Her parents ran an Indian restaurant and by all accounts they were a well-liked, well-respected family. When Alisha disappeared on her way home from school, her parents notified MisPer immediately. She was missing overnight, and the following morning her body turned up in the alley close to her parents' restaurant, propped up beside a pile of refuse sacks. Although several suspects were interviewed, none were charged and the killer wasn't found. It's a long shot but we need to check that none of those suspects have moved into the Watfield area.'

'You think we're dealing with the same killer?' Ian asked.

'We might be. Let's not rule out that possibility until we've checked their current whereabouts. It might even be a copycat killing – somebody who read about Alisha's murder. It was high-profile at the time, especially in the Manchester area, so our killer could have been living there in 2014.

'Ian, check up on those suspects. Lucy, once you've spoken to West Midlands Police, talk to Savannah's friends – Sally Gilmore and Holly Bradshaw – again and try to get more information about her online activities. Mention the Disappear website and see if you get a reaction. Find out if they or Savannah knew Harriet Long and press them again about who she might have been going to meet – a boyfriend, her stepdad, anyone. Murray, when you've spoken to Stu and the manager at Tenby House and Garden Services, interview Harriet's closest friends, especially Emily Rowley. I'll speak to the victims' mothers and tackle Kyle about that incident with Lance. Harriet's mobile is with Forensics. They're trying to work out where that last video was filmed and they'll send details of her online activity soon. Ian, let me know if anything raises any alarm bells. Finally, in case you aren't aware, the newspapers are full of Savannah Hopkins' murder this morning. It's going to be a media feeding frenzy, especially once they announce details of Harriet's death. I don't need to remind you to say nothing to the press. We can't have anything leaking that will prevent us from catching this murderer. That's it for the moment.'

With her head now pounding wildly, she made for the door and marched down the corridor, praying nobody would stop her. Once on the floor below, she sped up and only just reached the toilets in time before she threw up. She bent over the toilet bowl and heaved again until her stomach was empty, then pressed her palms against the wall and calmed her racing heart. *Bloody wine and lack of sleep.* She needed to smarten up her act sharpish. She had a team to lead. She flushed the toilet and crossed to the sink where she splashed cold water onto her face, staring at her reflection as she did so. Mike had been right when he commented on how jaded she looked. She'd aged five years in one night. *Fuck it.* There were more important things than wrinkles and baggy eyes. She waited while hot air blew her hands dry, then ran fingers through her hair, adjusted her jacket and strode back upstairs purposefully.

Lucy and Murray left headquarters at the same time. The rain was still tumbling and they jogged across the car park and halted beside Murray's Jeep, next to Lucy's Peugeot. 'You think she's up to it?' Murray asked.

'Natalie? Of course she is. What makes you think otherwise?'

'She seemed off her game today. She flew through that briefing and hardly took a breath. Not like her.'

'Well, Sherlock, I think you'll find that's down to working a straight forty-eight hours with no breaks and not enough food. It's amazing she can still function at all. I'd be dead on my feet.'

'One of the joys of heading a murder investigation.'

'There is *no* joy in leading a murder investigation,' said Lucy, her face suddenly serious.

'True. By the way, Yolande wanted you to know she's bought some outfits for Spud. She's taking them around to Bethany later today.'

Bethany was nineteen weeks pregnant with Spud, who'd acquired the nickname after Bethany had compared the size of the growing baby to a jacket potato she was eating. Spud was now approximately the size of a mango but the name had stuck.

'She didn't have to do that.'

'I think she did. She wants to treat it like she would any friend's new baby, as if it has nothing to do with me.'

'What about you? How do you feel about becoming a father?'

'I'm cool about it. You and Bethany needed a sperm donation and that's what I gave. I'm not really a proper father and I don't want any involvement either – only as a friend to you both.'

'It's going to be weird, though, isn't it? Seeing a baby that you helped create.'

'It's only weird if you let it be. We all agreed. Yolande was on board too. We'll be supportive mates and that's it.'

Lucy gave him a long look that he ignored. They'd talked and talked about this before Murray had offered a sperm donation, but now the baby was real and would be arriving in a few months, Lucy wondered if he and Yolande might not have changed their minds and want more involvement in the child's life.

He threw her a wide smile. 'Don't worry. We won't interfere. Yolande's bought some cute sleepsuits. She couldn't resist them even though you won't need them for months.'

'That's very thoughtful.' Lucy decided she'd have to wait to see how things developed after Spud was born and trust her good friends to stick to their promise.

'Yeah, well, as long as she doesn't get any ideas of us having kids yet. I couldn't deal with that. I'm not ready for such commitment.'

'She won't. She's already got one big kid in her life. She couldn't cope with two of you.'

Murray gave her the finger but she grinned and slipped into her car without acknowledging it.

Natalie hadn't yet left the building. Superintendent Aileen Melody had requested an update on the investigation and so she had dutifully raced upstairs to deliver it. She was surprised to see her superior in dress uniform, normally reserved for funerals or functions. Aileen was standing up behind her desk; her jacket, with the crown insignia displayed on epaulettes, was hanging on the back of her chair. Her hair was pulled back from her face and showed off sharp cheekbones and serious eyes. Aileen had fought her way to this position and took no nonsense from anyone, including Natalie.

Aileen wasted no time getting to the point. 'I've orders from above to hold a press conference and get media support. They might be able to reach out to witnesses who spotted either or both of the girls. I can't say it's what I would choose to do because I don't like admitting we have few answers and I don't want the son of a bitch responsible for these murders to even consider for one second that we aren't onto him. So, tell me… are you making headway?'

Honesty was always the best policy as far as dealing with Aileen was concerned. She could be firm but also fair. 'It's messy at the moment. We've got a few potential suspects, and as soon as we've done some more digging, we'll bring them in for interview. We're looking at several angles but it's not going to be quick or simple.'

Aileen stared at her without blinking. 'That's where we have the problem. This killer, who we assume has killed both these girls, is still out there, and the public will be extremely anxious about this situation, yet I can't reassure them that their children are safe until we have a suspect in custody. You don't have the luxury of time, Natalie. The perp kidnapped one girl on Monday and another on Tuesday. If one goes missing today, there'll be an almighty hoo-ha. Which is why I have to talk to the press and get the message out.'

Natalie stood with hands behind her back. There was nothing to add. Aileen was under pressure from above and Natalie was being press-ganged to perform, but she and her team could only work at their pace, and no amount of ear-bashing would change that. She cleared her throat. 'It's been a little over forty-eight hours since we discovered Savannah. We've worked through the night, and the investigation got sidelined by Harriet's disappearance, which we had to also investigate given her connection to one of our suspects. I have only got three officers, one who can't work to full capacity. If you want instant results, I suggest you supply me with a much larger team or a magician.'

She held Aileen's cool gaze. The super shook her head. 'I requested more officers and my request was denied. There's simply insufficient manpower and I can't reassign officers currently working on other cases to you at the moment.'

'Then we can only work as fast and as efficiently as we are. I have everyone working flat out and have a number of leads.' Natalie stood firm.

'Okay. It's been a tough morning. We're all devastated that two teenagers have been murdered on our patch and I've had to answer a lot of questions from the powers that be. I don't need to tell you how serious this is. All eyes are on us, Natalie. We can't be seen to be lacking in any way. None of us can.'

The subtext of her words was transparent. Natalie didn't profess to understand the politics that played out in the force but she was convinced Aileen was embroiled in them. If Natalie's team didn't get this right, it would reflect badly on Aileen, but as much as she respected her, she didn't give a stuff about her reasons for wanting a result. Natalie had her own – she had to catch the bastard. There was no way she was going to let them harm another child. She held her peace and waited to be dismissed.

Aileen did so with a wave of her hand and then called out, 'Natalie, how the hell did the perp manage to move Savannah to Western Park and Harriet to Bramshall woods without being spotted?'

Natalie stopped mid-stride and spun back around. 'We're checking CCTV footage and will follow up on all vehicles in both vicinities.'

The answer appeared to satisfy Aileen, who gave a brief nod and said, 'I want to be updated regularly.'

'Yes, ma'am.' Natalie left, wishing she hadn't gone upstairs and wasted time smoothing down Aileen's ruffled feathers. They hadn't enough manpower as it was, and keeping her away from the investigation was irritating. She thundered downstairs and into the lobby, ignoring the people gathered at the front desk.

She was halfway across the car park when she heard her name being shouted and turned to see the woman in the red jacket scuttling after her. Natalie strode away and reached her car before the woman caught up with her.

'DI Ward. I'm Bev Gardiner of the *Watfield Herald*. I saw you at Bramshall woods. Are you now also investigating the murder of Harriet Long as well as Savannah Hopkins?'

She waved a hand at the woman. 'No comment. You'll have to wait for the press conference.'

She yanked open the car door and eased onto the driver's seat.

The woman was still talking. 'How do you as a mother feel about these abductions? You must be deeply concerned that somebody is targeting teenage girls.'

Natalie opened her mouth to tell Bev if she mentioned her family in any article she'd sue the arse off the woman, then shut it again. Ignoring the woman, she reversed and drove away. *Fucking media!*

*

He turned up the radio and chuckled deeply as he listened again to Melissa Long's tearful plea for her daughter to return.

'She's not coming home alive, Melissa! Although you'll probably know that by now,' he said.

The interview she'd given earlier that day was still being played hourly on each news bulletin. Soon the presenters would take it off and replace it with a solemn announcement telling the listeners the tragic news that Harriet Long had been found dead in Bramshall woods.

He stroked his shoulder, caressing the snake. It had enjoyed the kill, easing around Harriet's throat slowly, so slowly, and watching the terror manifest in her eyes quickly, followed swiftly by resignation. She'd surrendered without a fight in the full knowledge there was no point in struggling. He'd whispered why he'd chosen her and he was sure he'd spotted a tear in her eyes before the light had gone out in them.

The news had ended and he still had plans to make. He'd enjoyed messing with the police. By now, they'd have found the video he'd shot and uploaded to the Disappear website. He'd made it easy for them and placed the mobile next to a message for the police to find. It would be interesting to see if the investigating team understood the clues he'd left for them. He doubted they would. They were no match for him and the snake.

*

Lucy sat with Holly and Sally in the head teacher's office once more. This time she spoke to the girls together and with their form teacher, Kirsty Davies, present; they seemed more at ease than they had with the head teacher, Mr Derry. Kirsty had warned Lucy the girls were more upset today. The realisation of what had happened to Savannah had sunk in and Lucy thought both girls looked paler and much more subdued. Sally's eyes were pink and Holly sported dark bags – the sign of a bad night's sleep. They'd gone back over everything they'd already told Lucy, and now she asked about Harriet.

'Do either of you know Harriet Long?'

Sally glanced at her friend and shook her head. 'Never heard of her.'

Lucy showed them a photograph of Harriet.

'Is she missing too?' asked Holly.

'She went missing yesterday,' said Lucy, not wanting to frighten or upset the girls further by telling them Harriet was dead.

'I might have seen her about town,' said Sally.

'Did you ever talk to her?'

'No, but I'm sure I've seen her.'

'Were you with Savannah when you saw her?'

'I don't think so. Savannah wouldn't have spoken to her either.' She suddenly reached for a tissue and blew her nose. The mention of her friend's name had set her off again and her eyes filled with tears.

'Did Savannah ever talk about Harriet or any friends from Lincoln Fields School?'

'We're not friends with anyone from that school. It's the other side of Watfield.'

'But you must bump into pupils from time to time in town or around Watfield, in cafés or the cinema or at the bowling alley. You can't avoid them all,' Lucy said.

Sally looked at her with big eyes. 'We don't hang out with them.'

'Why not?' Lucy asked.

Holly leapt to her friend's defence. 'She means there's an *us and them* situation.'

'A rivalry?'

'Not quite that but if you go to Watfield Secondary, you don't hang about with anyone from Lincoln Fields.'

Lucy shook her head in frustration. 'So, Savannah had no friends at all at Lincoln Fields that you know of?'

'She never said anything to us and we were her only friends,' said Holly, her bottom lip beginning to tremble with emotion.

Sally spoke up. 'Savannah didn't know many people at our school or in Watfield. She wouldn't know anyone from a different school. We were her only friends and she went off on Monday thinking I *wasn't* her friend. I think she might even have run away because she was upset with me.' She began to cry. Even though Kirsty had tipped her off, Lucy was surprised the girls were so upset this time round when they seemed more composed the day before. The explanation for their distress followed.

Holly put an arm around Sally and cast a baleful look at Lucy. 'She's convinced this has happened because of that stupid bracelet. She thinks Savannah took off because she lost it and if she hadn't lost it and they hadn't argued over it, Savannah wouldn't have gone. I keep telling her it isn't her fault.'

'But she was really angry with me!' Sally wailed.

Lucy leant forwards and spoke quietly to the girl. 'I don't believe you're to blame. I think she'd already planned to run off.'

Sally sniffed back tears. 'But I was horrible to her on Monday. I called her a silly cow.'

'Sally, this isn't your fault,' Lucy said firmly to end the tears.

It took a few minutes for Sally to be able to talk again.

'Can you think of anybody at all she might have gone to meet on Monday?'

She was met with head shakes and sorrowful eyes.

'Have either of you heard of a website called Disappear?'

'What's it about?' asked Sally.

'Have you not heard about it?'

Holly shifted in her seat. 'I have. It's a challenge website. I've heard about it but not from Savannah.'

'Who told you about it?'

'I don't remember who. We were talking about it on WhatsApp. Somebody said they'd like to try it out and go missing but none of us could think of how to hide without being found.'

'And you definitely didn't say anything to Savannah about it?'

'No. We were talking about the banana and Sprite challenge and somebody brought up the subject of Disappear. Savannah wasn't in the WhatsApp group.'

'Sally, you haven't heard of it at all?'

Sally shook her head and tears sprung again.

Lucy persisted for a while longer, but although the teenagers were cooperative, they were also upset and had no more to offer her. After half an hour, Lucy called an end to the interview and headed back to the station.

The Killers' 'Mr Brightside' came on the radio and she increased the volume, beating the rhythm against the steering wheel with the palms of her hands. Bethany loved this track. She was half-tempted to phone her other half. They'd both had a rough night, what with her getting in so late and then getting up again and then Bethany becoming restless in the early hours after Lucy had returned home for the second time. They'd have to get used to little sleep. Once the baby was born, there'd be no lie-ins or full eight hours of kip. Now Bethany had more of a visible bump, the baby was becoming a reality, and although Lucy had doubted her ability to be a good parent at times, she now had to admit to a sense of excitement that a new life would be joining them in a few months.

Her mobile rang and, muting the track, she answered. It was an exasperated Murray.

'No fucking joy! Stu was at work all day and got home at six thirty yesterday and stayed there. His mother confirmed he didn't leave the house at all. She couldn't sleep, so she was up until the early hours reading. Unless he managed to sneak out without her hearing, it's unlikely he managed to video Harriet, kill her and dump her body. Didn't get anywhere at Tenby House and Garden

Services either. Noel Reeves was highly affronted. Says they never fly-tip. He even showed me the skips they use to transport any leftover debris to the recycling facilities and invoices for them. I've located a couple of local building companies and I'm going to track them down but this feels like I'm on a wild goose chase. What about you? How are you getting along?'

'Same. Savannah's friends gave me huge doe eyes and burst into tears but they knew nothing. I don't think their acting skills are good enough to put on such a convincing performance of upset and confusion. I felt shitty asking them about the Disappear website and Harriet Long. Good thing their teacher was with them. She took them to the school nurse after the interview.'

'Where are you headed now?' he asked.

'Station. Going to help Ian trawl through hours of CCTV footage.'

'Better you than me. Makes my eyes sting like buggery.'

'Me too, but I've clearly got a much higher pain threshold than you and infinitely more patience with such matters – ah, soz, got another incoming call, Murray.'

'Okay. See you later.'

Lucy accepted the second call, this time from Ian. 'I can't reach Natalie, and Lance Hopkins is on his way to the station. Are you nearby or should I put him in a holding room until somebody gets back?' asked Ian.

'I can be there in a quarter of an hour. I'll interview him.'

'Cheers. Catch you in a while.'

Lucy started the music up again immediately after she ended the call. She pressed the accelerator pedal and listened to the wounded Brandon Flowers belting out the words in his anguished fashion. This time she didn't think of Bethany singing along off-key to it and dancing in the kitchen or of the baby. She ran through questions she needed to fire at Lance because, at present, he had to be considered as a suspect. With Natalie out of the station it fell to her to handle the interview appropriately. One thing was for certain: there could be no slip-ups. This might be their only shot at establishing if Lance had been in the vicinity, and she couldn't mess it up.

CHAPTER SEVENTEEN

WEDNESDAY, 18 APRIL – AFTERNOON

Natalie spent over an hour with Savannah's mother, Jane, along with the family liaison officer, Tanya Granger. Natalie hadn't gleaned anything new and Jane hadn't known about the pavilion or any website that dared teenagers to go missing. There were no words to describe the anguish on the poor woman's face as she struggled to answer Natalie's questions. Her world had imploded. Her only child was dead, her lover and employer had been charged for possessing child pornography, and the building yard where she worked had been temporarily closed, although it was fairly likely it would become permanent.

Now Natalie was on her way to Melissa Long's house and wishing she could get leverage on the case. Before she interviewed the woman, she drove past her home, towards the woods and to the turn-off. It was a tight turning with no sign and easy to miss. It would definitely be somebody in the know who had taken Harriet there, or somebody who'd stumbled across it when hunting for the perfect spot to leave her body – somewhere close to her home yet somewhere associated with waste. She couldn't shake off the feeling it was somehow connected to the Alisha Kumar case. There were similarities between Alisha's murder and the murders that had taken place in Watfield that she couldn't ignore.

The five-bar gate that had been unlocked last night was now padlocked as it apparently had been when officers arrived on the scene. If the killer had brought his victim's body here, he'd have had to climb either the heavy metal gate or the wooden-barred fence to gain entry. Mike's team had examined the area for signs that the body had been dropped or lowered into position but found nothing to support that theory.

Making a three-point turn, she retraced the route to the terraced houses and knocked on Melissa's door. A baby wailed – earnest anguished cries that increased in pitch and cut through her – and her heart went out to the mother inside, struggling to maintain some semblance of normality with two young children demanding her attention, while reeling from such a dreadful shock.

The door opened and Kyle shuffled outside. 'It's a bad time. The little 'un's playing up.'

'I understand but I need to ask further questions. Can I start by asking you a couple, regarding Lance Hopkins?'

'What about him?'

'I understand there was an incident in a pub last year.'

He looked around to make sure they were alone and pulled the door to. 'Melissa doesn't know anything about it. She'd go ape if she found out I'd been fighting with Lance.'

'What was the fight over?'

'He stitched me up. He did the job on the gutter I told you about and I paid him all I was prepared to pay him, but it was a shit job and I mean really shit. The bloody guttering was crap quality and three days after he supposedly fixed it, it leaked again. He'd charged me handsomely so I went to get my money back, only he wasn't prepared to admit he'd ripped me off and he got majorly pissed about me bawling him out in front of everyone in the pub. He swung for me. We wrestled for a bit and I got smacked in the nose, and then someone called the police and we got taken away. Melissa hates all that sort of behaviour, so I didn't tell her.'

'Was that the only time you fought?'

'The one and only. The man's a fucking gorilla. I wouldn't stand a chance if he'd really tried to hurt me. Besides, there was no way he was going to give me a refund. I only wanted others to know he was a cheat. I thought if word got out how he swindled people, he'd not get any more work.'

'And Savannah, you never met her?'

'Never.' A chill breeze whistled around them both. He bounced up and down on the balls of his feet to warm up.

'I'd really like to talk to Melissa. I know this is a dreadful time for you both but I need your help if I'm to catch the person who killed Harriet.'

'She's in a bad way. She won't talk to me or anyone. She yelled at the liaison officer to get out too and we've turned off all the phones because journos keep ringing us. Bastards. They ought to leave us alone.' He rubbed his hands together then tucked them under his armpits.

'I'd like to see her all the same.'

He pushed open the door wide and said, 'She's upstairs.'

The baby's cries had lessened to sobs, and Natalie climbed the creaky wooden staircase and headed towards the noise. The sobs were coming from the first bedroom door, which was ajar. She tapped gently on it. 'Melissa, it's DI Ward. Can I come in?'

She stepped into a single bedroom, a room that screamed 'teenage girl' to her and was filled with familiar clutter she'd also find in her own daughter's room. The décor was different to Leigh's room, with a découpage dresser against one wall, each drawer covered by different-coloured pieces of fabric, and above it, a white canvas picture, clearly home-made, on which was written in gold ink, 'Laugh as much as you breathe. Love as much as you can.' Several school books were stacked haphazardly on the floor next to a bright-red table lamp, which stood on top of a science textbook. A pink nightdress hung half in and half out of a wicker basket in the corner of the room. The shelves next to the bed contained a collection of plush animals: a pink monkey with long legs that dangled over the shelf, a fat cheerful hedgehog and a chubby baby rabbit. Her eyes alighted on a photograph of a young Harriet with a man Natalie didn't recognise but presumed was her father. She glanced at another white canvas, 'Wake up and make-up', hanging above a half-made bed on which sat Melissa Long, eyes unfocused as she rocked back and forth, the baby in her arms. Next to her sat a large blue toy elephant – Harriet's treasured possession.

The baby's nose was running badly and he snuffled noisily. 'Mine were like that when they were teething. My boy was the worst. Got seven teeth all in one go. I didn't get any sleep for months. I hear teething crystals are the way to go these days,' Natalie said. Her gentle words had the desired effect.

'I bought some but they don't seem to be working. He's fretful. Been worse today than ever.'

'Is there anyone who can come and help you out for the time being? Can Kyle's mum?'

'She's already looking after Jack. I couldn't dump this chap on her as well. He's too needy at the moment. My parents said they'd come but I can't... I can't speak to them. I can't face them. They'll be understanding and sympathetic but they'll blame me too. They'll say I should have looked out for her more. I know they will.'

'You can't be sure of that. They're grieving too and they're *your* parents. They'll want to be there to support you, not play any blame game. Melissa, it's really hard for you at the moment, why not let the liaison officer help you? There's a great deal of support for you. You don't have to go through this alone.'

Melissa blinked back tears. 'But I do. I feel so responsible. I had no idea of what was going on in her head. That's wrong. That's so wrong.'

'Teenagers don't like to share much with their parents. Harriet was no different to most.'

Melissa stopped rocking the baby, whose eyes had closed at last. 'I don't know what to think. I don't know what to do.'

'Help me. Help me find whoever did this to your daughter.'

'How?'

'Tell me what you *do* know about her. What sort of things did she talk to you about?'

'School, friends, clothes, make-up… she loved nail varnishes. She had so many she could have started her own salon. That's what she wanted to do. Become a nail technician.'

'You told me she was a little wild at times.'

'Rebellious streak, like her father.' A ghost of a smile played across her face as she reflected on some memory.

'What were some of the things she got up to?'

'Mostly arguing with teachers. I was called to the school on a few occasions because of disruptive behaviour – answering back, fighting, smoking. She wasn't a saint but she wasn't a demon either. She was a proper daddy's girl, and when Shane was sent down, she always believed the authorities were in the wrong, not him. She used to big him up to her friends, and getting into the odd spot of bother was her way of proving she was his girl.'

'Did she ever do anything that really worried you? Self-harmed, took drugs?'

'Not at all. She was keen on fitness – regularly used the gym at Watfield Sports Centre, and even played football for a while. I know she was caught smoking at school but it was only the once and only because her friends dared her to. She actually didn't enjoy it at all. For all her faults, she had strengths too and she thought anyone who took drugs was an idiot.'

There it was – the word Natalie had been waiting for: dare.

'Did Harriet ever talk about trying other challenges, or her friends doing dares?'

Melissa shook her head. 'I can't think of anything. Oh, she did the Ice Bucket Challenge with Emily. Emily tipped freezing-cold water over her. I came home and found them giggling over the video they'd made. Everyone seemed to be doing that challenge though – celebs, some of my workmates, everyone. It wasn't harmful.'

'What about her online activity? Was she on many social media sites?'

'She used to play a lot of online games and she liked the app where you can mime along to music as if you're singing it. She loved Instagram. She was always posting photos of her nails on it. She used to do mine for me when I had time, but not recently. It's difficult to keep them looking nice when you have little children to run after. That was our mother–daughter time – she'd happily sit down at the kitchen table and do them for me.' She swallowed heavily. The baby let out a soft snore and stirred. She stroked his cheek tenderly.

'How did she feel about her stepbrothers?'

'She pretended she couldn't be bothered with them but secretly she loved them. I've heard her reading to Jack or playing with his trucks with him. He doted on her and I think she was fond of them both.'

'And Kyle?'

'She didn't dislike him. She got on okay with him but there was a bit of tension at times. Only because she felt so strongly about her father. Nobody could replace Shane in her affections.'

'Did she visit her dad in prison?'

'Shane didn't want either of us to visit. He turned his back on us both once he was locked up and I moved on. Harriet turned him into some sort of a romantic figure that would one day come back into her life. She wouldn't hear otherwise.'

'Did Harriet ever mention a website called Disappear?'

Melissa shifted the baby to her other arm and flexed her fingers to get the circulation moving again. 'I've not heard of it. Is it a gaming site?'

'It's where teenagers are encouraged to disappear from families, friends and loved ones – to hide for hours or even a few days.'

'You think that's what she was doing? Trying to hide from us?'

'It's possible. You're certain she's never said anything about it?'

'Not to me and I doubt she'd have said anything to Kyle. They don't talk much at all.'

Natalie's phone vibrated in her pocket. She couldn't think of much else to ask Melissa, who picked up the blue elephant with her free hand.

'Why would she want to hide?' Melissa asked.

'It's a challenge – a type of dare. Do you think she'd be likely to try such a thing?'

'Why would she want to frighten me that way? She must have known I'd go out of my mind with worry. Why would she consider such a thing? You know, DI Ward, I wonder if I ever knew my daughter at all.'

Melissa retreated into her own world again and stared fixedly at the elephant. She wouldn't respond to any further questioning. Kyle came upstairs, forehead lined with creases. Natalie spoke quietly. 'I'll have to leave you again. I'll make sure the family liaison officer comes back. Talk to her, Melissa. She'll advise you on how to handle the press and what will happen next.'

Natalie checked her phone when she was back in the car. It was gone five and Lance Hopkins was being interviewed at the station. She pulled away from the line of houses and passed the turning to the fly-tipping area. There was so much more to do but her stomach felt full of acid, and tiredness tugged at her eyelids. She couldn't continue without some rest. She rang the station and asked them to contact the FLO for Melissa Long and let her know if there were any developments, then checked in with Graham to ensure there hadn't been any further reports of missing children, and finally drove towards Castergate and home, desperate for some sleep.

*

While Natalie was talking to the victims' relatives, Lucy and Ian were in the interview room with Lance Hopkins, who sat with his legs apart, head in hands.

'We have a witness who claims to have seen you in Watfield in recent weeks.'

'I've not been back since Jane and I parted company. There's no reason for me to return. I didn't even enjoy living in the place when we did. I never fitted in.'

'Why was that, Mr Hopkins?'

'Because people are petty-minded bigots. They assumed because we'd been travellers we were nothing more than a bunch of thieving, cheating crooks and they didn't give us a chance. They certainly didn't give me one.'

'Was it the same for Savannah?'

'Poor kid. She took some stick when she first started at that school. I told Jane it was a stupid idea to move to a place like Watfield. Most of the residents have lived there since birth. We weren't merely outsiders, we were *detested* outsiders. I did it for Jane. She couldn't fit in with my family, and when she said she had enough money to buy the house, I was willing to give it a go – last-ditch attempt to see if we could work things out. My mum was right. She said all along we weren't right for each other. We want very different things and ways of life. Jane stuck it out, got a job, tried to make friends, and Savannah seemed to settle a little, but I couldn't. Work was impossible to find and I missed my old life. I missed my family.'

'And you definitely haven't returned to Watfield since you moved away?'

'The day I walked out on Jane was the last day I spent there. I've been in digs in Sutton for a while and jobbing on a building site. I needed to lick my wounds for a while. I got in touch with

Mum and found out the family were headed to the area so I said I'd join them when the job's finished in a week or two.'

'You stayed in touch by telephone?'

'That's right.'

'Yet Jane didn't have a contact number for you.'

'That was probably cos I busted my phone. I had to get a new one and the number changed. I didn't pass it on to her. I didn't think we had anything left to say.'

'You weren't at all interested in Savannah, your stepdaughter? You didn't even want to know how she was getting along?'

He pushed himself upright and looked Lucy in the eye. 'I know it's difficult to believe, what with the kid living with us and then me becoming her stepfather, but she and I never really gelled. She didn't like sharing her mother. Jane had brought her up single-handedly with some help from her own mother, and she and Savannah were really close. There wasn't room for anyone else.'

'But she lived with you and your family for a couple of years. You must have got to know her really well and formed some bond with her.'

'Nope. She spent most of the time whinging about the other kids and getting up my mum's nose. She was a right prima donna and couldn't get along with the other kids in the group. If she wasn't with Jane, she'd hardly speak to anyone. When we moved to Watfield she became even worse. It was like she didn't want anyone in Jane's life.'

'You're saying you didn't get on?'

He rubbed a hand over his clean-shaven chin. 'We tolerated each other. Jane was the glue in our relationship. When we got a bit ratty with each other, Jane would step in, and if you're going to ask me if I'd ever hurt her, the answer is no – never. I didn't once touch or harm her. I might not have been close to her but I would never have hurt her.'

'You have a reputation, Mr Hopkins. You were involved in a brawl with Kyle Yates in September, last year.'

He snorted. 'That was nothing. The lousy shit had it coming to him. He came marching into a pub when I was having a quiet drink and shouted the odds about me ripping him off. I hadn't. He was abusive and I lost my rag. I went for him and he struck me first. I only thumped him a couple of times but someone decided the police ought to get involved.'

'What happened in the days after? Did you see Kyle again?'

He shook his dark hair. 'No. He was only out to cause trouble, make sure I wouldn't find work thanks to his bad-mouthing.'

'You didn't go to his house again?'

'Absolutely not. I had no reason to.'

'Did you ever encounter Melissa's daughter, Harriet?'

'I didn't know she had a daughter. I thought they had a little lad. Never saw a girl when I was working on the place. Still, it was only half a day's job.'

Lucy changed tack and, crossing her legs casually, asked, 'What did you do with the old guttering on Melissa Long's house?'

'Took it to the tip.'

'Where was this tip?'

'Just outside Samford, which is a bit of a drive away, so I stored it just outside our house until I had other rubbish to take. The salvageable stuff I can sell, I move on, and the rest goes to the refuse tip.'

'Were you ever tempted to dump it out of sight?'

He gave a loud laugh. 'Oh yeah, that'd go down well. Can you imagine if I got spotted dumping rubbish? I don't want to make life harder for myself, do I?'

Lucy couldn't find any tell or mannerism that made her doubt Lance wasn't telling her anything other than the truth. She uncrossed her legs and sat forward. 'I don't know if you've heard the news but Harriet Long's body was found this morning.'

Lance rubbed his hands up and down his thighs. 'I didn't know. I'm sorry to hear that and I'm cut up about Savannah. I thought I'd go and visit Jane. I bet she's in a terrible state.'

'I'm going to need a DNA sample and for you to tell us your exact movements for yesterday afternoon starting at three thirty.'

'I was at the building site all afternoon until gone six. After that, I went straight to the Wheatsheaf for a couple of beers and dinner, then back to my digs at nine and watched television.'

'Do you have any witnesses?'

'Plenty. I was at the pub with the lads from the site and I share digs with one of them, Gary Robinson. He was with me until we both turned in at around eleven.'

'I'll need Gary Robinson's contact details.'

'Sure.'

'And Monday afternoon, where were you then?'

'Same routine, same pub, same person who can vouch for me.'

'Then PC Jarvis will take those details and collect a DNA sample for our records in order to eliminate you from our enquiries.'

'Certainly.'

She'd asked him everything she could. She glanced at Ian, who'd remained silent during the questioning. He gave an imperceptible shake of the head to indicate there was nothing he had to add. Lucy thanked Lance for his assistance and turned off the recording device. She left Ian to get the details and headed back to the office. Murray was at a desk, staring at CCTV footage.

'Thought it hurt your eyes too much checking video footage,' she said, jokingly.

'There's nobody else free to do it so I'll have to suffer the discomfort. Yolande says I've starting squinting to watch telly and I ought to visit an optician. She might be right. Must be an age thing. No luck with Lance Hopkins?' he asked.

'Not a thing. I hope I read the situation correctly. He seems plausible enough. Ian's doing a DNA swab in case we need it but I'd say Lance has nothing at all to do with either murder.'

'Natalie's rung in. She's headed home for the night.'

'Unless we can come up with something soon, I think I might be doing the same. You can only run on empty for so long.' Lucy sorted through her paperwork and notes. If Lance had nothing to do with the murders, then who else was there left to suspect? Stu? Anthony? Or was there somebody they hadn't yet found? She yawned widely.

'Looks like someone else is ready for their bed,' Murray teased.

'Shut up!' She tried to focus on the notes again but they made little sense. She watched Murray, who was once again peering at the computer screen, his face screwed up in concentration. He might hate checking through the endless footage but at least he was trying to find new suspects. She stood up, stretched and then asked, 'So, old man, want a hand?'

*

He dried up the mug and stacked it back in the cupboard. The snake was restless, coiling and uncoiling against his flesh. It needed to feast again.

'Hush! In good time. We know where she lives. We'll take her.'

He might have had to change plans but he was once again in control. He would act later once the girl was alone. He knew what to do and say. It was all planned out. He smiled at his own cleverness.

He checked the time. It was close to six thirty. It was almost time to go and lie in wait.

*

The house seemed eerily quiet to Natalie, who sat on the bottom stair and pulled at her boots. She was dog-tired but she had to eat before she could turn in and she needed a bath or shower. There was no leftover smell of any cooking. If they hadn't yet eaten, she'd order takeaway. The door to David's office was wide open, his seat empty and his computer pushed to one side, abandoned. In its place was a classic car magazine. He clearly wasn't working on the new translation. She ambled into the kitchen and, finding no one, tried the sitting room, where she came across Leigh, lying full length on the settee, hugging a cushion and watching *Hollyoaks*, one of her favourite shows. Natalie was tempted to drop down beside her but that would mean asking her to move, and Leigh was glued to the programme.

'Hey!'

'Hi.' Leigh didn't look up.

Natalie waited a second then tried to raise a smile. 'What, no, "Hi Mum, how was your day at the cop shop?" Or, "Thanks for the super slushy text message?"'

Leigh shifted slightly and responded with a plaintive, 'Mu-um, I'm watching telly.'

Natalie gave up. It was maddening when Leigh froze her out like that. Up until a month or two ago, she'd have invited Natalie to join her, but something had changed between them and the atmosphere charged up whenever she spoke to Leigh, who'd become defensive for no apparent reason. She gave it one last shot. 'Where's Dad?'

'Grandpa's.'

'Why? Is everything okay?'

'I dunno. He didn't say.'

'Have you any homework to do?'

Leigh threw her an exasperated look. 'Some reading. That's all. I'll do it after I finish watching this.' She hugged the cushion more tightly and stared at the television. As Natalie was about to leave, she muttered, 'I'm having tea at Zoe's tomorrow. Dad said I could.'

Natalie didn't argue. Josh had football practice after school on Thursday evenings and usually David collected Leigh and either brought her home or treated her to a McDonald's. Josh's mate, Ethan, lived in a village outside Castergate, and Ethan's mum invariably dropped Josh off. Harriet's deception raced through her mind. Harriet had lied about going to stay overnight with her friend. It wasn't that Natalie didn't trust Leigh but she'd feel happier if she confirmed the validity of the arrangement. She'd ring Zoe's mum. She headed upstairs to her son's bedroom. As usual, the door was shut and, standing close to the door about to knock, she heard him mumbling in his usual fashion, then break into a sudden laugh. He was on his laptop, chatting to a friend. She hovered by the door, trying to decide if she ought to interrupt or not, then concluded she wasn't going to pussyfoot about in her own home. Besides, Josh should be studying for exams. As bright as he was, he couldn't afford to mess up his GCSEs, so a gentle reminder she was around wouldn't go amiss. She tapped lightly. The murmuring stopped and he called out, 'Yes?'

She put her head around the door. 'Just thought I'd say hello.'

'Hi.' He lifted his hand from the computer mouse. A paragraph of an essay was visible on the screen.

'I hear your dad's at Grandpa's house?'

'Yeah.'

'When did he go?'

'After we got home.'

'Why?'

'Don't know. Grandpa needed a hand.'

David had been gone a couple of hours. It was unusual for Eric, David's father, to request assistance. It was usually the other way around. David was hopeless at anything DIY.

'Did he say when he'd be back?'

Josh shook his head and glanced at the screen quickly.

'You doing a project?'

'Coursework.'

That was Josh – coherent, engaged conversation was beyond him these days. She hoped he wrote better than he spoke.

'You eaten?'

'Chips.'

David must have stopped at the chippie in Castergate on the way home. She'd have to throw together a casserole or something else more nutritious if she was going to keep pulling late nights. Her kids couldn't live on Indian takeaways and chips. David was actually a decent cook but didn't enjoy it and was reluctant to prepare meals. It was a shame because he made a mean chilli con carne. Her stomach grumbled at the thought. 'Okay, I'll catch you later. I'm going to get some food and then a bath.'

He'd already turned his attention back to his screen and Natalie pulled the door to. She stood for a few moments, listening once more.

'Nah. It was my mum… You're lucky. Try living with a mother who's a cop. She's into everything… Anyway, what did Charlie say to you?'

She couldn't face an argument but it saddened her to feel she was kept out of her children's private lives. She'd once been their most important person – the one they ran to and with whom they'd shared their secrets. Now, she was treated as an invader. She drifted away back downstairs and searched the fridge for some cheese, settling on a tomato and an unopened packet of cheddar. She slid the knife through the plastic covering and cut off a chunk, eating it without a plate. She bit into the tomato, which squelched horribly, almost dissolving into mush in her mouth. *Like baby food*, she thought. Josh had always hated tomatoes and refused to eat them. It was the pips he disliked most. The fruit was tasteless but it was food nonetheless and she needed some nutrition.

The sound of a key in the lock alerted her to David's arrival. She called to him, 'I'm in here.'

He appeared, eyebrows lifted. 'Didn't expect you home for a while.'

'Expect the unexpected. I won't be up for long though. I'm going to have a hot soak and then bed. Eric okay?'

'Yeah, fine.'

'What did he want?'

He dropped his car keys into the bowl on the kitchen top. 'Oh, only to change a hose and connector on that ancient washing machine of his. He needed a lift out with it. Look, I'll let you get that bath. I've got to work on that translation. I'm behind on it. It's been heavy going with it today and the client's getting antsy. I promised it by the end of the week.'

Eric could easily have pulled his washing machine out into the open without assistance from David; besides, he had his live-in girlfriend, Pam, to assist him. Neither of them was an invalid; in fact, Eric was extremely fit and sprightly for a man pushing seventy, and Pam was only in her mid-fifties. The image of the car magazine on David's desk flitted across her mind, and suddenly a thousand imaginary ants crawled over her scalp. David wasn't telling the truth. 'I suppose your work got interrupted, what with fetching the kids and then having to help Eric?'

'Yeah. It's impossible some days to get anything done. I'll go and crack on now.'

There it was: the same look Josh had given her when he'd pretended to be working on science coursework but was talking to a friend online instead. Another, more important, thought sprang to mind. 'Leigh says she's going to Zoe's tomorrow night for her tea.'

'That's right.'

'You checked with Zoe's mum, didn't you? I can ring to make sure she was invited if you like.'

'There's no need.'

'I was only asking. Don't get so defensive.'

David's jaw jutted. 'What's your problem, Natalie?'

Something erupted inside. Yesterday, David had been a different man altogether, and now, he was a belligerent arsehole! She'd been at work for hours and a fat lot of recognition she got for all her efforts to keep a roof over their heads and food on the table. Her voice climbed higher as she spoke. 'Problem? I don't have a problem.

I'm working an investigation where a schoolgirl lied to her parents about her whereabouts and as a consequence was murdered. It's not a fucking *problem*, David. It's called caring!'

'Then you'll be happy to know I've also been *caring*. Naturally, I double-checked with Zoe's mum. What do you take me for? I'm not completely useless, you know?'

'Oh, for fuck's sake! I don't need all this shit when I get in. Get off your sanctimonious high horse.' Natalie stormed out of the room and almost collided with Leigh. She halted mid-stride and took in the girl's miserable face. She'd overheard them arguing. She reached out to stroke Leigh's hair. 'Sorry. I shouldn't have lost my temper. It's been a rough day.'

Leigh returned a blank look. 'I'm used to it. You're always shouting at each other these days.'

Natalie's jaw dropped but Leigh moved off before she could speak. She called after her. 'Leigh—'

'I've got reading to do.'

Natalie ran a hand across her face. Things were spiralling out of control. She needed to get a grip on the investigation and then rectify this situation. She and David had to resolve their issues, whatever they were. She needed to stop being so suspicious of his actions. It was killing their relationship and she couldn't have her children involved in their petty arguments. For now, she was too fatigued, physically and mentally, to handle anything more than a bath and a long sleep. Tomorrow was another day.

CHAPTER EIGHTEEN

WEDNESDAY, 18 APRIL – EVENING

Katy Bywater slumped in her chair and aimed the remote control at the television, her empty mug by her feet.

'Katy, love,' her father, Christopher, said apologetically. 'It's not that I don't want to lend you the money, it's just that I'm a bit short myself this week.'

She turned on him. 'You always have enough to go down the pub every night. You want to know why I had to ask you for it? I need to buy tampons and pills for stomach cramps. Do you have any idea how embarrassing it is to ask you for money for that sort of thing? If Mum was here…'

She'd pressed the right buttons. He flushed to the roots of his hair.

'I understand, sweetheart. It's really difficult without her. I'm sorry. Look, I can stretch to a tenner.'

He delved into his pocket, drew out a battered wallet and pulled out a ten-pound note, which he handed her as a peace offering. She took it without any word of thanks. He smiled at her but she ignored him and stood up without a word.

'Where are you going?'

'My room.'

'I thought we could watch something together.'

'I've got stuff to do.'

'Oh, okay.'

'I hate you for making me move here, you know.'

He opened his mouth but said nothing and she stalked away, leaving the empty mug bearing her name on the floor next to her chair. He flopped onto the settee and flicked through endless channels before settling on a repeat of *Top Gear*. When it ended and *Red Dwarf* began there was still no sign of his daughter. He tried the other channels again but soon gave up and meandered upstairs, where he hovered outside the bedroom door before finally tapping gently on it.

'Yes.'

'Katy, I might pop out for a while.'

'To the pub,' she said flatly, her voice almost inaudible through the door.

He pushed it open. Katy was sat cross-legged on the bed, her mobile in front of her on the duvet. She didn't glance in his direction.

'I won't be long.'

'Whatever,' was the reply.

He left her to it and trudged back downstairs, where he picked up the pink sports bag she used for school and moved it next to her coat so it would be ready for the morning. Then he left the house, turning before he reached his car, to look up at her window. A crack in the hastily drawn curtains allowed a small ribbon of light to escape and he waited but no one appeared to wave at him. With a small sigh, he unlocked the car door.

It was eight o'clock when Christopher Bywater awoke to the sound of his alarm chirping. He yawned, stretched and kicked off the duvet then padded out onto the landing and tapped on Katy's door. There was no answer. He headed downstairs, expecting her to be in the kitchen, but there was no one. He climbed the stairs again and knocked once more. This time louder.

'Katy, love. It's gone eight.'

Still no answer. He pushed the door open and stuck his head in. 'Katy, it's gone…' The words froze on his lips. There was nobody there and Katy's duvet bore the indentation of somebody who'd sat on it but not slept beneath it.

The bathroom door was ajar and his daughter wasn't there. He raced back downstairs and flung open the sitting-room door. Her mug was still lying beside the chair where she'd left it. He ran a hand through his hair, walked back out to the hallway and stood stock-still. The realisation of what had happened was a punch to his solar plexus. Katy's pink bag wasn't where he'd placed it. She'd taken it. His daughter had run away again.

CHAPTER NINETEEN

THEN

There had been a general buzz on the playground the previous afternoon. Somebody had spotted a snake in the dump and several of the older boys had gone across to flush it out and kill it but returned empty-handed. The boy is more excited than most at the prospect of discovering it and adding it to his list of kills. If he could catch it and smash a rock on its head and bring it back, he'll be a hero. They won't snigger at his stunted form or squeaky, babyish voice any more. He is so carried away with the prospect, he doesn't hear the teacher ask him a question, and when he looks up, a vacant look on his face, and replies honestly, 'I wasn't listening, sir,' the entire class begins giggling.

The teacher becomes irritated and sends the boy to the headmaster's office for being insolent. He doesn't even know what insolent means, and it's unfair he's been sent to the head for simply day-dreaming. The boy decides to bunk off instead. He's already in trouble so he might as well be in trouble for doing something wrong. Besides, he has maths next and he hates maths. He'll be better off going home and then facing up to any anger the following day. He knows the drill – the head will tell him off and threaten to suspend him for a few days, and his mum will be asked to come to the school to fetch him. She'll be angry with him but eventually she'll forget all about it.

He has another reason for returning home ahead of the others: he wants to find that snake. The week before, he'd managed to trap a creature that resembled a mouse but turned out to be a shrew with a pointy nose, that screeched to be freed when he stuffed a plastic tub on top of it. Its screaming intensified until he decided it would attract attention from other kids and he crushed it. He'd killed another three cats – the last one, a manky old thing with matted fur and weeping eyes that was better off dead. It wasn't as much fun watching cats die as it had once been, nor the rabbits who he hit with well-aimed stones, or the dog that had snarled at him and bared sharp teeth until the sharp-edged stone had struck it between the eyes and it had yelped and then collapsed in convulsions. The boy had enjoyed its death throes for a short while but a snake… a snake would be far more satisfying to kill.

He hoists his bag over his shoulders and slips out of the school gate. It's unlikely that anyone will observe him running back to the flats via the lanes and fields. No one ever seems to notice him. He's like the invisible man. Veering off the route and onto the wasteland, he speeds towards the high fence where he'd seen Faye and her mates enter the dump. It doesn't take long before he finds the loose wire netting and pulls at it with eager fingers. He shoves his bag under it first and then, commando-style, wriggles under the fence on his belly. He stands up, bashes at the dusty earth clinging to his clothes and kneecaps and grins. He is in.

The smell doesn't hit him immediately. It's a sweet aroma similar to the stench of the dead cat he'd kept in a shoebox until the maggots inside it made its stomach explode and he had to get rid of it. It isn't unpleasant but it is a little cloying. Walking slowly, head turning left and right, he imagines himself to be a big game hunter in Africa, looking for signs of wildlife. He isn't sure what tracks a snake makes or where it might hide, but he lifts a solid, dark-red stone, ready to hurl as a missile should he spot the snake slithering into sight. The smell intensifies – rotting vegetables and something else he doesn't recognise that makes his nose wrinkle. It's emanating from a mountain of waste that is gradually coming into view. It isn't as high as the block of flats in which he lives but it is certainly as tall as a house, with sloped sides of garbage, cans, packaging and other unidentifiable pieces of rubbish.

This isn't as interesting as he'd hoped, and he ambles up to the foot of the slope and studies the peelings and assortment of boxes, wrappers and junk, feeling let down. None of it will be worth collecting. It is nothing more than garbage. He catches a slight movement in the corner of his eye and spins around, stone lifted. It isn't the snake. It's hard-faced Faye Boynton, in school uniform, with two of her friends.

'Whatcha doing here?' she demands.

He's no longer the brave hunter. Facing her cold, hard stare and the mocking looks from her friends, he mumbles a reply: 'Nothing.'

'He's got a weapon. He's brought some protection… against the snake,' chuckles Missy Henshaw, who is at least two feet taller than him. 'Why've you got a stone, little boy?'

'Scaredy-cat, scaredy-cat!' The third girl, Vee Patel, annoys him with her childish chant. He isn't afraid of a snake. He's going to kill it.

Missy joins in the teasing. 'Scaredy-cat! Were you frightened the snake would gobble you up? It's way bigger than you.' She bursts into laughter.

He shakes his head but the sight of Faye's face prevents him from speaking out. Two fire spots of red appear on her high cheeks. 'Why are you here? You spying on us?'

'No-oh.' The word came out like a faint bleat that makes the other two girls laugh again.

'Yeah he was. He's followed us here.' Vee approaches him and he takes an involuntary step backwards, stumbling on the uneven ground and landing on his backside.

'Whoops! He's landed on his scrawny arse,' says Vee in glee.

Faye continues to stare at him.

'I'm not afraid,' he pipes up.

Missy folds her arms and glowers at him. 'You ought to be.'

'Why aren't you in school?' Vee's words take him by surprise. He's momentarily forgotten all about school. The girls should be there too. They've bunked off as well.

'I decided to come here instead.' He pushes himself up into a standing position. Vee is far too close for comfort, staring down at him.

One of Faye's eyebrows lifts in interest. 'You skiving?'

He nods and receives a vague look of approval that emboldens him. 'I wanted to kill the snake.'

Faye glances across at Missy and then suddenly they both burst into laughter again. He becomes indignant. He might not be much to look at but he has killed animals and he will kill the snake. 'I did. I've killed before.'

Vee edges close enough that he can smell cigarette smoke on her uniform. She pokes him hard in the chest with a fingernail.

'Ow! That hurt.'

'What? This?' She pokes him again, harder still. He presses his lips together to prevent himself from making a sound.

'Pack it in, Vee.'

'Why? He's a nosy parker. He's followed us here and he'll dob us in to the teachers.'

Faye shakes her head. 'No, he won't. Will you? Cos if you do, we know where you live.' She doesn't need to say what she'll do. The fact she knows who he is and where he lives is enough to make him keep quiet about this encounter.

He shakes his head. 'I won't say nuffin'.'

'I won't say nuffin',' repeats Missy in a high-pitched voice, and she snorts in a derisory manner. 'Little shit. Why don't you fuck off home now?'

'What are you all doing here?' He doesn't know what has made him ask. Maybe he's feeling less threatened because he's keeping their secret or he's simply curious. His mother tires easily of all his questions and tells him he asks too many. 'You know, curiosity killed the cat,' she said after he'd bombarded her with questions about space and the planets for almost an hour. He'd merely smiled. It wasn't curiosity that killed them – it was him. Faye scowls at him, bringing him back to the present.

'None of your business what we're doing. Now, buzz off or I'll tell your mum you were skiving.'

'She won't care.' He isn't going to be cast off. He wants to find some of the treasures in the dump that he's heard other kids talking about, or the snake. 'Can I come with you? I'm good at killing things. I can look out for the snake.'

For some reason, this makes the girls laugh again and Faye rolls her eyes. 'What have you killed?'

'A big fat toad, some cats, a mouse-thing and a dog.'

Vee sniggers. Faye doesn't. Instead she gives him another look, like he's a strange object. 'Go on, then. You can come with us but you have to prove to us first that you're brave enough. You don't look very brave.' She winks at Missy, who gives a small nod. He doesn't understand its meaning but he's suddenly keen to join the trio. It's a new feeling, being part of something. 'You can be our lookout and kill the snake but only if you do a dare.'

'What sort of dare?'

'We'll show you.'

The girls stride off as one and he follows, his legs a blur in an attempt to maintain the same pace. They move around the stinking mountain of waste towards another pile, smaller and less smelly. This refuse isn't rotting. Heaped in front of him are household appliances: old dryers, refrigerators, washing machines, vacuum cleaners, ovens and other white goods he's seen when shopping with his mother. This is the treasure he's heard about. Although these are broken and disused, there's surely something that could be fixed or sold. His eyes dance over a silver electric kettle, complete with plug, the snake now forgotten. He could take back something for his mother and make her happy with him. He almost misses Faye speaking to him.

'There. You have to climb into that.'

Ahead of him is a large, glass-fronted washing machine. It isn't much of a dare. He's climbed into all sorts of spaces tighter than that. It's the advantage of being so small. He'd once hidden in a space behind the toilet for over an hour while his dad had searched for him to give him a hiding for stealing from the local shop. By the time he'd crawled *out, his dad had forgotten about the spanking and gone down the pub instead. That was before he got blown up by a bomb. He blinks away thoughts of his dad.*

'You're skinny enough to get into the drum. Go on. Whatcha waiting for?'

'Then I can come with you?'

'Sure you can.' Faye's eyes glitter dangerously but he doesn't mind. He can get into the machine. It isn't much of a dare at all.

'Okay.' He trots towards the white enamel machine, squeezes through the round hole and clambers into the drum, folding his legs up in front of his chest and clasping his arms around his knees. His head is at an uncomfortable angle but it's bearable. 'See. I'm in.'

'I knew you could get in,' says Faye.

'It's easy,' he replies with confidence.

'You have to stay there now until I let you out.'

He hesitates for a second. He's already done what she's asked so she should let him join them. He opens his mouth to say so but changes his mind. It won't be for long. The girls have to go home for their tea and they'll let him out before then.

He tries to nod but it isn't possible. The drum in the machine rocks slightly left and then right, making him think he's going to topple over.

Faye waggles fingers at him and shuts the door. It makes a click that sounds very loud inside the drum. He can't see through the glass door very well. It's blurry and he can't make out the three girls. They're now distorted shapes that stare in at him through the glass, faces that grow and change shape as they look and point. They remind him of when his mum took him to the funfair and they'd stood together in the hall of mirrors and laughed at their massive fat faces and round bellies and super-long arms. It was the only time he'd not looked like a toddler and his mum had hugged him and told him one day he'd grow up to look like the really tall, slim boy in the third mirror.

Faye's nose is massive and her forehead small like a weird cartoon character. 'You look funny,' he shouts. The reply is muffled. Suddenly

Faye's face disappears and he watches as the girls back away. The enclosed space suddenly feels really tight, squeezing the air from his lungs, like it's closing in on him. He calls out, 'Faye. I have to go home for tea soon. Don't leave me long.' The girls don't hear him. He watches as they become black specks and disappear from view. He tries to push open the door but there isn't enough room to move and the door is stuck fast. The drum slides to the left and his body sways to the right. He attempts to steady himself but it makes matters worse and he tumbles sideways. Now his head is cricked to the left and his legs too high and he can't sit up.

'Faye!' His voice, high and whiny, makes him more frightened than anything. He isn't a brave hunter. He's a scared boy trapped inside a washing machine.

CHAPTER TWENTY

Natalie was completely disorientated, her head thick from sleep. The buzzing drone that had woken her hadn't come from the cloud of bees she'd been dreaming about: it was her mobile. On sudden autopilot, she tossed back the bedcovers, forced herself upright and staggered into the bathroom, where she dropped down onto the toilet, thankful David always put the seat down after use, to take the call.

'Natalie, it's Lucy. Murray said you wanted to be contacted if there was a development.'

She wiped sticky sleep dust from one eye, instantly more alert. 'Yes, what is it?'

'We believe we have another suspect… Kyle Yates.'

'Kyle?'

'Murray's gone to fetch him.'

'Okay. Give me half an hour. Fill me in when I get there.'

She ended the call and sat for a minute, letting the cool air rouse her. It was 1.12 a.m. She'd managed five hours of sleep. She probably needed another five but that wasn't going to happen. She slipped back into the bedroom to collect her clothes, and as she reached for them on the chair closest to her side of the bed, David's voice reached her.

'You going?'

'Yes. They've pulled a suspect. Go back to sleep.'

'I'm not tired.' The bedside lamp lit up suddenly, casting a soft glow over his side of the bed, and David pushed himself into a sitting position. 'Sorry about earlier. I had things on my mind. I shouldn't have jumped down your throat.'

She pulled on her blouse and tucked it into her trousers. 'I wasn't in the best of moods. Leigh overheard us.'

'Want me to say something to her?'

'Let it drop for now. I don't want the kids involved in our spats.'

'Been a bit more than spats recently, haven't they? Don't give me that look. I'm not spoiling for another fight. I wanted to apologise, that's all. You're right to worry about them both and it's harder for you when you have to be out at all hours – I get it. I went off the deep end. I was uptight. The translation's proved harder going than I anticipated and I need to make the deadline tomorrow night.'

She finished dressing, ran a comb through her hair, secured it in a loose bun with a clip and then brushed her lips with a tinted gloss. She'd do. She faced David. 'Hopefully you'll get it done today, with both of the kids out of the way until later.'

'That's what I'm banking on.'

There was a pause before she said, 'We need to try harder. We can't be fighting in front of them.'

His face was genuine concern, a deep furrow between his eyes. 'I know. We'll fix this. See you later. Good luck.'

'Thanks… now go back to sleep.'

She felt more refreshed after the rest and was keen to talk to Kyle again. She crept onto the landing and past Leigh's bedroom. The nightlight illuminated her daughter's form, one arm dangling over the side of the bed, her fingertips grazing her bed companion, a large beige teddy bear called Sammy. Natalie tiptoed into the room, tucked the girl's arm back under the duvet, lifted the soft toy off the floor and slid it into the bed next to her before she stole downstairs.

*

One desk was filled with takeaway cups and empty packaging. A half-eaten egg sandwich had been thrown on top of a serviette. Natalie took a sip of water from the bottle she'd grabbed from her fridge back home and waited for Lucy to explain their findings.

'Murray was double-checking the footage from the CCTV cameras at the Aldi car park on Monday afternoon. He rewound from the point when we spotted Anthony Lane approaching Savannah and her two friends and noticed a van leaving the car park slowly… really slowly. He ran the vehicle registration through DVLA and got a hit – it belongs to Kyle Yates. We both searched through cameras to see when it arrived and then we got really lucky. We discovered it parked up ten minutes before we saw Savannah and her friends outside the supermarket… and… there were two people in it. We magnified the image and this is what we saw.'

Natalie squinted at the picture on the screen. There was no mistaking who was in the passenger seat: Savannah Hopkins.

'The lying bastard told me he'd never met Savannah. What else have you got on him?'

'We've not unearthed anything else. He was single and lived with his mum before he moved in with Melissa Long. He's never been in trouble with the police – other than the fight at the pub with Lance Hopkins – and his work record appears to be sound. He's worked as a courier for the last ten years with the same company.'

'There must be something. I was sure he was holding back the first time I interviewed him.'

The internal phone rang and Lucy answered it. 'We're on our way down.' She turned to Natalie. 'He's here and so is his lawyer. You want to interview him?'

'You bet I do.'

*

Kyle rubbed a hand under his nose for the fifth time since they'd begun the interview. Murray had been chosen to sit in with Natalie and maintained an icy glare, which was unnerving the suspect.

'Does he have to be here?' Kyle asked his lawyer, a young man in glasses and a suit, who looked equally intimidated by Murray.

Natalie was quick to reply. 'Are you referring to DS Anderson?'

'Yeah.'

'Then yes, he does have to be here during this interview. Now, let's go back over what you told me when I spoke to you outside your house yesterday afternoon. You'd been unhappy with work that Lance Hopkins had carried out on your property, and on encountering him at the Wheatsheaf pub, you accused him of cheating you. The exchange became heated and resulted in blows being thrown and you receiving a bloody nose.'

'That's right. It was over the guttering. He tried to charge us for cast-iron guttering but he put up PVC guttering, which was half the price.'

'And you tackled him on the subject?'

'He said the price he quoted was for PVC not cast-iron, which was bollocks and I refused to pay him the full amount.'

'And you had an argument in the Wheatsheaf pub over this matter on Friday the seventh of September?'

'That's right.'

'You didn't meet up again after the fight?'

He rubbed under his nose again then tucked a hand under his armpit and clamped it there but said nothing. It was a sure sign she was onto something.

'You didn't go to his house and talk to him about it?'

Kyle made no reply.

Natalie shuffled her papers into a pile and sat back. 'I believe you couldn't let it drop. It annoyed you enough to tackle the man in front of customers in a pub and all you got for your trouble was a bleeding nose. It obviously annoys you, even now… all these months later. Here's what I think: you went around to his house and asked for a full refund.'

Kyle still didn't respond.

'And I also think that's where you met Savannah Hopkins. Did she answer the door? Did you chat?' She waited but it was in vain. She pressed on. 'You knew Savannah even though she didn't live near you or attend the same school as Harriet. How could you be acquainted with a thirteen-year-old girl who lived on the far side of town if you hadn't met her when you went around to her house to challenge Lance Hopkins? You knew Savannah even though you denied it when I spoke to you last. You lied to me. Why?'

He swallowed hard and looked away.

'Kyle, there's no refuting it. We have proof you not only knew Savannah but were with her Monday afternoon, shortly before she disappeared. It's time to come clean.'

The man wouldn't look up. Natalie held on but he remained resolutely uncooperative.

'Why were you with Savannah Hopkins on Monday afternoon?'

Nothing. She cocked her head in the lawyer's direction but he made no effort to encourage his client to speak. She'd have to coax the information out of him one way or the other.

'Was this some sort of twisted revenge? Did you follow Savannah after she left the supermarket and attack her?'

Silence. Natalie suddenly thumped the table hard and Kyle looked up, eyes moist with tears. 'Answer me, Kyle, or so help me, I'll charge you.'

The lawyer whispered to his client, advising him to respond. Finally, Kyle drew a breath and replied. 'I was with Savannah on Monday afternoon but only for a few minutes. I knew who she was but not because I went to Lance's house. You're wrong about that. I never saw Lance again after the fight in the pub. Savannah's one of a few kids I see now and again.'

Murray spoke in a menacing low tone. 'What do you mean by that?'

His words were sluggish, tugged reluctantly from his lips by an invisible force. 'I deal a bit of weed… and Adam… from time to time. Savannah contacted me to buy some gear.'

'You sell ecstasy and cannabis to minors?' Murray spat the words out and glowered darkly at the man, who nodded.

'Can you speak up for the recorder?' Natalie said sharply.

'Yes.'

Natalie continued. 'How did Savannah know you sold drugs?'

'I approached her and her friends a few months back. They were smoking behind the supermarket. If kids are smoking, they're sometimes interested in buying from me. I told them if they needed anything, I could get it for them. The kids know I'm around the car park on a Monday afternoon after school. They find me. Savannah did. I sold her half a gram of weed.'

'How often did she buy from you?'

'Once or twice a month.'

'Where did you go after you left the car park?'

'Home. I went straight back home. I had to collect the babies from my mum. Melissa was working. She'd taken on an extra shift. We need the money. I only did it because we need the money.'

'What about Harriet? Did you ever offer her any drugs?'

'Christ, no. She was dead against substance abuse and Melissa knows nothing about this either. I didn't have anything to do with either of their deaths. You can ask my mum what time I picked up the children from her. She'll vouch for me. I didn't kill the girls. Can't you help me out here? I only sold a bit of gear. I never hurt anybody,' he pleaded with his lawyer.

Natalie shifted her paperwork again. Kyle might not be responsible for Savannah's death but he'd be charged for drug-dealing. His excuse meant nothing to her. They all needed to make ends meet and pay bills, but not everyone sold illegal substances to children,

children the same age as hers. Suddenly, she didn't want to listen to him any longer. He sickened her. It wasn't the result she'd hoped for. It was yet another dead end.

CHAPTER TWENTY-ONE

THURSDAY, 19 APRIL – MORNING

Mike caught Natalie alone in the office. She'd sent both Murray and Lucy home. There was little point in her returning to her house for such a brief time. She'd only add to the morning chaos.

'Morning. You not got a home to go to?' Mike leant against the door frame, a takeaway coffee cup in one hand. He lifted it up. 'If I'd known you were here, I'd have brought you one in. The barista was having a bad morning, he renamed me Mark.'

'Got to admit, Mike's a really tricky name to spell.'

He smiled. 'You been here all night again? You need to watch it. You'll make yourself ill at this rate.'

'I grabbed five hours' sleep. I'm fine.'

'Good. Okay, I'm headed upstairs to sift through our mammoth pile of potential evidence.'

'What are your thoughts on this?'

'I have to say, it isn't the easiest investigation I've worked on. The killer's wily. They've not given us anything to go on. So far the painted wood we found under Savannah's nails is all we have. It might indicate where she was held captive.'

'Who am I dealing with, Mike?'

'Somebody who's planned it. Whoever is responsible has been extremely careful to leave no trace.'

'But if anyone can find anything, it'll be you and your guys.'

He stared at the cup. 'Glad you have faith in us. I fear it might take us longer than I'd like. An investigation such as this requires a huge number of man hours, and… I'd better go and put mine in.'

He left her to her thoughts. They were all racing around chasing evidence and suspects, and a second girl had died on their watch. Was the killer ensuring they were overworked – so overworked that they could continue their killing spree for a while longer? The thought chilled her to her bone.

*

He doused his hands with his favourite Boss aftershave and patted his cheeks lightly, getting an immediate hit of citrus followed by a slight scent of ginger. It wasn't overpowering like many other aftershaves, yet it was fresh and made him feel clean. The snake wriggled across his chest restlessly. He checked his image in the long mirror. Nobody could possibly imagine what he'd been up to overnight. No one would know, certainly not the middle-aged detective who'd been put in charge of the case.

He'd watched the news first thing that morning and the appeal made by Superintendent Aileen Melody, who'd asked for the public's support and vigilance in finding the person or persons responsible for the deaths of Savannah Hopkins and Harriet Long. He'd moved closer to the television set to look into her troubled eyes and saw she was panicked. The police had no idea of who was behind the murders and they didn't even know there was now yet another missing girl to search for.

He had been irked to discover the detective leading the investigation reminded him of Faye Boynton. Faye, who bossed people about and let them do her dirty work. He'd searched for information on DI Natalie Ward online and discovered, thanks to a newspaper article, that she was married with two children, and one was a fourteen-year-old girl. Wouldn't it be something if he brought the investigation even closer to her doorstep? The thought amused him. He might just do that. However, for now he had to keep up appearances and enjoy the havoc he was causing.

*

Natalie was reading through the case file from Manchester when Ian arrived for work. One suspect had stood out more than the others: an out-of-work drifter named Brendon Jones, who'd been living on a canal boat close to the Kumars' restaurant. With no alibi, he'd been their prime suspect for a long time, but due to lack of evidence he had been released. Ian noticed the file open on her desk.

'I checked out all the suspects in that case. None of them appear to be in the area but I couldn't locate their main suspect, Brendon Jones. I asked a colleague up there to look into it and see if he's still around.'

'Okay. We'll keep an open mind for now.'

'I spoke to Murray downstairs. He brought me up to speed. I hear Kyle's been charged.'

'Yes, we handed him over to the drug squad. He apparently had a stash of drugs and dealings with a number of schoolchildren in the area.'

'Bastard. Hope they lock him away for a long time.'

'Who's that?' said Murray, before adding, 'Morning, Natalie.'

'Kyle Yates.'

'Oh him! What a bloody waste of time it was chasing about after him. Thought we'd nailed our killer for a while there. Got anything new?'

Natalie shook her head. 'I was going back through the Manchester file on the off-chance I spotted something. Mike might have some news if we're lucky. At the moment, we'll have to continue to slog through CCTV footage.'

'Where do you want me to start?'

'The cameras on the main road to Bramshall. There are two camera points I'm interested in: one before the turning into the woods and one after the estate where Harriet lived. Check vehicles, registrations and timings. You're hunting for anomalies – any vehicle that might pass either camera only to reappear a short while later. It's just a theory but one of the vehicles' occupants might have stopped at the turn-off to discard Harriet's body.'

'Any timeframe I should be looking at in particular?'

'Start at midnight and work through to when she was discovered.'

Lucy was next to arrive and was about to get to work when Natalie received a call from Graham. Another fourteen-year-old, Katy Bywater, had gone missing in Watfield, and although he was conducting a full search for her, he thought Natalie should be involved.

'When did Katy disappear?' Natalie asked.

'Her father, Christopher, doesn't know. She was at home when he got in from work. He's a tyre fitter for A1 Tyres. They had a meal together and then she went upstairs to her room, which was usual. He went down the pub at quarter to eight, and when he returned home at about ten thirty, her light was off, so he assumed she was asleep. This morning, she didn't get up when he called her, and when he went to wake her he found her bed hadn't been slept in. He thinks she's run away.'

'Where was her mother at the time?'

'She died a year ago. There's only him and Katy. You'd be best off speaking to him and making your own judgements, but it seems things have been strained between them recently and she's run away before. This might not have any bearing on your investigation but I thought you ought to know all the same. She's got an iPad, which we're checking out at the moment for any leads, but I'll make sure you get it.'

'We're on our way.'

'I'll meet you at their house in about forty minutes.'

All faces in the room had turned in her direction. 'You probably gathered we have another potential victim – Katy Bywater. She attends Watfield Secondary School, the same school as Savannah, but is in the year above her. Lives about four streets away from her. Her father thinks she might have run away. She went missing sometime last night while her father was out, so it might not be linked to our investigation, but let's not take any chances. Ian, find any useful information about Katy that you can and let us know.' She picked up her jacket and threw it on. Lucy and Murray were right behind her as she clattered downstairs and outside into the bright sunshine.

The Bywaters lived on a seemingly never-ending road of semi-detached houses that began at the main road where the Hopkins family lived, curved past Watfield Secondary School and the Aldi supermarket, and ended up feeding into Church Street. Officers were walking the length of the street, talking to residents on their doorsteps, and the faces of concerned bystanders turned as Natalie and her team approached and joined the numerous vehicles now lining the road.

A small group of people was gathered by Christopher Bywater's gate, talking to a man in blue overalls bearing the name of the tyre-fitting company. Natalie let out a groan when she recognised two of them: Bev Gardiner, the reporter from the *Watfield Herald* and her sidekick photographer.

'What the fuck's he up to?' Natalie muttered before leaping out of the car and striding in his direction, where she spoke assertively. 'I'm going to have to ask you to move away, please. We need to talk to Mr Bywater alone.'

'It's okay,' said Christopher. 'I don't mind talking to them. They might be able to help find her.'

'Sir, you ought not to speak to anyone at the moment. Weren't you advised of that?'

'Yes, but I thought it would be okay.'

'DI Ward, do you believe Katy has been snatched by the killer stalking the streets of Watfield?' Bev asked in a loud voice.

Natalie was aware of the anxious looks being cast in her direction. These concerned citizens needed to move away and let them get on with their jobs. Christopher Bywater shouldn't be outside holding private press conferences and he ought to have an officer with him. 'No comment. Mr Bywater, can we talk inside, please?'

Christopher shook his head. 'But—'

Natalie moved in front of him, blocking him from the reporter. 'Sir, we need to talk inside, please. It's very important.'

He lifted a hand to thank the reporter, and Natalie and Lucy guided him towards the house while Murray waited by the gate to ensure everyone dispersed.

The house was a modest affair, built in the 1960s and in dire need of redecoration. The front door opened onto a hall, barely large enough for one person let alone two. Natalie couldn't ignore the brown and orange carpet – a leftover relic that not only covered the stairs directly in front of her but extended through to the room on the right, which served as both a dining room and sitting room. Someone had tried to make the place more homely by adding deep-orange cushions to the brown-leather settee and matching chair that was turned towards the television in the corner of the room, along with a faux-fur rug that hid the ghastly swirling pattern on the carpet. A round table with two chairs took up the rest of the space, along with a dresser housing ornaments and photographs. A couple of well-thumbed teen magazines lay beside the chair next to an empty mug bearing the name Katy.

Christopher pressed fingertips against his forehead. 'I'm a bit confused. I've already spoken to DI Kilburn. I thought he was in charge of the search for Katy?'

'That's correct but we are assisting. We've been investigating recent disappearances ourselves and it was thought prudent we got involved.'

Christopher dropped down onto the chair with a heavy thump. 'Oh, lord, no. You're in charge of those murders, aren't you?' He dropped his head into his hands then let out a quiet groan.

'We don't know what's happened to Katy but it would help if you could tell us everything that happened last night, so we can work out when she left the house.'

He pushed himself into a seated position and rested his elbows on his knees. 'I came home from work at five thirty and she was sat here, watching telly. I cooked dinner – pasta – and we ate it watching *The Simpsons*. Then after that, she went upstairs to her bedroom. I sat alone for a while and then I decided to go to the pub at quarter to eight.'

'You left her alone in the house?'

'She's not a child,' he retorted defensively.

'She's only fourteen.'

'She doesn't act like she's fourteen some days,' he replied. He placed a hand behind his neck and rubbed, his face screwed up as if in pain. 'She doesn't need watching over. It makes her worse.'

'Worse in what way?'

'Moody, argumentative – I can't handle her tantrums. Ever since her mum passed on, she's become hard work and there's the whole growing-up thing that makes it more difficult. I can't get through to her.'

'DI Kilburn said you argued last night.'

'That's right. She wanted me to give her an advance on her pocket money and I refused because I hadn't got enough money to shell out on extras, and she laid into me because I've been down the pub a couple of times this week. Made me feel a right shit. She needed it for personal hygiene stuff and said it was dead embarrassing having to discuss matters like that with me and how she wished her mum was still alive. I can't tell you how rotten I felt. I gave her ten pounds but she was still angry. She said she hated me for making her move to Watfield and stormed off. I couldn't stay in after that. I told her I was going out for a couple of hours and went down the pub. She had my number if she needed it.'

'Was it usual to leave her alone?' Lucy asked.

'I've left her before. She's usually busy online with her mates whether I'm there or not. She doesn't need supervision. It's really not been easy since her mum died. We both need space.'

Natalie could imagine how difficult it was to communicate with a resentful teenage girl, especially with no support from a partner. 'What made you think Katy had run away?'

'Her sports bag and phone are missing. The bag is always by the front door and she doesn't go anywhere without her mobile. I don't know what clothes she was wearing or took with her, but I told DI Kilburn what she was dressed in when I last saw her.'

'Has she run off before?'

'After we first moved here, she disappeared. She caught a bus to Northampton and ended up at a friend's house. The kid's mother rang me and I drove down and collected her. Katy was missing her friends badly. We talked it over and she didn't do it again. She's stayed out late on a couple of occasions but not gone missing.'

'And you passed this information on to DI Kilburn?'

'The first thing I thought of was that she'd gone to Northampton again. I called a couple of her best mates but they've not heard from her for a while. DI Kilburn said he'd contact all her old friends and they're looking at ways she might have travelled there.'

It seemed to Natalie there was a strong possibility Katy might have caught the train that ran from Watfield to Samford and then another from there to Northampton. DI Kilburn would definitely be looking into that possibility. Maybe that's why she needed money and was disgruntled when she only received ten pounds. Her concern, though, was that Katy hadn't actually run away and had, in fact, been taken by the killer. 'Where did she go when she stayed out late?'

'She was in Western Park, of all places.'

On her own?'

'Yes. That worried me even more. I told her she couldn't do that. It was far too dangerous to be out alone in a place like that and I grounded her. She got the message. That's why she carries her phone – so we can stay in contact. She isn't picking up at the moment. I've tried her loads of times. It goes straight to the messaging service.'

It had been the same with the other girls. Nobody had been able to reach them on their phones. 'Did your daughter ever talk about Savannah Hopkins?'

'I can't say that she did. I heard the name on the news but it's not one Katy's mentioned before.'

'They were at the same school.'

'Then she might know her but her name didn't crop up.'

'What about Harriet Long?'

He rubbed the back of his neck again and then sat forward. 'No.'

'We'll need a list of her friends to talk to.'

He gave a sad shake of his head. 'She doesn't seem to have any.'

Lucy's eyes widened and she chipped in. 'No friends? Who does she talk to online then?'

'Her old schoolmates in Northampton. We moved from there soon after Lisa died. I thought it was better for us both to make a fresh start.'

'She must have one friend here at least!' Lucy exclaimed.

Natalie was equally surprised the girl laid claim to having none, and felt a pang of sorrow for the seemingly friendless teenager. Savannah too had been unpopular.

'That's one of the things we regularly fell out about. She refused to make an effort. It was a deliberate move on her part. She was manipulating the situation so I'd give in and we'd return to Northampton, but I wasn't the pushover she hoped for. The thing is, she can't understand why I'll never be able to return. It's way too painful for me. When I lost Lisa, I lost everything apart from Katy, and I took the decision to move. I didn't make it lightly but I honestly thought she'd get used to Watfield in time. It's a really nice town and kids don't have trouble mixing, do they? Not somebody like Katy. She's a bright girl and very sporty so I was sure she'd fit in more easily than she did.'

There was a moment of lucidity. Natalie's head snapped up. 'You said Katy took her sports bag with her?'

'That's right.'

'Did she use Watfield Sports Centre?'

'A few times. They have all sorts of events there and she went to a couple. I encouraged her to join the girls' football team but she wasn't keen. Actually, I think she was but she was holding out in an effort to persuade me to leave Watfield.'

Harriet had liked sports and played football too. Maybe they had met or known each other after all. There was another possibility.

'Katy has a mobile phone. Is it on a contract?'

'Pay-as-you-go. Bought it at the phone shop in town.'

The phone shop kept cropping up. Duffy must have seen or known all three of the girls. That was quite some coincidence. The question was, how well had he *really* known them? All of a sudden, Natalie was keen to interview Duffy again. She had enough information to get started and no time to waste. She thanked Christopher and moved towards the front door. A young officer was waiting for her on the doorstep. He stepped forwards and held out an iPad. 'I've been instructed to stay with Mr Bywater once you leave, and to pass this to you. DI Kilburn sends his apologies but he's too heavily involved to talk to you personally and will contact you as soon as possible.'

'What do I do now?' asked Christopher from his chair.

Natalie answered him. 'I'm sorry but all you can do is wait and let the police do their job. We'll do everything we can to find her. In the meantime, if you think of anything that might help us find her, tell this officer.'

*

Back in the car, Natalie switched on the iPad, checked the history and, without saying a word, handed it to Murray. He looked at the page and said, 'Shit. She's been on that Disappear site.'

Natalie nodded. 'She intended on hiding. She took her sports bag and phone and went when she knew her dad was at the pub and unlikely to check up on her.'

Lucy leant her elbows against Natalie's headrest. 'And she didn't go missing on the way to school like the others did. She might actually be hiding out somewhere and not in danger.'

'True, but it bothers me that she's been on that bloody website. And there are other coincidences: she's at the same school as Savannah, she goes to Watfield Sports Centre – as did Harriet – and all three girls visited the phone shop. We really have to follow this up.'

While Natalie and Lucy talked, Murray scrolled through the browsing history on the iPad. He shook his head and said, 'She's been searching through information on dares or challenges and for information on how to avoid being found. She was definitely interested in this disappearing challenge. She's been on the Disappear website every day, sometimes twice a day, checking videos and the questions and answers section, but there's nothing in her search history about timetables or routes to get from Watfield to Northampton.'

'She might have decided that Northampton would be the first place her dad would think of. He told us she came back late from Western Park. That place seems to have some sort of attraction for these girls.'

'You saw the pavilion. No one could possibly hide out there.'

'Maybe there's somewhere else in the park we don't know about. I'll ask DI Kilburn to send officers to it in case she is hiding there.'

Lucy had pulled out her smartphone and was looking at Google Maps. 'The park's close to the sports centre. Think she might have bumped into or met Savannah or Harriet there?'

'Yes, that's possible too.' Natalie took the iPad from Murray and made the decision. 'First stop is the phone shop. Murray, we'll drop you off on the way. Head to the sports centre. Take photos of the three girls with you and find out if they were ever seen together.'

She picked up the comms unit as they pulled away and spoke to Ian. He had made some progress.

'Hi, Natalie. I've sent the information on Katy and Christopher Bywater across to your email. Her mum, Lisa, passed away in May 2017. One month later, Katy was suspended from school for unruly behaviour, and she and her father moved to Watfield in late July last year.'

Natalie was no psychiatrist but the date of Katy's suspension was close to her mother's death, and undoubtedly the two were linked. Katy was a very unhappy girl.

Ian continued, 'I've got something else too. Mike's passed me information from Harriet Long's phone. She bragged on social media that she was going to perform a dare that would stagger them all.'

'She didn't say what it was, did she?'

'No, only that it would make a few people take notice of her and would definitely make her dad proud.'

The poor girl had really wanted her imprisoned father to pay her some attention and not cut her out. Natalie mused they now had yet another connection between the three girls: they were all unhappy teenagers, each vying for attention.

'Mike's also managed to enhance the video of Harriet screaming. It's still not clear but they think it's a dark-grey door.'

Natalie thought of the specks of wood found underneath Savannah's nails. The girls might have been held captive in the same place.

'Cheers for that. I need you to do something else. Mark out a one-mile area around Katy's house and search for rubbish dumps, bins, areas associated with waste, skips or any other such places where a killer would leave a body.' She caught the look Murray threw her. She hoped fervently that it wouldn't come to it, but if Katy had been taken by the killer, her body would be somewhere close by.

CHAPTER TWENTY-TWO

THEN

It's hot and cramped in the washing machine. He can no longer see out of the door or hear any voices. He kicks against the glass but his foot strikes it feebly.

'Faye!' The weak cry takes a lot of effort. There's no answer. He tries to breathe in but he's in an awkward position and his chest feels crushed. He can't move his head to work out how to escape, and although his foot connects again with the door, it isn't enough to open it.

He's becoming light-headed, disconnected from reality like when he had a fever and been in bed, his mother by his side. He has no true memory of the event, just a series of shifting scenes: his mother crying; a bowl that smelt awful; a damp cloth; his father – no, it couldn't be him, because he's dead; a hand on his head and a deep voice; his head being lifted to help him sip water. This feels similar except he's really uncomfortable and there's no one to help him. His arms are numb and everything is slowing down except his breathing. He can't inflate his chest as normal, each breath no more than a gasp. 'Faye!'

There's nothing from outside. The girls have left him. He's going to spend the night here. He rolls his eyes upwards, straining to work out how to get out, and catches sight of a movement – something long and black. His pulse quickens. It's the snake. The snake is actually inside the machine above him, and he has no stone to crush it. That's why the girls were laughing. They've shut him in with the snake. The scream dies in his throat. If he moves or makes a noise, it will attack him. He knows about snakes. He watched a programme where a man had caught one. Snakes don't like movement. If they feel threatened, they'll attack. He has to remain still. The effort is almost impossible and waves of pain shoot through his upper body, but he doesn't flinch and instead closes his eyes. His chest hurts with the effort of breathing, and in spite of trying to remain quiet and not annoy the snake, he starts to rasp as he inhales small amounts of oxygen. He must stay still. He must not anger the snake.

He thinks about his mum who'll have his tea ready and will be wondering where he is. A lump rises in his throat. He wants to go home and tell his mum about the snake and how he knew to keep still. His mum is always telling him how clever he is…

'God might not have given you a big body, but he gave you big brains.'
'The other kids laugh at me all the time and call me horrid names.'
'If they had any idea of how much you have inside that head of yours, they wouldn't laugh. Your body will change and grow eventually. It's had to wait its turn while your brain takes up all the growing energy first. You wait and see if I'm not right.'

He really wants his mum now. The snake is making a hissing noise. It's coming for him and he won't be able to attack it, not here, not all squished up in the machine. Maybe it's a huge boa constrictor that will crush the life out of him, or a smaller snake with a flickering, forked tongue that will suddenly dart out and strike him and then his body will fill with poison and his skin swell until it bursts. Tears well in his eyes and trickle down his cheeks. He doesn't want to be trapped in the machine with the huge snake. He releases a little whimper.

'Help!'

His voice is a mere whisper. He's alone apart from the snake and he's going to die. There isn't enough air. He attempts to move but can't.

His limbs are heavy and glued to the metal drum in which he is stuck. Small sparks of light flitter across his vision. His chest is getting tighter. The realisation hits him hard. The snake is a boa constrictor. It's coiled around him and is crushing him bit by bit as it tightens around his bony chest. Soon he'll hear the sound of his ribs cracking. He can't move. He squeezes his eyes shut. He doesn't want to see the snake. He can't bear to see its scaly body. It's terrible enough having it gradually squeeze the air from him. He's terrified it will slither over his face. Fear – a deep, terrible fear – replaces the knowledge of what is happening, and he moans quietly as his breaths became increasingly shallow.

He wants to tell his mum he's sorry and that he'd only wanted to get her something nice from the dump – the bright, shining kettle or something similar – but it's too late. He won't wake up tomorrow and make up some excuse as to why he didn't see the headmaster and eat his favourite cereal, Rice Krispies, while his baby brother rhythmically thumps his plastic cup against the tray on his high chair. Tears break through his lashes. The pain is almost unbearable in his chest. The snake is killing him.

The door springs open.

'Ha!' Faye's bark of laughter is loud to his ears.

He draws in a painful, ragged breath. 'Snake. Help!'

Faye giggles. Vee appears beside her and shoves her face into the gap. She's upside down. As oxygen pours into his lungs again, he registers it is him who's upside down, not Vee.

'Snake,' he repeats.

'Where?'

'On me.'

'There's no snake,' Faye says.

Behind her, Missy is snorting with laughter. 'You look a bit stuck. Want a hand?'

He can barely move. Every part of him is stuck in the drum. He manages to move a hand towards his chest. There's nothing restricting it. The snake has slithered away again, probably scared of the girls.

A pair of hands reach for his calves and pull at them. He howls at the rush of pain that pours into them.

'Pipe down, you baby. We're helping you out. Shut up for a second.'

The girls yank at his shoes and get them outside the machine, so they're touching the ground.

'You're going to have to slide the rest of you out yourself. We've helped you enough.' Faye sounds cross now. 'And you stink of piss.'

'The snake.'

'What snake? There isn't a stupid snake. It was a story we spread about to keep kids like you out of our area.'

'There's a snake in the machine.' He wriggles and twists and turns until he flops onto the ground, exhausted, snot running down his chin.

'Yeah, sure there is. Go home, scaredy-cat. We don't want you around here. If we find you here again, we'll put you back in there and never let you out.'

He pushes up onto his knees and, turning 180 degrees, faces the open door. Where has the snake gone? He looks upwards and then downwards and spots a length of black hose coiled sinisterly.

'Go on. Shove off.' Missy is advancing again with a mean look on her face.

He staggers to his feet and stumbles away.

'Scaredy-cat!'

The taunts follow him as he trudges off. He'd almost died. It wasn't a snake that had been killing him but lack of air. He knows that now. Tears roll down his face. He is dirty and smelly and very, very angry. The girls will pay for what they've done.

CHAPTER TWENTY-THREE

THURSDAY, 19 APRIL – LATE MORNING

A faint buzzer sounded, announcing Natalie and Lucy's arrival. No one was behind the counter and they waited for a minute until they heard footsteps and Mitchell, the phone shop owner who lived in the flat above it, appeared.

'Sorry, I was upstairs.'

'Morning, sir. Is Duffy in?' Natalie asked.

'Not yet. He had to wait for an engineer to call. There's a problem with the boiler. He'll be in soon though.' He rubbed at his chin and then said, 'I've been thinking about things since we spoke yesterday and I was going to ring you. It might be something or nothing but…' He crossed the shop and turned the key in the door.

Natalie waited for him to speak again. Mitchell looked out of the window before facing her. He wrung his hands together and looked at the floor. 'It's awkward… I think highly of him and I'm sure he wouldn't…'

'Mr Cox, are you talking about Duffy?'

He nodded miserably. 'My office upstairs overlooks the backyard and I've seen him outside on the odd occasion with some of the kids. I've been giving it a lot of thought since you were here last and I can't be a hundred per cent certain, but I suspect he might have been outside with the missing girls. It was a week last Saturday. I'd been to the warehouse to collect some stock. I came in via my private side entrance, and once in my office, I heard laughter outside. I glanced out of the window and onto the tops of their heads. One might have been Savannah and the other wore her hair in two buns. There was a third girl too with Duffy.'

'Did she have short brown hair?'

His eyebrows lifted. 'She did. How did you know?'

Natalie lifted her mobile to show him a photograph of Katy Bywater. His head bounced up and down. 'That's her. I'm sure of it. I really don't know what to make of it though. Duffy's a popular young man. You don't need to be Einstein to work out that he's attractive, and lots of our female customers gravitate towards him. I don't want to cause him unnecessary grief. I was lucky he wanted to come and work for me.'

'Did you ask him what he was doing outside with these girls?'

He looked down for a second. 'I must confess, I didn't. He's such a good employee, very good technician as well – better than me at fixing computers – and we get a huge amount of repeat business thanks to him. As far as I could tell they were only talking, but…'

Judging by his facial expressions, Mitchell was experiencing an internal struggle. He had information but wasn't sure if he should impart it. Natalie tried to nudge him along. 'Is there something else you'd like to tell us? It might not seem to have any relevance but it could well help us. You see, Katy Bywater has gone missing.'

Mitchell's hand flew to his open mouth. 'Oh!'

'Anything you can tell us might help us find her.'

He recovered his composure. 'I can't think of anything but… I've had a few concerns recently…'

'What sort of concerns?'

'Probably not connected in any way but I think Duffy might have been tampering with some of the youngsters' phones.'

'In what way?'

'Again, I can't be certain. It only came to light a couple of days ago. I spotted a group of boys hanging around Duffy and he appeared to be doing something to their phones, one by one. I couldn't tell what but it seemed odd, although I'm not sure if that's relevant to your enquiries.'

'What do you think he might have been doing?'

'I really couldn't say but it looked suspicious. If I had to guess, I'd say it looked like he was fiddling with the settings.'

'Where were you when you saw him performing these actions?'

'Upstairs. I have a monitor so I can see when the shop is busy and I need to go downstairs to help.'

'Does it record?'

'It's linked to the CCTV camera.'

'And does Duffy know of the monitor's existence?'

'Yes… Oh, I see what you're saying. He can't have been doing anything untoward. He knows I can watch him from my office.'

'You don't watch him every minute though, do you?'

He gave a sharp laugh. 'Goodness, no. I'm usually too busy. I glance at it from time to time. The front door buzzer alerts me to customers and I check on it to see if I'm needed.'

'He's here,' said Lucy, who'd been watching the front door.

Duffy, immaculate in a dusty-grey coat and dark trousers, peered in through the glass.

Lucy unlocked the door and he stepped inside, the smile on his face fading rapidly. 'What's going on?'

'We'd like you to come along to the station, Duffy. We need you to assist with our enquiries.'

'I've told you everything I know.'

'Some new information has come to light so if you wouldn't mind accompanying us.'

Mitchell's shoulders slumped and he couldn't look his employee in the eye. Natalie asked Lucy to drive Duffy to the station in the squad car, then contacted Murray, still at the sports centre, to arrange transport to get them both back to Samford.

'You won't charge him, will you? I couldn't manage to run this place as efficiently without him,' Mitchell said.

'We'll have to see what he has to say for himself. Could I take a quick look upstairs at your office, please?'

'Certainly.'

She followed him up the steep wooden stairs to the flat above the shop and into a sitting room, where her gaze was drawn immediately to a painting dominating the wall. It was of a woman with ivory skin, large dark eyes and a beautiful smile that lit up her face. Mitchell caught her staring. 'That's Cosmina, my partner.'

'Lovely name.'

'Cosmina Balan was lovely in every way. Sadly, she died of cancer a few years ago.' His voice thickened with emotion and he turned away briefly before saying, 'This is my office.'

A desk, cluttered with a laptop in pieces, stood under a window. She peered out onto the yard below, surrounded by brick walls, with no exit and containing nothing other than a wrought-iron table and two chairs.

'I never use it. Duffy sometimes takes his lunch outside to eat. It's only small but it catches the midday sun.'

The monitor he'd mentioned was on a filing cabinet, the screen visible from the desk. The shop was empty and the camera was trained on the counter area and a door fitted with a keypad. Undoubtedly a stockroom. The remainder of the office was taken up by shelves of box files appropriately labelled for tax purposes.

'What happens if Duffy needs to go to the stockroom to fetch a new phone? Does he leave the shop unattended?'

'He buzzes or calls for me to go downstairs.'

'And if you're not here?'

'I'm almost always here during opening hours. He's rarely alone.'

Natalie thanked Mitchell and left him to join Murray at the sports centre. She met him outside.

'One of the football team coaches is in this morning and remembers Katy going off with Harriet after a practice session. They definitely knew each other.'

Natalie experienced a familiar buzz that indicated they were onto something. The girls had been acquainted and they'd all been spotted with Duffy outside the phone shop.

Duffy stared at Natalie with wide blue eyes, his palms open. 'Katy's gone missing?'

'That's what I said and you've admitted to knowing her so I'd like you to tell me everything you can to help us find her.' Natalie was determined to drag out every piece of information he had. Duffy glanced first at Lucy sat opposite him and then over at Murray who stood by the door. He swallowed hard and shook his head before looking directly at Natalie once more.

'Her dad bought her a phone and she's been in the shop once or twice. I don't *know* her. I certainly had no idea she'd gone missing.'

'Cut the bullshit. You were seen with her, Savannah and Harriet in the yard behind the shop a week last Saturday. You were well acquainted with all three of these girls and even saw two of them the day they disappeared.'

'I don't know what you want me to say. I had nothing to do with them disappearing.' His blue eyes rested on her.

'You can drop the pretence. You lied to me during an important murder investigation – the murder of teenage girls both known to you. What were you up to in the yard, Duffy? Tell me or you'll have to call a lawyer smartish because I'll have no choice but to charge you.' Her words had the desired effect.

'I wasn't doing anything illegal. I was just talking to them.'

'More bullshit. You could have talked to them inside the shop. It doesn't add up, Duffy. You had no reason to be outside with three teenage girls unless you were up to no good, so let's try again, and this time, tell me the real reason you were outside.'

'Okay… okay. We were smoking. I can't smoke in the shop.'

Natalie rolled her eyes. It was logical but there was more to this than smoking.

'No. I don't buy it.'

'It's true. Savannah was already in the shop looking at phone cases when Harriet wandered in with Katy. They'd met at the sports centre. Both fancied themselves as footballers. The shop was quiet. We had a chat about football and stuff and then Savannah asked if Mitchell was around. I called upstairs but he didn't answer so I figured he was out. Savannah pulled out a packet of fags and passed them around. Katy took one. Harriet refused but joined us outside. I left the back door open in case a customer came in. That's all.'

'You didn't think it was wrong to accept a cigarette from a minor?'

He snorted. 'Leave it out. Loads of young people smoke. I started when I was thirteen. I didn't offer the cigarettes around. Besides, she and I had shared smokes once before.'

'When Mitchell was out?'

'Yes, on a couple of occasions.'

'When we talked to you about Savannah, you claimed not to know her very well yet now you're admitting to standing outside and smoking with her.'

'It was a quick fag and a few words.'

Natalie was getting nowhere with this line of questioning so she tried another. 'I'd like to ask you about another matter. We suspect you might have been tampering with the settings on juveniles' phones.'

'That's utter bollocks.'

'You deny it?'

Duffy went silent for a moment and rubbed the palms of his hands on his thighs – a giveaway he was nervous. Natalie picked up on his actions. He'd had a chance to come up with a plausible explanation but instead was displaying signs of guilt.

'You deny tampering with the settings?'

'I…' He couldn't respond.

'Let's say you did. Why would you do that? Why would these teenagers come to you to change settings? Most of them are tech-savvy and can sort out their own mobiles. The only settings I can think of that they couldn't change would be ones put in place by their parents. Am I close?'

Duffy opened his mouth then shut it again.

'Did you lift parental controls, Duffy?'

No reply.

'Let's say you did actually lift these controls. Why would you do such an irresponsible thing? Don't you think they're in place for good reason? Children need to be protected and it's your duty as an adult to ensure they don't gain access to sites, games or apps that promote violence or pornography, or anything else that is unacceptable for kids this age.'

A dark look crossed Duffy's face. 'You've no idea! These kids see violence and worse on the news every day, on television programmes and films and sometimes in their own homes. They know what goes on in the streets – stabbings, drugs, drink. They're not blinkered to it. They may be teenagers but they're not blind. You talk as if I've committed some crime but I haven't. They didn't want me to download porn or videos of how to make bombs or anything. They just wanted access to some of the games that have a stupid PEGI rating. Some of those ratings are crap, like film ratings… Kids might not be able to go to the cinema to see an eighteen-rated film, but if their friend or their parents has it on DVD, they can watch it. Being able to play a game suitable for over-sixteens isn't going to turn them into maniacs so I don't see what the problem is. I played lots of eighteen-rated games when I was their age and it did me no harm. Kids have too many controls and restrictions placed on them and these games aren't as harmful as some say.'

'And that's how you justify your actions? You're not their parent or guardian. You have no right to decide what they should be able to play or watch. Their parents were being responsible and put controls in place and you…' Natalie bit back further angry words. They were not helpful. She inhaled deeply.

'You tamper with phones and give minors access to applications and games they shouldn't use. You smoke with underage teenagers and you lied to us. There's not a lot to commend you on at the moment, is there? You knew these girls and you've been withholding evidence during a murder enquiry. Am I getting through to you? You're in trouble, Duffy. Two girls are dead and I need to locate Katy quickly before something dreadful happens to her, so quit stalling me and spit it out. What do you know about these disappearances?'

He shrugged. The action angered her further but it also triggered a hunch. Her last word had resonated with him.

'You know about the Disappear website, don't you?'

She'd been right. He slumped in his seat.

'Want to ring a lawyer now?'

His voice was quiet. 'No. I admit I told them about Disappear. They all thought it was cool. We'd been discussing dares and Harriet had done a few of them. She boasted her dad was some gangster in prison and that she wasn't scared of anything and showed us a video she'd taken of her doing the choke dare. She was really into them. We were only chatting about them – the types of stuff you could do – and I mentioned Disappear. Next thing, they were discussing actually taking up the challenge. Savannah was the keenest. She said it would make her mum sit up and notice her. Katy hated living in Watfield and thought maybe going missing for a bit would convince her dad to return to Northampton, and suddenly Harriet dared them both to go missing. She egged them on and they made a pact to do it.'

At last, they had the link they'd been searching for. Natalie almost sighed with relief.

'Did they agree on which days they'd take up the dare?'

Duffy nodded. Savannah was going first, on Monday, Harriet on Tuesday and Katy on Wednesday.'

'Who else knew about this dare?'

'I don't know. After we talked about it they went off to the coffee shop to discuss how best to go through with it. I wasn't party to that conversation. Savannah came back a while later and said it was all sorted.'

'Did she say where she was headed? Was it the old pavilion in the park?'

'That's right. How did you know?'

'Doesn't matter. Carry on.'

'The first I knew of it again was when Savannah walked past the shop on Monday and gave me the thumbs up. I guessed she was going through with it. Harriet came to see me on Tuesday because her mobile wouldn't work. She was pissed off because she wanted to film herself doing the dare and then post the video to the website. When I tried the phone, it worked the first time. After what had happened to Savannah, I told her she ought not to go through with it but she wasn't having any of it. Said it was even more of a reason to do it and she'd get even more attention if people thought she was in danger. We argued about it. I thought that was a stupid reason and it was too risky. I advised her to forget about the dare and go home but she got all moody, picked up her bag and stormed off in a huff.'

'Was she going to hide out at the pavilion too?'

'I honestly don't know what she'd planned. It was her big secret and she was full of it. I hoped she'd taken my advice and I actually believed she had until the following morning when you interviewed me. I didn't think anything serious had happened to her – I mean, whoever murdered Savannah would have had to know about the dare and where Harriet was going. It didn't add up. I figured Savannah had been in the wrong place at the wrong time and been targeted by some lunatic. It wasn't likely the same thing would happen to Harriet. Besides, she was street-smart and she could look after herself.'

Lucy suddenly piped up. 'What utter bollocks! She was only a kid not a bloody ninja warrior.' Natalie gave her a look that was ignored.

'You let her go off into the evening alone, knowing full well Savannah had been murdered.' Lucy folded her arms and glowered at Duffy.

'I keep telling you I didn't know any of them well. I only told them about the website but I didn't force them to take up the challenge – it was their decision, and I tried to prevent Harriet from going through with it.'

'What about Katy? Did you see her yesterday?' Natalie asked.

His brows furrowed as he digested Lucy's words. 'Maybe I should have phoned the police but I didn't imagine anything like this would happen. It was only a stupid dare.'

'A stupid dare that cost two girls their lives!' Lucy retorted.

'What about Katy? When did you last see her?' Natalie repeated, giving Lucy a look that silenced her.

'Yesterday afternoon. She was heading to the supermarket to get some provisions for the dare and I ran outside to talk to her. She came into the shop for a few minutes. She was terrified by what had happened to Savannah and Harriet but also desperate to get her dad to move back to Northampton. I told her the same thing I told Harriet and she finally agreed it was madness to go missing given both the others were dead. On my life, she wasn't going to go through with it.'

Natalie pursed her lips. She wasn't here to dispense judgement but she was furious about Duffy's lack of responsibility. 'You don't seem to appreciate how foolish it was to encourage these vulnerable girls to take up this dare. It was completely irresponsible.'

'I didn't encourage them! They wanted to do it. If you're going to hold anyone responsible, then blame their families who made them feel so miserable they wanted to run away to draw attention to themselves. I'm not the guilty party in this. I didn't drive them to their deaths.'

'You played your part though,' Lucy mumbled.

Duffy scowled at her.

Natalie pressed on. 'You have absolutely no idea where Katy might be hiding?'

'None. I was totally convinced Katy had given up on the idea and was going home.'

'If I find out you're lying again, you know what I'll do?'

'I know. I'm not lying. Believe me, if I knew anything at all, I'd tell you. I want you to find her alive.'

'Let's hope we do. Based on the fact you lied about the website when I asked about it the other day, I need to confirm a couple of other things with you. You went to the dentist on Monday afternoon and then went home and played video games with your nephew.'

'Yes.'

'And you spent Tuesday evening with Jaffrey McCarthy and other band members.'

'That's right. We practised in his garage until about twelve and then I drove home.'

'Drove home from where? Where does Jaffrey live?' asked Natalie suddenly.

Duffy's face clouded over. 'Bramshall. Look, you know all this already. You've already checked out my alibis. I didn't have anything to do with these deaths.'

'Then you have nothing to worry about,' Lucy replied.

Natalie had been processing the information and gave him a cool stare. 'You say you were near Bramshall until about twelve?'

'That's right.'

'And did you pass the woodland area on your way home?'

'I did,' he replied warily.

'Did you travel with a friend or alone?'

'I was on my own.'

'We'll need your car registration to confirm that.'

'Why?'

'Because you happened to be close to where Harriet Long lived and where we found her body.'

'I didn't know she lived in Bramshall! I went to see Jaffrey and the band like I usually do on a Tuesday. Honestly.'

'I'm sure we'll be able to confirm all of that. I might also need to have somebody examine your car.'

'What?'

'It's usual procedure.'

'Hang on a sec… What's usual about that?'

'As I explained, you happened to be near Harriet's house late Tuesday and you knew she'd made plans to disappear.'

'For fuck's sake! I didn't have anything to do with this.'

'Then you'll want to make sure we eliminate you from our enquiries, won't you? I appreciate your full cooperation. If you wouldn't mind waiting here, we'll get back to you as soon as possible,' Natalie said smoothly and stood up.

In the corridor, she spoke to Murray and Lucy. 'Leave him to stew for a bit. See if you can find his car on any cameras over in Bramshall and check the CCTV camera in Watfield again. We might spot him or Katy on it.'

'If he's guilty, he's putting up a good performance. I had him pegged as a bloody idiot, not a murderer,' said Lucy.

Natalie rubbed her chin and said, 'I can't make my mind up if he loved the attention from these teenagers and played to his audience or was setting them up. If it's the former, he's a complete halfwit; if the latter, he's a dangerous individual. Let's see if we can find out which.'

CHAPTER TWENTY-FOUR

THURSDAY, 19 APRIL – AFTERNOON

'That's him,' said Lucy, pointing to grey trousers and shiny brogues, all that could be seen of Duffy as he stood in the street talking to someone out of shot. Natalie squinted at the screen and sighed. He'd been wearing that same outfit when she'd spoken to him the previous day. They waited for movement and both he and Katy Bywater, in her school uniform and carrying a pink sports bag, came into shot and vanished again.

'And that's definitely Katy,' said Murray. He wound the footage on and a full five minutes later, Katy passed the camera again.

Natalie studied the map of the town layout on the desk. 'She's headed in the direction of Aldi. Try the camera in the car park and see if she actually went to buy provisions. If she did, it means she paid no attention to Duffy's warning.'

Murray headed to his terminal to do as bid. Lucy had phoned Duffy's fellow band members and confirmed he was on the out-skirts of Bramshall, several streets away from Harriet's house. His Toyota GT86 had passed a camera at ten past twelve, but even after blowing up the image, they could only make out Duffy in the driver's seat and no sign of Harriet.

Lucy shook her head and commented, 'I know he denies any involvement but he could have hidden Harriet in the boot or on the floor in the back.'

Natalie was in agreement. They'd have to run tests on his car to see if there was any trace of Harriet's DNA. She set about making the arrangements.

Ian was hunched over his screen, rewinding and slowing down grey footage of vehicles headed along the main road that passed the turn-off to the fly-tipping spot. He squeezed his eyes tightly and rubbed his forehead.

'You okay?' Murray asked.

'Bit of a headache.'

'Take a break for five minutes.'

'I'll be fine.' He rolled his shoulders a couple of times and returned to the job at hand.

Murray's phone rang. 'DS Anderson… Yes… Yes, I did ask about that appointment. Oh, okay. Thank you. Twenty minutes, you say? Thanks again.'

He looked up. 'That was the dentist's surgery. Apparently, although the screen showed Duffy attended his appointment scheduled for four o'clock, he didn't get there until twenty past four. That was the receptionist I spoke to. She wasn't on duty Monday evening and mentioned to her colleague that we were checking on Duffy. Her colleague was on duty that day and actually checked Duffy in. He was late for his appointment by twenty minutes.' He turned his attention back to the footage.

'Oh, really? So now we have some time unaccounted for – the twenty minutes immediately after he saw Savannah. I'll talk to him again.'

Ian wandered across with a printout on which were several red crosses. 'I've sent this across to DI Kilburn. The council has provided us with the locations of business premises that have large recycle containers for waste and any individual waste bins along roads that are emptied regularly by operatives. I've contacted all skip hire companies and asked for information regarding their skips. I'm waiting for the last place to respond. Those we've located are on the map too. Only one's been hired within a one-mile radius of Katy's house.'

'Good work. I just hope they don't find her in any of those places.'

'Natalie…' Murray's voice was guarded.

'You found Katy on the CCTV at Aldi car park?'

'Yep, and a familiar face.'

Natalie bounded across and grimaced. 'Not Anthony Lane again?' The image was clear and showed Anthony Lane looking directly at Katy Bywater as she headed into the store.

'Okay. I know we're looking into Duffy's involvement but this man keeps showing up too. He might even be harbouring Katy. I'll arrange a warrant to search his flat. Lucy, head over there with it, take a look and then bring him back for questioning while I talk to Duffy again.'

Natalie raced upstairs to obtain the permission she needed from Superintendent Aileen Melody. A copy of the *Watfield Herald* was open on her desk and she rested her palms either side of it.

'I'm glad you're here. I was going to let you know the *Watfield Herald* has printed a disturbing piece in its evening edition about the monster preying on teenage girls. They've drawn attention to the fact you're heading the investigation and pointed out that as a parent of a teenage girl, you have a vested interest in finding the perpetrator.'

She slid the paper towards Natalie, who skimmed through the article and stopped at the fifth paragraph that talked about her.

'How dare she bring my family into this! It has nothing to do with the investigation.'

'She thinks it has a bearing – a detective with a daughter of the same age as the missing girls, who is motivated to catch the killer. Flattering in one sense.'

'I find it intrusive. If the killer is reading this, they'll now be aware I have a daughter.'

'You know this Bev Gardiner who wrote it?'

'She's been hanging about crime scenes. I moved her on without comment but she's been tenacious. Must have done some research. She even managed to interview Christopher Bywater shortly after Katy went missing before we got to the scene. Goodness knows how she found out about Katy's disappearance so quickly.'

'Yes, that was a cock-up and should never have happened. I've already been questioned as to why Christopher didn't have an officer with him at the time. We need the media behind us on this so best not to make a ruckus, although I have to admit I'm pissed off about it. I could have done without the media jumping on Katy's disappearance and shouting about it being linked to this "Watfield Monster". It's blown up too quickly and the press office is under siege. I really don't want our investigation compromised but I've been ordered to cooperate with the media. So, what are your thoughts?'

'The disappearances *are* related,' said Natalie.

'Oh shit, Natalie. We're going to have to find something or someone pretty damn quick if we're going to appease the public.'

'We've got a potential suspect, Nick Duffield, helping us with our enquiries. He knew about the Disappear dare they were all undertaking and not only saw all three girls on the days they went missing, but he drove through Bramshall in the early hours of Wednesday morning, and passed the spot where Harriet's body was dumped. We're also about to interview a second potential suspect – Anthony Lane, who is on the sex offenders' register. I need a warrant so we can check his flat in case Katy is there before we bring him in for questioning.'

'At least I can give the press office something, then – that we are questioning two men in connection with the girls' murders. You think either of them are responsible?'

'I don't want to jump the gun, Aileen. We don't have strong enough evidence yet to convict anyone.'

'Then find some. This article is only the beginning. We'll have people baying for blood if we don't start coming up with results. They won't be patient.'

'We're working as hard as we can but there haven't been enough hours in the day to sift through all the footage and information we've amassed.'

'We have to be *seen* to be proactive, Natalie.'

'I'm aware of that but we're not superhuman, Aileen. We've limited time and resources and a huge ask: we're not dealing with one murder here – it's two, and now a third child in danger. There should be more officers assigned to this.'

Aileen stared into space. 'I've already explained that isn't possible. You have Forensics to assist you and MisPer are out in force trying to locate Katy. I'm fully aware of the difficulties you're facing and know you're giving it your all, but we need to reassure the public that we're in control. They want to see us doing our utmost to protect them and getting results so… bring me some.'

Natalie didn't interrupt. This didn't sound like Aileen talking at all, and she was more convinced than ever that her super was under considerable pressure. She waited for the warrant and raced back downstairs to hand it to Lucy. Calling Ian to join her, she hastened to the interview room where Duffy was still waiting.

'When can I leave?' he asked as soon as they appeared.

Natalie took her time before responding. 'This is PC Jarvis. He'll be sitting in with us and operating the recording device. If you feel you would like a lawyer to be present, you must say so now before we begin.'

'I don't need a lawyer, do I?'

'It's up to you but I strongly advise you to get representation.'

'No, I've not committed any crime. Let's get this over with.'

'Then we'll begin the interview.'

Ian switched on the machine and introduced those present in the room. 'Thursday the nineteenth of April. Interview with Nick

Duffield, known as Duffy, begins at four fifteen. Those present are PC Ian Jarvis and DI Natalie Ward. For the record, note that Nick Duffield has refused a lawyer.'

'Duffy, you saw Savannah on Monday afternoon. According to your statement, it was about three forty p.m. Does that still hold true?'

'Yes. I think so. It was about the time I had to leave for a dentist appointment.'

'This was the appointment you had at four p.m. that lasted a full hour.'

'That's right. I had a tooth prepared for a crown. There were impressions and X-rays. It took forever.'

'We've spoken to the surgery.'

'And my appointment was for four p.m., right?'

'It was but you didn't show until almost twenty past four. Can you explain what you were doing between three forty and four twenty?'

'I got waylaid. I was chatting to someone I bumped into.'

'That wouldn't have been Savannah, would it?'

'No. I'd already seen her. I told you.'

'You were so busy talking you forgot what time it was?'

He shrugged. 'As it happens, yes. I lost track of time.'

'Who was this person that held you up?'

'Just a girl.'

'Another girl? A customer?'

'Yes, she is.'

'Another teenage girl?'

'She's eighteen, okay? I don't go out with kids.'

'You're going out with her?'

'Not officially.'

'Okay, Duffy. Give us a name.'

'I'd rather not. I don't want you to interview her and give her the impression I've done something wrong. I've been trying for ages to chat her up and we've only just started seeing each other.'

Natalie wasn't going to waste any more time. 'A name,' she urged. He kept silent.

'Duffy, we need a name. Without it your alibi doesn't hold up. With no alibi you will be in the frame for Savannah's murder. You've already admitted to being in Bramshall, where Harriet lived and… where her body was found. Don't be stupid. Give us her name.'

'Lily Curry. She works at the shoe shop in Watfield. Can you be discreet? I don't want to blow my chance with her.'

Natalie glared at him. Two girls had been murdered and one was still missing, and all he could think about was himself. 'Thank you. Would you mind staying here while we check this out?'

'Do I have a choice?'

Natalie stared him down. 'No. You don't.'

*

Anthony Lane ran his mug under cold water, placed it on the draining board then wiped his hands with a tea towel.

'I don't see why you have to come barging in while I'm eating. I haven't done anything wrong.'

Lucy cast about the small kitchen. 'I didn't barge in. You gave me permission to enter and I see you've already finished your meal. This piece of paper gives me the right to search the premises, so please sit down and let me do my job.'

He sighed heavily. 'If you must. Don't mess anything up.'

She moved from the kitchen into the sitting room, a functional space with grey walls, large enough for a two-seater settee, a television, a square table and a dark-grey writing desk on which stood a small computer and keyboard. A large black-and-white framed photograph of the Eiffel Tower on a misty morning was mounted on one wall, and on another, the Arc de Triomphe at night. The place lacked warmth, and apart from several embroidered cushions and a large flowering cactus in a black earthenware pot, it was unwelcoming.

Behind the sitting room was a bedroom, containing nothing more than a single bed and a tiny inbuilt wardrobe; off it was a brown-tiled shower cubicle and toilet that had seen better days. There was one remaining room: a closet-sized space, no bigger than a walk-in wardrobe, being used for storage. It was stacked high and she lifted clear-sided boxes packed with clothes that didn't fit into the wardrobe, checked box files of old letters and bills and pulled out a head-and-shoulders portrait of a sad-faced young woman studying a daisy in her hand, then replaced it. Nobody was hiding or hidden in his flat.

'Find what you were looking for?' he asked, leaning against the door frame.

'I'll need to check the computer.'

He let out a sharp laugh. 'Hoping you'll find out I've been downloading kiddie porn?'

'I'll have to take it in to be checked.'

'Sure, why not? You'll be sadly disappointed though. There's not much to interest you on it.'

Lucy unplugged the computer. 'Time to go,' she said.

He scowled at her. 'You really have it in for me, don't you?'

She ignored the comment and waited while he collected his coat and followed her to the door.

*

'You can let Duffy go. It all checks out. Lily met up with him before his dentist appointment. She also went to Caffè Nero with him afterwards, and even commented his lips were so numb he had to drink his coffee through a straw. His mother's confirmed he was at home at six p.m. and played video games with his nephew until one of the Missing Persons unit visited and he went out to assist in the search for Savannah. Forensics have seized his car but it'll take some time to process it, so until they come up with something, we have to release him.' Natalie tossed the file on the desk. It was late-afternoon and there was still no news of Katy. Anthony Lane was being awkward and resentful and had requested a lawyer, who had yet to appear, before he would speak to them.

Natalie headed downstairs to the vending machine, and as she crunched her way through the bag of salt and vinegar crisps, she went over the facts. Unless Forensics turned up something from Duffy's car, Anthony Lane was now their only suspect. If he wasn't the killer, she couldn't think who else might be. She rammed the last of the crisps into her mouth and threw the bag into the bin. The action caused her thoughts to flow faster still. *Bins. Rubbish.* There was some reason the killer dumped the girls' bodies in locations to do with rubbish. Once again, the idea that this was somehow related to the Alisha Kumar murder flashed through her mind, but how could she join the dots?

Mike was standing on the bottom step as she turned to go back upstairs. She hadn't been aware of his presence.

'Have you seen the piece in the *Watfield Herald*?' he asked.

'I have – the cow!'

'Don't let it get to you.'

'I'm trying not to. Cheer me up. Tell me you've found something promising.'

'I won't lie – we're not faring too well. We've found no blood, no prints and no traces of DNA on either girl's body, not on their clothing or anywhere in the vicinities where their bodies were found.'

'Nothing at all?'

'I know. It's the first time I've been this stumped. The killer knew what they were up to when they dumped the bodies outside, especially on a rubbish dump. There's almost too much for us to go through. It'll take days – weeks even – to sift through it all.'

'Think they did it on purpose then?'

He nodded. 'Pretty sure that's the case.'

'Anthony Lane's downstairs, waiting for his lawyer to turn up. I'm not going to be able to charge him with anything other than loitering at this rate. But every time a girl has gone missing, he's been spotted watching her. He might have something to do with this.'

'If he has, his DNA isn't on their clothes or bodies.'

'This is getting increasingly difficult. I don't think we've ever had a case with so little evidence.'

'I don't think we have either. We will find something but it'll take time. I wish I could speed things up for you but it is what it is.'

'I don't have the luxury of time. I'm worried about Katy's safety.'

'I can tell you are. There's a huge search going on for her. It was on the early news.'

'But what if it's already too late? Savannah and Harriet were killed soon after they went missing. If the killer is sticking to the same MO, she's probably already dead.'

'There's no body yet, Nat. Keep the faith. If the perp did kidnap her, then they already changed their MO. They snatched her at night rather than on her way home from school, which also means they might not have harmed her.'

'I'm desperately clinging to that hope, Mike.'

'Getting anywhere with CCTV?'

'Apart from spotting Duffy's car, no.'

'We've prioritised his Toyota but it'll still take a while to examine it thoroughly.'

'So I was told. I've let him go for now. Apart from his car we haven't got anything. I could do with some extra help on this but every department is stretched to the limit.'

'Tell me about it. We're struggling too. Talking of which… I only came down for some chocolate – food of champions,' he joked.

He pressed a pound coin into the slot and tapped out three numbers. The machine whirred into action – a series of clatters – and threw a bar of chocolate into the drawer. He retrieved it, peeled back the outer wrapping and offered it to her. She snapped off a section with thanks and, waving it in the air, said, 'The killer must have driven Harriet's body to the fly-tip down that lane. They can't have carried her through the woods.'

Mike mumbled his accord through a mouthful of chocolate. 'They'd definitely have left behind some forensic evidence if they'd come through the woods.'

'And they must have moved her into position after the Missing Persons unit had passed through that area. They were taking a huge risk of being spotted. It was the same with Savannah. Her body wasn't in Western Park when the search teams were looking for her. The killer moved her body there after the search party had cleared away.'

'Sounds logical to me.'

'Somewhere on that CCTV footage is a vehicle driven or owned by the killer.'

'All I can add is whoever it is, they're methodical. Can't find a shred of evidence on either body. We haven't even found the little star earring Savannah was wearing.'

'Do you reckon it could be somebody who understands the way we operate?'

'Could be but let's face it: there are enough crime dramas on television to give whoever it is sufficient information about how the police go about their business, or they could even find out from Google.'

'But to leave no DNA, they must know what they're doing.'

'I'd say that's the case. They've covered themselves up well, probably worn gloves, or even shaved their body so they left no hairs. I've seen it before but we've always found something eventually, no matter how clever they were in covering their tracks.'

Natalie popped the chocolate into her mouth and licked her fingers clean, tasting a mixture of rich cocoa and the salty residue from her crisps. It was an agreeable combination. 'This killer's confident. To dump a body when there are officers close by takes bare-faced nerve.'

'Then they're either an arrogant git or supremely confident,' Mike said. He offered her the last piece of the bar and she shook her head.

'The latter worries me most. I'm anxious they're playing us, and worse still, they're one step ahead of us.'

Mike balled the wrapper and sucked his gums. Natalie pointed out a blob of chocolate on the corner of his mouth and wiped it off for him. He studied her for the longest second. 'They'll trip up. They always do.'

Natalie thought about Alisha Kumar lying by the rubbish bags close to her parents' restaurant. 'Not always, Mike.'

'Work the facts, Nat. That's all you can do.'

'Aileen's breathing down my neck for instant results, like I can magically find a killer with only three team members.'

'Firstly, you have three phenomenal officers and you have quite a reputation here for results, and secondly, the rumour mongers are saying Aileen might be replaced.'

'You're kidding! She's one of the top superintendents in the force.'

'Makes no odds. We operate out of one of only four special headquarters in the country. We are the crème de la crème, and if we don't get the best results, we are all in danger of being moved along.'

'Shit! I'd never have expected anyone to be brought in to replace Aileen.'

'Seems like there's a chap in London they're considering, but it's only rumour.'

'I hope that's all it is.'

'Speaking of being replaced, I'd better get back.'

They parted on the first floor and Natalie ambled along the corridor towards her glass-fronted office. The door was open and she could hear Ian's and Murray's raised voices. The truce that had fallen between them following Ian's stabbing seemed to be over.

*

He peeled off his shirt, damp with perspiration, and admired the snake in all its glory. It was satiated for now. It'd been a long wait since the day he had squeezed the life out of Alisha Kumar. Vee Patel, who'd married Ali Kumar, would never know why her daughter was killed. It was a shame she would never understand the message he'd sent: her daughter's strangled body left by rubbish bags. How fitting.

After the first victim, the snake had been cunning and lain low, biding its time, amassing information on its other victims. It had tracked both of them down using the all-powerful Internet and waited calmly. Revenge was a dish best served cold, and this dish was so icy no one would ever guess who was behind it.

Vee wouldn't mock anyone ever again. Her soul had been destroyed. The snake had slithered away back into hiding… plotting carefully before striking again.

Missy wouldn't be able to work out who was behind the murder of her wild, rebellious daughter – a girl who showed off and acted brashly and who took after her mother. Although the snake had already been plotting to murder the girl, it had been delighted when Harriet had decided to take up a dare of all things and go into hiding and, moreover, given him two further sacrifices that the snake took as reward for his patience. That had been most exhilarating. It was a shame Missy, who'd been the thickest of the trio, would never work out the significance of three girls being strangled and found in areas associated with rubbish. Maybe he should send her a letter to explain it to her.

He laughed at the thought of her distress and the snake joined in, its jaw opening and closing in appreciation of the joke. And for Harriet to die while doing a dare! The universe had truly been generous to the snake.

Suddenly his eyes narrowed. He had not quite succeeded, and he had a thirst that needed to be quenched. Faye's recent death due to overdose had been unfortunate and hugely frustrating. Apart from anything else, he'd been saving her for last. She had been the leader, the brains of the gang that had tormented him, and would have presented a far greater challenge. As it was, her death had left the snake feeling unfulfilled.

The snake hissed something and he understood. The *Watfield Herald* was lying open on the table. He wandered across and read it then smiled. DI Natalie Ward, as arrogant as Faye, made a wonderful substitute. The snake had enjoyed killing so much it seemed churlish to spoil the spree.

CHAPTER TWENTY-FIVE

THURSDAY, 19 APRIL – AFTERNOON

'Go and take a break for fuck's sake.' Murray scowled at Ian, who was rubbing his eyes.

'What's going on?' Natalie asked.

'The martyr here thinks he should keep working even though he's in agony.'

'You feeling rough?' Natalie had to admit Ian's face had turned quite grey.

'Headache, that's all. Murray's making a fuss.'

'Okay, bugger off home. You're no use if you can't be fully focused. You were only allowed back if you took up light duties. I don't want to be responsible for your recovery going into reverse.'

'But, Natalie—'

'Go on. Come back tomorrow morning if you feel better.'

He stood reluctantly and swayed slightly.

'See, you're not in a fit state to work. You need a hot meal and some kip,' Murray commented.

'You're worse than my mother… and nowhere near as good-looking.'

Murray grinned. 'Ah, good. Banter again. That's more like it. You'll live. I'll take over here.' He waved Ian off airily.

Lucy passed Ian as he was leaving. 'You look like shit,' she said.

'I told him that too,' Murray shouted.

'You want a lift home?' Lucy asked Ian.

'No. I can manage. Thanks.' He trundled away down the corridor.

Lucy breezed in and dropped a box on the first desk. 'He really does look like shit. Here, got a box of Krispy Kreme doughnuts. There'll be more for everyone now Ian's gone.'

'Any news on Anthony's lawyer?' Natalie asked.

'I think he's on his way.'

'And his computer?'

'With Forensics. They fired it up straight away but there wasn't anything of concern at first glance. He's a funny one. His flat was almost empty, like he doesn't live there full-time, and very tidy.'

Natalie collected a doughnut from the box and took it to her desk. 'Mike says there's no DNA on either victim. He's struggling to find any evidence.'

Lucy licked yellow icing from her first doughnut. 'None at all? That's unusual.'

'Isn't it? This killer's intelligent – three girls in three days, two dead already and their bodies returned almost under the noses of the Missing Persons unit. The bastard is messing with us – showing us they're better than we are. I bet they also called MisPer anonymously to tip them off about seeing Savannah in the park the morning her body was found, and I expect they knew full well Harriet's phone would give off a ping when that video of her was uploaded. They deliberately hung around close to Harriet's house before turning it on and uploading it – that's how fucking clever they are!'

Murray chipped in. 'Or they live near Harriet.'

'Yeah, that's a possibility but I can't shake off the impression they're enjoying all of this... this... taunting us. Harriet's phone was smack bang next to a bag marked rubbish. The fucker set it up, maybe even before they moved Harriet's body to the fly-tip.'

Lucy agreed. 'Unless the perp's a crazed maniac who gets off on a daily killing spree and has just been fortunate enough not to be discovered, this has been in the planning for a while.'

Natalie nodded. 'I agree. The fucker's avoided detection and hasn't left any prints or forensic evidence at the crime scenes. The other thing that bugs me is that we've no idea how this person even knew that the girls would be taking up the Disappear dare, not unless they overheard them discussing it in the coffee shop Saturday before last. Does that coffee shop have CCTV?'

Murray shook his head. 'Katy's not been found dead. Maybe the perp hasn't got her and only ever intended killing Savannah and Harriet.'

All of a sudden Natalie couldn't face the sticky cake on her desk. 'Christ, I hope for Katy's sake that's true. See if Anthony's lawyer is here yet, Lucy. I really want to crack on. He's the only suspect we've got at the moment.'

Lucy said, 'And he swears he's innocent.'

Murray reached into the box and snorted. 'Innocent, as in he was only hanging about the supermarket because he likes staring at teenage girls? I suppose that's possible. It would marry up with his past record.'

Lucy phoned downstairs to see if the lawyer had turned up. Natalie continued talking to Murray.

'Past record or not, Anthony *could* be involved in this, after all, he was in Aldi car park just before each of the girls went missing.' Even as she spoke, Natalie had a feeling Murray could be right. Anthony had no history of violence. Then Mike's words *work the facts* came back to her. That's what she had to do.

*

The snake was lying in wait. This was the street where DI Natalie Ward lived. He drove past the houses slowly, reading the numbers until he reached the one he had been looking for, with its unremarkable frontage but neat garden filled with trimmed rose bushes and shrubs. Surely DI Ward didn't have time for gardening?

There were no cars on the driveway. DI Ward wasn't at home and it didn't look like her husband was either. He wanted to take a closer look at the house and peer through the windows but that would only draw attention to himself, and he had managed to stay well under everyone's radar so far. Best not to spoil it by being greedy. It was enough to have visited and get an idea of where she lived. He had seen enough to be able to picture her here, in this average house, tears streaming down her face when she learnt her daughter had gone missing.

*

It was 5.45 p.m. when Natalie got word Anthony's lawyer had finally arrived.

'Thank fuck for that. I'm suffering from a massive sugar overdose,' said Lucy, jumping up and brushing crumbs from her trousers.

Murray didn't lift his eyes from the screen. 'Leave the doughnuts there. I'll make sure they don't provide any further temptation for you.'

'Geez, you are too good to me.'

Natalie was already by the door. She'd sorted through all the questions she wanted to ask Anthony. She hoped they wouldn't be too long with him. She could do with going home. She tucked a file under her arm. 'Ready, Lucy? Oh, wait a sec. I'd better take this call.'

It took several seconds for Natalie to understand what was being said.

'Hi, Natalie. It's Rowena, Zoe's mum.'

'Hi, Rowena. What's up?'

'Nothing major. I tried your home line but no one picked up. I just wanted to say if Leigh's feeling better maybe she'd like to come bowling with Zoe tomorrow night after school. Zoe's disappointed she couldn't come today.'

An icy cage formed around Natalie's lungs, squeezing them and stealing her breath for an instant. She tried to make sense of it. 'Rowena, I'm sorry… I don't understand. Isn't she with you?'

Rowena's voice was suddenly filled with concern. 'No. She's with you, isn't she? She told Zoe she'd started her period and had bad stomach cramps, so she was going to see the school nurse and request that you pick her up early. You didn't get a call from school?'

It didn't add up. 'No. I'm at work. She'd have rung David.' Her head was telling her that's exactly what would have happened but a nagging voice made her ask, 'Zoe didn't see Leigh go off anywhere, did she? Get into a car maybe?'

Rowena spoke to her daughter – an urgent exchange. The girl came on the phone. 'Hi, Mrs Ward. We were in the playground after lunch and Leigh had stomach cramps. She said she couldn't face classes or coming home for tea and was going to the school nurse. I offered to go with her but she said she'd rather go on her own and I didn't see her after that.'

'She hasn't said anything to you about being unhappy at all, has she?'

'No.'

'Zoe, this is very important. Has she ever mentioned running away and hiding or disappearing to you?' Natalie held her breath, waiting for the response.

The girl seemed genuine. 'No. She just had cramps and wanted to go home.'

Her mother came back on. 'Is everything all right? I didn't intend causing any anxiety.'

'No. It's fine. She's probably with David. It'll be some miscommunication. I'll give him a call.'

'You will let me know she's okay, won't you? And about tomorrow if she's up to it.'

'Yes, sure.'

Natalie rang home but no one answered the phone and Leigh's mobile went directly to answerphone. She left a message for her daughter then tried David's number. She listened to his voice asking her to leave a message. Anxious thoughts tumbled over themselves but she picked through them. Leigh had come home, rested up and then David had taken her out as usual, and neither of them had a signal wherever they were. She should calm down. There was no logical reason for David to ring her to say Leigh had come home early. He wouldn't bother her over something like that. She inhaled deeply, regaining control of her spiralling emotions and thawing the icy fingers that raked her insides. That made perfect sense. If she hadn't been working this investigation, she wouldn't have been so anxious, yet still an inner voice told her this situation didn't feel right. She spoke after David's message, trying not to sound panicked.

'David, is Leigh with you? Zoe's mother said she left school early with a stomach ache. Please ring me as soon as you get this message. I'm worried.'

She glanced up at Lucy. 'Can you start the interview? I need to make another call.'

'Is everything okay?'

'I hope so. I'm probably overreacting.'

'I'll deal with Anthony. You check it out.' She took the file from Natalie, who sat on the settee in the corridor and called Eric, David's father.

'Eric, it's Natalie.'

'Hi, Natalie.'

'Is David there?'

'No. He popped round for a few minutes yesterday afternoon but I've not laid eyes on him today.'

'Yes, he said… You get the washing machine fixed?'

'Washing machine? You've lost me there. It's working fine. Erm… is everything all right?'

'I'm trying to track him and Leigh down. They aren't answering their phones. Look, if he rings you, get him to call me immediately.'

'Certainly. What's going on? You sound… anxious.'

'Leigh supposedly went home after lunch with a stomach ache and I'm checking on her whereabouts.'

'Maybe she's at home now.'

'No one's picking up there. I'm at work.'

'I could drive over if it would help, see if they're in.'

'I've left messages. They'll ring me. Besides, Josh will be back home soon. I can ask him. Thanks, Eric.'

'No problem. Kids, eh? Such a worry – even when they grow up. Try not to get overly concerned. She'll be fine.'

She pocketed her mobile and reasoned David had the matter in hand, but the knowledge that the *Watfield Herald* had mentioned her daughter didn't help matters. She was getting jittery and she couldn't afford to get distracted. Anthony was waiting for her.

Anthony was looking more confident with his lawyer by his side, a woman in her late forties who acknowledged Natalie's arrival with a small tilt of her head. With the recording device in operation, the lawyer spoke up.

'My client, Mr Anthony Lane, would like to make it clear that he is here to assist you with your enquiries but had nothing to do with the disappearance of any teenager. He feels you have victimised him since the start of this investigation and would like it put on record he is unhappy with your treatment of him. He has paid for his past indiscretions and has not reoffended since.'

Natalie took the open file from Lucy and said, 'It is duly noted. Sergeant Carmichael, how far were you in this interview?'

'I'd just asked Mr Lane why he was outside the Aldi supermarket yesterday afternoon.'

'To which I replied I was buying food,' said Anthony with a self-satisfied smirk.

Natalie let the smug remark wash over her. 'That may well be the case but if we examine the footage taken from the CCTV camera, in particular this image, you can see quite clearly you weren't making any move towards the supermarket. You were, in fact, standing still and staring at this girl.'

'For the recorder, DI Ward is showing Anthony Lane a photograph taken from the CCTV camera outside Aldi at ten past four.'

'I was looking past her at something in the distance.'

'And still looking at that same something a few minutes later? You can see by the time clock in the top left-hand corner, you watched her for a full five minutes until she entered the supermarket, and you remained glued to that spot until she re-emerged, four minutes later.'

'DI Ward is showing Anthony Lane three more photographs showing the interviewee staring at Katy Bywater.'

Anthony glanced at his lawyer. 'I wasn't doing anything wrong.' The lawyer nodded to urge him to explain.

'I like looking at teenage girls and I don't mean in a perverted way either, before you jump to conclusions. I simply admire them – their confidence, their arrogance even. They have a way of acting, standing and talking that fascinates me. This girl exuded a sadness that was evident in the way her head was bowed and the way she walked. I was just observing her.'

Natalie was quick to respond. 'That sounds very poetic. You certainly seem to enjoy observing teenage girls, don't you? This is the third time you've come to our attention, and all three girls you were watching have disappeared – two have been found dead.'

He heaved a sigh. 'It's a tragedy. They were all lovely in different ways. I'll level with you. After I finish work, I shop at that supermarket every day at about the time the schoolchildren finish for the day. I don't mean any harm at all. I'm not preying on them or following them. I look out for subjects I think are interesting.'

'Can you clarify what you mean by *subjects*?'

'I paint women, mostly young women on the cusp of woman-hood, and try to capture their emotions as they struggle to develop into maturity. I take my inspiration from those girls I see hanging around the supermarket. They are all very different in looks, man-nerisms and attitudes.'

Lucy cocked her head to one side like a sparrow. 'You're an artist?'

'It's a hobby but I've become quite good at it. I've even sold a couple of portraits. I go to classes every Wednesday evening.'

'Did you paint the picture of the girl with the daisy that's in your storage room?' Lucy asked.

'Yes, that's one of mine. The canvases are too big for me to keep in my flat so I store them in my art teacher's garage along with all my painting equipment.'

The sour combination of vinegar and chocolate rose in Natalie's throat as she realised Anthony was unlikely to be the killer. 'And you went to art class last night?'

'That's right. It's from eight to ten every Wednesday at the Methodist Hall in Church Street. I've been attending since I arrived in Watfield. It began as therapy and has grown into a real passion.'

'What did you do after art class?'

'I hung around chatting to the others for a good quarter of an hour, then took my equipment back to Chad's house – that's my art teacher – and then went home.'

If the timings were correct, and Chad vouched for him, it would have left no time for him to drive to Katy's house and kidnap her. Anthony stared at her, his eyes bright. Could he be involved? Was he working with somebody? Did he identify a potential victim and then alert a partner? Natalie's brain was having difficulty processing that theory and there was something about the way he spoke with such passion about his painting that made her believe he was telling the truth.

'I want to make it clear that although I'm on the sex offenders' register, I've not reoffended. Following my release, I saw a therapist who helped me work through my issues. Painting transformed my negative emotions into creative positives. I swear I've never approached any of these girls with any intent to harm or shock. I've only ever observed them at a short distance for my artwork.'

Natalie paused for a moment. Did she believe him? Facts were facts. Did he simply study teenagers in order to get ideas for his paintings? It sounded plausible. 'Do you have many of these paintings?'

His face transformed as his eyes crinkled with pride. 'Over twenty canvases now. Chad says they're good enough to exhibit and is going to try and arrange to have them shown in a gallery in Repton.'

Natalie had a choice to irk him and make him uncooperative by insisting he had something to do with the disappearances, or appeal to him. She chose the latter. 'Anthony, on three separate occasions you saw the girls who disappeared, soon before they actually went missing. Did you notice anyone else watching them, or even following them? Think carefully. You might be able to save this girl's life.' She tapped her finger on the photograph of Katy.

He screwed up his face. 'I tend to get lost in my own world when I'm watching, imagining how I'd paint their eyes or their expressions.'

'I understand but if you cast your mind back to yesterday afternoon, did you see anybody you recognised going in or coming out of the supermarket at around that time?'

'I can't think of anyone.'

Natalie sat back in her seat, allowing him time to think. Eventually he shook his head. Her phone vibrated in her pocket – an incoming call. She pulled it out. The screen flashed David's name.

'Sorry, I can't think of anyone. I was fixed on her sorrow and how I could paint her in shades of blue and purple.'

'Give it some more thought, and if anything springs to mind, let us know.'

'Will there be anything else, Inspector?' the lawyer asked.

Natalie wished it were otherwise but she had no reason to hang onto Anthony Lane. 'Not at the moment. Thank you for your time.'

They ended the interview and Natalie left Lucy to see them out. She walked on ahead to the bright lights of the foyer. She had nothing to give Aileen. There were no suspects and the clock was ticking. BBC News was showing on a screen in reception and she paused as a familiar reporter came into view, The ticker tape headlines read: *Watfield Monster strikes fear into town… Katy Bywater believed to be third victim… Police urge public to remain vigilant.*

She stood directly in front of the television set and listened to the report.

The land and air search for fourteen-year-old Katy Bywater continues into the evening amidst growing concerns for her safety. Katy went missing from her home here in Watfield yesterday evening and there has been no word of her whereabouts. Katy is the third teenager to have disappeared this week. Thirteen-year-old Savannah Hopkins' body was discovered only a few hundred metres from her home on Western Park Road on Tuesday morning, and following her disappearance on Tuesday afternoon, the body of fourteen-year-old Harriet Long was found in woodlands behind her house on Wednesday morning, which leaves the question on everyone's lips: is Katy the killer's third victim?

She couldn't watch any more. The killer had murdered his victims soon after snatching them. How long would the bastard keep Katy alive, and was it already too late for the girl? She walked outside, away from the broadcast, and rang David, who'd obviously got her message and was ringing to reassure her. He picked up on the second ring and she strained to hear him.

'Nat, I'm so sorry.'

'David?'

'It's all my fault.'

'David, what are you saying?'

'Leigh. She hasn't come home. I don't know where she is.'

CHAPTER TWENTY-SIX

THURSDAY, 19 APRIL – EVENING

'I'll have another officer assigned to the investigation,' said Aileen.

'No way. I've been leading this from the off and it's my daughter who's missing. I'm best suited to be in charge.'

'You're personally involved.'

'All the more reason to stick to it.'

Aileen shook her head. 'I'm sorry, Natalie, you'll have to step away from it. I need a detective with a clear head. You're too emotionally wrapped up in it.'

Natalie gritted her teeth. 'She's *my* daughter and I'm one of the best you have. Not only that, I've been eating and breathing this case since it began. If you bring somebody fresh to it, we'll waste valuable time. I don't need to tell you how imperative it is that we jump on this now. Aileen. I'm not asking… I'm begging.'

Aileen fell silent for a few minutes then said, 'All right.'

'Thank you.' Natalie spun on her heel.

Mike had joined Lucy and Murray in the office. 'I'm going with you.'

She gave a brief nod.

Lucy looked across. 'DI Kilburn's already at your house. He's got units looking for her.'

'Right. I'll speak to David and you carry on here. If the perp has Katy, we need to stick to facts and evidence if we're to get her back safely.' She couldn't bring herself to add that the killer might also have her own daughter.

'On it,' said Lucy.

Natalie marched out beside Mike, head held high, aware of eyes trained on her. The news had spread quickly. She wasn't going to forget for one second that she was a mother, but she was also a detective – a bloody good one, as Mike had reminded her – the crème de la crème. If some bastard had taken her daughter in the hope she'd lose focus, they were wrong – very wrong. She'd nail them, and when she did, they'd wish they hadn't messed with her family.

She'd also had a chance to process her thoughts since David's phone call. Leigh might well have decided to take off – probably to punish her and David for their fall-outs. There was not necessarily any connection between the investigation and Leigh going missing. For a start, she didn't attend any school in Watfield, nor did she know Savannah, Harriet or Katy. Natalie held onto that hope. It wasn't the best of scenarios but it was way better than the alternative – that Leigh was in the killer's hands.

They drove in silence. Just outside Castergate, Mike cleared his throat before saying, 'Go easy on him.'

'David?'

'He'll be cut up.'

'I know.'

'He'll blame himself.'

She sighed. 'I know he will.'

'Good. Then don't go all hard ball on him.'

She nodded. If it had been anyone other than her own husband, she'd have probed and demanded and pushed for answers, but on this occasion, she'd be met with guilt and even self-loathing, because for all his faults, David loved his family.

Her street was swarming with officers conducting door-to-door enquiries and neighbours, people she'd known for years. Concerned faces looked up as she arrived in the squad car and she swallowed hard. The hunt for her daughter was on. Mike double-parked on the street outside her house and stood by the vehicle – a silent sentinel – as she got out. A familiar voice yelled, 'DI Ward!' Natalie bristled. Bev Gardiner was here.

'How the fuck did she hear about this?'

Mike placed a hand on her shoulder. 'Leave it,' he warned.

'Get her out of my sight,' she hissed.

'Will do. Go in.'

Her home, her family's refuge, had been invaded. Uniformed police moved about upstairs. Josh's school bag hung from the banister but Leigh's untidy mess of shoes and bag were absent. Her stomach lurched. A female officer bounded down the stairs and drew to a halt on seeing Natalie. 'Ma'am.'

Natalie nodded a response. She straightened her shoulders. She had to be strong. Voices were coming from the kitchen – Graham and David. She swallowed hard and strode towards it. David was at the kitchen table, his head in his hands. He lifted his face, a contorted mask of agony.

'I'm sorry,' he said.

'We'll get her back.' She'd said the very same words to other parents in the past and watched the hope spark in their eyes. David continued to watch her, his eyes pleading for forgiveness. 'You weren't to know.'

Graham stood up. 'We're talking to all her friends. The school nurse didn't set eyes on her so it's likely Leigh lied about the stomach ache and has taken off of her own accord.'

'Any footage from the school?'

'There's nothing on the cameras by the entrances so the only other route she could have taken was across the playing fields.'

The playing fields were flanked by hedgerows but it was feasible Leigh had squeezed through a gap and made her way onto the lane that ran beside them, thus avoiding detection. Graham continued,

'She might not even be far away. We've pulled in all camera surveillance footage from the Castergate Secondary School vicinity. Her phone is switched off so we can't track it but we've notified the provider and we're hoping for a ping.'

Natalie knew the Missing Persons unit was doing everything in their power to locate her daughter, but if Leigh had left at the end of lunchtime, she'd already been on the move for over five hours and might have covered quite a distance. She had confidence in Graham's abilities. He'd tracked many teenagers. He'd be fully aware of all possibilities. The main question was, did he have sufficient manpower to track two missing girls?

He must have guessed her thoughts from her expression. He spoke gently. 'We've intensified the search for Katy Bywater but we've pulled in extra squads from Derbyshire to help us man both operations. We've got everyone, including those off-duty, to help us with this.'

She gave him a tight smile of thanks.

'One of my team is talking to Josh and we're examining Leigh's browsing history on her iPad. Your husband gave us permission to examine her social media sites as well.'

They seemed to have it all covered but there was one important question to ask. 'Has she been on the Disappear website?'

'Yes, she has, several times over the last couple of weeks.'

Her chest started to ice over again at the thought of a connection that linked her daughter to the other victims, yet Leigh didn't know the other girls. This had to be a coincidence. She waited for the sensation to subside and silently prayed her daughter was safe. Mike was once again behind her. 'Bev Gardiner has left,' was all he said.

'Mike.' David sounded like a wounded animal. It was almost too much effort to speak.

'How are you holding up?'

'Badly, mate. Thanks for coming.'

Mike crossed the room. 'You want to talk it through with me?'

Natalie was grateful. It would be harder for David to tell her
what had happened. She moved to the sitting room, where she
found Josh with Eric and a policewoman. She acknowledged them
all. Her son jumped up and gave her a warm hug. It had been a
couple of years since they'd shared a proper heartfelt embrace like
this. Eventually he pulled away.

'Is she going to be okay?'

Natalie nodded, not trusting herself to speak for a second. Eric
watched her with sad eyes.

Josh continued, 'She never said anything about running away.
She's been proper moody lately but I didn't have a clue she was
planning this.'

'She kept it from us all,' said Natalie. 'She might even have done
it on the spur of the moment. They think she slipped through the
hedgerow along the playing fields and onto the lane. Josh, do you
know about a dare called Disappear?'

'Sure, I've heard about it. It's a bit of a craze. Kids go missing
for as long as they can manage. They opt to do a twenty-four-hour
challenge or longer. If they last the full five days without being
discovered, their names go on some leader board. I haven't looked
at it. Somebody mentioned it in a chatroom.'

'Did you talk to Leigh about this dare? Or did she bring it up?'

'No. There are loads of stupid dares on social media, like the
one where you pour vodka into your eye. Leigh never said anything
about them. She doesn't do Facebook. Says it's for oldies. She hangs
out on Snapchat. Do you think she's taken up the dare?'

'She might have done.'

He looked confused. 'She's got more sense than that.'

Josh had a point, but an unhappy, hormonal teenager didn't
necessarily pay attention to any sense when they felt trapped and
unwanted. It seemed Leigh had planned to disappear.

'Where might she try to hide, Josh? I can't think of anywhere
she'd go. She wouldn't stay outdoors. You know how much she

hates the dark. Do you know of any places maybe your friends have mentioned?'

'She'd most likely stay with a friend.'

'She hasn't got a boyfriend I don't know about, has she?'

'Leigh? No.'

'Okay, thanks, love. What time did you get home?'

'After football practice. About quarter to six. I let myself in. Dad and Leigh weren't about so I thought they'd gone out together. I went upstairs to mess about online and then Dad came rushing in and asked if Leigh was at home.'

'You didn't see Leigh at school?'

'No. She never hangs about with me.'

Eric spoke up. 'Leigh's not silly or irresponsible. She'll soon realise that whatever's made her take off like this isn't as bad as she thought, and she'll come back.'

'Did she say anything to you about being unhappy?' Natalie asked.

'I'm afraid not. She's been a bit withdrawn the last couple of times she came around. I put it down to her age.'

'Okay. Thanks, Eric. You'll stay, won't you? Keep an eye on David and Josh for me?'

'You going looking for her?'

'DI Kilburn will take over that side of things. I'm going to work it from my end.'

'But you're working a murder investigation, Mum,' said Josh, slowly.

'We're also looking for another girl, Katy Bywater, who's still missing. They might even be together,' said Natalie, not wanting to frighten Josh.

'I don't know anyone called Katy Bywater.'

'Leigh might know her though.'

The boy's eyebrows sank low. He was looking more and more like David every day. She gave him a tender smile. 'Try not to worry too much.'

Natalie headed upstairs to her daughter's bedroom to see if anything was missing: Leigh was incredibly untidy and her nightdress, socks and a school blouse with a stain on it had been left on top of an unmade bed. Sammy the bear was flat on his back on the floor and the charging lead for her mobile phone was still connected to the socket. Natalie opened drawers but could spot no missing clothing. Her favourite black sweater was folded up, and her ripped jeans that she loved wearing were tossed on the back of a chair. Leigh's collection of trainers and boots were higgledy-piggledy at the bottom of her wardrobe and her only two coats hung on a hook behind the door. If her daughter had planned on running away, she'd intended doing so in her school uniform. Natalie lifted a bright-orange box marked with Leigh's name and shook it. It rattled. She looked inside. There were about forty pounds in coins and notes in it, the equivalent of four weeks' pocket money. Leigh had been saving up for some new clothes and it seemed she hadn't taken the contents. The silver necklace that she'd received for her thirteenth birthday was in its box in her bedside drawer. After staring at it for a moment, Natalie decided she couldn't tell if her daughter had planned to run away or not, but either way, she'd taken nothing she valued with her.

Natalie checked the hiding place where she kept the children's savings account books and then returned downstairs, where she found Mike and David in deep conversation that stopped as soon as she entered the room. 'I can't tell if anything has been taken. It all seems to be in its usual place.'

'Shit. Is she just in her school uniform, then?'

'Looks that way and I don't think she has much money. Her building society account book is still here and she's left her pocket money behind. You didn't give her any money, did you?'

His gaze fell downwards. 'No.'

'She appears to have no clean clothes, no money and she's afraid of the dark. It smacks of an impulsive decision and she might be hiding out at a friend's house. I'll tell DI Kilburn what I know.' A hiatus fell during which David couldn't look at her. 'I've got to go,' she said eventually.

'I don't know what to say, Natalie. I didn't pick up on anything unusual this morning. She wasn't any different to other days. I couldn't have guessed what she was planning.'

'Me neither, David. We're both at fault.'

Mike patted his friend's hand and stood up. 'Ring me if you need me.'

'I'll be okay. I just hope Leigh is.' His eyes rested on Natalie. He was expecting her to comfort him or at the very least say something further to assuage his guilt, but she couldn't. She wanted to but she was prevented from speaking by two thoughts: David wasn't at home working as he said he would be, and he'd lied about helping Eric. Eric hadn't known what she'd been talking about when she asked him about the washing machine and had divulged that David had only been with him a few minutes. David knew how strongly she felt about people lying to her face. It was the one thing she could not tolerate and had stemmed from the ghastly incident with her sister, Frances, many years ago that she tried to forget but couldn't – the incident that had resulted in them never speaking to each other again.

She cleared her throat and mumbled that she'd stay in touch and left her house. In the car, she didn't speak again until they'd cleared Castergate and were headed back to Samford. Mike reached for his cigarettes and lit one, then wound down the window a few centimetres. A breeze found its way inside and chilled her cheeks but couldn't cool the heated fury that was building up inside.

'Did he tell you why he wasn't at home when Josh got back?'

Mike pursed his lips and blew smoke out of the small gap. 'Yes.'

'And where was he?'

'Don't do this to yourself, Nat. Leigh is missing. That's what's important here not where David was.'

'He should have been at home, working. That's what he told me he'd be doing but he wasn't. If he had been, he'd have picked up his mobile or answered the house phone when Rowena called, so it is important.'

'It'd be best if he tells you.'

'Why? Is it another woman?'

Mike snorted silently. 'No, not another woman.'

'Then where the hell was he with his phone switched off?'

'It's not important.'

'Mike, for fuck's sake. Don't hold back on me.'

Mike held the cigarette between finger and thumb and dragged on it, then after he'd released the smoke said, 'He was at the bookmakers. He laid bets on some of the races at Cheltenham this afternoon and was waiting for the outcome of the five thirty-five race.'

'Betting shop. I should have guessed,' she said, softly.

*

The snake was oiled and ready for action. Tiny electrical currents pulsed through his veins, warming his body. This was so perfect. DI Ward would soon find out what it was like to be up against somebody far cleverer than her, somebody who could outwit and outsmart her without trying too hard. She hadn't a clue what was about to happen. He stroked the snake's head tenderly and wondered how loudly the detective's daughter would scream once the snake coiled around her throat.

*

As soon as Natalie got back into the office, she dumped her bag on the floor and addressed Lucy and Murray.

'Just so you know, Missing Persons are looking for Leigh. I've every reason to assume she's taken off of her own accord and I want us to remain completely focused on finding the person or persons responsible for killing Savannah and Harriet, and who might have taken Katy.'

Lucy was first to respond. 'Anthony's computer was clean and his alibi checked out. He was with Chad, his teacher, after art class. As he told us, he paints portraits of young women and Chad believes he is quite a talent. He also said he's very dedicated to his artwork.'

'We can rule out Anthony then, and unless Forensics come up trumps with the Toyota, we have nothing on Duffy. Bloody great!' Natalie pulled a face and stalked to the window.

'We're still examining CCTV footage in Bramshall and Watfield. There are no cameras near Western Park but there's a camera on the roundabout as you leave Watfield. We're trying that. I requested assistance from Forensics and they're using the latest technology on it,' said Murray.

'Okay. That's good.' Aileen had come through on her promise that they'd receive some help. There had to be another way to track the killer down. What hadn't they followed up? The answer came in a flash: the Alisha Kumar investigation.

'Ian was waiting on some information from a colleague in Manchester, regarding one of the suspects in the Alisha Kumar case: Brendon Jones. Can you chase that up? I want to know where the guy is.' She stared out into the inky sky and watched the silvery trails of raindrops sliding down the glass. If her daughter was outside, she'd need shelter. The rain was beginning to fall heavily. The idea of Leigh alone in the darkness ate away at her and she lost several minutes to morbid thoughts until she dragged herself back to the here and now. Worrying wasn't going to bring Leigh home. She had to trust in the expertise of Graham and his units. She returned to her desk and thumbed through her notes, annoyed she had so little to go on. Katy could even now be in the killer's hands and they were no closer to working out who it might be. She ran through everything they'd done so far. Was there something she was overlooking?

Lucy came off the phone. 'Brendon Jones, the main suspect in the Kumar investigation, lived on a narrowboat called *Swinging Rose*. It was moored on a canal only a couple of streets away from the Kumars' restaurant. Manchester police haven't been able to locate Brendon but they have had word the boat was moved away and is somewhere in Staffordshire.'

Natalie's pulse beat quickly in her temple. This could be the break they'd been waiting for. The only problem was that Staffordshire was at the heart of the inland waterways with more miles of canal than any other shire, not to mention the numerous marinas dotted throughout the county. The boat could literally be almost anywhere on their patch.

'It's a vast area but we'll begin with waterways closest to Watfield. If Brendon is behind these killings, he needs to live somewhere nearby.'

'I'll get onto it. I'll start with the marinas and see if the boat's been spotted.' Lucy headed to her terminal and hunched back over it. Natalie rubbed at her forehead. The urge to ring Graham and ask how they were getting on was great. Too great. Her daughter was somewhere outside. She ought to be at home, curled up on the settee, watching *Hollyoaks* or a film, or teasing her brother. Natalie swallowed the lump that formed in her throat. Her phone rang. She snatched it up.

'Just wanted to tell you there's no news yet.' David sounded flat.

'They'll keep up the search for her.'

'Is that what they do? Keep searching?'

'That's right. They won't give up.'

'I feel useless. I ought to go and help search for her. I can't sit here like this.'

'You need to be there in case she rings or comes home.'

There was a silence followed by, 'Why did she go?'

'I don't know but when she comes home, we'll make sure that whatever it was is resolved and never happens again.'

There was another silence.

'I have to get on, David. Is Eric still with you?'

'Yes, he's here.'

'Good. We have to wait and let the experts handle this.'

'Sure. Sorry. I'll see you later. Natalie…'

'Yes.'

'I love you.'

She wished he hadn't rung. She didn't need such distractions. She turned her attention again to Savannah and the day she disappeared. They'd appealed for witnesses but nobody apart from Duffy had seen her that day. Duffy. It kept coming back to Duffy.

'Duffy is still troubling me. Apart from him, and maybe an unknown who overheard the girls in the coffee shop, who else could have known when the girls were going to disappear and follow them?' she said to Murray.

'One of the girls might have let it slip to somebody else.'

'I considered that but they all wanted to keep it secret. They didn't even share with their best friends.'

'Duffy has alibis for Monday and Tuesday.'

'I'll admit that's a bit of a puzzle but there's a potential weakness in his alibi for Tuesday. He was only with his band mates until twelve. After that, we don't know where he went.'

Murray nodded.

'And what if he had an accomplice?'

'That's true but why would he want to kill the girls? From what we've seen, he rather enjoys female attention.'

Natalie couldn't refute that. The man was a charmer. She'd observed the effect he had on teenagers, so why would he murder them? 'Why does anyone murder? Maybe there's more to what he does than merely remove parental controls.' She was clutching at straws and she knew it. 'Shit! I can't think straight. I need to do something proactive. Which terminal's set up with the Watfield roundabout footage?'

'The one on the left.'

'I'll look at that. You stick to Bramshall and maybe one of us or Forensics will get a result.' She clicked onto the footage and started noting registrations and times the cars passed over it towards Watfield. This was going to take a long time, but while her daughter was missing, she had time. She wasn't going anywhere until she knew Leigh was safe.

CHAPTER TWENTY-SEVEN

FRIDAY, 20 APRIL – EARLY MORNING

The evening had turned into night and then into the next day, and even the adrenalin and sugar couldn't prevent Natalie's officers from fading. Lucy had tried in vain to locate *Swinging Rose* and Murray was red-eyed from staring at the screen. By one thirty they'd gone off for some rest, leaving Natalie staring out of her office window.

A car drove past, its headlights illuminating the fast-falling rain. Leigh only had her school jacket with her. She'd be cold unless she'd taken shelter. She pulled up David's number then changed her mind. He might have dozed off, and even if he hadn't, what was there to say? Leigh had run away because they had failed her.

She turned swiftly at the sound of Mike's voice.

'I guessed you'd be here. I brought you a hot chocolate.'

She took the offered drink with thanks. 'Why are you still here?'

'Working overtime. There's a very important investigation that needs my attention.'

She had no energy to smile. Steam spiralled like a corkscrew from the cup and she inhaled sugary aromas. 'David and I fucked up big time. We drove Leigh away,' she said.

'No, you didn't. She'll come back. You know the stats in these cases as well as I do. Most teenagers reappear of their own volition within twenty-four hours.'

She blew on the drink, causing a small indentation in the foam. 'What if she doesn't come home by then?'

'Plenty of kids come back unharmed. Don't believe the worst. You can't stay here all night, Nat. You should go home even if it's only for a short while. You need to present a united front when she returns.'

'I don't want to.'

'Sometimes we have to do things we don't want to do,' he replied and stroked her cheek, fingers grazing it gently. 'Go home. Be there for her when she returns.'

She looked away, blinking back tears. His tenderness had touched her deeply and he was right. It would be better for Leigh if she turned up overnight and found both her parents waiting with their arms open. There was little to be gained by staying at the station.

'Thanks,' she said.

'You're welcome. I'm at the end of the phone if you need me.'

He gave her a smile that lit his eyes and she remembered the passion she'd once seen in them when they'd been in a similar situation – her hating David for lying and him giving her what she craved. It couldn't happen again – not in similar circumstances. She finished the warm chocolate and picked up her car keys.

A light burnt downstairs and Natalie padded into the sitting room. Eric was lying on the settee, a blanket over him, reading the car magazine she'd spotted in David's office.

'Hi. Any news?' he asked.

She shook her head.

'I thought I'd wait up in case she came home – friendly face and all that.'

A wave of affection threatened to bowl her over. Eric had been a rock throughout their marriage and played a huge part in the children's lives. 'You need anything? A whisky? Hot milk?'

He chuckled. 'I already had two large ones. We opened David's last bottle of best malt.'

'He asleep?'

'Maybe. He's in bed.'

'Thanks for being here.'

'Where else would I be? You're family.'

She moved across the room and planted a kiss on his head.

'What's that for?'

'Being family.'

She plodded up the stairs and went directly into Leigh's room. Dropping onto her bed, she picked up Sammy the bear and, holding him to her chest, let the tears roll, all the while silently begging the universe to send her daughter home.

CHAPTER TWENTY-EIGHT

FRIDAY, 20 APRIL – MORNING

Natalie had left the house at eight. David had tumbled into the kitchen just as she was planning on leaving and was dismayed she had spent the night in Leigh's room.

'I didn't want to disturb you.'

'I wanted to be disturbed.'

'David, we're too wound up to talk or discuss anything. Our priority is Leigh.'

'Don't you think I know that?' he begins, then stops himself.

'I've got to get to work but I'll stay in contact with Graham. If Josh doesn't want to go to school today, keep him at home but it might be best if he sticks to the normal routine.'

'How can you be so calm about this?' David asks.

'I'm not. Believe me, I'm in no way calm but we have to go about business as usual for the moment. She's not been gone twenty-four hours yet and there's a good chance she'll appear today.'

'I hope to God you're right. I don't think I can go through another day of this.' He rubs his already red-rimmed eyes and it grieves her to see him so powerless. Losing Leigh has shocked him to the core but can she ever forgive him? She chooses not to think about it, and with promises she'll stay in contact with him, she leaves.

*

Murray interrupted her thoughts. 'Natalie, there's something strange here. I'm looking at the footage taken at Aldi car park when Katy disappeared. I've been rewinding to see if anyone else was around when Katy was in the shop and I noticed a van that drew up close to the entrance, sat for a while and pulled away. I've just run a DVLA check on the personalised number plate and it belongs to Mitchell Cox.'

Natalie jumped to her feet. 'We've been hunting for somebody who knew all three girls and maybe knew they intended to disappear. Mitchell Cox might just be that person. Come on. We're going to talk to him.'

The shutters were down on the phone shop even though it was almost nine but Natalie remembered the side entrance, accessible via a brick archway that led to a small car park. Mitchell's white Peugeot van with its personalised number plate was in the far corner. She pressed the buzzer marked 'Phone Shop' and waited for Mitchell, who was a few minutes before opening the door. 'Morning. Is everything okay? Have you found Katy?'

'We'd like to ask you some more questions if we may?' said Natalie.

'Most certainly. Come inside. It's not too warm out there.'

He beckoned them inside and, taking the lead on the staircase, said, 'Come on up.'

Classical music was playing in his sitting room and he muted it with a control so they could talk. He dropped onto his chair that made a sound like a soft sigh. Natalie glanced at the painting of solemn-faced Cosmina, the woman he'd once loved, whose eyes seemed to follow her as she moved forwards into the room.

'Were you here Wednesday afternoon, Mitchell?'

'Yes, I was.'

'You didn't go out at any point?'

He wrinkled his forehead than raised a forefinger. 'I popped out to buy some glue. I was working on a laptop with a broken case and I ran out.'

'Where did you go to buy the glue?' Murray asked.

'I was going to try the supermarket, but when I got there, I suddenly remembered I had a spare tube in my toolbox, so I came back home.'

'You drove to the supermarket.'

'Yes.'

'It's only a few minutes on foot. Why did you drive?'

'The supermarket was my first stop. If they hadn't stocked the type of adhesive I needed, I'd have driven to the retail park.' He looked at Natalie with a puzzled expression. 'Why?'

'We understand you were in the car park about the same time as Katy Bywater was in the supermarket.'

His eyes grew large. 'Really?'

Murray spoke again. 'Did you see Katy while you were there? Maybe going in or coming out of the supermarket.'

'I don't think I even looked in that direction.'

Murray said, 'Are you sure?'

Mitchell lifted a finger to his lips as he pondered the question then said, 'No. I can categorically say I didn't notice her. Or anyone else. I drove into the car park and was about to get out of the van when I thought of my toolbox. I started the car back up and drew away again. I had no idea.'

'Did you return immediately?' Natalie asked.

'Yes, of course. I had to mend the laptop. The customer wanted it back urgently. In fact, they collected it first thing yesterday. It turned out to be fiendishly more difficult to repair than I'd anticipated. It took several hours. I almost didn't finish it in time.'

'Can I go back to a week on Saturday when you saw Duffy outside with the girls?' Natalie asked.

Mitchell looked her in the eye. 'Yes.'

'Did you hear any exchange at all between them?'

'Nothing. I heard a laugh. I think I mentioned that to you. That's what attracted me to look out the window but I couldn't hear what they were discussing.'

All the dead ends were draining Natalie's patience and energy. Katy had been missing for over a full day and they were no closer to knowing what had happened to her. She decided to wrap it up. Mitchell stood up. A loud whirring and clicking suddenly filled the flat.

'That'll be Duffy. He has a remote control to open the shutters. I ought to have done it. I'm glad you didn't charge him. I didn't want to fire him. He's a rare find. Not many people with his computing and technological skills are willing to serve in a phone shop. Was he tampering with phones?'

'He was unblocking parental controls so underage children could play games with an eighteen-plus rating. He didn't sell them the games, so what he was doing wasn't technically illegal, but it's a grey area. We warned him if he did it again we wouldn't be so lenient. You might want to talk to him yourself.'

'Yes. I'll do that. Thank you. I'm very pleased he's nothing to do with what's happened. He's a lovely young man.' He flushed at his words. 'I'll leave you to make your way out.'

As they walked down the stairs, Murray commented quietly, 'I think he's got a crush on Duffy.'

The shop bell sounded as they made their way downstairs and a loud voice said, 'You're open then?'

Duffy replied. 'Yes, of course.'

'You weren't here on Monday afternoon when I came by.' The voice sounded irked.

Natalie drew to a halt and listened.

'I had a dentist appointment—' Duffy began.

'And I needed a top-up. I've been out of credit and had no phone all week because I couldn't get back in before today. Can I have twenty quid's worth, please?'

Natalie pushed the door to the shop open and walked in. Duffy's eyes widened. 'What are you doing here?'

'Could I have a word with you, sir?' Natalie directed her question at the man.

'What about?'

'Did you just tell Duffy you tried to buy a top-up for your phone on Monday but the shop was closed?'

'That's right. There was a "back in ten minutes" sign in the window so I waited outside the shop but no one came back. It's the only phone shop in the area and I've been at work all week and not able to get to town until now.'

'What time was this?' Natalie asked.

'Ten to four. I waited for twenty minutes but nobody showed up and I had to go back to the car because my car park ticket was only for thirty minutes.'

Natalie stood for a second. 'And you're certain you were here at ten to four?'

'Yes, I came straight from work.'

'Thank you. Do you live locally, sir?'

'Over the other side of the railway lines – Lichfield Green. Number three.'

'If I need to talk to you again, I'll be in touch.' Natalie gave him a smile.

Murray, behind her, had witnessed the exchange and joined her as she climbed the stairs and tapped on the door to Mitchell's flat. The man appeared quickly, an anxious look on his face.

'You've not been honest with us, Mitchell,' said Natalie.

The man's mouth opened in protest but Natalie lifted a hand to silence him. 'Monday afternoon you supposedly took over from

Duffy when he had a dentist appointment, but you didn't. You put up a sign saying you were out and would be back in ten minutes.'

'Surely, that's not important?' He rubbed a hand over his face, screwed up in confusion.

'You told us you were in the shop but now it seems you weren't.'

'But I was. I was in the shop in a manner of speaking. I had the most awful headache from eye strain and I nipped upstairs to take a couple of paracetamol and use my ice bag. I keep it in the freezer for whenever I get a bad head. It helps relieve the tension. I sat with it over my eyes for ten minutes or so, then went back downstairs. I didn't leave the shop. I was here all the time!'

'But you told us you were in the shop,' Murray persisted.

'And to all intents and purposes I was.'

'We have a witness who said you were gone at least twenty minutes.'

'That's rubbish – I can't have been that long. I'm sure it was no more than fifteen minutes tops. I really didn't think it was important to mention it because I was upstairs the entire time. I didn't leave the shop.' He levelled his gaze at Natalie.

She couldn't prove otherwise, and as tempted as Natalie was to bawl him out for withholding information, it would not achieve anything. All the chance encounter with the customer had achieved was to delay her further, and another quarter of an hour had been lost. Chasing facts only worked when you had useful facts to follow up. They left the phone shop empty-handed and frustrated.

Natalie jumped into the passenger seat and said, 'Dig up some background information on him.'

'He seemed genuine enough.'

'I know but check him out all the same. I know he was out of the shop for only a few minutes but they're now unaccounted for.'

Towards the roundabout leading out of Watfield, traffic began to slow. They crept past Jane Hopkins' house and Western Park, and as they slowed to a halt, Natalie glanced across at the closed gates.

The railings and gates were a colourful display of flowers, gifts and cards. The girl who had been shunned in life had become popular in death. A cloak of sadness enveloped Natalie as she considered the irony of that scenario. If only Savannah had been more readily accepted by people in the town, she might be alive today.

It had been three full days since Savannah's body had been left behind those railings and placed by a waste bin. Someone had used the cover of darkness and had been cunning. They edged closer to the roundabout by which stood the CCTV camera they'd been examining. Had the killer come through it or had they approached from the town side? They might find out very soon. It still wasn't soon enough for Natalie. The bastard who'd murdered these girls had planned this fastidiously: they knew how to dodge cameras and people, where to place the victims' bodies, and they were still one step ahead of her. A sudden tremor ran through her body. Had that somebody deliberately snatched Leigh to get to her? She fervently hoped that wasn't the case. She forced images of Leigh out of her mind. It wasn't productive to dwell on what might be happening to her daughter, as hard as it was. Traffic was flowing again, and as she looked at her wing mirror, she could just make out the last of the line of houses. Inside number 21 lived Jane Hopkins, a mother who needed answers, and Natalie had to help her find them. It was too late to help Savannah or Harriet but Katy was still out there somewhere, and as long as there was no news of her death, there was still hope, and Natalie clung onto it.

*

Lucy had tried two of the five marinas in the county – those closest to Samford and Watfield. So far no one had recognised the photograph of Brendon Jones she'd obtained from Manchester Police, or spied the narrowboat, *Swinging Rose*, in the area. It had moved from its long-term mooring at Castlefield Basin in Manchester several months after the Alisha Kumar case, but seemed to have slipped away unnoticed. The last sighting of it had been along Caldon Canal, which ran from Etruria, north of Stoke-on-Trent, and had last been spotted near Froghall Tunnel in January of this year. She'd ascertained it was a fifty-seven-foot narrow beam boat, built in 2004, trimmed in oak and painted blue, but more than that she did not know.

It wasn't as simple as she'd imagined given not only the number of waterways in the county but also the fact there were several more neglected areas and canals where those who did not wish to pay for moorings hung out, often moving their boats regularly. It required more than one officer to track it down.

The marina at Barton-under-Needwood, approximately thirty-five miles away from Samford, was far larger than she anticipated and home to 300 berths, a thriving visitor area of shops, bars and restaurants and new-build apartment blocks. If Brendon Jones was using an alias and had changed the name of his boat, he'd be able to remain undetected for some considerable time. She glanced again at the photograph she carried. The man had dark-brown hair and a beard that covered most of his face. It would be simple enough for him to remove the facial hair, reveal his features and become instantly unidentifiable. He could become invisible.

A text message lit up her phone. It was from Bethany.

Spud just jabbed me.
Don't forget – 2 p.m.
X

Lucy smiled to herself as she typed out a reply. This was the second time the baby had poked Bethany. *A proper little fighter*, Lucy mused. It would be truly difficult to leave such an important investigation, especially with Natalie's own daughter also missing, but she'd do whatever she could to be with Bethany today and see their child.

Will try my very best.
Love you both.
X

If she was honest with herself, it was going to be nigh on impossible to get away, even though the hospital was only a few minutes down the road from headquarters. She'd play it by ear and hope she had some free time to scoot off at 2 p.m. for half an hour.

She sat in her car and tried to fathom out what to do next. If she were the killer, where would she hide out? Would it be somewhere like Barton Marina, or would she choose to hide away on the less-used routes and stay on the move? It would be the latter.

She studied the map of the canals closest to Watfield on her smartphone and sighed. There were thirty-eight miles of waterways between Samford and Watfield. It would take her at least fourteen hours to march it out. There had to be an easier way. Brendon certainly wasn't going to walk it. There had to be bridges and exit points along the route where he could collect a vehicle to get in and out of Watfield. She'd drive the length of the canal and check each one. It wasn't going to be an easy task but it had to be done and she was nothing if not tenacious. She put the car into gear and wondered if Natalie had heard any word on her daughter. Her boss constantly surprised her with her ability to soldier on regardless, and Lucy wasn't sure that if she were in that unenviable position, she would have as much grit. Her admiration for Natalie had hit new heights and the only way she could assist was to locate Brendon Jones.

CHAPTER TWENTY-NINE

Murray and Natalie were only five minutes out of Watfield when Graham rang her with news of the discovery of Katy's body. Natalie could hardly speak. She'd been clinging to the belief the killer had changed their MO and Katy was alive. It had kept her spurred on and motivated and had helped her from going crazy with worry about her own daughter.

'She was found in a skip.'

Natalie blinked back tears. The idea that a human being could discard these girls so callously was more than she could bear in her heightened state of anxiety. 'Was it close to her house?'

'Two streets away. The house owners hired it a week ago because they're having their front drive dug up and replaced. It was half-filled with rubble. The builders, a landscaping and gardening outfit from Watfield, came on-site at ten and that's when they discovered her.'

'Who were the builders?'

'Tenby House and Garden Services. The lad who discovered her is in terrible shock – Stu Oldfields. Had to get paramedics out to him. We interviewed him when Savannah went missing.'

'He's known to us too.' The killer was playing a complicated and twisted game and it sickened Natalie further. 'We're not far from you. Where exactly are you?'

He gave her the address. Murray cast a sideways glance at her. 'You okay to go and do this?'

'I'm fine.' She knew she wasn't. They'd not saved Harriet and now they'd let down Katy too. They'd all done everything possible and yet the girl had still been murdered. The sadistic bastard was taunting and tormenting them all and had taken three girls and killed all of them. Would Leigh be next?

The sight of Katy's body in situ almost broke her but Natalie kept a poker face and gravitated towards Stu Oldfields, who was sat in the back of an ambulance, his face the colour of putty. Natalie sat on the bed opposite him. 'Must have been a horrible shock for you.'

He pulled the blanket tighter around his shoulders and nodded.

'Think you can answer a couple of questions?'

'Yeah.'

'Who ordered the skip?'

'The boss – Noel. He arranged everything. We just got told what the job was and when to go to it. We shouldn't have been here. We should still be working on Jane Hopkins' house. We're only doing this driveway because we couldn't finish that job.' His teeth were chattering as he spoke, a reaction to shock.

'I understand you found the body?'

'Yeah, we'd done all the prep work yesterday so we had to wait for the bricks to be delivered. They weren't coming until ten so we didn't arrive until almost half nine. We sat inside the cab with a flask of tea until the delivery arrived, and once it was offloaded, we started work. I don't know how long it was before I went over to the skip to toss out some cement and the girl was there, looking up at me with bright-red eyes.' He began to shake at the memory.

'I take it the owners weren't at home when you arrived?'

'No. They're away for the week. There was no one at home.'

'Did you know the victim?'

Tears began to roll down his face. 'I never saw her before.'

'She was one of Harriet's friends.'

'Was she?'

'Did Harriet ever mention her name to you – Katy? Katy Bywater?'

His head swung side to side and he clenched his teeth. Natalie studied his reaction. Stu was nothing like the arrogant, swaggering young man she'd met on Tuesday. There was little doubt he was not responsible. This was either an unfortunate chance event or the killer was even cleverer than she'd imagined. She left Stu in the care of the paramedics and joined Murray, who was awaiting instructions and observing the crime scene from the pavement. The skip dominated the front garden and was almost the same height as a medium-sized car. Katy had been well-hidden. Only somebody peering out of a bedroom window might have spotted her body, and the house owners weren't there. The pathologist and Forensics had yet to arrive, and everyone was keeping their distance so as not to contaminate the scene. Natalie could guess how Katy died. Graham had told her there was visible bruising to the girl's neck. She'd been strangled.

Her mobile rang and she made a grab for it. A sudden, urgent hope that it was David to say Leigh was home rose from deep inside her. It wasn't her husband but Ian who spoke excitedly.

'I've got important information on Brendon Jones. He's related to Mitchell Cox. They're cousins. Brendon's mother, Gabrielle, and Mitchell's father, Craig Cox, were siblings.'

'Wait up, Ian. I'm putting you on speaker so Murray can hear.'

Ian repeated what he'd just said.

'You have got to be kidding. What else have you found out?' Murray asked.

'Hang on a sec, give me chance to check this…' His voice trailed away for a second. Natalie assumed he was typing. He returned with, 'Gabrielle Cox married Gareth Jones in Manchester in 1976 and Brendon was born in 1978. He worked as a supervisor at a small logistics company until late 2012 when he began claiming sickness and unemployment benefits. He's been out of work since.'

'Any clue as to why he's receiving medical assistance?' Murray asked.

Natalie had read the files and took a guess at the answer. 'During one of the interviews, it came to light that Brendon had been receiving treatment for depression following the death of his parents.'

Ian spoke again. 'They were killed in a motorway accident in August 2012. The investigating team were concerned because Brendon not only lived on a narrowboat close to where Alisha had last been spotted but he'd been drinking heavily and had little recollection of the events of that day. He stood by his claim that he fell unconscious sometime late morning and didn't see a soul. The team couldn't prove otherwise and there was no forensic evidence on either his boat or his person that linked him to the girl.'

'That's right,' Natalie said.

Murray dragged his eyes off the skip and said, 'I wonder why he felt the need to move here after four years moored in Manchester.'

'Maybe Mitchell knows,' Ian replied.

'We'll talk to him. Does Brendon have any other family, Ian?' Natalie asked.

'Only Mitchell.'

'What about Mitchell's dad? What happened to him?'

Ian read aloud, 'Craig Cox was a freelance reporter, one of those on board a DC-10 travelling from Brazzaville, in the Republic of the Congo, to Paris when it exploded and went down in Niger in 1989.'

Natalie recalled the tragic event. It had been in the newspapers and on television. It had been claimed the attack was the work of Libyan agents in retaliation for France's support of Chad during the Chadian-Libyan conflict. Mitchell must have lost his father when he was a child.

Ian continued searching through databases, leaving Natalie and Murray discussing how best to use this new information.

Natalie ran through her thoughts. 'Brendon wasn't found guilty of Alisha Kumar's murder but the police had serious doubts about his innocence at the time. Now we have three victims, we believe his narrowboat is in the area and the girls all visited Mitchell's phone shop. This feels like we're onto something at last. We need to establish if these two are close. Ian, do you have anything else on Mitchell?'

'Yes… just looking at that info now. He was born in Salford in 1985.'

Murray's eyebrows lifted in surprise. 'What? He looks way older than thirty-three or thirty-four. I had him pegged as forty at least.'

Ian carried on. 'His mother's maiden name was Jenny Pullman. She married Craig Cox in 1983. Oh, there's a brother – Andrew Cox, born 1992. No. He's dead too. Mother and son both died in 2005.'

'How did they die?'

'Car accident.'

Natalie shook her head. Motor vehicle crashes accounted for a huge number of mortalities each year.

'Mitchell worked in Manchester as a computer technician for a tech company from 2006 until February 2013, when he purchased the phone shop and flat in Watfield. Been there ever since. Hang on… The tech company was on the same trading estate as the logistics company where his cousin worked.'

'So, Mitchell and his cousin worked near each other. Maybe they were chummy too. Ian, Mitchell had a girlfriend, Cosmina Balan. See if you can find out anything about her that might be useful. I understand she passed away shortly before he bought the shop,' said Natalie.

'Will do.'

She faced Murray. He spoke first. 'Back to Mitchell?'

'You got it.'

*

Duffy let out a soft groan when he saw Natalie and Murray for the second time that day and adopted a defensive pose, arms folded across his chest. His hair was styled and shining and he was dressed in a blue suit with skin-tight trousers and the same brown brogues he'd been wearing the day before. It seemed style was everything to Duffy.

'We'd like a word with Mitchell.'

On cue, Mitchell appeared at the door behind the counter. 'I saw you on the monitor screen.'

'Could we speak upstairs, please?' Natalie asked.

Mitchell nodded and disappeared from view. Natalie and Murray followed him to the flat, which smelt of melted cheese and toast. Steam rose from a mug on his table.

'I'm sorry to disturb your lunch but some information's come to light regarding Brendon Jones.'

Mitchell stiffened at the name.

'We understand he's your cousin.'

'He is but I haven't seen him in years.'

'When was the last time you saw him?'

He shrugged. 'Ten... twelve years. I couldn't say.'

'You're not close, then?'

'Not at all.'

'You don't keep in touch?'

'Christmas cards... the odd phone call.'

'Did you attend your uncle and aunt's funerals in 2012?'

His face darkened momentarily. 'Yes. I did.'

'And did you see your cousin after that?'

'Maybe once. I can't remember. We really don't have anything in common.'

'But you both worked at companies on the same trading estate. I find it odd you wouldn't have seen more of each other.'

Murray gave her a lengthy stare. 'We don't get along. Now, you've wasted enough of my time today. I think I've been more than helpful, on a number of occasions, and I'd like to be left alone to finish my lunch.'

'You are aware your cousin was a suspect in a murder case, aren't you?'

'I have nothing further to say to you.'

'Earlier, you wanted to help bring the person who's murdered these girls to justice. It won't hurt to answer my questions. You might hold a vital piece of information we need.'

'I don't. I haven't spoken to Brendon in a very long time.'

Natalie tried one last time. 'Have you set eyes on him at all since you moved here? I don't need to stress how important it is that you tell us what you know.'

'I've nothing to tell you. Now… leave me alone.'

Natalie squared up to him but backed off at the last minute. There might be a reason he'd become so defensive – he was hiding something. She marched outside, ignoring looks from passers-by as she threw open the squad car door. Murray got into the driver's seat and commented, 'That was a sudden change of attitude. Where did Mr Helpful disappear to?'

'I think our phone shop owner just revealed his true colours.' She pressed the button on the comms unit and spoke to Ian. 'Pull out all the stops. I want everything on Mitchell Cox.'

'Roger that. I've just established Brendon Jones doesn't own *Swinging Rose*. He's living on the boat but it's registered to somebody else.'

'Then who the hell owns it?'

'Wait a minute…'

It was over a minute before Natalie realised she'd been holding her breath. The comms crackled and Ian said, 'It was bought in 2011 by a woman – Cosmina Balan.'

Natalie thumped her thigh with her balled fist. 'I knew he was keeping something back. That's what he didn't want us to know. Cosmina was Mitchell's long-term girlfriend. When did she die?' There was another pause as Ian hunted for the information.

'March 2012.'

'And who did the boat pass to after her death?'

'I don't know but there seem to be no named relatives. She was a Romanian refugee who came over to the UK in 2001 when she was eighteen. That's all I have for the moment.'

'That'll do for now. Keep looking and let me know when you find something.'

'Will do.'

She turned to Murray. 'He's involved in this somehow.'

'Maybe they both are – him and Brendon.'

Natalie made a rapid decision. There was no more time to waste. Her daughter was still missing and a fast action might save her life. 'We'll tackle him about this. Now.'

Natalie grabbed her mobile and rang her superior for a warrant to search Mitchell's premises. With assurances it was on its way, they got out of the car and headed to the phone shop. This time they weren't coming away without answers.

CHAPTER THIRTY

Lucy dashed into the office. It was already 1.45 p.m. and she ought to get to the hospital to be with Bethany. She'd almost covered all the exit points along the canal from Samford to Watfield but had yet to try Watfield to Castergate.

'What's happening?' she said, breathlessly.

Ian filled her in with the details he had. The news about Katy knocked her for six.

'Oh, fucking hell! I really hoped Katy was going to be okay. What about Leigh?'

'No news. I don't know about you, but I think the killer's taken her too.' Ian stared at her with sunken eyes.

'I bloody well hope not.'

'Well, there was that article in the newspaper about Natalie. I think the killer might have read it. This person loves playing games and the attention they're getting. What could be more attention-grabbing than kidnapping and then murdering the lead detective's daughter?' His concern was evident. Lucy chewed it over. There was a good chance that was the case. She made a quick decision then rushed upstairs to the roof terrace, where she rang Bethany.

'Hey, look, I know how important today is but how much would you hate me if I said I couldn't make it?'

'I wouldn't hate you. I'm guessing you aren't going to make it.'

'We just found a third victim. I'm needed, Beth.'

'You found another girl?'

'Yes, and Leigh still hasn't returned home.'

'Then you can't leave the team. I'll get a recording of the baby and we'll watch it together.'

'Thanks. I feel really bad about this.'

'It's okay. You care, Luce. That's what's important. You care. See you later.'

She pocketed the mobile with a heavy heart and an, 'I'm sorry, Spud.' She had to get back to the canal and track down the narrowboat. She couldn't let anything happen to Leigh.

*

Natalie held up the warrant. Mitchell maintained a guarded look.

'I don't know why you feel the need to search here. I haven't done anything.'

'You failed to tell us about *Swinging Rose*.'

His shoulders drooped and he hung his head.

'It would have been helpful to know it belonged to your girlfriend, Cosmina, and that after she passed away it fell into your hands. Given your cousin lives on board, I'm sure you've had occasion to speak to him since 2012. Where is the boat, Mitchell?'

He held up his hands, palms open. 'Honestly? I don't have a clue. Cosmina left the boat to me. She'd always wanted to live on a narrowboat. She fell in love with it the second she saw it and bought it with a little help from me. We were going to use it for holidays and weekends and travel the locks of the UK, but we didn't. She became ill very soon after she bought it.'

His eyes had misted but he continued. 'Have you ever lost somebody you felt was part of your very being? That's how I felt about Cosmina. She and I were two halves of the same person, and after she died I was ripped apart, like some vital part of me had been sucked out. I couldn't function properly, and the boat… it filled me with such unhappiness she couldn't be there. I can't explain it any more than that. It was painful to go on board. Brendon's always had mental health issues but after his parents died, they became worse. He lost his job and started drinking heavily. He spiralled into debt and couldn't afford the rent on his flat. At the same time, I'd decided to jack in my job, move from Manchester and try to start afresh. I'd bought this place and had no use for the boat. He came to see me before I left, begged me to take him with him but that was the last thing I wanted to do, so instead, I let him live on the boat, free of charge.'

'I asked you before when you last saw him. I'm asking again now – when did you last see your cousin?'

Mitchell drew himself up to his full height and said, 'At his parents' funeral and once afterwards.'

'Were you aware he was questioned by police in 2014 over the disappearance and subsequent death of a teenage girl.'

'I wasn't.' He scratched casually at his neck.

'He didn't contact you at the time?'

'Why would he?'

'Because he was probably anxious, had few people to turn to and you were his only relative.'

Mitchell snorted. 'I'd already been generous enough. He's a difficult man – an unstable drunk who doesn't want to face up to the real world. I suffered painful losses too but I didn't drown myself in self-pity and turn to drink and drugs. By gifting him Cosmina's boat, I gave him a golden opportunity to sort himself out and still he made no effort whatsoever. I visited him a few weeks after he'd moved in and the place was a pit – a stinking mess that made my stomach turn. He'd violated everything I loved. I told him he'd have to sort himself out or I'd evict him, and you know what the ungrateful git did? He attacked me. Went for me like a crazed animal, got me by the throat and said if I tried to make him homeless, he'd kill me.'

'Yet you still let him live there. You could have involved the police and had him moved out.'

'It wasn't worth the effort.'

'But he's living on a boat that your girlfriend owned. It isn't his. I'm sorry but I find this very hard to believe. Why would you allow a man you despise or have no contact with to stay on somewhere so filled with memories of her?'

'I was also at a low point in my life. Grief makes you behave in bizarre ways, which is why I decided on the spur of the moment to let him live there. Arguably not the best decision I've made but one I made nevertheless and *that* is the truth.'

While Natalie was questioning him, a stony-faced Murray searched the flat. Mitchell's story sounded plausible and his mannerisms and facial expressions appeared genuine, yet Natalie wasn't giving up. Brendon could be their killer, but if he was, why had he moved to Watfield? There were two possibilities: Mitchell was working with his cousin to kill the girls, or Brendon was trying to make it seem as if Mitchell was the murderer – some peculiar vendetta on his part.

'You haven't made any further attempts to have him removed from the boat?'

'I should do. Maybe I will now this has happened. I'm mentally stronger than I was back then.'

Natalie still couldn't accept what was being said even though her own personal experiences with Frances had proved that relatives could come to despise one another. Facts. She needed facts. Someone had dropped Katy's body into the skip near her home off Church Street earlier today. A pulse quickened in her neck.

'Where were you this morning, Mitchell?'

'Here. You saw me.'

'That was coming up for nine o'clock, and as I recall you hadn't opened the shop shutters. You admitted you were running late. Why was that?'

'I slept in.'

'Was your van here when you got up?'

'I think so. I can't see it from my windows.'

'You'd have heard it if it had left the car park.'

'I'm afraid I wouldn't. I sleep with earplugs in. That's partly why I was late. I didn't hear my alarm go off.'

He had a response for everything. Thoughts of her daughter again filled her mind. Could he or Brendon have snatched her?

'Where were you yesterday afternoon?'

He scratched at his neck again. 'What time would that be?'

'Lunchtime – about one thirty.'

He gave an apologetic smile. 'I was here. I had to look after the shop because Duffy was in custody.'

Her phone rang, interrupting them. She took the call on the staircase. It was Mike.

'There's something curious about the CCTV footage. We identified all the vehicles coming into and going out of Bramshall, and there was one we believed to be an unmarked SOCO van, the same make and model as on our fleet. We checked the log book and it wasn't in the vicinity that night. It was in Stoke. The camera in Church Street is working again, and we discovered the same vehicle passing by at five this morning. We established our van was parked up at headquarters at that time, and we suspect the van on the CCTV footage is bearing false plates and belongs to the killer.'

'What type of van is it?'

'A Peugeot Expert.'

It was the same make and model as Mitchell's. She hastily thanked Mike and returned to the sitting room, where Mitchell was now standing in front of the portrait, tears in his eyes.

'Do you own a Peugeot Expert van?'

He nodded. 'It's in the car park behind the shop.'

'And can I confirm you are the only person who uses it?'

'No. It belongs to the shop and sometimes Duffy takes it out if we get a request for a call-out for a computer repair. The keys are up there.' He pointed towards a wooden key holder by the front door, from which dangled various keys including a set belonging to a vehicle.

The keys could be accessed by anybody who came upstairs.

'Is the door to the side entrance kept locked?'

'Only when I'm not in.'

A person could get to the stairs from the side entrance and not be heard. There was a possibility that Brendon was setting up Mitchell, but it seemed like a long shot. He'd need to know the van was free if he took it without Mitchell's knowledge and would have to be certain he wasn't seen. And could Duffy actually be involved? Had they missed a vital clue? She had no time to process all her thoughts. If the girls had been in Mitchell's van, there ought to be forensic evidence to prove it. There was only one way to find out. 'We need to examine your van.'

There was no outward sign of unease at the statement. He nodded in the direction of the keys and said, 'Go ahead.'

Murray appeared and shook his head to indicate he'd found nothing to assist them. They'd have to hope the van yielded some trace that the teenagers had been there at one time. Protocol dictated a forensic unit examine it in case officers contaminated it, but she didn't have sufficient time to wait. Her daughter was missing and Brendon Jones was in the vicinity.

⌐   *

Lucy slammed the steering wheel with the flat of her hand. She'd spent a fruitless couple of hours stopping at every possible point where the canal met the road and asking about *Swinging Rose* and Brendon Jones. She'd missed her baby's scan and she'd nothing to show for her efforts. The canal network was a fucking labyrinth.

She had two more stops to make but was fast losing hope. *Swinging Rose* wasn't on the canal and she was beginning to wonder if it hadn't moved out of Staffordshire. Her next stop didn't look promising. She drew off the road onto a pavement next to an Audi dealership. The canal ran under a humpbacked bridge and was reached by a slippery grass track that hadn't been used very much. The water was muddy and brown. Volunteers hadn't cleared this section and tall weeds grew along the towpaths and plastic bottles floated in grime. She had a choice: to head left and towards a narrowboat that appeared to be moored there, or go right and follow the overgrown towpath that curved away from the dealership. She chose the lesser-used route. If she wanted to hide from everyone, she'd lurk here. Clouds of midges hovered above the stagnant water and she flapped at the odd one as it buzzed around her. *Bloody canals.* If Bethany ever decided they ought to try a canal boat holiday, she'd veto the idea immediately.

She reached a short brick tunnel, dark and musty, its ceiling glistening as if damp with perspiration. She wrinkled her nose as she walked through it. Beyond lay two narrowboats – the first called *Black Pearl* was a sooty black boat with faded flowers painted on its hull and planters on its roof full of weeds. The window shutters were closed, and when she banged on the door there was no response. The owner wasn't there. The next boat, *Jenny*, had smoke coming from its stack. She called out and was greeted by a scrawny man with a Jack Russell that bared its teeth under his arm.

She flashed her warrant card. 'I'm looking for a boat called *Swinging Rose.*'

'Not here,' he replied.

'Have you seen this man around here?' She held up the photograph of Brendon Jones and the dog growled threateningly.

'No. Don't see many people around these parts.'

Lucy put the photo away. It was hopeless. 'Are there any more boats along here?'

'One further up. It's empty. Been here a while.'

'How long?'

'Couple of months, I'd say.'

She thanked the man and continued around the bend, where she stopped. The boat wasn't *Swinging Rose*. It was a slate-grey boat with no markings or name. She'd drawn a blank.

CHAPTER THIRTY-ONE

FRIDAY, 20 APRIL – AFTERNOON

Mike had arrived as quickly as he could and, together with one of his team, set about examining the Peugeot in the small car park. 'Just so you know, they've almost finished with Duffy's car,' he said as he shone a light under the passenger seat, its intense beam picking out a small piece of fluff, which he lifted and bagged.

'And turned up nothing.'

'You got it.'

Natalie had asked Mitchell to remain inside and been met with no resistance. Murray was keeping an eye on both him and Duffy and had taken up position near the phone shop where he could keep an eye on both entrances. She checked the time again. It was almost three o'clock and Leigh had been missing for over twenty-four hours. She ought to ring David. He'd be as drained as her. School would be coming to the end of another day. She'd give anything for Leigh to turn up in her uniform, a sorry expression on her face – anything.

The car park was little more than a cobbled courtyard surrounded by a mix of old buildings, once a collection of warehouses. It was large enough for only six vehicles, with spaces allocated to the businesses that backed onto it: a chartered accountant who, according to the sign in his window, was out, a hairdresser and a kebab shop that only opened evenings. A yellow Ford Fiesta was the only other car there at the moment. She watched Mike peel away the carpet in the van's footwell. She wasn't sure what they'd find but any trace at all would link Mitchell or Duffy to the killings. If there was nothing, then she was a long way from working out who other than Brendon could be responsible. She tried Lucy's phone to see how she was getting on but it went immediately to answerphone. She left a message asking her to ring back.

Standing with her back to the phone shop wall, she shivered. She should call David. Before she could act on her thoughts, her mobile rang. Ian could hardly get his words out. She tried to make sense of it. 'Slow down. I can't make out what you're saying.'

'I've had a call from Manchester. They found a body in the canal a month ago. It was badly decomposed and they've only just identified the victim. It's Brendon Jones.'

Natalie couldn't hear anything else for the buzzing in her ears. Brendon Jones was dead but *Swinging Rose* was in Staffordshire. Mitchell's cousin couldn't be responsible for the teenagers' deaths. However, somebody had moved that boat. She raced out of the car park under the archway and dashed over to Murray. 'I'm pulling Mitchell in. Stay here in case he makes a run for it.'

She scooted to the side entrance and took the stairs two at a time. She flung open the door to Mitchell's flat and called his name but was met with silence. Mitchell Cox had disappeared. She bounded back downstairs and into the shop, where Duffy was unpacking a box.

'Where the fuck is he?'

Duffy pointed at the door with the keypad. 'In the stockroom. Went in a few minutes ago.'

Natalie had a bad feeling. There was no good reason for Mitchell to go inside the room. 'Open it up. Now!'

Duffy sprang towards the keypad and punched in the code. The door opened into a galley-sized room filled with shelves of phones and laptops. Several boxes lay in a heap on the floor along with an enormous poster advertising Nokia phones. A table had been moved away from the rear to reveal a small door. She rattled the knob but it was locked.

'Where does this lead to?'

Duffy's mouth was agape. 'I didn't know there was a door. There was just the poster…'

Natalie cast about but there was no sign of Mitchell. He'd escaped. She hurtled out of the front door, yelling for Murray as she ran. There was only one direction he could have taken, into the tiny alleyway between the kebab shop and his premises. The alleyway was only a few paces from the shop, but when they reached it there was no sign of Mitchell. He had vanished. Murray darted off to scout about for him but he could have hidden anywhere. Natalie let out a long groan then screwed around at the sound of her name being called. Mike was waving at her. She headed back to him.

'Mitchell's done a runner. I need to call it in.'

'You better get a team on it quickly. We came across this in the back of the van.' He opened up his hand to reveal a star-shaped earring, the twin of the one Savannah had been wearing.

CHAPTER THIRTY-TWO

MONDAY, 16 APRIL – AFTERNOON

Savannah Hopkins is sick of Watfield. She hates school and detests her mother's new boyfriend, Phil, even more than she'd hated Lance. After Lance had packed his bags and left, she'd thought it would be her and Mum again – the two of them, just like it had been before Lance had come on the scene, but her mum had had other ideas. Phil is slimy and gawps at her whenever her mum isn't around, and it's disgusting listening to the pair of them going at it in her mum's room. It makes her want to puke.

It's been a really bad day. She got into a fight with Claire Dunbar and argued with Sally, one of her best friends, except she isn't her best friend or any friend. The silly bitch had taken off her friendship bracelet and pretended she lost it. Savannah has had it with them all. She is going to show them and teach her mum a lesson.

She smiles to herself as she sidles along the pedestrian high street. The chance meeting with Harriet and Katy in the phone shop has given her the opportunity she needs to make people notice her. Harriet is amazing and her dad is a gangster in prison. She doesn't give a shit about anything or anyone, and when all three have done the Disappear dare, they'll be in a special gang of their own. No one will mock her any more.

They've chosen which days they are going to do their dares and she is going first. She feels important – like a leader or something. She's even hidden her best clothes in her school bag so she can change into them and look grown up and glamorous like Harriet when she films herself for the Disappear website.

She knows where to hide. They'd discussed the best places to go and she told them about the pavilion. Harriet knew of it too and thought it would be awesome if Savannah hid there. Savannah is certain there's a room at the back of the pavilion. She only has to break in, and she's brought a hammer and screwdriver she's stolen for just that purpose. It's going to be so cool to upload her own personal video and show everyone she isn't afraid and can stay hidden for three days. Her mum will go mental and then she'll be scared. When Savannah gets home, her mum'll be so relieved that Savannah will be able to tell her to dump Phil or she'll go again and this time not come home. It will be the two of them again.

She slows as she walks past the phone shop and spots Duffy rearranging stock in the window. He knows what she is up to and winks at her. She gives him a thumbs up and carries on, her heart fluttering in excitement. Maybe Duffy will be impressed and start thinking of her as more grown up now. She really fancies him. He is like a boy band member or a film star to look at and really friendly. He's been so nice to her. Not like many of the others. He likes the rebel in her and she saw the way his eyes sparkled when she offered him a cigarette or told him she'd nicked something from Aldi. After this, he might even ask her out. The thought warms her. She steals towards her house. This is going to be the hardest part as she might get spotted but she doesn't need to worry – neither her mum's car nor the workmen's van is there. This is too easy!

She jogs on and has almost drawn level with the park gates when the van draws up. The window lowers and Duffy's boss beckons her over. She's spoken to him a couple of times in the phone shop. She edges towards the van, anxious her mother might well be driving in the opposite direction and see her.

'Duffy sent me. He had a brilliant idea of where you can hide. He's had to go to the dentist but he'll meet you there later. He asked me to take you.'

Duffy is going to meet up with her later. She flushes at the very thought.

'Quick, climb in the back before anyone spots you.'

She rushes around to the passenger side and crouches in the footwell. He puts the van into gear, gives her a quick smile and pulls away. This is going to be even more mega than she'd anticipated.

CHAPTER THIRTY-THREE

FRIDAY, 20 APRIL – AFTERNOON

Lucy was halfway back to her car when she was struck by a sudden thought. Forensics had found slivers of grey painted wood under Savannah's nails. The last boat along the canal had been painted grey. Could somebody have repainted the boat?

She turned on her heel and jogged back towards the boat and ascertained how long it was by striding out with measured paces. It was approximately the same length as *Swinging Rose*. She clambered onto the deck behind the cabin, maintaining her balance as the boat rocked. The rear doors were locked and covered by a heavy curtain preventing her from seeing inside, and like *Black Pearl*, the exterior shutters were fastened from within. She called out and listened hard but there was no sound. Studying the deck closely, she made out slight scuff marks in the dust and grime. Someone had been here recently.

She dismounted and stood beside the boat, her eyes inching forwards, section by section, searching for evidence of blue paint under the slate-grey but could see nothing. Then, taking out her penknife, she scraped away gently at the hull to uncover the original colour. It wasn't long before her eyes widened.

*

Officers were searching for Mitchell but Natalie suspected he'd always had an escape plan. He'd been one step ahead of them right to the very end. The question was where he would go next. If she could work that out, she might also find Leigh.

Lucy's call couldn't have been better timed.

'I think I've found *Swinging Rose*. I can't be certain but it's certainly a boat matching the description that's been painted over in dark grey. I've picked away some of the paint and it's cobalt-blue underneath. I can't get into it without smashing the doors and I haven't detected any signs of life inside.'

'You think it's the boat?'

'Yes.'

'Than that's good enough for me. Let's make sure. Where are you?'

Lucy gave her location and Natalie ran to the squad car to join Murray. 'Lucy, we're on our way. Mitchell's escaped and he might be headed your way. Make sure he doesn't see you.'

'Okay. I'll keep out of sight and let you know if he appears.'

Murray turned on the siren and they sped away. Natalie rang Aileen and told her what they were up to then sat back and tried not to dwell on the fact that Lucy had said she couldn't raise anyone on board. If Leigh was there, she'd have responded if she could. Natalie rubbed sweaty palms on her trousers and once again silently begged for her daughter to be safe.

*

That wretched policewoman had got onto him. He couldn't understand how she'd made the connection. He'd been so damn careful. The boat had been Cosmina's gift to him. She knew what darkness lay hidden in his heart and loved him all the more for it…

'You want to exact your revenge soon?' Cosmina smiles her secret smile at him.

'It's no more than they deserve.'

She traces his face with one of her long fingernails, sending ripples through his body. Everything about Cosmina excites him. She's like him — strong, independent and wilful. She's stared death in the face and made a fresh start in a new country, and together they are perfect.

'You will soon be able to put your plan into action,' she purrs. 'It won't be long now until you are ready.'

She slips on her rubber gloves, lifts the needle again and presses the foot pedal to continue her work on the snake. The tattoo of the serpent is her idea. For years he has been haunted by the memory of the day in the washing machine when he believed a boa constrictor was squeezing the air from his lungs. She was horrified by the tale and now she's turning that fear and anger into power. He controls this snake and together they'll finally be able to get payback for that day.

The tattoo is a masterpiece and she has truly brought the creature to life. It has taken many hours of pain and patience but they are both at the end… or should it be at the beginning? The familiar buzzing of the machine fills the studio and he relaxes his muscles as she works, admiring her beautiful dark eyes and fine cheeks as she puts the finishing touches to her creation.

*

Cosmina had been his partner in crime, helping him to not only plan the murders but find out where the three women lived. The boat had been part of the plot, as had convincing Brendon to live there. Her dying had not. Even now the thought of her body ravaged so quickly by the evil disease that took her from him made him want to howl like a deranged animal. Cosmina, his Cosmina, had been everything he could have hoped for. He shook himself. This wasn't the time to dwell on what might have been. He'd been caught out and it was time to make his escape. He had planned for this eventuality. There was just one thing he wanted to do before he left.

*

The man with the Jack Russell was ambling down the towpath in Lucy's direction. She remained hidden in the undergrowth and hoped the dog wouldn't sniff her out. It was rushing left and right, picking up scents, its tail wagging nineteen to the dozen. She hoped she'd made the right call and that Mitchell would head here. Leigh could be on board the narrowboat and he'd come back to fetch her. She hoped the team would outsmart him this time and the others would be in position before Mitchell showed up. If he showed up before, she'd need to be quick. The man was more slippery than an eel and her only advantage would be that of surprise.

The dog's snout came into view and she grimaced. This was a breed that could lock its teeth onto you if they felt so inclined. She didn't stir. The dog snuffled past. She kept perfectly still in case any slight rustle attracted its attention, then suddenly froze as the owner shouted, 'Hey!'

She thought for a second the man had seen her but soon realised he'd turned away and was speaking to an approaching stranger. The Jack Russell whooshed past her and hurtled towards the person, barking angrily until he was told off and scooped into his owner's arms. The man's loud voice carried across to her. She caught snippets of his conversation, 'Police… looking for *Swinging Rose*… you seen it?'

The reply was mumbled. She edged forwards to see who was speaking and recognised the neat man with the placid face. It was Mitchell Cox. Whatever the dog owner had said had spooked him and he'd already turned around and was retracing his steps towards the tunnel. She couldn't lose him. She sprinted out of her hiding place. The dog began a volley of startled barks that caused Mitchell to glance back and increase his speed. He was quicker than her and outrunning her. The dog owner shouted after her but she ignored him and drove herself onwards. The distance between them was increasing. Mitchell was creeping away from her, an inch at a time, and was now almost at the slope leading to the road. He began to scurry up it. She was in danger of losing him. Once he reached the main road, he'd get away.

Her head screamed at her legs to pump faster but she didn't have the speed required. She pushed harder still and was almost at the slope when Mitchell came hurtling back down it, pursued by Murray. She threw herself at him and he stumbled. It was enough for her to grab his left leg and yank on it. Murray was on him instantly, knocking the air out of him and flattening him against the ground. His face was twisted to one side as Murray's large palm rested on his head, and Murray cautioned the man before cuffing him and dragging him to his feet.

Lucy hadn't noticed Natalie's arrival. She sucked in lungfuls of air and promised herself she really would give up smoking. When she'd regained her breath, Natalie asked, 'Where's the boat?'

'Down there, through the tunnel and beyond the bend.'

'Hand it over, Mitchell,' Natalie said.

'What?'

'The key to the boat. Hand it over or I'll smash the doors open. It's up to you. I'm sure Cosmina wouldn't have wanted to see her boat in bits.' Her words had the desired effect.

'My jacket pocket,' he replied.

Murray felt for it and passed Natalie the key.

Murray led Mitchell away, leaving Natalie and Lucy to check out the narrowboat. The dog owner was still where Lucy had last seen him, mouth open. The dog snarled at Natalie but the man reprimanded it with a smack on the snout.

Natalie climbed onto the deck first and, with a trembling fingers, unlocked the door. With the shutters over the windows, the boat was in darkness. Natalie switched on her Maglite and ran it around the cabin, letting the beam fall against a small log stove and simply furnished interior, offering everything one would find in a compact flat. She tried the light but it didn't work.

'Careful of the steps,' she said to Lucy as she descended. 'Leigh!' Her voice sounded loud and brash to her ears. 'Leigh, can you hear me?' she said again, trying to sound more like the girl's mother. Behind her, Lucy's torchlight fell on the kitchen sink and bright-blue curtain below it. They moved forwards, step by step, to a door. It opened to a bedroom containing a double bed with a storage drawer underneath it, large enough to contain a body. She dropped to her knees and, placing the torch on the bed, tugged at the drawer, pulling it out as far as she could. Lucy shone her light on it. An object wrapped in plastic bags was inside. Lucy dragged it out and unwrapped it. It was a pair of number plates – those used to disguise Mitchell's van. There were a shower and toilet next to the bedroom, and only one more room remaining. It was painted dark grey.

'Let me,' said Lucy but Natalie refused. The key was in the lock and she swallowed hard before turning it. The door opened into a room no bigger than a wardrobe. It was empty apart from a pink sports bag that had been left on the floor.

'She's not here.' The words were little more than a whisper. If her daughter wasn't here, then they were probably too late.

Natalie sat opposite Mitchell Cox. His lawyer was present and Lucy was operating the recording device. Behind them, watching through the one-way mirror, were Aileen Melody and the rest of Natalie's team. Mitchell had not held back, keen to show off his intelligence. As far as he was concerned, he'd outwitted the police.

With his confession and the amount of evidence they'd amassed, they'd be able to present a sound case, yet he didn't seem to care.

'You don't seem overly concerned that you will be going to prison,' said Natalie.

He shrugged lightly. 'I've done what I set out to do – avenge those bullies from my childhood – and there'll be other rewards.'

'What do you mean by that?'

'There are always those people who admire the audaciousness of somebody like me who can outsmart seasoned detectives like you. Not everyone appreciates the establishment. There are many who will revere what I've accomplished. I've murdered teenagers and a grown man and you only captured me by chance. By rights, I ought to have got away. I was ahead of you all the time. There are those who will want to follow in my footsteps. I might even get a book deal or sell my story to the magazines.'

'There will also be those who will make your life a living hell while you are in prison for murdering teenage girls,' said Natalie.

'We'll see about that,' he replied, confidently.

He'd confessed to all the murders, including that of his cousin, Brendon Jones. He'd run though how he'd set his cousin up to be the fall guy for Alisha's murder, and was disappointed when the police didn't charge him. He'd ensured his cousin was so drunk the day he murdered Alisha that he couldn't remember if Mitchell had visited him or not.

'Brendon was wasted most days. It wasn't hard to reduce him to a comatose state, lay him out in the bedroom and rip and dirty a few of his clothes. I should have planted evidence on him. As it happened, it didn't matter that he wasn't charged. It was better that he lived on the boat while I looked for Faye Boynton and Missy Henshaw. Melissa Long,' he added. 'I eventually tracked down Faye but by then it was too late. She'd already died of an overdose.'

'But you still went ahead and punished Melissa Long?'

'Too true I did. I'd already planned to kill Missy's daughter, Harriet, but when I heard the girls outside my office window discussing the disappearing dare, I couldn't believe my luck!'

'How did you know of their exact plans?'

'They couldn't help themselves. They told Duffy every detail of what they were planning and about their mundane little lives.

They were all crazy about Duffy, and him, well, he bathed in their adoration.'

'How did you hear the conversations?'

'I listened in. The monitor connected to the CCTV camera also contains a listening device. I could hear every word through my earphones as I sat in my office upstairs.'

'Could you run through how you knew Savannah was on her way to the park?'

He sighed dramatically. 'I heard Duffy call out "good luck". He was about to leave for his dentist appointment anyway, so I told him to get going and I'd mind the shop. As soon as he left, I put up the sign saying I was out for ten minutes and drove to the park. I figured I'd be in time to pick her up and I was. I tempted her into the van with tales that Duffy had come up with an even better place to hide and would meet her there, and she got in! How gullible. I drove her to the boat, where she insisted on first getting changed for the stupid video she was going to make for the website, and then I locked her in the room. I dispatched her sometime later after she'd worn herself out screaming.'

'And Harriet?'

'Pretty much the same thing. She actually came into the shop because her phone wouldn't work, so I listened in. Duffy tried to convince her to go home but she wouldn't listen. Feisty girl, that one, and liked to think she was streetwise. She still hopped into my van once I told her Duffy had sent me and would meet up with her. Tsk!'

'But Katy didn't take up the challenge?'

'No. She went home and almost screwed up my plans. Luckily her father went out and I dropped by her house and was able to persuade her that Duffy had had a change of heart.'

'You used false number plates on your own vehicle to get around unnoticed.'

He grinned suddenly. 'Genius, wasn't it? And I wore a full forensic outfit bought from the Internet. No one suspects an officer of the law and it ensured I left no evidence.'

'But you were sloppy about your van.'

He scowled. 'Yes. I thought I'd dealt with that. I covered the seat, floorwell and back of the van in plastic, and I cleaned thoroughly after each girl had been deposited. I don't know how I missed the earring.'

Natalie only had one more question. 'Where is Leigh?'

His face lifted in sudden delight and he casually crossed one leg over the other. 'Oh, dear. Has she gone missing?'

'Cut the crap. Where is she?'

'DI Ward, I don't have any idea where your daughter is.'

'How do you know she's my daughter?' Natalie growled.

'I read the article in the *Watfield Herald* and then did a little research of my own.'

'If you've hurt her…' Natalie began.

'My client has told you that he doesn't know of her whereabouts.' It was the first time the lawyer had interjected and Natalie glowered at him.

'Did you take my daughter?'

Mitchell pulled a face. 'I'm hurt you'd even think that.'

'Do not mess with me, Mitchell. Where were you yesterday afternoon?'

'In the phone shop. I'm sure I can conjure up a few names who'll confirm that for you, although I'm flattered you think me capable of such duplicity to be able to be in two places at once and kidnap your daughter. Yes, very complimentary. It shows you appreciate my abilities.'

Natalie did not react to his goading. If she wanted to know where Leigh was, she had to handle him carefully. 'You certainly out-foxed us during the investigation.'

He smiled again. 'I did, didn't I?'

'You planned everything meticulously.'

He beamed at her.

'I don't understand where Leigh would fit into this plan. It isn't... tidy... well thought out, not like taking three girls who were planning on disappearing. Snatching Leigh is... well... messy.'

He shifted in his seat. His ego had been massaged and then pricked. 'Exactly. Which is why in the end I decided not to kidnap your daughter. Now, my lawyer thinks it might be a good idea if I give you a statement and we request I have psychological assessment, so I think we're done here.'

Natalie leant across, her face close to his. 'Where is she?'

He shrugged and said, 'Wherever she wants to be.'

There were white flashes and a hubbub of noise as journalists jostled to question Superintendent Aileen Melody further, but she put up her hand to silence them. 'That's all I'm prepared to say for now. We *have* charged a thirty-two-year-old man for the abduction and murder of Savannah Hopkins, Harriet Long and Katy Bywater, and there will be more information in due course. Thank you all.'

There was a clamouring of raised voices then one louder than the others shouted, 'What about DI Ward? Have you found her daughter yet?'

Aileen faced the journalist, Bev Gardiner, and spoke directly at her. 'We have units searching for her.'

'Do you believe she could be the killer's fourth victim?'

Aileen's eyes blazed. 'We sincerely hope that is not the case.' She walked off back into headquarters and upstairs to the office where Natalie was helping pull together everything they'd discovered. Aileen spoke gently to Natalie. 'Has Mitchell said anything at all about Leigh or her whereabouts?'

'Only that he doesn't know where she is. There are dive teams searching the canal. They've unearthed a bag containing Savannah's clothes and school bag. We expect them to find Harriet's too.' She paused before she said what was on all their minds, that maybe Leigh had been dumped in the canal too, in a bin bag much like the discarded clothing.

Aileen put a hand on Natalie's shoulder. 'You've done brilliantly. You have to stop now. Go home. Be with your family.'

'I need to be here in case—'

'Go home. That's an order.'

Lucy looked across and spoke up. 'We're nearly done here. We just got confirmation from Bart Kingsley over in the technical division that they're closing down the Disappear website and that the video of Harriet was uploaded onto the site from her mobile phone.'

'He admitted he'd taken it and sent it to the site to try and confuse us,' said Natalie.

Aileen patted her arm. 'Murray and Lucy will question him again and see if we can get anything more out of him about Leigh,' she said.

'Thank you.' Natalie stared into space for a moment then, with a brief nod, picked up her bag and keys and stalked out of the office.

CHAPTER THIRTY-FOUR

FRIDAY, 20 APRIL – EVENING

Mike drove Natalie home. The Missing Persons unit was still searching for her daughter and she couldn't function properly any longer. They had their killer but he refused to tell her where he'd hidden Leigh.

'You want me to come in with you?' he asked.

'I have to face him at some point. Now is as good a time as any.'

'Not really. You're mentally and physically drained and should deal with it all when you have focus again.'

'I don't care about the lying, the gambling, any of it. I don't give a shit. I just want to know where that bastard has taken Leigh.'

'Get some rest. It'll seem different in the morning.'

'It won't. I'll still be married to an addict who promises but can't deliver, and Leigh will be out there somewhere. My life is in tatters, Mike.'

'Listen to what David has to say, and for now at least, pull together. You need each other.'

'You're very good to me.' She put her hand on top of his. He lifted it and pressed it to his lips and then released a heavy sigh.

'You know how much I care about you but I'm not going to make waves. Not while you're going through this horror.'

She understood. She was in emotional turmoil. 'I don't think I can forgive him this time.'

'Nat, he isn't a bad man. In truth, he's a better man than me. I cheated on Nicole and I didn't treat her or Thea the way I ought to have. I didn't give her a chance. David loves you. You and the kids are his life. He's isn't wicked or bad. If anything, he's ill. He has a sickness and that's all there is to it. He needs you more than ever.'

She looked into his eyes and saw her own desire reflected there, but this wasn't the right time for such fantasies.

'I'm not strong enough to carry us both.'

'That's nonsense and you know it. You are amazing and you can ride this storm out. You're no quitter. Me, on the other hand, I'm a coward when it comes to relationships and especially commitment. I knew my marriage was sound but some screwed-up part of me didn't want that safety, or that love. It suffocated me, and instead of sitting back and counting my blessings that I had an understanding wife and a beautiful daughter, I ruined it. Don't make the same mistake. David is an arse at times but he's also a top bloke. I wish I could have been half the father to Thea that he is to Josh and Leigh.'

She stared into the night and said what had been on her mind for the last few hours. 'What do I do if he's killed Leigh? What do I do?'

'You can't think that way so don't punish yourself. Go home, be with your family. Wait it out.'

She gave him one last look then left the sanctuary of his car and headed inside. David and his father were sat at the kitchen table.

Eric threw her a wan smile. 'I'll get off. Call me if you hear anything.'

'You don't have to go, Eric…' Natalie began.

'It's best if I do. You need time together and some rest.' He lifted his hand in farewell.

David looked at her through red-rimmed eyes. 'I have to talk to you about this mess I've created.'

'I can't do this now, David.'

'Please. Please, Natalie. It's all bottled up inside me and if I don't explain I feel like my head will explode.'

Mike's words swam in her head. She sat down opposite him. He rubbed a hand over his face again and she noticed how old he suddenly looked. Lines had appeared on his forehead and around his eyes that hinted at the David he would become. Her grabbed her hands and held them between his own sweaty palms and she listened.

'I swear this will *never* happen again. I have to clarify why I was at the bookies yesterday afternoon.'

She studied his face as he fought to find the right words to justify his gambling. He wet his lips and began. 'I've not been able to get any translation work recently. I've only had one contract since March.'

'But what about the big—'

He shook his head and spoke over her. 'There was no big contract. There was no conference. I went to meetings at a couple of agencies in Birmingham on Monday purely to try and get some work, but it's tough, and with all the translation software programs available, people like me are finding it harder. They had nothing for me. I came home disillusioned. I didn't know what else to do. I went to the pub and then the bookies, placed a small bet and it came up trumps. I won five hundred quid, and all of a sudden, I felt like the king of the world. I felt so alive. It was like a wonder drug. I got carried away and wanted to share this good fortune but I couldn't tell you the truth, so I came up with total bullshit that I was going to earn a packet on some new translation. Shit! I don't even know what made me say that – maybe it was simply because I wanted to see the look of pride you used to have for me in your eyes again.'

She didn't interrupt, mindful only of Mike's suggestion that David was ill. He certainly had an illness – gambling, an addiction that wouldn't leave his body.

'The following day, I put all the remaining money I'd won on more races thinking, no... *believing*, I could get the couple of grand I told you about and pass it off as my translation fee, but I lost. I lost it all. I was out of pocket and even that didn't stop me. I was desperate to win money that you'd believe had come from my work so I visited Dad and told him I needed to borrow some cash for a surprise gift for you. I didn't help him with any washing machine on Wednesday night. I went to scrounge betting money from him. You'd know if I took anything from our account so I needed to get it from elsewhere, and after the loan debacle I couldn't try that option.'

'You utter idiot.' Her words were soft but accompanied by the further hardening of her heart. Poor Eric had fallen victim to his compulsion too – dear, faithful Eric who had never let either of them down.

'I know how awful that was. Believe me, I feel dreadful about it. I took five hundred quid from him. I told myself I shouldn't do it but there were some really good runners on Thursday so I went to the bookmakers while the children were out. I had a couple of small wins on the first two races and was convinced luck was on my side so I placed a large bet on the third race and lost. I couldn't give up, Nat. I'd lost most of Dad's money but I was sure I knew which horse to back for the last race of the day. It was a dead cert and I stayed to watch the race, just to be certain I'd clawed back what I'd lost, but it didn't win. I was in the betting shop watching horse races, desperately hoping I'd come away a winner. That's why I didn't have my phone switched on or know that Leigh hadn't gone to Zoe's house. And now you know what a horrible, shallow person I am. I'm so ashamed of myself but I promise you, Natalie. This time I *shall* stop. I'll get a job doing something, anything, but I'll never gamble again.'

'Did you tell Eric about the horse racing?'

He nodded and his hands clung to hers more tightly still. 'If I'd been here, Natalie, I'd have known about Leigh. I'd have gone searching for her. If I hadn't been so wrapped up in thoughts of winning money, I might have even noticed she was unhappy. I've been the worst sort of father to her… and husband to you.'

Her thoughts stuck together like damp cotton wool balls. David had been weak-willed. He'd wanted self-esteem and to bring them closer again, as they once had been. Instead, he'd only caused a bigger rift. She could never trust him again. They'd limped along since the first time he'd gambled and lost all their money. They'd managed to overcome that hurdle and had been on the path to recovery, but if David had to find a solution in gambling every time he had a moment of self-doubt, they'd never recover from this. As it was, with Leigh missing, it was unlikely they'd manage a future together.

'You shouldn't have lied to me, David. If you'd told me you were gambling or that you had no work, I could have coped with it. If you'd become unemployed and just stayed at home with our children, I'd have held you in as much esteem as I did when you worked for the law firm. What you earn isn't important. What I can't cope with is being lied to, and you knew that. You knew how I'd react but you did it all the same. You knew, after what Frances did, I'd never be able to forgive you if you lied to me, but you still did it.' Every ounce of energy drained from her body.

'Natalie, if Leigh comes back, please forgive me. Please try. For her sake.'

She couldn't answer. Leigh had been gone twenty-nine hours and there was every chance Mitchell Cox had killed her and dumped her body.

'I don't know if I can.' She pulled her hands away and went to the sink. She ran the cold water tap and filled a glass. Mike had told her she should try. She'd been trying to hold the family together ever since the first time David had let them all down. How much more could she take?

'I'm going to watch television,' she said.

'I'll come with you.'

'No. Stay here. I need time alone. Where's Josh?'

'In his room. He didn't go to school. He's been online asking Leigh's friends if they have any idea where she might be.'

She headed up to see her son, who was sitting on his bed, arms wrapped around his knees. He looked up hopefully.

'No news yet,' she said and sat on the edge of his bed. 'Dad said you've been helping to find her.'

'No one knows where she is. I tried all her friends and mine too. She's vanished.'

'Somebody knows where she is, Josh. It's almost impossible to stay hidden in this country. We'll track her down.'

'Did you find the other girl – Katy?' His lip trembled and Natalie's heart went out to him. Her big, grown-up, sixteen-year-old son was as frightened for his sister's well-being as they all were.

'We were too late,' said Natalie. 'But we caught the killer.'

'Did he admit to having taken Leigh too?'

'No.'

'You think he took her, don't you?'

'In all honesty, I don't know what to think.'

He pulled his knees in closer. 'If she comes back, I'm never going to tease her again.'

'She didn't run away because you teased her, Josh. Please don't think that for one second.'

'Then why did she go?'

'Probably because your dad and I have been fighting a lot lately. You must have noticed.'

He shook his head. 'Not really.'

'Well, Leigh noticed. I'm going to watch television. Do you want to join me?'

'I'd rather stay up here. I don't feel like doing anything.'

'If you change your mind, come down. And don't blame yourself. Okay?'

He gave a brief nod and she kissed his forehead. She noticed his cheeks were stained with dry tears. He missed Leigh too.

*

Lucy was glued to the image on the screen. Bethany had downloaded the scan and Lucy couldn't tear her eyes away from the small form lying on its back. It had the tiniest hands and feet and it actually looked like a baby. She took Bethany's hand and squeezed it.

'She's beautiful,' she said.

'What makes you think it's a girl?' asked Bethany.

'I just know she is.'

'We'll both have to wait and see.'

Lucy lifted up a hand and touched the screen. She was looking at her future daughter and she hoped with all her heart she could keep her safe. It was a big ask. Natalie was a great mother, and her daughter had gone missing. None of them knew what the future held for their children. All they could do was be there for them and hope they navigated the dangers and terrors that were out there.

Lucy would do her utmost to bring her child up so she could stand on her own two feet and be aware of all the pitfalls life had to offer, and she'd pour every ounce of love she had into the child. She stroked the baby's cheek, the screen cool to her fingers, and whispered, 'Hi, Spud. I'm your other mummy.'

*

Natalie's eyelids were heavy but she didn't move. She wasn't even sure what she was watching. It was just sound and movement, anything to stop her thinking too hard or feeling too deeply. David sat in the other chair. She'd given in and let him sit with her in the same room although they hadn't spoken since. He'd dozed off, exhausted by the events of the last few days, and she was glad. She couldn't bear looking at his guilt-ridden face.

Some gaily coloured birds flew across the television screen and a gazelle bounced behind them. She had no energy to turn the set off. Had Mitchell taken her daughter? Where would he have left her? Natalie's body gradually shut down, little by little, worn by fatigue. She was beginning to sink into oblivion when the doorbell sounded, jolting her awake.

David jumped from the chair then froze. 'What if…?'

She pushed herself up. 'I'll go.'

'We'll go together,' he said.

Josh had heard the bell too and was already at the bottom of the stairs, his face ashen. Natalie made out the distorted head and shoulders of Graham Kilburn through the glass of the front door and drew a breath.

She opened the door but her eyes weren't drawn to his sombre face. They fell onto the lowered head of the person standing next to him. 'Thank goodness. Oh, Leigh! Leigh!'

She pulled the girl into her arms and held onto her, shaking with relief. She bent to kiss her head and whispered, 'You okay?'

The girl nodded dumbly.

Natalie caught David's eye and beckoned him to join them. He moved swiftly, wrapping his arms around them both and holding them tightly.

'It's going to be fine,' he said, tears trickling down his face.

They pulled away from Leigh and Natalie wrapped an arm around the girl's shoulders as she walked into the house.

'Hey! Welcome home. Missed you,' said Josh, looking awkward.

Leigh gave him a smile. 'Missed you too.'

'Come on. Come in and I'll make you your favourite, a banana milkshake. How about that?' said David.

The girl edged forwards.

Natalie looked at Graham, who spoke. 'She walked to a village outside Samford called Loxley. She was making her way back home when we picked her up. She'd walked a fair way – almost eleven miles.'

'Where did you stay, sweetie? Where did you spend the night?'

'A church.'

'A church?' Natalie repeated.

'I wanted to pray that you and Dad would stop arguing,' she said quietly.

Natalie blinked back tears of her own. Leigh had run away on their account. Mike had advised her to pull together with David. He had regrets for not trying harder with his own marriage, and now he only got to see his daughter on odd weekends. Nothing was more important to her than her family. For the time being, Natalie had to put those she loved first. She pulled her daughter closer to her, felt the girl's bony shoulder against her ribcage and was reminded of the day she'd first held her precious child in her arms.

'Your prayer worked. We've stopped arguing,' she replied.

David stepped forwards and enveloped them both in an embrace, grazing Natalie's cheeks with his stubble. They remained motionless for a moment before breaking away.

Leigh looked from one parent to the other. 'So, everything's okay again?' she asked.

'Everything's good,' said David.

Natalie swallowed hard and managed a smile. She owed it to her children to forgive David – they were the most important thing in her life. But she wasn't sure she could. Not this time.

A LETTER FROM CAROL

Hello, dear reader,

Thank you for buying and reading *The Dare*. I truly hope you enjoyed it.

If you'd like to keep up to date with all my latest releases, just sign up at the following link. Your email address will never be shared and you can unsubscribe at any time.

www.bookouture.com/carol-wyer

This is the third book in the DI Natalie Ward series and actually the twentieth book I've written, so it holds a special place in my heart – a landmark, if you like.

The idea for the book came about after reading several disturbing reports regarding teenagers' obsessions with social media dares. Like many parents, I worry that our children are not policed or protected online, and that as vigilant a parent might be, there is always a chance they don't know what their offspring is actually up to when they're using their smartphones or computers.

Teenagers can be very secretive and aloof, and I drew on my own experiences as a parent for some of the scenes in the book.

If you enjoyed reading *The Dare*, please would you take a few minutes to write a review, no matter how short it is? I would really be most grateful. Your recommendations are very important.

I love hearing from my readers – you can get in touch on my Facebook page, through Twitter or my website.

I hope you'll join Natalie and her team again later this year.

Thank you,
Carol

📺 www.carolwyer.co.uk

◼️ AuthorCarolEWyer

🐦 @carolewyer